IN THE ENEMY CAMP

Clements brought the pistol up, steadied it in both hands until the muzzle was right in the centre of Powell-Owenby's face. He remembered quite vividly the moment of Lang's death, that second when the young man ceased to be. He pulled the trigger . . .

'Oil, money and power versus the value of human life is at the heart of this sophisticated tale of political intrigue, betrayal and assassination set in oil-rich Indonesia'

Kirkus Reviews

In The Enemy Camp

ROBERT L. DUNCAN

SPHERE BOOKS LIMITED

First published in Great Britain by
Severn House Publishers Ltd 1986
by arrangement with Sphere Books Ltd
Copyright © 1985 by Robert L. Duncan
Published by Sphere Books Ltd 1987
27 Wrights Lane, London W8 5TZ

TRADE
MARK

Set in Century Schoolbook

Printed and bound in Great Britain by
Cox & Wyman Ltd, Reading

To my friend and colleague, Angus Ross, of Harrogate, North Yorkshire, with affection and respect

1

JAKARTA

Sangre could not sleep. The small room of the *losmen* stank of urine, betel-nut sweat and the rank odor of the goddamned cheap *kretek* cigarettes. The noise seeped through the walls of the old hotel, the high-pitched giggling of the transvestites who picked up men on the street below, the shrill arguments of the whores in rooms down the narrow hallway trying to get more rupiahs out of their Japanese johns who came all the way from Tokyo to Jakarta for girls advertised by tour directors as 'unspoiled.'

He could not sleep because of the waiting. Tomorrow, or the next day at the very latest, there would be a telephone call to the fifthy fat Indonesian who ran this *losmen* who would send his wife up with a penciled message on a piece of brown paper which she would slide under the door. It would have a number for him to call from a safe telephone, and the voice would give him final instructions and let him know where to pick up the second half of his money.

He already knew where it was going to happen. He had spent the afternoon going out to the port, where he watched the workmen erecting the platform that would hold the dignitaries, and he wandered along the docks, sheltering a joint in a cupped hand, knowing he should stay off the stuff until the job was finished, but there was a rising feeling within him, a mixture of excitement and dread that had to be controlled, and the pot was enough to keep it in check for the moment. He found a warehouse right behind the platform, a ruin of a warehouse undergoing reconstruction. There was already a bamboo scaffolding along one side, ready for the workmen who would remove the cracking bricks and stones and repair the walls.

He himself was dressed in rags, invisible in this pesthole of a city, and when he climbed the scaffolding to the roof of the warehouse he found a gaggle of naked kids playing there, potbellied from malnutrition, bodies riddled with every conceivable type of intestinal worm and body lice that this hothouse environment could engender. They were playing a game with pebbles and they looked up at him with wary eyes as he approached. He kicked out at one of them, a little boy about six who darted away reflexively.

Sangre swore at them in Indonesian, told them to get the hell off the roof and stay off or he would cut their feet off and leave them to beg in Merdeka Square. The children cleared the roof in less than thirty seconds and would not be back, because they knew the stories of families who cut off the hand or the foot of a child and used the mutilated kid to coax money out of tourists in China Town or near one of the big hotels. Then he settled at the corner of the roof, into the right angle protected by the abutting parapets of old hand-carved Dutch stones which had been allowed to fall into disrepair. It was an excellent height. Sitting down, he could see through a gap where a stone was cracked and half missing, a good view of the platform. He could calculate the angle that the short rifle barrel would have to make to give him a perfect shot, not just a killing shot, but an absolutely perfect one. For in this part of the world, hiring a killing was nothing, and he himself could go down on the street and pick out a stranger and within five minutes find a man who would take the life of that stranger, cut his throat for very little money. No, the fact of killing was nothing. People died all the time, and there was not one of those workmen down below in the rain who would not die sooner or later. The seeds of destruction were built into every living mechanism, but Sangre was an artist, a perfectionist, and that was the reason he was being paid so much money.

He remembered a contract in Sicily. He had picked a large-caliber pistol for the job. It was at a wedding, and the groom was a paunchy old man with coal-black hair who was putting his hand over the cool young fingers of his child bride, ready to cut the multitiered wedding cake, grinning toward the cameras when the bullet removed his face, simply sheared it away, just as the flashbulbs popped.

And later, in a roundabout way, he had come into possession of one of those pictures, which was a classic of abstract art in that all that was caught on the emulsion was the wedding cake, part of which had been blown away, giving it the appearance of a volcano which had just erupted, and in a crease down the side of it ran a tide of red, like lava.

Since then he had taken his own pictures.

He finished the joint and put the shreds of paper into his pocket. He was tidy. That was why he was still alive.

He went back to the *losmen* to find a girl in his room who had managed to pick the rickety lock on the door and was working on the lock of his tool kit with a nail file when he grabbed her by the hair. He threw her backward on the floor where she began to beg and plead. He kicked her in the ribs then bodily threw her out into the hall, yelling that the next thieving whore who came into his room would end up dead. She wailed her way downstairs to complain to the fat man who ran the *losmen* who would sympathize with her and end up doing nothing because he was afraid of Sangre.

Unable to sleep, bothered by the amplified high-pitched wail of the muezzin from the new mosque across the square, by the slow ticking of his own clock, Sangre finally fished out his bottle of pills, sorted out a red and a yellow and washed them down with a mouthful of warm gin, settling back with his head resting on his duffel bag, one arm over the metal toolbox, knowing that whatever happened, that however far out the pills carried him, he would still have the presence of mind to protect his possessions if they were attacked.

Closed his eyes. Oh, that goddamned gamelan music, that orchestra of chiming cymbals and gongs and flutes which was not music at all and before he left this part of the world, he would find some village back in the jungle where the gook Javanese were squatting on the ground, banging their instruments, and he would take an automatic weapon and make one slow sweep, an arc of exploding bullets which would kill them all in one unbroken movement of his arm.

The pills were having an effect, because the gooks became three dimensional and he could smell them and the dung of their village and their water buffalo and the stink of stagnant water, and they were no longer playing instruments but suddenly dispersed, taking the shapes of trees and grass and the reeded sides of hootches and he was excited and exhilarated because the game was about to begin, and they would be trying to kill him before he could kill them. But as they had taken the liberty of assuming shapes, he had now given himself time to prepare by becoming invisible. He took his rifle from the duffel bag and began to field strip it in the darkness, polishing each piece with a fresh, clean cloth, because the care of the weapon was all-important and his life depended on whether that rifle was going to work, to stand between him and death when the time came. And cleaning it was almost a religious rite, an act he could do in total darkness, as if by touching the metal pieces he communicated with them, groomed them, was reassured by the solidity of them and the way they clicked together, all for the purpose of firing a bullet, a series of bullets, little carriers of death.

He had seen photographs of bullets in flight, a slight blur of motion, because the bullet is death and nobody can get a clear picture of death, just that little blurred line of Death About to Happen.

He clicks the cartridges into the automatic clip, a whole nest of them, and slams the clip into the holder in the rifle with a sharp metallic click, and now he can see the shapes of the gooks in the trees and grass and he begins to fire as they fire at him. A surreal quality, intense yellow light falling through the narrow dapple openings in the trees, and one by one, in slow motion, he fires and explodes the little brown men running toward him. There is no sound to the rifle, nothing except the high singing of the bullets cutting the air, inaudible to any ears but his, and the whomp of those bullets striking flesh and bone. The enemy is firing at him, but they cannot touch him. They cannot even come close. He fires from a chamber that will never be empty, toward an endless supply of men rushing him from the brush, and the killing will go on forever. . . .

He came awake to find the sun streaming in through the window of his room, falling across his face. His mouth was dry, his mind still furry from the pills. And then he stirred and felt the weight across his stomach. The rifle. In his drugged sleep he had taken the pieces out of his tool kit and put them all together. Jesus. In his sleep.

He took the rifle apart and put the pieces away, then took an upper to bring himself awake. Sometime during the night he had decided on the kind of kill he would make this time. He would use a simple copper-clad bullet that would leave no more than a small, black entry hole, the size of the bullet itself, one that would not expand in the brain but make an exit of roughly the same size. The implication, of course, although his employers would never know it, would be that of an execution without malice, a murder of convenience, the bullet designed to sear through a brain and obliterate pieces of memory which might be compromising. He could achieve an artistic balance with a shot like that, depending on whether the head was canted at exactly the right angle. It would take skill to put the hole halfway between the center of the ear and the corner of the eye.

That would depend on the size of the head, of course, the size of the head and the angle and the distance. Sangre listened to the noisy traffic on the street outside the window. He thought about breakfast. He was not really hungry. He would probably fast today, eat nothing, spend his time waiting for the slip of paper to come sliding under the door so he could make his telephone call and find out just who he was supposed to kill.

2

SINGAPORE

'I was rather hoping it would be in the old Chinese section of town,' Lang said as he looked up at the imposing marble facade of the bank on Orchard Road. 'The smell of joss sticks, the click of abacus beads. I even had the faint notion that this Mr Wu I'm supposed to see might not speak English so I could try my basic Chinese on him.'

'Of course he speaks English,' Christie said, pulling her red sports car to the curb. 'He wouldn't be vice president of such a bank unless he spoke perfect English. How long are you going to be?'

'That depends on how cooperative he is and how efficient his staff is. I don't think it'll take very long for him to give me the status of an account, do you?'

'I'm just a secretary,' Christie said. 'A *secretary* secretary who takes shorthand. You're an ambassadorial aide, after all.'

'A dogsbody,' he said.

'That's English.'

'Then what would you call it in Australia?'

'The same thing you would in America,' she said. 'A highlevel gofer.'

He straightened his tie, climbed out of the car before he put on his suit jacket in the heat. 'I shouldn't be any longer than fifteen or twenty minutes. Can you come back for me? I'll buy you a drink and *dim sum*.'

'I'll wait,' she said, and she fished around in the glove compartment and came up with a card bearing the seal of the Australian Embassy and DIPLOMATIC BUSINESS in gold lettering across a white background. She placed it in the window.

'You're kidding,' he said. 'No cop in Singapore is going to buy that.'

'It works,' she said. 'You wait and see. I'll pay for the drinks if I'm forced to move by as much as an inch.'

'You're on.'

He retrieved his attaché case from the backseat and as he went up the walk caught a glimpse of himself in the glass door of the bank, partially silvered to screen out the rays of the tropical sun. It startled him to see how businesslike he looked, a tall young man with perfectly groomed hair, and he thought about the letter he would write to his mother when the day was over. Here he was, James Lang, aide to the American ambassador in Jakarta, coming to Singapore on official business, with a perfectly smashing Australian secretary waiting for him in a red sports car and a couple of days of leisure time just waiting for his business to be finished. He had met Christie in Jakarta, gone with her briefly before she was transferred to Singapore, and he would have to admit to his mother that she was quite right when she had predicted that one day a girl would come along who would be as exciting as his job.

The inside of the bank was impressive, white marble, subdued, almost as elegant as the Peninsula Hotel in Hong Kong, and he presented his card to a receptionist on the general offices side, a beautiful young Chinese girl. 'I'm James Lang from the American Embassy in Jakarta,' he said. 'I have an appointment to see Mr Wu.'

'Ah,' the girl said. 'If you will please have a seat. He will be with you shortly.'

Lang sat down on a white upholstered divan. He was aware of an incessant clicking sound. By leaning forward slightly, he could see down a long corridor into the open door of a bookkeeping section. He half hoped that the sound was the rattle of abacus beads, but the Chinese bankers had joined the twentieth century. He had a partial view of rows of women sitting at computer terminals, punching data into their machines, and now he could distinguish the whir of the computer printers spewing out financial statements.

He straightened up as a young Chinese in a Western business suit came out of a door behind the reception desk, extended a hand to greet him. 'Mr Lang?' he said with a smile.

'That's right. You must be Mr Wu.'

'No. I'm his assistant, Tom Li. Mr Wu is going to be busy for a few more minutes, but if you'd care to wait in my office we can take care of preliminaries.' He spoke to the receptionist in Chinese, led the way into a small office, impeccably furnished with Chinese antiques, in which the computer terminal on the teak desk looked out of place.

'I'm not aware of any business which would require preliminaries,' Lang said, pleasantly. 'Actually, it's not even necessary that I speak to Mr Wu. I sent a letter a week ago, asking for a printout of an American foreign-aid appropriation which was routed to the Bank of Indonesia through your bank by Chase Manhattan.'

Li waited while the tea tray was trundled in and Lang was served coffee while Li himself went through the anglicized ritual of tea and hot milk, stirring the mixture with a small silver spoon, an expression of great interest on his face. 'What was the problem?' he said.

'Without being technical,' Lang said, 'this part of the appropriation was to have been four million dollars. It was to have been received by the Bank of Indonesia approximately one week ago. In short, it was delayed. The excuse was computer error, if I remember correctly. The embassy telexed your Mr Wu, who said there was a bookkeeping problem and our figures didn't match your figures.' He sipped his coffee. It was hot, black. 'I was coming to Singapore anyway for a couple of days vacation, so I was asked to stop by and see what the problem is. I wrote, telling him I was coming. I believe the appointment was confirmed by telephone.'

Li smiled reassuringly. 'I'm sure it's something very simple,' he said. 'Communications in this part of the world are not all they should be. The American currency was probably changed into Singapore dollars by Chase Manhattan and then the Singapore dollars converted into Indonesian rupiahs at the rate most favorable to your government. We had an account last week, you'd know the name if I mentioned it, which suddenly showed a balance of one fifth what they should have, and I'm talking megabucks. It turned out that the computers were printing in American dollars when they should have been showing Singapore dollars, which exchange at the rate of five to one.' He drank his tea. 'What balance did the Bank of Indonesia say you had coming?'

Lang consulted a notebook. 'About ten million.'

'My goodness,' Li said, the smile on his face implacable. 'I can see your dilemma. An error of six million dollars is ridiculous. And you're sure the balance was listed in American dollars?'

Lang opened the attaché case, showed him the Xerox copy of the original cable to the Bank of Indonesia. 'Definitely American dollars.'

Li patted the tips of his fingers together soundlessly, as if this problem were a technicality which would amount to nothing in the end. A light flashed on his desk and he picked up the telephone and spoke Chinese, deferentially. It was obvious that his superior was on the line. He put the telephone back on the cradle with great care. 'Mr Wu desires to take care of this personally.' He stood up and turned toward the door and Lang had a feeling of *déjà vu*, remembering the instructor at the Foreign Institute who had given the lectures on Chinese manners.

When dealing with the Chinese, and if you quote me on this, ladies and gentlemen, I will deny saying it to my dying day, but whenever a Chinese begins the long process of apology you can be pretty goddamned sure that first, he has something to apologize for, and that secondly, check your wallet and your watch when he gets through. Just remember that as Rule Number Fifty-three and if your suspicions are not well founded, then no harm done, but if you're savvy, you may be saving yourself and the United States a lot of trouble.

So almost reflexively, with a curiosity born of prudence, Lang glanced at the file folder on Li's desk, read the reference number upside down, 11076, and stored the information away in case he should need it. And now there came into the room the most obsequious little man Lang had ever met, Mr Wu himself, dressed in an expensive dark blue silk business suit, his skin pale yellow, as if he were

9

jaundiced and had spent a lifetime in windowless rooms, his thinning hair clinging to his shining scalp, an expression of great chagrin on his face as he bowed first, satisfying the Chinese formalities before he shook Lang's hand, apologizing profusely in a steady stream of London-accented English, ushering Lang into the inner office, a magnificent room full of colorful tapestries and ancient woods.

'I take full responsibility, dear chap,' Wu was saying, blotting his broad forehead with a linen handkerchief. 'We pride ourselves on handling the moneys entrusted to us by the truly great nations of the world, and nothing like this has ever happened before. Would you care for a cigarette?'

'No, thank you.'

'Some wine, perhaps.'

'I won't take up your time, Mr Wu. If you could just give me the adjusted figures and a statement I can show to my ambassador . . .'

That was enough to launch Wu on a long-winded explanation and the promise that he would send an official letter of apology to the Department of the Treasury of the United States of America, and another to Ambassador Clements in Jakarta. Lang had the most peculiar sense that the instructor who had given the lecture was now being proven absolutely correct, for Wu was dissembling, filling the air with words as if they would fall on the floor and provide a solid base for the explanation he was about to propose. He sat down behind his desk and inserted a cigarette into an ivory holder, then lit it. 'I feel terrible that your country would have to send you all the way here to straighten out something which is most simple. Now, if you wish, I can have a typed statement prepared for you this afternoon and I wish most sincerely to make amends by having your stay in Singapore written to the expense of the bank itself, since we are fully responsible.'

'That's very kind,' Lang said, enjoying himself now, not with the apparent discomfort in the man but with the ingenuity he was displaying. 'But that's not necessary. If you could just tell me about this mix-up, I won't take any more of your time.'

'It is quite simple,' Wu said, repeating himself, his eyes

settling on a decoration in a wall tapestry, an archer ready to launch an arrow at a deer. 'There were two transactions which were mixed together, so to speak, because they were going to the same place at roughly the same time. There should have been two separate transactions, one for the four million dollars from your country and the second for roughly six million dollars from the other client.' He inhaled the cigarette, held the smoke before he let it out. 'So I have already spoken with officials at the Bank of Indonesia and the transaction has been straightened out there. The four million has been credited to the American trustees account for the Indonesian Department of the Interior, and the remainder of the money has reached its proper destination.'

'I would very much like to be able to report to my ambassador the name of the other client whose funds were mixed up with ours.' Wu would not answer the question, of course, but his discomfort was visible.

'Unfortunately, sir, the banking laws of Singapore require confidentiality, and without the permission of the other party . . .' He shrugged, forced a thin smile. 'But it has all come right after all. I can assure you and your country that I personally will examine the most favorable of the exchange rates among the currencies involved, and your country will have them.'

'I respect your rule of confidentiality,' Lang said. 'But the ambassador will certainly want to know the name of the official at the Bank of Indonesia who has been involved in this mistake.'

There was a slight tremor in Wu's face, a faint negative motion which foreshadowed what he was about to say. 'Believe me, sir, he had nothing to do with all this. I am admitting the mistake in the name of our bank. I take full personal responsibility.'

'I understand that,' Lang said. 'But I'm sure the ambassador will still want to know.'

'I will have to see whether that too falls under the rules of confidentiality, Mr Lang. But I wish for your country to be fully satisfied in this matter, knowing the extent of the appreciation we have for the trust your country puts in our institution.'

11

'I'm sure you do,' Lang said. 'I'm sure you do.'

'I think you're terrible,' Christie said when he was back in the car and she was pulling out into the flow of traffic. 'He sounds quite sincere to me.'

'A classic piggyback,' he said, looking through his wallet to make certain he had enough money for lunch.

'A what?' she said. 'And where do you want to go?'

'To your apartment, love. If you have air-conditioning.'

'*Dim sum*, first,' she said. 'And you pay. A policeman stopped and I explained I was waiting on diplomatic business and he told me to take my time. Now what is this piggyback business?'

'A classic maneuver for somebody's transferring funds between countries when they don't want to be caught at it,' he said. 'In this case, four million dollars was to be forwarded from the United States account here to the United States account in Jakarta. Now, a bank official here added an amount to it, in this case, six million dollars, and it was sent to the Bank of Indonesia. A bank officer was supposed to have separated the funds, depositing the four million to our account and the other six to where it was supposed to be going.'

'There's a marvelous restaurant down near the docks,' she said, making her way expertly through the traffic. 'That's where we're heading. But I still don't see the point.'

'What point?'

'To this piggyback business.'

'It's simple. The other six million dollars was sent to Indonesia illegally. Maybe to finance a terrorist organization, maybe for bribe money on a massive scale. The money could be financing dope. Who knows? But the embassy made an inquiry about the funds at the wrong time, before the Indonesian bank officer had a chance to separate the money. If we had waited a couple of days, the proper amount would have been put into the computers, and in essence the other six million dollars would simply have disappeared.'

Christie frowned, a lovely endearing frown which he found irresistible. She was caught behind a truck now, and the fact of that truck blocking her progress was of far more import than the fact that she had only a vague idea what he was talking about.

He put his hand beneath the long blond hair that cascaded down her back, touched her neck. 'You're a marvelous girl, you know that?'

She stepped on the accelerator. The sports car leaped around the truck and she darted back into the thick traffic, into a spot with scarcely a foot to spare in front or back. 'You say that because I'm such a hell of a driver.'

'Better than I am, actually.'

'So this piggyback business is illegal, is it?'

'Massively. But it's done all the time. For the big-time illicits, it's standard operating procedure.'

'And what will your ambassador do about it?'

'Nothing,' he said, and he felt the faint stirrings of curiosity, combined with a slight urgency. 'Within the next hour or two, since I've stirred up a hornet's nest, the proper data will be entered into the computers and there won't be any accessible records on that other six million.' He looked over his shoulder at the traffic. 'Take a left at the next corner,' he said.

'That's out of the way.'

'We'll miss the peak lunch crowd this way. I want to go back to the bank. Humor me. There could be a promotion in this for me. Advancement follows initiative.'

She did as he asked, made a signal followed by a swift dart of a turn that almost upset a bicycling noodle vendor. 'You're not going to do anything illegal, are you?' she said. 'If you're out to impress me with an act of derring-do, it's really not necessary.'

'I don't think it's illegal,' he said. 'Besides that, it may not even work at all. But there's no harm in trying.'

'You're sure?'

'Of course.' He was not as sure as he sounded, nor would he admit to her that what he was about to do came from the great sense of caution and discretion he was forced to display day in and day out as aide to Ambassador Clements, He was low man on the totem pole at the Jakarta Embassy, and he could see the logic of his position there, an entry-level post in the foreign service in which he was to observe, to make himself useful to the ambassador. If he asked the ambassador for permission to do what he was about to do, he would get a negative. There were certain things a new foreign service officer did not do, foremost among which was the central rule, If It's Not Your Business, Leave It Alone.

But he wasn't going to leave it alone. He had her pull to the curb fifty feet down the street from the bank, and he hopped out of the car, taking his attaché case with him. As he approached the bank two Chinese men in business suits came out of the bank, carrying on an animated conversation. He stopped on the sidewalk to let them pass, in that moment reconsidering what he was about to do. This was not New Haven and he was not embarking on a practical joke at Yale in which the worst that could happen would be a dressing-down administered by a professor.

He would make a deal with himself. He would take a crack at it and if there were any complications at all he would simply back away and admit to himself that the rule was indeed a good one and that the extra six million was none of his business.

It was also possible that the word had already gone out of Mr Wu's office and the whole thing had been corrected in the computers so there was nothing to be found there anyway. In that case no harm done and he would let it be.

He came into the bank lobby and waited near a marble column at a counter where he pretended to be writing out a deposit slip while he kept his eyes on the receptionist at the desk in front of Mr Li's office. She seemed to be firmly established in the seat behind the desk, answering an occasional telephone call, doing a little typing. He set himself a maximum time limit. If she was still at the desk in five minutes, he would abandon the whole idea, because the afternoon was passing and he was hungry and Christie awaited him and this might not be such a hot idea after all.

Three minutes passed. An intercom buzzed on the girl's desk and she went into Mr Li's office. In that second Lang made his move and went past her desk and down the corridor, hurrying only until he was beyond sight of her desk before he slowed to a saunter, took a black notepad out of his attaché case and a ballpoint pen out of his shirt pocket. He entered the computer room, where ten rows of girls were at work and on the far side of the room a supervisor's office with a glass window overlooked the whole work area. It seemed to be empty at the moment. His presence disturbed none of the girls, who continued to punch away at the keyboards.

He examined the back of one of the computers, found a serial number which he jotted down laboriously in his notebook, then examined it from the front, squinting at the screen and the columns of numbers. The operator was a Chinese girl in her early twenties who noticed his frown and bowed slightly to him as she stopped working, keeping her eyes on her demurely folded hands.

'Do you speak English?' he said.

'Yes, sir.'

'Now, then. What's gone wrong with your machine?'

'I don't understand. Nothing is wrong.'

'Then why did you report it?'

'I didn't report it, sir.'

'Well, somebody did,' he said in mock exasperation. 'I'll have to check it out. Are the characters on this machine English or Chinese?'

'English, sir.'

'All right. Can you save the material you have in the machine now and access a file for me?'

'I think you have the wrong machine, sir. This one is fine.'

'Jesus,' he said, rolling his eyes toward the acoustical ceiling. 'If there's nothing wrong with the machine, then just go along with what I want. Otherwise, I'll have to send the thing to the shop. Now, what's it going to be?' He consulted his book. 'Access a file at random, say 11076.'

For a moment, he thought she was going to refuse, in which case he would simply mumble something and abandon the whole thing, but she punched the keys and then entered the number. And momentarily the format flashed on the screen, just enough words that he felt jolted by what he saw before the masculine hand reached out and switched off the machine and he looked up to find Li standing there, face impassive but angry enough that there was a spasmodic tic in his jaw. He let loose with a stream of vituperative colloquial Chinese to the girl at the machine, who turned pale and sat perfectly motionless, as if she thought he was going to strike her.

'It's not her fault,' Lang said. 'She thought she was doing the right thing.' Li just looked at him, glaring eyes, black, shining with anger.

'You don't know what you're doing,' Li said. 'You will cause yourself more trouble than you ever thought possible.'

'Are you threatening me?'

'You can be arrested for what you did. In Singapore this is the same as theft.'

True, Lang thought. Oh, goddamned true, especially with the information that was burned into his brain now, so unsettling as to be totally unforgettable, and his only thought now was to get out of the bank, not to be detained here where they could draw him into rooms from which he could not gain egress. They might very well get him on the street, but he would have a better chance out there, for he did not think that this bank was going to press formal charges when he had seen what he had seen. But he had to get out now, without causing a scene, without calling down on his head the phalanx of bank security people.

'I'm going to walk out of here, Mr Li, and I don't think you're going to have me arrested.'

He turned and left the computer room, knowing that Li was right behind him, and he could almost smell the man's indecision. They reached the lobby and Li's hand reached out and grabbed his arm.

'Take your hand off my arm,' Lang said.

Li's hand dropped away and Lang left the bank.

As he approached the car, Christie let out a small cry of alarm. 'What's the matter, love? You look white as chalk. Are you sick?'

'No,' he said, keeping his voice even. 'You're to do exactly as I say. In one minute you're to drive off without me. Don't even . . .'

'You're having me on,' she said. 'You're frightening me.'

'Just do as I say. I don't want you mixed up in this. You drive off. If anyone asks you how I left you, you say that I insulted you, any story you like, but you don't know a damn thing.'

16

'I really *don't* know a damn thing,' she said. 'Get in the car. We'll go someplace and talk.'

'Time's up,' he said. 'Get the hell out of here. I'll be in touch from Jakarta when I can.'

'But . . .'

He saw the look of desperation in her eyes. 'Now. Go.'

He turned away from her and approached the taxi stand, not even looking back. He told the driver to take him to the airport. He would not even risk going back to the hotel to get his things. If he was lucky it would take them a little while to get organized, to decide what to do about him, and by then he could be out of the country. But the first thing he would do would be to call Ambassador Clements and tell him that there was far more to what was happening here than the concealment of a transfer of funds. He was not sure exactly what he had, but he was sure that certain people would kill to keep him from figuring it out.

If they had the chance. Which he would not give them.

The moment Lang left the bank Mr Li composed himself and went to a private office where he put in a call to Jakarta.

3

JAKARTA

Ambassador Clements came awake slowly, aware that it was early in the morning and for a moment he thought that Alice was lying next to him, for he had been dreaming about her and he was caught in a brief melancholy because the dream had been so real, and they had been sitting on the porch of the small house in Austin, Texas, where they had lived while he was going to school, talking about nothing in particular. The melancholy was transient. She had been dead a long time and only infrequently did she inhabit his dreams now. She had died and over a period of time he had adjusted to her absence and the pain had passed. Special times, he thought, but those days had been spent in a different world.

He turned his head, looked at the woman beside him. Madeleine was still asleep, turned away from him so that her nude body was a pale island in the semidarkness of the room, the curve of her shoulder down to the narrow waist, the rise of hip like the contours of a landscape. The covers were in a shambles around her and her smooth arms embraced a pillow. There was no need to awaken her. He eased himself out of bed and went into the luxurious bathroom which years ago had been added to this ancient Dutch house in the old Batavian section of the city. Somehow it characterized Madeleine Rooseno that she should have had the bathroom done in antique hand-decorated tiles from the Netherlands and at the same time added solid gold fixtures of a functional modern design to the marble tub and the shower.

He took a hot shower and then toweled himself dry, found that the servants had cleaned his suit during the night and left it on a teak valet in his dressing room, the shirt freshly laundered, the shoes shined to a high gloss.

As he dressed he went through his schedule for the day. It was a rather heavy one with a large part of midday consumed by the dedication ceremonies to be followed by routine meetings at the embassy. He knotted his tie and then opened the door to the bedroom gently, so as to make no noise, but Madeleine was already up, sitting at the dresser in the sheerest of peignoirs, brushing her long black hair, and the drapes had been drawn to admit the morning sunlight. A silver coffee service had appeared on a hand-carved French table at the foot of the bed. He came to her and kissed the top of her head. She smelled of sleep and her face glowed in the mirror as she raised her arms and put them around his neck. She smiled, proud of herself and her body, the breasts small and golden brown. He looked at her face in the mirror, washed by reflected light from the tall windows which flooded across a lovely oval face with wide, full lips, high cheekbones, almond-shaped eyes an unusual shade of green. She had always described her ancestry as a cross between Chinese and Javanese, but he was certain that there was a European somewhere in the past to account for the color of her eyes. She sat gracefully, her long fingernails painted gold, and from the way she held her hands, with the delicate fingers splayed outward, in the manner of a classical Balinese dancer.

'You were going to leave without awakening me,' she said with mock chiding.

'You said you didn't have to be in the city until ten.'

'I don't,' she said. 'But I hate to wake up and find you gone. You do have time for coffee.'

'Not much, I'm afraid,' he said. 'My car should be here any time. G. D. Majors is staying at the temporary residence and he'll be along.'

'He's asking for special favors from the government,' she said. 'How much money does he have?' She poured the coffee, hot and black, then sat down opposite him, her eyes sparkling with delight as if she enjoyed watching the most common things about him, and yet a part of her mind was always tuned into business.

He tasted the coffee, an Indonesian blend, very strong. 'Madeleine, I have the feeling you could make love and talk business at the same time.'

'I would find the combination very exciting,' she said. 'Now, does he have a lot of money?'

'Yes. And I've known him since my college days.'

'You know that I have to make a ruling on him at the Finance Ministry.'

'We won't discuss that,' he said.

'Why?'

'I love you but G. D.'s business dealings with the Indonesian Government are his own affair. I won't interfere.'

She smiled. 'You're a very strange man,' she said. 'Why don't you ever use your influence?'

'That's not my job,' he said. 'I'm hired to represent the United States.'

She poured coffee for herself, mixed it with chocolate. 'Is that the reason why you won't move in with me? Everybody in the capital knows we're lovers anyway.'

'You know damn well why I don't move in with you,' he said with a smile.

'The hypocrisy of the Western mind,' she said, without malice.

'Nonsense,' he said.

'I don't think so.'

'Unofficially the diplomatic community recognizes that I'm a man as well as an ambassador and I can do anything I damn well please as long as it doesn't interfere with my capacity or my official judgement. So I'm free to come here and everybody looks the other way. But you know damn well that if I moved in it would all hit the fan. Your country would ask for my recall if my country didn't yank me out first, which they would. Moral turpitude. I think that would be the call in Washington.'

'Have you ever been asked to explain about me?' she said.

'No.'

'What would you say if you were asked?'

'I'd say you are my very good friend.'

'Is that all I am?'

'What?'

'A very good friend. Like G. D. Majors.'

'You know better than that.'

'You used the words.'

'Because that's the way I would have to defend the relationship if official notice were ever taken of it. I would have to say, "Madeleine Rooseno is a very good friend and a deputy minister in the Finance Ministry and she's related to the ruling class of Indonesia. She's of great help to my staff and of course I see her whenever I can."' He sipped the coffee and then heard the discreet tap on the door which meant that his car had arrived. He put the cup back on the tray and stood up, embraced her, drawing her very close against him. He kissed her, then stood looking into her eyes.

'Now, no more of this testing business,' he said. 'You know how I feel about you.'

'Can you come back tonight?'

'I don't think so. But I'll call you.'

She kissed him again and then released him. 'Go take care of the world,' she said. 'And remember that you can ask favors of me whenever you wish. This is my country, not yours.'

He went down the elevator and out the private entrance to the street where the limousine was waiting. G. D. was lounging in the backseat, grimacing as the chauffeur opened the door and inadvertently let in the sunlight as he admitted the ambassador. Clements realized that he had given Madeleine an inadequate description of the relationship between G. D. and him, for G. D. was like the brother he had never had and they had jockeyed through the University of Texas together, each in a different way.

Clements had been eternally red-eyed from cramming the night before exams and G. D. was always cool, rested. Yet at the end, when Clements scored in the mid-nineties, G. D. was never more than a few points lower, in the high eighties, when Clements knew he had never cracked a book.

'How in the hell do you do it?' he had asked him once. 'You don't even take notes in class.'

'Easy,' G. D. said. 'I pay a guy at the frat house fifty bucks for a copy of the test.'

'Where does he get it?'

'He pays a part of the money to the department secretary who types it up.'

'If you go to that much trouble, why don't you make a perfect score?' Clements had asked.

'Shit, they'd catch me for sure,' G. D. had said with a lopsided grin. 'They know I'm not an A student. So I don't push my luck. You want copies of the tests from now on? We could split the cost.'

'No, thanks.'

'I didn't think you would or I would have offered a long time ago. That's the difference between us, buddy. You take all this seriously and I know it's bullshit. But college won't matter to me in the long run.'

And it hadn't, Clements thought. As far as he knew, G. D. had never read a book since college and was none the worse for it financially. When Clements had married Alice in his senior year and then gone back East to graduate school, G. D. had gone into the oil business, had made and lost three fortunes and four wives before Clements had his first important post with the foreign service, had houses all over the world and was currently immensely wealthy from brokering oil in Southeast Asia. He was a physically large man who exuded a sense of expansiveness, from the solid-gold belt buckle he wore to the custom boots and the modified Stetson. He did his best to project the image of a 'good old boy,' and perhaps beneath the layerings of rough and tumble in which he had been engaged for thirty years, he still was that. *But woe be to any business adversary who bought that package and underestimated him*, Clements thought.

At the moment G. D. was suffering a hangover. His eyes were bloodshot and he was chewing on an unlit cigar. 'You talk to her about me?' he said.

'No.'

'Fine goddamn friend you are. Besides that, you're out of bourbon at your place.'

'You look like hell,' Clements said with a smile.

'I feel like hell,' G. D. said. 'I was going over some production reports. The more I read the more depressed I got. The more depressed I got, the more I drank.'

'It's going to get worse before it gets better,' Clements said. He tapped the glass, told his chauffeur to drive on.

Jakarta was a subtle city, totally overlooked by tourists except as a place to pause between Singapore and Bali, a vast plain which had been torn between wealth and poverty for centuries, occupied by the Dutch until the great battles which had burst it free in 1949. It was still a vast sprawl of urban poverty, tiers of huts rising like walls along the banks of the filthy canals which crisscrossed the city. The flood of recent oil money had made it possible for the government to begin to clean up the worst of the slums, and then the recession had hit, the rampant inflation which had slowed the social progress to a crawl.

Now there were new high-rise buildings existing side by side with shacks, new buildings which seemed to age overnight, fitting in with the widened avenues, lined with street stalls, the masses of traffic, buses, motorcycles, the eternal trucks, mopeds, *betjaks* (the three-wheeled motorized taxis, cheap to hire), the smell of diesel exhausts, the stink of the brackish canals which laced the city with a network of barges and single-masted boats, drawbridges on even the smaller streets to allow them passage.

Ordinarily, Clements enjoyed his morning ride to the embassy. As a rule, he required his Indonesian driver to follow a different route each day so he could keep in touch with what was going on in the city. He had learned to do that early in his career, to move away from official government circles as much as possible to know what was happening in the country itself, what the people were thinking, how the economy was actually functioning instead of accepting at face value the pronouncements of press secretaries and official papers.

There was much to be learned from graffiti painted on walls, the spontaneous outbursts of folk art that demanded reform in government or instructed the Yankee fuckers to go home, and he could often guage the mood of a government by how long graffiti remained in place before it was scrubbed away or painted over. Society here was a hurly-burly mixture of Muslim and Hindu and a dozen animistic religions, and despite the government's efforts to project Indonesia as one big united country, there were dozens of highly vocal factions constantly demanding change.

But this morning Clements instructed the driver to go straight to the embassy because G. D. had early meetings and was scheduled to go back to Bangkok before noon. The car slowed at the congestion on the street, great masses of people just milling about the intersections. G. D. peered through the tinted window at the crowds.

'Every time I come to this damn place, I think the population has doubled,' he said.

'A thousand new people a day,' Clements said, rather sadly. 'They come out of the jungle or make it here on boats that shouldn't even float. They sleep on the streets and drink the contaminated water in the canals and they scrounge enough food to keep from starving.'

'Then why do they come?'

'Because as bad as things are here, they're better than where these people come from.'

G. D. turned away from the window. No social conscience at all, Clements thought, without judgement. 'The Indonesian Government could feed all the immigrants with the money they lose by being so goddamned stubborn. They've got the American oil producers by the balls. They set the rules and then they change them. What kind of game are they playing, Charlie?'

'You make a big mistake if you think this is a game,' Clements said. No, he went on, this was a complex reality involving money and pride. The Indonesians had been poor until the vast fields had been tapped, and the new wealth had brought an increased sense of nationalism on the one hand and a corrupt bureaucracy on the other. It was foreign investments that had developed the oil and gas fields, yet now the Indonesians were putting the squeeze on their Western partners, trying to compensate for the declining price of oil. And lurking in the background, always there despite the official disfavor of the Indonesians, was the Soviet Union, waiting for the current alliances to fall apart so they could move in, establish a new partnership in this part of the world.

'I don't give a damn about the Russians,' G. D. said. 'A lot of British and American oil companies are hurting, Charlie.' He leaned back, lit the cigar. 'Give me the straight stuff,

Charlie. Is it going to change? What are the Indonesian nationalists going to do?'

'Win,' Clements said.

'And throw all of us out?'

'I think so, yes. At least, that's my personal opinion. Officially, I'm told to express official approval every time the economic ministers put out a rosy press release and ignore the belligerence of the state oil company. But off the record I believe that Pertamina Oil is going to win out and eventually the oil holdings in Indonesia will be nationalized. If I had any oil holdings anyplace within a thousand miles of Jakarta, I'd get rid of them. When the takeover comes the Indonesian government might pay fifty cents on the dollar, probably less.'

'I think you're wrong. The big boys aren't going to let that happen. They invested a hell of a lot of money here. They're not going to let it go that easily.'

'I hope you're right.'

'I know I'm right.' G. D. shrugged. 'Have you given any more thought to the old proposition?' G. D. said.

'You're still serious about that?' Clements said.

'Hell, yes. We'd make an unbeatable team. I'd sell off all my holdings in this part of the world and we'd go back to Texas. M and C Enterprises. You remember?'

Clements remembered all right. He had been at Yale when his father died and he and Alice had come back to Austin to make the arrangements for the funeral, for Clements was an only son and his mother had died when he was in his teens. G. D. had been right there, all the way, a great comfort. And when Alice spent a few days visiting her parents, Clements and G. D. had gotten drunk together and in a bar had decided to form a corporation, an oil company to end all oil companies, offshore drilling, the Anadarko basin, shale oil in Wyoming, riches and power beyond belief, because G. D. had already hit big and Clements had inherited a staggering amount of money from his father's oil interests. Together they could parlay their assets into the biggest damn oil company in the world.

And somehow, after the drink that was one too many, there had been an argument which, after all these years,

Clements could only vaguely remember, despite his attempts at times to reconstruct it. It seemed to him now that he had said something like 'Alice is coming back tomorrow and after I talk to her, we'll make the deal final.' And he remembered the stunned expression on G. D.'s flushed face, as if he had been poleaxed. 'What the hell does she have to do with this?'

'She's my wife. She has an equal say.'

'You're shitting me,' G. D. had said, grinning. 'Hell, no woman's ever going to lead me around by the nose. I dumped Linda when she tried that. This is just us, buddy. Nobody else. I know this business upside down and backwards. I paid ten thousand dollars to a geologist from Texaco to slip me reports on a hot property under the table. Only while they were farting around, I moved. A thousand acres of the hottest damn leases in Texas.'

They had been hot, all right, and G. D. had made millions, but the greatest oil company in the world had never materialized. For by the next morning Clements had sobered up and Alice was back from her parents and it was time to catch a plane and G. D. was on hand to help with the baggage and to remind him of the offer, which would remain open.

But now, just short of his fiftieth year, with Alice dead, there was something about that old plan which still appealed to him. For he could resign his post here at any time and open the blind trusts into which all his assets had been placed.

'You tempt me,' Clements said.

'Anytime,' G. D. said, sincerely. 'We could do some great things together.'

'One of these days, I may take you up on it,' Clements said. But not now, he could have added, for Jakarta lay at the exact centre of the rebellion which was to come, sooner or later.

'When you going to come up to Bangkok again?' G. D. said. 'I've been adding to the compound, and now I've got a whole damn zoo. And Bangkok's got more beautiful women per acre than any other spot short of Hong Kong. You come up and I'll guarantee you a private good time like you've never had before.'

'One of these days,' Clements said.

G. D. nodded, as if he understood. 'I keep forgetting. You already have the most beautiful woman in Indonesia.'

'Just good friends,' Clements said.

'Still, come up to Bangkok.'

'Sure.'

In the blink of an eye the Boulevard Jalan Hayam Wuruk changed names and became Jalan H. Hackjrudin. Momentarily the limousine was turning into the gates of the embassy, which closed behind it. At one time the American Embassy in Jakarta had had a certain amount of charm about it, or so it seemed to Clements in retrospect, back in the pre-1965 days when he and Alice had visited here on infrequent occasion en route to a consular post somewhere beyond. It had been a compound with a sense of grace about it, the chancery in front, other buildings across spacious lawns and beds of exotic flowers, the American flag dangling from a tall metallic pole which glinted silver in the sunlight, 'pointing democracy toward heaven,' as one poetic ambassador had put it.

He remembered a time when Alice had been interviewed by a local reporter here who was definitely anti-American and paid by the Soviets for any propaganda pieces he could get into print. He had picked her for a story simply because she seemed to be so vulnerable. The reporter had been an ash-brown little man with darting eyes who asked her if she and her husband did not feel ashamed to be getting rich off the economies of the poor countries of the world. Alice hadn't blinked and her sweet smile had not faded.

'I'll make you a trade,' she said. 'We'll have an impartial third party come in and then we'll gladly disclose our net income if you'll disclose yours.'

The reporter blinked. 'Then you deny that you represent the lackeys of capitalism.'

'I'm not sure what a lackey is,' she said. 'But if lackeys are the thousands of people who gave money to build a clinic in a small country in Africa, a country that lacks the resources to have any import or export trade, with people who will be saved from disease because people from America felt compassion for them, then perhaps my husband and I do represent lackeys of capitalism.' The smile remained constant. 'And now, sir, I would suggest that if you print anything at all about me that you quote exactly what I've said. Otherwise I will contradict you, in print, and your government will have the choice of backing you or offending the United States of America.'

A spunky woman, Clements thought, and perhaps it was his marriage to her which had shaped his career, because she was so world-minded, so aware of the need for good people to represent America. The journalist had backed down, of course, but that was before the temporary Communist coup, student terrorists running amok in the streets, before the British Embassy had been burned to the ground and the American Embassy was spared only by circumstance from the same fate.

At that point the American Embassy had gone through extensive reconstruction, with heavy use of cement and steel, control gates for limited access, Marines on duty around the clock at the new and heavier walls. In the parlance of State, the embassy had been 'hardened,' and now it was a veritable fortress, bristling with electronic gear that would warn of attack.

Inside the chancery Clements took time to introduce G. D. to Barkley, the first economic counselor, then excused himself and went down the long corridor to his suite of offices and the omnipresent Lucy, who had been his private secretary for the past ten years. Once he closed the door to his private office, he noticed that she had the thermos of coffee ready for him on the large free-form desk, and there was a vase with freshly cut tropical flowers atop a bookcase. The dispatches from Washington had been laid out on his blotter, and a separate sheet contained his schedule for the day, all of it the work of the faithful Lucy, who stood near the door, ready to give him the briefings she had not had time to record on paper.

He poured himself a cup of coffee from the thermos, sat down in the large swivel chair. 'Well, Lucy,' he said. 'What do we have on tap for today?'

'The cables from Washington are all routine,' she said. 'But I was sure you'd want a look at them anyway. And Jim Lang called from Bangkok.'

'Bangkok? What the hell is he doing in Bankok?'

'He sounded very upset. Something about airline schedules and the first plane he could get out of Singapore. He wanted to talk to you but you were en route and he won't have a chance to call back. He should be in by noon and he wants to see you immediately. I told him you would be at the dedication ceremony. He said he'd come out there. Do you think he could be in trouble?'

'You have to stop mothering my aides, Lucy,' he said with a smile. But of course she would not, for Lang was the young idealist, ready to tilt at any visible windmill, and in many ways Lang represented the son he had never been fortunate enough to have. 'You don't need to worry about him. He was looking into some illicit funds that supposedly came into Jakarta along with some of our aid money.'

'He sounded desperate.'

'Everything's dramatic when you're as young as he is.' He sorted through the papers on his desk. 'Is the draft of my speech here?'

'You won't be making a speech. Just a few informal remarks about the wonderful cooperation between the two countries and the blend of Indonesian and American resources which have made the new port facilities possible. No more than six or seven minutes.'

'Who else is speaking?'

'Oil Minister Rooseno.'

Clements moaned inwardly. Rooseno was Madeleine's uncle. He had been a radio commentator at one time before he had risen in the Suharto bureaucracy. He loved the sound of his own voice and never made informal remarks of less than an hour's duration. On one occasion, an afternoon when the temperature was close to a hundred and two degrees Fahrenheit, Rooseno had carried on for close to an hour and forty minutes. 'Then what?' he said.

'I told Jim Lang he could ride back from the dock with you in the limo. Then you have lunch with the American Women's Association. They're issuing a new guidebook to the city. This afternoon, the Country Team at three, an informal meeting in the garden with members of the Aberdeen, South Dakota, High School Band that's on its way to perform in

Australia. Then you have the evening free. I supposed you would want to have dinner with Mr Majors.'

'He's flying back to Bangkok this morning. And don't fill in the evening. I want to catch up on my reading.'

'Yes, sir. And one more thing. Mr Kemper would like ten minutes.'

Ah, Kemper, Clements thought, a most unusual mixture of positions. For Kemper was not only chief of station for the CIA here but also head of security. 'I'll see him in an hour or so. What time do I leave for the dock ceremony?'

'Eleven o'clock. Mr Rooseno is coming by for you in Pertamina's new limousine. I've seen that your morning suit is in your dressing room.'

'How would I do without you, Lucy?'

'Probably poorly,' Lucy said in one of her rare flashes of humor. 'But I'm still a good many years away from retirement so you don't have to worry.'

Clements was reading circular memos from State and routing them through the embassy when G. D. stopped in to say goodbye. He shook hands like a football player. 'I ordered you a case of I. W. Harper,' he said. 'I told them to deliver it to your house.'

'You trying to get me thrown out of office for taking bribes?'

G. D. grinned without humor. 'The way Indonesia's kicking me around while you sit around with your thumb up your ass, no court in the world would believe that you were being bribed. Besides, it gives me something decent to drink when I drop in.'

'Take care of yourself,' Clements said.

'You can count on that. But honestly, buddy, if you get the chance, set the Indonesians straight. I want enough money left to hold up my half of the proposition. The greatest oil company in the world. Don't forget that.'

'You can count on it,' Clements said. 'And many thanks for the bourbon.'

Clements was changing his clothes in the dressing-room suite adjoining his office when he heard the intercom buzzer and flipped it on.

'Yes?'

'Mr Kemper is here, sir.'

'Send him in. I'll talk to him while I'm dressing.' He had just put on the fresh shirt and was inserting the gold cuff links when he heard the slight tap on the door and Kemper came in, and he could tell from the serious expression on Kemper's face what the general tone of the conversation was going to be. Harry Kemper ran his staff with great efficiency and, for the most part, Clements allowed him the greatest possible latitude in his operations, for he had served in embassies where the tension was so great between the chief of station and the ambassador that the work of the embassy was seriously impaired. There was a perpetual paranoia at work in every chief of station, Clements realized, and especially in Kemper. Perhaps rightfully so, for they were perpetually in the midst of an enemy camp regardless of where they were stationed.

Kemper was wearing a safari suit with short sleeves, a permissible uniform for this part of the world. His arms were tanned a deep brown and he looked extremely fit. Clements gave him a nod in the mirror. 'Which cap are you wearing today, Harry,' Clements said. 'Security or intelligence?'

'Out here, there's not much difference between the two.'

'Let me ask you a question before you begin. You know about the piggyback money, the extra six million?'

'Of course.'

'Jim Lang seems to have uncovered something in Singapore that has him spooked. Is there any possibility he could have found anything on the money?'

Kemper showed a half-smile. 'He has a girlfriend in Singapore.'

'So?'

'I know Jim pretty well. If a little derring-do could impress the girl, he's not above it.'

'Then you don't believe he might have stumbled onto something accidentally.'

Kemper shook his head. 'Not a chance. I've had some of the best people in the business trying to trace the path of illegal money coming into Jakarta for a long time. They

31

haven't been able to do it and I'll bet you a hundred dollars that all this is one of Jim Lang's courtship dramas.'

'You're probably right,' Clements said. He looked at himself in the mirror. 'Let's change places one of these days, Harry,' he said. 'You wear the formal morning clothes and give your remarks to ten thousand Indonesians who have been assembled by the government to show respect and don't give a damn, and I'll wear the comfortable clothes and stand guard.'

'If I had my way, you wouldn't even be participating in mass meetings like this,' Kemper said. 'They're dangerous.'

Clements knotted his tie, a conservative dark blue. 'You might as well sit down. There's cold Perrier in the minifridge. And get me one while you're at it. Not that anything's going to keep me cool. I'll be drenched through with sweat before I even get to the platform. And I've drawn long-winded Rooseno as my speaking counterpart today. No surcease for the wicked.'

Kemper occupied himself taking two bottles of Perrier from the minifridge. 'You want ice?'

'Not even a glass,' Clements said. 'Now, what's on your mind, Harry?'

Kemper handed him a bottle and then sat down and poured his mineral water into a glass. 'I want you to insist that Rooseno ride with you in your protected car.'

'You don't understand the protocol,' Clements said. 'Today he's making a special point of impressing me with Pertamina's newest limousine. He has to demonstrate that the current Indonesian Government is progressive and not on the edge of bankruptcy. Unless I'm wrong, the limousine will be a Mercedes, and that in itself will be another communication to me that Indonesia does not have to buy all its automobiles from the United States.'

Kemper sipped the Perrier, took a sheet of paper out of his pocket. 'A call came this morning. Eight forty-two to be exact. A threat on your life from a shrill-voiced representative of a splinter group of the Indonesia Communist Party.'

'Denouncing American imperialism,' Clements said. He stood in front of the air conditioner while he put on his trousers. 'Calling for the Yankee capitalists to leave

Indonesia forever. How many calls does this make in the past six months? At least one a week, isn't it? And what does this group call themselves?'

'The Red Brigade.'

'Not very original,' Clements said. 'It's always "The Red Brigade" or "The Red Watch" or even "The Red Army."'

'We're not going to underestimate any threat, especially one as specific as this one,' Kemper said. 'This fanatic said that if you appear in public today, you will be killed.'

'Why today?'

'According to this crazy, the Red Brigade has boasted to the press that they have the power to coerce the United States, that this power will be demonstrated by the cancellation of your appearance at a public event.'

'You're not suggesting that I stay home?'

'I'm suggesting that we take extra precautions,' Kemper said. 'I've checked. The Pertamina limousine is a Mercedes and it's not reinforced, even though it has bulletproof glass. So let's play it safe and use our limousine with our lead car and our backup. The Indonesian military, their special police can work the flanks, the point, and bring up the rear.'

'Do you know how the Indonesian Government would interpret that?'

'At this point, I don't give a damn.'

'Which is exactly what your attitude is supposed to be,' Clements said. He sat down, put on the shoes, the surface of the leather so perfect he could see his own reflection. 'I appreciate your efforts, Harry. But the Indonesian Government would take all that as a vote of no confidence in their ability to protect foreign dignitaries. And what happens in the crowd at the docks? I'm exposed there. You know that area. It's bedlam, totally impossible to police.' He stood up, sipped the Perrier. 'You know the odds. Reagan's protection is the best in the world, and a crazy got him. Even the Pope, for God's sake.' He shrugged. 'We just have to take the chances.'

'All right,' Kemper conceded. 'We'll go with their limo. But I want permission to change the route.'

'Not even that,' Clements said. 'This is a Muslim government and military to boot and that means their own particular brand of macho. They're easy to offend and I don't intend to offend them.' He finished the Perrier. 'I appreciate your concern, Harry, but this is the way it has to be.'

Kemper stood up. 'Maybe this is another false alarm, Mr Ambassador. But I would like to take some time to review with you the whole security system here at the embassy, not only the defensive structure here, but the patterns of movements of key personnel.'

'We'll do that,' Clements said. 'Now, if you'll excuse me, Harry, I think I'd better take a look at the remarks I'm supposed to make.'

Sangre had been awake at dawn. The pills had worn off and there had been a confrontation in the street outside the *losmen*, shrill voices yelling, the Jakarta police using their nightsticks on one of the roving night gangs. He had stood at the window with his camera and watched the fighting quite dispassionately, with the disdain of a professional watching amateurs, the nightsticks used like clubs, no finesse. He took only one picture, that of one young man who stood propped up against a lamppost, the blood streaming out of his matted hair to cover the whole side of his face, the police pounding away at him while he hugged the lamppost and refused to go down.

Stupid.

The young man should have gone down with the first blow and then taken out a knife and slashed across the back of the boot of the nearest cop, right through the soft leather and the tendon which controlled the foot. One smooth slash of a razor-sharp blade, a smooth movement of the arm, graceful, a certain beauty there, and the cop would have been crippled for life.

And when he turned away from the window, he stopped short. Because beneath the edge of his door was the paper, brown, rectangular, slid in the space beneath the door at an angle, even as he had been looking out the window. The fat man's wife had put the paper there and not even knocked to alert him because she was afraid of him. And ordinarily she would have had good reason to fear him because he had told her he would cut off one of her ears if she failed to rouse him when the message came. But now he was diverted by the paper and he snatched it up and memorized the telephone number. 512007. Easy to remember.

He felt high now, a tingling sensation in his fingers, and he went over the room very carefully, making sure that there would be nothing of himself left behind, not so much as a trace of a fingerprint or a scrap of paper. He picked up his duffel bag and his tool kit and went down the narrow stairs, knowing that no one would ever trace him back to this place, back to this filthy hole full of whores and budget travelers.

In the office he fixed the fat man with a stare, picked up the telephone and dialed, waited until he heard the voice on the other end, and then, lowering his voice so the fat man could not hear, simply said 'Yes' in English, and then waited for the instructions, given to him in sparse language, no frills, and to show that he understood, he simply said 'Yes' and put the grimy telephone back on the cradle. He took the loose bills out of his pocket, counted out the rupiahs he owed and put them on the counter, then went out onto the street without a word.

The sunlight was so bright that it hurt his eyes. He slipped on sunglasses and with the handle of the tool kit in one hand and the duffel bag in the other he stood on the sidewalk for a while, watching the police rounding up their victims into a van, bloody young men who had been beaten into submission. He watched only because it might draw attention to himself if he did not watch, and once the van drove off, he nodded toward the driver of one of the three-wheeled motorized *betjaks*, which in Bangkok he would have called a *tuk-tuk* from the sound that the motor made, and it reminded him of the sound of gook boat engines, the tuk-tuk-tuk you could hear in the dark of the night and not know where it was coming from. And one night, so dark he could not even see shapes, he had sat beneath a tree and fired tracers skimming across the muddy river toward that goddamn tuk-tuk-tuk and, after a hundred rounds, the sound of that putting engine receded into the distance, the boat never glimpsed.

The driver was a tall, stringy man, wearing nothing but shorts and a straw coolie hat, and he bowed and tried to help his passenger with the baggage, but Sangre pushed him aside, put the toolbox in the back at his feet and the duffel bag beside him and then told the driver where he wanted to go.

There was a canvas shade covering the top of the seat and he leaned against the duffel bag, trying to let himself go limp, because he would do this right, one shot, no mistakes, perfectly placed, and that took perfect concentration and insides that were at peace, controlled by the mind, not by drugs. He soaked in the sunlight which poured through a rip in the canvas, and he closed his eyes, listening to the roar of the traffic on the streets, the smell of diesel stinging his nostrils, and then he began to shut them out, the noises first, reducing them until he achieved the equivalence of silence, knowing the noise was there but not allowing it to affect him. And he filtered the air through his nostrils with such concentration that all odors were left outside himself. And now, against the inside of his closed eyelids, he pictured the events that would come in the next two hours, rehearsing them with no sense of panic, no feelings at all, just seeing them without any sounds or pressures, as if he had closed off the sound on a television set and was aware of nothing but the picture.

The roof, the killing (and that was a special pleasure which would not be considered now, not in this rehearsal) and then a picture or two and the proper disposition of the gun and the quick change into the clothes inside the duffel bag which would transform him, the exit from pandemonium, like Orpheus escaping from hell, calmly, for that's what it would take. Perhaps he was magically protected after all, because he should have been dead at least a dozen times but was not, a number of times from gook soldiers on patrol and the rest by police who should have had him, back in the days before he had perfected himself so that he made no mistakes.

Tuk-tuk-tuk.

Weaving through the traffic toward the north, and he was as invisible as if he did not exist at all, because everybody in this pit of a city was hustling to stay alive so they saw nobody else. And within two hours, when he had become the new person, he would have fifty thousand dollars in cash, and once he was on the jet, he would spring into a sudden identity and the stewardesses would notice him, and if they started a conversation with him and he had the chance to talk about himself, he would tell them that he was an artist.

It took him an hour to reach the docks and he did not haggle with the man, paid him in rupiahs so grimy that they were about to disintegrate in his hand, then climbed the scaffolding to the rooftop with little effort, even hampered as he was by the toolbox and the duffel bag. There were no children here today, nobody, and he put his things in the corner of the roof and then leaned on the stone parapet and smoked a cigarette, looking down on the decorations, red and white bunting on one side of the platform, the Indonesian national colors, and one small American flag on the right side. Workmen were putting up folding chairs on the platform and he checked his angles, making certain that the speakers' podium was not obscured by any stray scrap of cloth. The crowds were already beginning to gather on the docks, filthy street people who had nowhere else to go. A few soldiers were passing out small Indonesian flags, and he could see other soldiers passing out free *kretek* cigarettes to ensure that there would be large crowds of people here.

He made another survey of the roof, restless. He took a knife from his pocket and severed the hemp that bound one end of the top row of bamboo scaffolding, the long sections of bamboo swinging downward, making access to the top of his roof difficult. Then he took his scope from his duffel bag and zeroed in on the heads of a dozen people in the crowds below, in turn, the cross hairs placed in the center of multiple foreheads. In his imagination he pulled the trigger, squeezed it off ever so gently, a number of times, and watched each of the heads explode. He imagined the visual patterns each would make. He could remember one man he had killed in Algeria who had been sitting at a sidewalk cafe when the bullet smashed into his head, and the spectacular pattern his blood had made on a painter's drop cloth, almost like an abstract flower, blood red.

He sat down in the corner. As the morning went by, the heat of the day increased and the humidity soared. He found a piece of cardboard, a large square from an old packing carton which the children had managed to carry up on the roof and he leaned it up against the parapet where, by edging very carefully into the triangular space, he had a partial shade. He could smell the approaching monsoon rains, not that far off, and his right knee began to hurt him. *Okay, knee, straighten up, none of this shit, because we all work together, and when the time comes, you're damn well going to do your part.* He realized he should have brought water with him, because the dust was already beginning to settle in his mouth. He remembered a professional he had met in Africa, a slight man who looked like a hymn singer instead of a contract hit man, who never ate food or drank water or screwed a woman for twenty-four hours before a killing, claiming that deprivation sharpened a man's senses. Maybe so. But he still should have brought the water.

Every half hour he made the route around the roof again, went through his mental rehearsal, checked his gear yet one more time. It was impossible to have too much preparation, to make certain everything was in place. His life would depend upon it.

Shortly before noon he removed the pieces of the rifle from the toolbox, unwrapped each in the proper sequence, went through the ritual of cleaning each one before he snapped it into place. Then he put the magazine in the slot, drove it home with the palm of his hand and tucked the rifle into the duffel bag. He kept the scope separate and, while he smoked a cigarette, he checked his camera one last time, then looked through the scope toward the speakers platform. The magnification was so great that he could see a fly on the end of a workman's nose. The workmen had rigged a canvas cover which hung like a shroud behind the bunting, a cover which could be hoisted into place should the rain break before the dignitaries were through with their speeches. Through the scope he could place the cross hairs on every seat on the platform, even if the canvas cover was in place. He estimated the distance at twenty-four to twenty-six meters. He would not even have to adjust for elevation or for wind at this distance.

He placed the cross hairs on the head of a bearded workman who reminded him of his father, a man who stood in profile conducting an animated conversation with a young man who was trying to tighten the ropes that supported the bunting. The scope revealed an interesting angle. He wondered if he could fire a bullet that would enter the side of the right eye, pass through the bridge of the nose on a horizontal plane and remove the other eye as well without killing. Probably so. But that was pure conjecture because he was here to work and it would be an American head that would fill the circular eye of the scope and he would be shooting to kill, not to maim, not to demonstrate his skill or his artistry.

A money shot.

He heard the distant beating of helicopter rotors. He halfway expected them and he located the Indonesian police helicopter out over the water, hovering checking all the ships. Sooner or later it would make a swing around the warehouses. He stuck his duffel bag beneath the protective lean-to of the cardboard, then lay down on the roof in a rim of shade projected by a parapet, his toolbox by his side, his arm over his eyes as if he were sleeping. The sound of the helicopter came ever closer and there was a moment when he knew it was hovering above him by a hundred feet or so while military eyes looked down at what was apparently a workman asleep on the job.

He had to control himself to keep from grabbing the rifle out of the duffel bag and trying a shot at the sons of bitches who would be looking down on him with such scorn, never knowing that he would make more for this day's work than they would make for a whole year. He could see in his mind's eye the copter centered in the scope, not on the plastic bubble of the window, for the curved reflective surface could distort and it was too easy to miss the pilot, but on the aluminum skin that covered the high-octane gas tank, where the bullet could rip right through to the volatile heart of the machine and explode it in a ball of flame.

He reveled in the thought, in the mental picture. He did not stir. The helicopter moved on. He edged the arm away from his eyes a fraction of an inch to look into the glaring sky, make sure it was gone. Then he sat up, checked his watch.

Another hour or so to go. He settled down in his corner to wait.

On Kemper's advice, Clements had agreed that Minister Rooseno would pick him up at the chancery in the new limousine, for according to custom, since the American Embassy was technically American soil, only the limousine would be pulling through the wrought-iron gates while the escort of police and military vehicles waited outside. And Kemper would be able to gain his desired protective position without incident.

The limousine was indeed a white Mercedes and when it came to a stop beneath the portico, a driver popped out of the front seat, dressed in chauffeur's livery that resembled a military uniform without the markings of rank. He opened the back door with alacrity and Minister Rooseno himself came out of the car and up to the door to meet the waiting Clements, to shake his hand and conduct him out to the waiting limousine, obviously anxious to impress Clements with his new machine.

'If you don't mind, Mr Ambassador,' Rooseno was saying. 'Perhaps the two of us might ride without the usual aides. We haven't had a chance to talk privately lately.'

'Of course, Minister Rooseno,' Clements said.

The backseat of the limousine was cavernous, upholstered in white leather, outfitted with a portable bar, a small color television, which was showing a test pattern at the moment, a minirefrigerator and a telephone replete with a dozen different buttons. Clements suspected that Pertamina had indeed paid for this limousine but that it had been designed for the President's wife, Madame Tien, and that within a month or two would be relegated to the presidential garage. Rooseno pressed a button and a smoked glass arose to separate the back compartment from the driver's seat. As the limousine started forward one of Kemper's cars moved in front of it and another fell in behind so that, as they emerged onto the boulevard, the limousine was encapsulated by American vehicles, leaving the Indonesian forces to clear the traffic out of the way and to bring up the rear.

The air-conditioning in the Mercedes worked well and almost absorbed the faint odor of violets which Minister Rooseno wore as a pomade on his thick black hair. He was taller than the average Indonesian and his Nehru jacket bulged with the effort of containing a paunch. He was not Clement's favorite government minister for he had a tendency to distort conversations in the reports he made to his superiors and Clements dared not use anything but the most direct language with him so that his intent would not be misinterpreted.

However, Rooseno represented a useful faction in government, for he was a bureaucrat from an extended family of bureaucrats which had a tendency to stay in power when the generals were playing musical chairs. Today, Rooseno was a little edgy, slighty uncomfortable, as if he were seeking out information which might be unpleasant. He held up a clove cigarette, looking to Clements for approval.

'Do you mind if I smoke, Mr Ambassador?' he said.

'Not at all.'

'Do you care for one?'

'No, thank you.'

Rooseno removed a gold lighter from his pocket. A delicate flame extended from it, touched the tobacco. Rooseno inhaled deeply. The cigarette smelled medicinal. 'I wish to have a private and unofficial conversation with you,' he said.

'How can I help you, Minister?'

'A potentially unpleasant situation is developing,' Rooseno said, sucking on the cigarette. 'We are told that the oil production is declining, and with the new rulings which require replacement of foreign workers on the rigs and in positions of responsibility, we feel maybe production isn't declining, but that your countrymen are deliberately slowing down the production of oil in protest. In short, we believe you are not acting in good faith.'

'I'll give you my personal opinion, Minister. But this doesn't reflect the official policy of my government in any way.'

'I would appreciate your candid opinion.'

'I doubt that, sir. I think your government has overextended itself quite badly. You thought the oil prices were going to hold up and you mortgaged your future and now you're caught in a bind because you owe more than you can pay without cutting down on social programs. And you're attempting to get off the hook by convincing your people that the Americans and the British are at fault. Their presence is all that's keeping your oil production even at the level it is now. Every time you stick an untrained man on a rig in the name of nationalism before he knows what the hell he's doing, you're losing money.' He could see Rooseno bristling slightly, but he did not let up. 'I will ask you straight out, sir. The American oilmen believe that, sooner or later, Indonesia will nationalize the whole of the petroleum industry. Are you prepared to deny that?'

'If that day ever comes, and I'm not saying that it will, then any foreign interests will be bought out at a fair rate.'

'And there you have your problem, Minister. Your fair rate could bankrupt a lot of the smaller operators and seriously penalize the large companies. I have to tell you, if I were an American oilman working under your policies, I'd cut my losses and go home.'

'Taking your tremendous profits with you.'

'You know better than that, sir. Your government controls the books. The loss on the capital investments would be enormous.'

Rooseno's hand trembled slightly. He was having difficulty controlling his anger. 'If the Western oil companies cooperated more fully, we wouldn't have these problems.'

'With all respect, that's nonsense, Minister. The oil companies are bending over backward to keep oil production up without offending the incompetent people your oil ministry is forcing into the business.'

Rooseno forced himself to be calm, smoked the cigarette in silence, and suddenly Clements could see his problem quite clearly. As chief oil minister, the generals were holding him responsible for declining revenues, and it would be personally disastrous for Rooseno if the generals decided that another minister might be able to pry better cooperation out of the Americans.

The telephone buzzed. Rooseno picked it up, answered in Indonesian, then looked to Clements. 'It's for you, Mr Ambassador.'

Clements took the receiver impatiently. 'Yes?'

Lang was on the other end of the line, so out of breath as to be almost incoherent. 'I'm sorry to break protocol, Mr Ambassador. But my God, all hell's about to break loose. And I couldn't get through.' 'Calm down, Jim,' Clements said. 'You'll hyperventilate. The last I heard you were in Bangkok.'

'I don't know where to begin. Do you know anything about "The Six Ravens"?'

'The what?'

'"The Six Ravens."'

'No. Where are you?'

'I just got in at the airport. I saw their schedule, sir. The whole damn thing.'

'This isn't a good place to discuss it, Jim.'

'Yes, sir. I'll come out to the port. We'll talk then. And for God's sake, sir, make sure you have plenty of security. Keep a low profile. Jesus.'

'I'll see you after the ceremony. We'll talk.' He handed the telephone back to Rooseno, who placed it in the cradle.

'I want to know if you are willing to help,' Rooseno said with a sudden change of tone, a tinge of desperation in his voice.

'In what way?'

'I have arranged a conference,' Rooseno said. 'Not just Indonesia, but all of the oil-producing countries in ASEAN. I would like to have all the American companies there as observers. The discussions would be frank, candid.'

'That might be helpful,' Clements said, 'as long as it's not just another anti-American propaganda forum.'

'Then may I inform my government that your government will approve of such a conference and cooperate fully?'

'You can inform your government that I am amenable, Minister, but only as a private citizen, not in my capacity as an ambassador. This request will have to come through your foreign minister's office.'

'I see,' Rooseno said. He looked out through the window, realized that they were approaching the dock area. 'We had better go over the ceremonies today. If that meets with your approval?'

'Of course.'

'As to the order of the events,' Rooseno said. 'There is a

platform built near the new oil dock. The welcoming ceremony will begin with a young girl presenting flowers on our arrival at the docks. Then you will make your remarks and I will give a short talk of appreciation for what the United States is doing, a promise that the technical assistance which you are giving to the Republic of Indonesia will be well used. There will be a picture-taking opportunity for your information service and our newspapers. Is that convenient with you?'

'Fine, thank you.' Through the window of the car he could see the limp bunting which decorated the street along the docks. There was too much slack in the wires from which the banners were suspended. The air was full of diesel fumes and the stench of the harbor. From the look of the sky Clements was certain they would not make it through the ceremony before the skies opened to a monsoon downpour.

The Indonesian Government was very good about turning out crowds of people for official functions. The streets were so clogged near the docks that the limousine had trouble making headway, despite the police cars with their whining sirens. Like water, the tides of people closed in on the procession, slowing it to a crawl despite the howling sirens at the lead, the cars inching ahead through a solid wall of people.

The limousine rounded the corner of a warehouse onto the dock itself and here the foot police had formed a corridor to push back the crowds. Clements braced himself, already moving past the next couple of hours to his meeting with Lang. He could count on Lang to make even the most routine matter larger than life and it was probable that Kemper was right about the perpetual romantic drama that Lang created around any incident which defied a ready explanation. But this time there had been an incipient hysteria in his voice. Whatever Lang had seen had shaken him badly. But there was nothing Clements could do about it now.

The harbor itself was like no other in the world that he had seen. There were similarities perhaps between this harbor and Hong Kong in the old days, or even perhaps Singapore before Dr Lee had cleaned it up. For this stretch of water was filled with every conceivable type of fishing boat and ship and freighter built over the past fifty years, makeshift masts and rusty boiler plate, scows and barges with interconnecting gangplanks to form a floating city, and in the foreground the slab of concrete with special fittings for the loading of oil onto tankers from the termination of the West Java pipeline.

Rooseno snuffed out his cigarette in the ashtray, straightened his business jacket, his tieless collar. The limousine pulled to a stop in front of the decorated wooden platform near the gangplank. A red carpet had unrolled, the strip leading up a short flight of steps under the canopy set with a microphone and chairs. The television crews were on hand with their minicams from Indonesia's single television channel. Crowds of Indonesian girls surrounded the limousine, dressed in school uniforms, two of them with their arms full of tropical flowers, ready to present official greetings to the ambassador as well as the minister. Rooseno was helped from the limousine first, an automatic smile spreading across a brown face beaded with perspiration as he leaned down to accept the flowers from a girl.

And then Clements followed, allowing himself to shift into neutral and the approaching boredom with a forced graciousness that seemed almost natural.

Clements's talk took less than ten minutes, informal remarks which he gave in almost flawless Indonesian, frustrating the official Indonesian interpreter who stood nearby, ready to step in at the first sign of difficulty. He was aware of the Indonesian television crew with their minicams below the platform. The inanities which were to be said here today would be bounced off the Indonesian television satellites and sent to the people inhabiting the thousands of islands over the three-thousand-mile stretch of ocean that contained the Republic of Indonesia to be viewed by people who would have only the vaguest of ideas as to where Jakarta was.

Then Clements took his seat, watching the wall cloud of the thunderstorm moving across the distant bay as Rooseno took his place before the microphone and began his patriotic oration on the spirit of Indonesia and the fine work being done by the current administration. Clements feigned attention. The Indonesians were great believers in form. Later, when the generals looked at the television tapes of this speech, they would be gratified at the seeming interest of the United States ambassador.

But Rooseno was less than ten minutes into his speech when the wall cloud swept overhead and the dump of rain came down, a great deluge, and aides popped out with umbrellas to shelter Rooseno and the American ambassador while the workmen snatched at the ropes to pull the canvas cover into place over the speakers' stand. Part of the crowd scattered as the rain hit but there were thousands of people who remained politely in place as Rooseno's strong voice continued to carry over the docks, unfazed, pausing only once when his words were drowned out by thunder and then he repeated what he had already said before. Umbrellas came out to cover the television crew. The minicams continued to whir.

Clements noticed a stir back near the cars where the Indonesian police had formed a protective cordon. An argument was taking place between a whole squad of policemen and a tall, bedraggled young man in a complete state of dishevelment, his suit soaked through. It took a moment for Clements to realize that this wild-eyed man was Lang and that the police were not going to let him pass. He turned to the protocol officer to his left and nodded toward Lang.

'Tell the police to let him through,' Clements said.

'It might be more politic to wait until the speech is finished. The television cameras are still at it.'

There was no time to explain that Lang was distraught and that it might be preferable to have the minor disruption of Lang's arrival on the platform to the major brawl that would take place if Lang were pushed much further.

'Do it now, if you please,' Clements said, under his breath, keeping his voice down despite the fact that the rain pounding on the canvas had become a roar.

The protocol officer slipped out of his chair. Raising an umbrella, he went down the wooden stairs to the concrete and over to the crowd of policemen who were hustling Lang toward a police van. Clements watched. The showing of credentials and the perfect manners of the PO had a marvelous calming effect. In a few moments Lang came up the wooden stairs and sat down in the folding chair next to the ambassador. And it was only when he got close that Clements could see how truly upset he was. He needed a shave and he sat as if he were exhausted, shoulders sloped inward, hands trembling. He began to shiver.

'Are you ill, Jim?' Clements said, and then he saw Lang's eyes, wild. Not sick but so full of fear that he found it hard to sit here and control himself.

'We have to talk, Mr Ambassador,' Lang said, in a low, strained voice. 'They're going to kill us.' And then he looked around as if to see if anybody was listening, and he said something more which Clements could not understand. Clements shifted in his chair to be able to hear Lang better, and in that moment his eyes happened to sweep the top of the warehouse that flanked the platform and he thought he saw the shape of a man standing up there, exposed to the full fury of the rain. Yes, definitely a man, and what was he doing, pulling up a stick, a telescope, a camera? Ah, Jesus, and then he knew, too late, and with the thunder and a bolt of lightning he saw the flash of the rifle, and for a moment felt the jolt of adrenaline, knowing beyond doubt that the bullet was meant for him. The telephoned warning. Death. And yet in that second he heard the groan, the sound of lead impacting bone, and a part of the back of Lang's skull flew away and at that moment the sound of the rifle shot turned the platform into pandemonium.

Clements grabbed Lang, held him, shouted to the police that the gunman was on the roof. The crowd broke and scattered, ran for cover and the Indonesia police ran amok, following some sort of crazy drill which saw one team rushing to surround the oil minister and get Rooseno back to his car while the rest started firing at all the windows on the buildings flanking the dock, raking the stones with submachine guns.

Harry Kemper was on the platform immediately, pistol drawn, his team around the ambassador, who still held Lang in his arms while the medic on the American team took one look at Lang's head and motioned for a car to be brought up, on the double. 'We'll get him to the nearest hospital,' Clements said to Kemper.

'Not you, Mr Ambassador,' Kemper said, eyes sweeping the roofs. 'We don't know how many of them there are. We'll follow regular evacuation drill. You take car one.'

'To hell with the drill. I'm going to the hospital with him,' Clements said, and he supported one of Lang's shoulders while the medic put a temporary compress on his head, and two more men helped carry Lang to a car where Clements sat on one side of him and the medic on the other. Miraculously, Kemper had commandeered a police escort, sirens which blasted away the traffic in front of the car through the flooding streets toward the hospital.

Lang was partially conscious, eyes glazed, on the edge of darkness, but his mouth was moving, little pieces of sound, aspirations of breath, trying to make words. 'Liss,' he said, eyes trying to bring the ambassador into focus.

'I'm here, Jim,' Clements said. 'We're on our way to a hospital. You're going to be all right.'

Another sound, faint hiss of air. 'Liss-ten.'

'Yes, I'm listening.'

'Six,' Lang said, with great effort of will.

'Six what?'

'Six ray-vens,' Lang said, breaking the final word into long syllables.

'Ravens,' Clements said. 'The birds?'

'Yes.'

'What about them, Jim?'

'Kill us all.'

'We'll be at the hospital soon,' the medic said. 'It's better if he doesn't talk.'

'Conspir . . .' Lang said to Clements, pushing the syllables out.

'Conspiracy?' Clements said.

'Yes.' Only the 'yes' was a sibilance, a long exhalation of breath, and at that moment Clements was sure that Lang was dying and he was about to push the medic to do something when he saw the hypodermic in the medic's hand, thumb squeezing the air from the syringe before he plunged

48

the needle into Lang's arm. In a moment Lang jerked, his mouth gasping for air before he started breathing again, rapid, shallow.

He said nothing more. His eyelids drooped, half open, unseeing. They were close to the hospital emergency ramp now, the police car clearing the way up the lane, and the emergency technicians were at the car before it stopped. They hustled Lang onto a gurney, whisked him away with the medic keeping pace until elevator doors closed upon them all. Kemper took hold of Clement's elbow and hustled him down the hallway to an office which had been cleared out in a hurry, a half-eaten bowl of rice testimony to a meal interrupted, and an American doctor was suddenly examining Clements, putting a blood-pressure cuff around his arm while a nurse placed a terry-cloth robe around his drenched shoulders.

'I wasn't hurt,' Clements said to the doctor, who proceeded to take his blood pressure anyway.

'The pressure is elevated,' the doctor said. 'Do you feel any symptoms of dizziness?'

'No. I want word on Lang's condition as soon as possible.'

Kemper came into the room and waited until the doctor and nurse left, then he closed the door and produced an old-fashioned silver hip flask. 'Brandy,' he said. He handed it to Clements, who drank, felt the brandy burn its way down into his stomach. He shivered slightly. 'The bullet was meant for me,' he said, quietly.

'We proceed on that assumption, yes,' Kemper said. 'So we have to also make the present assumption that this represents a follow-up to the telephone calls and the threats against your life. It could be the work of one man or a dozen. We don't know. It may be part of a coup against the government but we're covering that angle, just in case. We also have to assume that this could be a part of an attack on the embassy or embassy personnel. So I've moved the embassy Marines into siege posture, put guards on all embassy personnel.'

The telephone in the office rang and Clements picked it up. 'Yes?' he said.

The voice was Indonesian, low-pitched. 'Is this the ambassador?'

'Hold on,' Clements said, evenly, then covered the

mouthpiece. 'I think you had better monitor this one,' he said to Kemper.

'Give me a second,' Kemper said, on his feet instantly and out of the room. Clements uncovered the mouthpiece.

'What do you want with the ambassador?' he said.

There was a low chuckle on the telephone. 'I know who I'm talking to. Your voice is much too famous. The bullet today was meant for you, by the way.'

Clements's hand was sweating. He had to stall. 'I don't talk to cowards,' he said.

'We are not cowards.'

'Anybody who won't give his name is a coward. Anybody who ambushes from a safe position is a goddamned coward.'

'We are Red Brigade. And the martyr has already been captured and will gladly sacrifice himself for what he believes in. His only regret is that he did not kill you.'

'What do you want?' Clements said. 'Why are you calling me?'

'To claim credit. To issue a warning. Americans will leave Indonesia within thirty days. Or you will be killed. You won't be so lucky next time.'

Clements could restrain himself no longer. 'Listen to me, you son of a bitch,' he said. 'It's pretty goddamned easy to be brave over the telephone or when you're hiding behind a wall with a rifle . . .'

The line went dead. The man had hung up on him.

Kemper was back in the office momentarily. Clements took out a handkerchief, realized it was as wet as the rest of his suit. He mopped his face anyway.

'I'm sorry I lost my temper,' he said. 'I didn't give you time for a trace, did I?'

'The Jakarta telephone system is so fucked up, we couldn't have made a trace in an hour. But that's the same voice that called me before.' He picked up the telephone. 'We'll see if he's telling the truth about a man in custody.' He dialed, asked to speak to a Colonel Mustafa. Clements only half listened, distracted by sounds in the hallway, wondering what was happening in the operating room. 'Yes. Go ahead,' Kemper was saying. He took a ballpoint pen out of his pocket as if to make notes but he did nothing but doodle on a sheet of paper, rows of interlocking circles. 'What kind of rifle? Say again.' More circles. 'All right, keep on it. I'll check it out myself later. And for God's sake, make sure that they set up a security force. I don't want him touched. Let them know that they'll make brownie points with us by keeping him in good shape until we can talk to him.' He put the telephone down. 'They have the assassin,' he said.

'Who is he?'

'They're running a check on him now,' Kemper said. The man's name was Oni Saud and he had been caught at the opposite side of one of the warehouses, trying to kick-start a motorcycle in the rain. He was carrying the rifle, but when he saw the police approaching, he threw the rifle down onto the street and put his hands on top of his head. He had been taken to the local police station where he made a statement on his own. He gave his name, said he was a resident of Jakarta but refused to give an address. He had formerly been an employee of the Indonesia state-owned oil company, Pertamina, until he had been discharged for political reasons about a year ago. He had not worked since. He said he had tried to kill the ambassador in the name of the Red Brigade because the Americans were ruining his country and it was time for the Communists to start a revolution.

'Jim was trying to tell me about a conspiracy,' Clements said.

'Oh?'

He told Kemper of the telephone call, the behavior at the speakers' stand, the words pushed out in the car. Kemper nodded, rubbed his chin. 'Do they mean anything to you?' Clements said.

'No. Whatever he got must have come from Singapore. I want his girlfriend's name, where he was staying, anything else you have. We'll run down all the leads.'

Clements took another pull at the brandy flask. 'Certainly.'

'I don't know what's going on here, Mr Ambassador,' Kemper said. 'But we'll follow total security procedures for at least twenty-four hours, then we'll reevaluate. And right now, you have to deal with some rather distasteful choices.'

'Such as?'

'The American press is outside. They want a statement from you with pictures of you in your present condition.'

'My God. With Lang's blood and brain matter all over me?'

'The United States Information Service agrees it will make effective propaganda.'

'That's a negative,' Clements said. 'Get me a raincoat out of the car. I'll be damned if I'm going to play this as a media event.'

'The PO suggests you go along with the press. The Indonesians would be pleased.'

'This is one time I don't give a damn. We'll have a press conference in the morning. Ten o'clock.'

'I suggest you hole up at the embassy for tonight.'

'Agreed. But I'm going to stay here as long as there's a chance that Lang can make it.'

'He's in surgery now. They have their best brain men on it. Lang evidently turned just as Oni Saud fired. The bullet penetrated the skull in the right rear quadrant and broke loose a portion of the bone matter. How he does depends on how deeply into the brain the bullet penetrated.'

'Where's the best brain surgeon in Southeast Asia?'

'Singapore,' Kemper said, without hesitation.

'I want him flown in.'

'Sure,' Kemper said, and in the way he said it, quickly, without thought, he expressed the way he felt about Lang's chances of living through the night. None at all.

The door opened and the medic appeared, dressed in a green surgical gown, the mask dangling down around his throat. 'They're a damn good team, Mr Ambassador. I have to admit, I didn't have much respect for Indonesian medicine before, but they did everything any team in the United States could have done.'

'Dead, then,' Clements said, suddenly numb.

'He was technically dead before they got him to the table. The bullet fractionated bone, sent it into the brain.'

'I want to see him.'

'I'd recommend waiting until they clean him up, sir.'

'No. I want to see him now.'

He followed the medic into an elevator, up three flights and down a corridor to an operating room where the nurses were just beginning to clean up. They vacated when the ambassador came into the room. Clements looked to the medic. 'I want to be alone with him,' he said.

The medic nodded, left the room and Clements looked down on Lang, who lay on the table, blood everywhere, the side of his head a mess, his face contorted in death, already gray.

He wanted to speak, to say something, even though the young man on the table could not hear him, would never hear anything again, but all he felt was the terrible sense of personal loss, of waste. Lang was dead for no reason except that a crazy man had missed the ambassador and hit him instead, a whole bright future wiped out, and that pretty young girl who waited in Singapore for him would never hear his voice again.

I would have been proud to have had you for a son.

No tears. They had been used up a long time ago. An infinite sadness and beyond that, down the line, he knew that there would come a raging anger which would have to be expressed.

The son of a bitch meant to kill me, not you.

He touched Lang's hand, skin already cold. He went outside the operating room. Kemper was there with a raincoat. The expression on his face was forlorn. 'A damn shame,' he said. 'A goddamned shame.'

'Yes.'

'We'll go down the back way, Mr Ambassador. I have a car waiting.'

'Thank you, Harry,' Clements said. 'Thank you very much.'

4

The embassy had been turned into an armed camp and Clements's usual round of purely social obligations had been sharply curtailed for the time being. He wrote the obligatory report to State the morning after the shooting, and received the personal calls of condolence from the diplomatic community in general and the Indonesian Government in particular, from the various ministries and even a personal call from the President himself, who declared an official day of mourning for Lang.

Clements sat in his office, waiting for the call to be put through to the States, to Lang's mother, who lived in Santa Barbara, and another call to his girlfriend in Singapore, whom he had met once, a proud introduction made by the in-love young man who was obviously full of emotion and working hard not to show it.

He had a call from Kemper, who was working with Indonesian Intelligence to set up an interview with Oni Saud, and against Kemper's better advice Clements insisted on being a part of that interview when the time came. Lucy brought him a fresh pot of tea, her eyes red from weeping, for she had been as fond of Lang as he himself had been. But she had turned her grief to energy, which she poured into her work, and he knew he could count on her.

When the call was put through to Singapore and Christie was on the line, Clements felt entirely inadequate as he expressed his sympathies and told her of the loss he felt. Christie's voice was brave and tremulous, and she thanked him and told him how much Lang had thought of Clements, had almost regarded him as a father, since his own had died young. The fumbling between the generations and the sexes, and then Lucy took over the conversation with Christie when the ambassador was off the telephone, and Clements could hear her weeping from the reception room, and he knew that the young girl would be crying on the other end of the line, and in their tears was more genuine healing than he could ever bring about.

He read a press release that had been drawn up by his staff to replace the canceled press conference, which he had decided not to hold this morning. Lang's death was a tragedy, but Clements did not want to see it accelerated into an episode which would cause a breach, however minor, with the Indonesian Government. For this was an Asian culture, after all, and technically the American ambassador and his whole staff were under the protection of the Indonesian military, including the police branch, and the authorities had allowed an Indonesian national to get close enough to fire a shot and kill an American. They had lost face. The two pilots who had operated the helicopter that had spotted the shooter on the roof had already been cashiered from the military with loss of pay and rank, even though Clements himself considered such actions not only extreme but unfair.

For the man on the roof had looked like a sleeping workman to them, and in this city of millions of indigents, there was no way they could have guarded against this attempt on Clements's life. But it was not too many years ago that the two men in the helicopter would have been sacrificed, executed in expiation, seeking to restore a balance, giving blood for blood.

Soon Lucy appeared at the door to let him know that Mrs Lang was on the line from Santa Barbara. He sat down and picked up the telephone.

'I know that you were notified earlier,' Clements said. 'But I had to call and give you my personal condolences, Mrs Lang. We were all very fond of Jim. He was a fine young man and he leaves a hole here which can't be filled.'

Her voice was controlled but troubled. 'I had no details from the State Department, Ambassador Clements,' she said. 'I want to know how he died.'

'We were at a dedication ceremony for a new oil dock,'

Clements said. 'A radical gunman took a shot at me and hit your son instead.'

There was silence on the line and he felt the pressure over the thousands of miles that lay between them, the bewildered hostility which had been generated within her. 'I don't understand,' she said, finally. 'You mean that he was killed by accident, then?'

'A terrible accident.'

'And why did it have to be him?' she said, the pain distorting her voice. 'What was the point of his dying? What did it serve? He loved his government, Mr Ambassador, and he would gladly have died for it if there was a cause he believed in. But to be struck by a stray bullet . . . Wasn't anybody protecting him? Don't you take better care of the young men who work for you?' And now she was weeping uncontrollably, her words lost in the torrent of grief. He was struck dumb, having no words that made sense. He sat and listened to her pain and felt his own pain and knew there could be no answers, that even the questions were hollow. And presently she brought herself under control and the weeping stopped, choked off by an effort of will. 'I apologize,' she said. 'He was an only child, Mr Ambassador. His father died years ago, in the Vietnamese War. So I need to discuss the practical matters. Maybe I should take this up with one of your aides.'

'No,' he said. 'I'll handle it.'

'I would like him buried next to his father in Arlington National Cemetery, if that's possible.'

Clements did not know what was usual, but he would make it happen. 'Certainly,' he said. 'If you like, we'll have Jim's body sent to Santa Barbara for a memorial service and then have a government plane take both of you to Washington.'

'No,' she said. 'He really didn't know anyone here in Santa Barbara. I moved here after his father was killed and Jim was away in school. And I would like a private funeral. I don't mean any disrespect, Mr Ambassador, but I don't want any condolence calls from members of the government who didn't even know him. When my husband died, I had a call from a colonel at the Pentagon who was supposed to be comforting me, but I found out he hadn't ever even known my husband. That was his only job, making condolence calls. It's a terrible feeling to lose somebody you love for no reason.'

'My wife died five years ago,' Clements said, knowing he was stepping beyond the lines of protocol. 'In an automobile accident. She was hit by a drunk driver. I don't know why I'm telling you this, unless it's to let you know that I understand. There was no reason for her to die, none that I could see.'

'Have you reconciled your loss?' she said. 'Have you found an answer?'

'No,' he said, sadly. 'I've just accepted that life is random, unpredictable and unjust. And there aren't any answers. Time passes and the pain subsides, but there aren't any answers.'

'James liked you very much,' she said, finally. 'I apologize for the bitterness.'

'You don't need to apologize,' he said. 'I have my own.'

'How soon will his body be sent back?'

'I'm trying to clear it with the Indonesian Government to send his body tonight. An air force jet is flying in from Clark Field in the Philippines. I'll clear everything in Washington and then I'll get back to you, Mrs Lang. It will all be done as soon as possible. We'll also have you picked up in a government plane and flown to Washington.'

'I thank you for your call, Mr Ambassador. I thank you for being good to my son and adding your caring to the short life he was allowed to have. And I thank you for your honesty. Goodbye.'

The line went dead. Across the Pacific her hand had severed the connection. He made the note on a blank sheet of paper.

'NO FUSS'

Lucy buzzed him on the intercom. 'I have a call from Mr Majors in Bangkok on line one. Do you want to take it?'

'Put him on,' Clements said as he picked up the phone.

'Are you okay?' G.D. said.

'Yes,' Clements said. 'Comparatively.'

'I had the hell scared out of me. We had word up here that someone took a shot at you, that somebody got killed, but the news didn't say who.'

'Jim Lang,' Clements said.

'Shit,' G.D. said. 'I only met him a couple of times but he was a good one. And I know how fond you were of him. Is there anything I can do for you, buddy?'

'Nothing. But I appreciate your concern.'

'What are friends for? Did they catch the man who did it?'

'Yes.'

'You watch out anyway, you hear? I want you alive and healthy when we leave this asshole of the world and start our supercompany. And by the way, that case of bourbon should be delivered within two days. You stay on the lookout for it. If there's not a full case, you let me know. I don't tolerate any of my contractors holding out on me. Hey, I just thought of something. You want me to come down there?'

'No, I'm all right. Really.'

'You need anything, you whistle. Anytime you want a little R and R, come on up. The latch string's always out.'

'Right.'

The minute G.D. was off the line, Clements buzzed Lucy on the intercom, gave her instructions to forward on to State. 'And I need a liaison with the Indonesian Government to expedite the shipping of Lang's body.'

'They've assigned one,' Lucy said, an edge to her voice. 'A Miss Rooseno. She's in reception now, I believe.'

Ah, how like Madeleine, he thought, *to show up when he most needed her.* Lucy would think it scandalous, of course, to see *that* woman actually coming to the embassy. He played it down.

'I'll meet with her in the garden,' he said. 'I'm tired of being cooped up.'

'Yes, sir.'

There was a Marine lance corporal at the door leading into the garden. He was in full-dress uniform but he carried a loaded carbine. He was clearly uncomfortable in the ambassador's presence.

'You can be at ease with me, Corporal,' Clements said. 'Is there any reason why I can't have the use of the garden?'

'No, sir,' the corporal said. 'We've added a metal screen to the top of the wall on the east so there's no view from any building into the garden. But I'll be required to be in the garden with you at all times.'

'That's fine,' Clements said. He went on through the French doors into the formal garden and over to the shade of a gazebo surrounded by a fantastic array of tropical flowers. But the usual platoon of gardeners was missing. 'What's happened to the grounds keepers?' he said to the corporal.

'A standard security check, sir. We're running all foreign nationals through a screening again. They should be back by tomorrow.'

Yes, Clements thought. A state of siege and nothing would be taken for granted, and young Lang was still dead, beyond all the protection that any of them could muster. The corporal excused himself, took his station by the door, and Clements could hear the crackle of the walkie-talkie as he checked in with his control. He sat down in a wicker chair, leaned back, studied the addition to the high east wall, another six feet of interwoven steel ribbons that blocked off the outline of an office building. The rest of the walls were topped with coils of razor-sharp steel that would cut an intruder to ribbons. He sat fortified in the middle of an enemy camp.

Lucy appeared at the door to the garden, Miss Rooseno in tow, and the Marine lance corporal went through the formalities of checking the papers handed to him before he would allow them to pass through. Clements stood up to greet them as they approached. It was obvious that Lucy approved of none of this, but she would handle it with discreet disapproval.

'Mr Ambassador, this is Miss Madeleine Rooseno from the Financial Ministry. She has been assigned to expedite Mr Lang's funeral arrangements.'

'Madeleine and I are old friends,' Clements said with an open smile. He took Madeleine's hand, held it. 'Would you have a bottle of champagne brought to us, Lucy?'

'Champagne?' Lucy said with a start, and he could tell she was about to ask if champagne was appropriate but she thought better of it and retreated across the garden, muttering to herself.

Clements took Madeleine in his arms, kissed her lightly, beyond caring about the proprieties for the moment. 'God, you don't know how good it is to see you right at this moment.'

'I couldn't stay away,' she said, concerned. 'Are you all right?'

'Physically, yes. How did you get yourself assigned to this?'

'I simply called my Uncle Rooseno and told him to arrange it,' she said. 'I can't believe that Jim Lang is dead. It all seems like a bad dream.' She opened her purse, took out a cigarette and leaned forward to allow him to light it for her. 'I know something about what happened to Jim in Singapore,' she said, rather wistfully. 'But I feel as if I'm caught in the middle.'

'How are you in the middle?' he said. 'And how could you know what happened to him in Singapore?'

'Many of my relatives are Chinese bankers. Some of them know how I feel about you. I don't want to see them lose money because of anything I say to the most important American in this part of the world. So the question is whether you understand the concept of losing face sufficiently well to be able to interpret correctly why they've acted as they have.'

He shrugged. 'I've spent the better part of my professional life in this part of the world. I speak Indonesian, some Mandarin. Try me.'

'First, I want you to promise that you won't take any action against the man I mention to you.'

'I would trust you with my life,' he said. 'But I want you to understand how I feel. I'm a diplomat in a sensitive position. But I also happen to be a very vindictive man and I can carry grudges forever. Somebody tried to kill my yesterday and Jim Lang literally got part of his head blown off. Now, if the man you're talking about has the slightest responsibility for what's happened here, then don't tell me anything. Because if he does, I *will* take action. You can count on it.'

60

'He has nothing to do with it. But I think he frightened Jim.'

'How?'

'I have a Chinese cousin named Tom Li. He was the Chinese banker that Jim Lang talked to in Singapore.'

'How do you know?'

'Tom Li called my Uncle Wong. He was very upset and wanted advice. Because Jim Lang had come to his bank, looking for information concerning the mixed-up accounts and Tom Li answered his questions and told him the matter would be corrected and thought he was satisfied. Tom Li introduced Jim to his superior and thought the matter was settled. But then, quite by accident, as Tom Li was passing through the bookkeeping department, he saw Jim talking to one of the computer girls and realized that Jim had talked the girl into accessing a file.' She tapped her cigarette and the ashes broke and showered into the grass.

'Go on,' Clements said.

'So my Cousin Tom Li panicked,' Madeleine said. 'Do you know what it would mean to his reputation or the reputation of the bank if word was passed around that the secrecy of the files and the accounts was not maintained? He could have lost his job. Even worse, he would have lost face in the community of bankers, and there wouldn't have been anyplace in this part of the world where anybody would hire him. The Chinese community is very close. He would have been disgraced forever. So he said some very harsh things to Jim and to the computer operator. He told Jim that what he was doing was against the law in Singapore and that he could be arrested. He followed Jim into the lobby, put a hand on his arm, quite panicked, because it was my cousin who was in the terrible trouble by this point. If Jim let it be known that he had looked at an account of the bank, it would be Li's fault.' She looked directly at Clements. She had the clearest eyes he had ever seen. 'So Jim may have been frightened of the Chinese bankers but there was nothing to it. Jim was very young. He was impressionable and dramatic and he didn't understand.'

'Will your cousin talk to a man from the embassy?'

'Of course. And he will make a full disclosure of the information Jim wanted. He has nothing to hide from you. But I would appreciate it if the appointment is made through me and the conversation is held quietly.'

'Have you ever heard of anything called "The Six Ravens"?'

'No,' she said. 'What is it supposed to be?'

'I don't know.'

'It would make a good name for a Chinese restaurant,' she said. 'Ravens are supposed to be good luck, a good omen, but the "six" is not a lucky number. I'll ask around if it's important.'

'I would appreciate it,' he said.

'But you won't tell me why.'

'Only that Jim mentioned it, was upset by it.'

He fell silent. She looked up as a white-jacketed waiter carried an ice bucket and the champagne into the garden on a silver tray. He removed the cork, went through the formality of allowing Clements to sample it before he poured, then he disappeared back into the building. She sipped the champagne, then leaned back against her chair. She inhaled the smoke from her cigarette, crossed her long legs. He wondered if she was aware of the sexuality she generated, the self-confidence which was close to insolence at times, the terrible sense of vulnerability at others. She was the exact opposite of what a beautiful young woman in this part of the world was expected to be. That would put off the Indonesian males. 'Now, my dear,' she said. 'What can I do to help you, officially?'

'Something to shortcut the miles of paperwork, for one thing.'

'I took care of that before I came,' she said. 'I had my secretary fill out the forms requesting the export of a deceased, and the necessary reports to the various government departments. And you would be surprised at the expressions of true regret from people in the Financial Ministry where Jim was doing his research. They were genuinely sorry about what happened and they all came to me asking what they could do to express themselves. I told them I would tell you how they felt.'

'I'll drop a note to his mother and tell her how highly he was regarded. I talked to her earlier.'

She finished her drink. 'I don't want to make things more difficult for you. So after the paperwork, what next?'

'We need permission for an air force jet to land at Kemorakan airport to pick up the body, sometime late this evening. It will refuel and be on the ground no longer than two hours.'

'That's no problem,' she said. 'You have permission.'

'You don't have to clear that through your military?'

'I cleared that too before I came here.' She held her glass out for more champagne, sighed. 'I'm so tired of people dying,' she said. 'I am so tired of the threat of death, one group always threatening to kill another.'

He drank the champagne, especially heady in the heat of the day. It slipped past his fatigue and his grief, eased him. 'Jim would have been promoted at the end of this year. It isn't often that somebody like him comes along.'

She seemed to be perfectly relaxed in the warm sunshine but she was not. Her eyes were on the Marine lance corporal standing at the garden door, but she was not seeing him. Her expression was thoughtful. 'When Jim used to do research at the ministry, we would have lunch once in a while. Did you know that?'

'No.'

'I think he was one of the few people in the world who really didn't know about you and me.' She smiled sadly. 'He used to tell me how wonderful you were and he talked to me sometimes about his girlfriend in Singapore and how he was going to marry her someday. I envied him in some ways.'

'How so?'

'That he could trust life sufficiently to make plans like that, such a fine feeling of security.'

'And you don't trust life?' Clements said.

'No. I could have lost you yesterday. Everytime you leave me, it's always possible that you won't come back, that I'll get a telephone call. Or maybe not even that. Maybe just an announcement on the radio.'

'Nothing's going to happen to me.'

'You can't guarantee that. Jim is dead, along with his fine feeling of security.'

He realized she was in pain. He touched her arm, her flesh warm in the sunlight. 'We're going to have a long time together.'

'You don't have to promise me anything. I was trained for calamity here,' she said. 'I spent many of my childhood years in Vietnam and Kampuchea. There were always wars, always intrigues, coups, assassinations, the possibility of dying at any moment or starving unless you were tough enough and clearheaded enough to look ahead.' She finished her champagne. 'I should never drink champagne in the middle of the day, especially on the one day I come to your embassy to help you. But as my Uncle Wong says, "Live each day as if you are to die at sunset," and on my last day, I would certainly have champagne in the morning.' She gathered her purse to her, stood up, kissed him on the cheek. 'You take very good care of yourself, darling,' she said. 'If you let anything happen to you, I'll never forgive you.'

'It means a lot to me that you came here today,' he said. 'I love you. I'll call you when things lighten up. And now, I'll see you out.'

'Please don't,' she said 'I think we should preserve some appearances.'

He watched her walking away, and then he sat down and studied the walls around him and realized at this moment how very much he wanted to be free, away from international intrigues and concealed emotions. He could go into business with G. D. and marry Madeleine, everything on the surface, nothing hidden. Soon, he thought, very soon.

Midafternoon, Clements received word that an Air Force 707 would be landing at Kemorakan airport at nine o'clock that night. He gave his deputy the information and asked him to call the mortuary and have the body transported to the airfield, then he called Kemper.

'I'm going to the airport tonight to see Lang's body off,' he said. 'Will that create problems?'

'A great many,' Kemper said. 'it's too early to tell the extent of the conspiracy.'

'It won't be a media event,' Clements said. 'We'll cover it with USIS photographers and feed the pictures to whoever wants them. I'll have Washington informed of the arrival time there but Lang's mother wants no ceremony. I will want a color guard at the airport tonight.'

'Then I suggest we transport them in a separate convoy,' Kemper said. 'We'll send your regular car with a decoy. You'll be transported in an ordinary civilian car. That's the safest way, if you insist on going.'

'I do. And I would like for you to arrange for me to talk to the assassin afterward.'

'I'm not sure that's such a good idea, Mr Ambassador,' Kemper said.

'I appreciate your concern, Harry. But arrange it anyway, if you can.'

'Yes, sir.'

After the ambassador had made the request, Kemper sauntered over to government house to see Colonel Mustafa, head of Indonesian Intelligence, a wiry little officer who had been befriended by Kemper and sponsored for training in the United States and then sent home with a sizable equipment grant when his training was complete.

Mustafa was delighted to see him and they drank coffee laced with chocolate, slipping in and out of Indonesian and English without being aware of it. They talked about the weather and the pity of the aide being killed at such a young age but the infinite wisdom of Allah in sparing the life of the ambassador at the same time. The ceiling fan made lazy circles overhead; the air-conditioning was out of whack again. The exchange of pleasantries continued over the refreshments.

Kemper was very careful to avoid putting Mustafa into a position where Mustafa would lose face if he could not comply with Kemper's request. So he sipped the chocolate-flavored coffee and picked his words very carefully.

'I have been asked by my ambassador to inquire into the state of the assassin's health,' Kemper said.

'He received no wounds in the capture,' Mustafa said.

So Kemper could now take it for granted that Oni Saud was still alive. 'My ambassador is naturally very curious about the man who tried to kill him and shot his aide instead. He would appreciate the opportunity to have certain questions put to the prisoner. He would also like to be present for the answering of those questions.'

Mustafa studied the white porcelain of his cup. He was equally roundabout in his answer. Indonesians tended to shy away from even the hint of confrontation. Mustafa blotted the crystal beads of perspiration off his furrowed forehead with a linen handkerchief. 'I can understand why your ambassador would be concerned and it is to his credit that he should have an interest in this man who has committed an unspeakable act. I hope that you will assure him that my men are quite competent in matters of interrogation and that a complete transcript will be made of all answers to questions.'

'My ambassador has the greatest regard for the competence and thoroughness of your men,' Kemper said. 'It is a matter of moral concern that he should face the man who tried to kill him.'

Mustafa lit a cigarette with a sigh. 'To allow a non-Indonesian to question a prisoner would amount to subordinating the Indonesian judicial process to the interest of a foreign government. I'm afraid that this must be considered an internal affair,' he said in conclusion.

'Oh, I understand completely,' Kemper said. 'Wouldn't think of overstepping the line.'

Colonel Mustafa lifted the delicate cup even with the line of his thin mouth, the steam rising up across the middle of his face. 'Of course, there would be nothing wrong with your ambassador observing the prisoner, I suppose. And if he has specific questions' – a delicate sip – 'they could be passed along to me.'

'Very kind,' Kemper said, knowing damn well the ambassador would be allowed to do anything he liked as long as it was made clear that Mustafa appeared to have the final say. 'My ambassador would like to see the prisoner sometime after nine o'clock tonight.'

'That will be very difficult.'

'I understand. My ambassador would be grateful to you personally if it could be arranged.'

'I'll see what I can do,' Mustafa said. 'I will contact you later.'

'At your convenience, Colonel. At your convenience.'

Kemper held a meeting with his intelligence staff at the embassy. He sat at the head of the polished table with his omnipresent notebook opened before him to the page on which he had listed the questions which still concerned him.

He was currently understaffed but he was well satisfied with his people, all dedicated, thorough, hardworking. They were the best in the business, fiercely loyal, and he could count on them all the way. Houghton, with his infectious boyish charm, had been assigned to track Oni Saud's end of the conspiracy. 'I'm covering wife and first family and updating his vita,' Houghton said. 'Nothing worth noting yet.'

The completely bald Oberlin, massive-jawed, pugnacious, was covering 'commercial ramifications.' As far as he could determine, the death of Ambassador Clements would have changed absolutely nothing in the business world, either here or elsewhere. It would have given no group or company any advantage whatsoever.

Atkinson was a bushy-headed psychologist who was covering terrorist groups as well as what he called 'singular aberrants,' the personal motive boys who killed for their own reasons. 'I've drawn a blank on any Red Brigade connected with the Indonesian Communists. That doesn't mean a damn thing except that it has to be a new faction and they couldn't put together a widescale conspiracy without my knowing about it.'

'Thank God for little blessings,' Kemper said, and looked toward Wiznoski.

Wiznoski was the Soviet analyst, a beak-nosed man who would eventually sniff out any possible Russian connection with the shooting or the shooter, if such existed, and he was vigorously picking at the relationship the ambassador had with Sergei Ludov, his Russian counterpart. Always possibilities there. 'I'm running my string of agents to see if there's any connection between the Soviets and this particular Red Brigade. So far, nothing but a blank.'

'I think you'll find a connection,' Kemper said.

The fifth member of the team was Thomasina Mims, a striking brunette in her early thirties with deep brown piercing eyes. She had become Kemper's good right hand the moment she was posted in Jakarta, a woman who coordinated, took notes, made sense of seemingly unrelated facts, kept the others from duplicating their efforts, stretched the budget and drafted Kemper's reports. But within a month of her arrival the relationship between them had become a good bit more than professional, and as it was a joyous union as far as he was concerned, he was aware that things were not going as well with her. As he looked at her now, she doodled on a notepad, did not meet his eyes.

'Tommi,' he said. 'Care to comment?'

'Not at the moment,' she said.

'So far we've little to work on,' Kemper said to his group. 'But we have at least two conspirators. We have Oni Saud and we have the man who made the telephone calls. Let's give it another intensive twelve hours and see what happens. Cover all the bases. No more surprises. That will do it for now. Tommi, if you have a minute, I'd like to talk to you.'

The rest of the group drifted out and Tommi remained in her chair, still doodling, but when the others were gone, her eyes lifted and met his. He leaned back in his chair. 'Are you okay?' he said.

'In one way, I'm fine. In another way, not so good,' she said.

'You want to talk about it?'

'I truly love you, you know,' she said, her fingers twisting the pencil.

'Yes, I know.'

'What's going on between us is interfering with my work,' she said. 'I think too much about you and not enough about my assignments, and sooner or later that's going to prove damn costly.'

'I haven't seen you make any mistakes.'

'Not yet. But I might, Harry. And on top of which, there's

no future for us. I like what I'm doing and sooner or later I'm going to be the first woman chief of station with the agency. But it's going to be a clean climb, on merit, not because I had an affair with a supergrade in Jakarta when I was thirty years old.'

'I'm a sexist,' he said. 'I don't want you to be a chief of station anywhere except in my house when we get back to the States. I want you at home, safe, with a houseful of kids.'

'What you're saying is the old barefoot and pregnant business.'

'Hell, yes, and I don't deny it.'

'Then we work together and we stay friends and that's it.'

'If you insist.'

He was still thinking about her when he took a taxi to an apartment he kept just off the Jl. Thalim. She was right, of course, for they were part of a dangerous business where a misstep could result in calamity, but she had filled a place in his life which had been empty for a long time and he hated to see that part of the relationship between them come to an end. But she was right. It was not only against the agency code but counter to common sense as well.

He had a cold shower, changed clothes, then went to a cafe near Freedom Square, sat in the shade of an umbrella on the street (his unofficial office, he called it) and ordered his usual coffee, looking out at the tall phallic obelisk in the square. 'Sukarno's Last Erection,' the journalists called it. The cafe was a perfect place to meet with his informants inside the Sukarno government, because there was no hint of the covert here. This place was nothing more than a local watering hole where many government officials stopped to sit and take refreshment and exchange gossip.

He checked his watch, certain that Colonel Mustafa would be by within a half hour, and he had waited no longer than ten minutes before the good colonel made his appearance.

'Would you care for something to drink, my friend?' Kemper said.

'A little mineral water, perhaps,' Colonel Mustafa said.

'It's been a long day.'

'A good one for you, I trust.' He summoned a white-aproned waiter, ordered a bottle of chilled mineral water.

'Our song bird is reluctant,' Colonel Mustafa said. 'He withstands pain too well. There are a great many informants who sing with very little persuasion. The mention of an electric shock, a mere glimpse of a razor-edged blade and they are off and running. But not this one.'

'Does he admit to the killing?' Kemper said, wearily.

'He admits to everything we ask in a general way, but he will give us none of the specifics. "Are you associated with the Red Brigade?" we ask. "Yes." he answers. "And just what is the Red Brigade?" we ask. "Who are your comrades?" and we get nothing out of him. Perhaps your ambassador might be able to get answers from him.' The bottle was served with a frosted glass. Mustafa made a ritual of pouring the water as if it were beer, a slow trickle down the side of the glass, to preserve the effervescence. Kemper understood the significance of the pause. There was another ritual to be observed now. He removed a small envelope from his pocket which contained three crisp one-hundred-dollar bills. The flap was sealed, no writing on the front. He laid it next to the bottle of mineral water and the colonel pocketed it with a deft sweep of his fingers.

'After nine o'clock, then,' Kemper said.

'I shall be going out there anyway.'

Out there. A country compound. 'My ambassador will appreciate this,' he said. 'The embassy?'

'Certainly.'

At eight o'clock Kemper found Tommi still at her desk, munching away at a sandwich supplied her by the kitchen while she thumbed through papers. She was a thin, almost delicate woman, but he had always been impressed by her remarkable stamina, her ability to keep her mind keenly toned when most of his people were fuzzy with fatigue. He pulled up a chair, sat down and put his feet up. 'Can you really do it?' he said.

She glanced up at him, startled. 'Do what?'

'Turn your emotions off. Just like that.'

'No,' she said.

'Then?'

'I still have the feelings. I simply don't act on them anymore. There's really not that much difference between us.'

'It's the damnedest thing,' he said, staring at the ceiling. 'But sometimes when I finish a piece of an assignment, I think about the place where I grew up, just north of San Francisco, the most incredibly beautiful hill in the world. And I say to myself, "When I get through with this next one, I'll go back there. I'll cash in and maybe buy a horse farm and watch the grass grow."'

'You won't,' she said, brushing the crumbs off the table. 'Someday I might quit and go back to Rhode Island, but not you. I'm proving something to myself but you're not. You enjoy the work too much.'

'Maybe so,' he said. 'So what's your summary of what we have?'

'There's something funny about what's going on here,' she said, making the transition to work almost gratefully.

'How's that?'

'The prelim reports don't make any sense at all,' she said, adjusting a rubber fingerstall before she riffled through the sheets in front of her. 'The telephone calls give every indication of conspiracy. Even after the killing, the Red Brigade called in to take the credit. But Houghton has very fine nets and they report absolutely nothing. If Oni Saud is a revolutionary, he became one overnight. Nothing in his background except a sudden good fortune.'

'Oh?' Kemper said, with interest.

'His young wife has a new motorcycle. Doesn't know where her darling man got the money for it, but blessings be to Allah.'

'Interesting,' Kemper said.

'He didn't get it from working. He was laid off by Pertamina Oil some time back. Got hit by a car, off the job. No workman's comp here. He was a translator for them.'

'Get Houghton on the money end,' Kemper said. 'I want a record of every penny they've seen for the past year and any money that might be stashed away, if he's a professional assassin.'

'I took the liberty,' Tommi said. 'I figured that's the direction you would take.'

'If he needs help, give him Oberlin. Oberlin can sniff out illicit cash like a bloodhound.'

She nodded. 'Did the good colonel go along with your request?'

'Three hundred dollars and we get a good look at Oni Saud tonight.'

'I've drawn up the sticking points,' she said, glancing through the papers until she found the one she was looking for. She yanked it from the stack and handed it to him. He studied it, made a mental check of her handwritten points against the list in his notebook. She was on his wavelength. It was no wonder they were so good in bed together. She overlooked nothing, the original nitpicker, the collector of odd pieces of string that everyone else overlooked, and she had but to make truncated little pieces of notes for him to understand completely.

'One shot medallist . . .' 'PKI credo . . .' 'One hour seven minutes . . .'

'You haven't missed a thing,' he said.

'That's what I'm here for,' she said. And now, for the first time, he could see the fatigue in her eyes as she laid her pencil down for the evening, the signal that her work was finished for now. 'There's something else I should have told you before,' she said. 'I was more abrupt than I meant to be. If conditions were different, I wouldn't have let anything stand between us.'

'If conditions were different, I wouldn't have let you,' he said.

She nodded. 'Much luck tonight,' she said, changing the subject. 'Maybe we'll get a break.'

'Yes,' he said. 'Maybe we will.'

He drove out to the airport to meet the ambassador. It was shortly after nine o'clock and he was aware of the increased security around the side gate where he gained admittance onto the field, a couple of American Marines and a complement of Indonesian national police. The Air Force 707 glistened silver in the light at the far end of the field where the honor guard was carrying the casket across the tarmac. And Lang had his Marines with flags all right, the banners limp in the still night air. The ambassador stood nearby, a woman by his side, and it was only as Kemper got out of his car that he recognized her, the Rooseno woman. There were great advantages, he thought with some resentment, to being rich in this world, for to a man with lesser resources and rank than the ambassador to have a well-known affair with a local would lead to repercussions. And then he remembered that she was the official liaison and under that cover could go anywhere and do anything either she or the ambassador damn well liked. He decided that when he had the time he would do a little nosing around and request further information on her.

A rattle of drums, sharp commands barked across the field and the honor guard paid a last tribute as the casket was loaded. The loading door on the 707 hissed shut. The engines revved up with an earth-shaking roar and the jet moved out to the runway, and then, after a short wait for clearance, gained speed and lifted off into the tropical darkness.

The ambassador spotted him. 'Mr Kemper, have you met Miss Rooseno?'

'I don't believe I've had that pleasure,' Kemper said, and he shook hands with her in a very formal manner. Then Miss Rooseno said good night to the ambassador and he thanked her for coming. Everything cool, well under control, as if the relationship between them did not exist at all. She climbed into the Mercedes that was waiting for her.

'A beautiful woman,' Kemper said, fishing.

Clements ignored the remark. 'Did you make the arrangements to see Oni Saud?' Clements said.

'Yes, sir. We're to meet Colonel Mustafa back at the embassy.'

'Very good,' the ambassador said. And he walked off toward Kemper's car without another word about the woman.

Mustafa's official car was waiting at the embassy and he was properly deferential to the ambassador, who climbed into the backseat. Clements said little during the long ride, still feeling slightly numbed from the difficulty of putting the casket of Jim Lang into the hold of a jet which would carry it across the Pacific. He had been grateful for Madeleine's presence. At least two people who had known Lang had been there to see him off.

But now he turned his attention to the man who had killed Lang and the anger began to rise within him.

Oni Saud was being held in one of the penitentiary compounds, a scooped-out place in the jungle with coils of sharp wire surrounding regular barbed-wire fences, guard towers with lights, individual pens inside the larger ones, wooden huts with heavy metal bars across wire-mesh windows, brush-covered shade arbors dotting bare ground to offer a minimal shelter for prisoners allowed in the larger yards.

Tidy, Clements thought, economical. A penitentiary compound could be expanded to accommodate thousands or shrunk to take care of a few, with little effort or expense either way. In this case Clements could see no prisoners at all as Colonel Mustafa stopped the vehicle at a gate and showed his papers to a pair of soldiers with carbines. There were guards in the wooden towers, a concentration of army and police vehicles around a square wooden building in a fenced area of its own. Mustafa rolled across the yard. A second gate opened and he parked inside.

The wooden building was a single large room, a quarter of which had been converted into a cell, iron bars stretching from floor to ceiling, a poorly ventilated room with a foul, scorched smell to it, as if something had been burning. And then Clements saw the man who must be Oni Saud, a thin and bony man in his forties, hanging from ropes attached to his wrists and the ceiling. A bored guard stood with a tape recorder next to him and said something to Oni Saud. Then, receiving no answer, he nodded to another guard who applied two exposed wires to Oni Saud's genitals. There was an arc of electricity, and the prisoner jerked on the ropes as if trying to get away. He screamed. The smell of scorched flesh.

'Cut him down,' Clements said.

Kemper saw the expression in Colonel Mustafa's eyes. 'The ambassador would like to talk with the prisoner, if you would be so kind as to interrupt your interrogation,'

Kemper said, trying to soften what would be perceived as a command coming from the ambassador.

Colonel Mustafa cleared his throat. 'May I remind the ambassador that this miserable human being tried to kill him and in the process killed his aide.'

'I said cut him down.'

Colonel Mustafa paused, as if considering, then shrugged, gave instructions to a guard who climbed on a stepladder, swung with a kris to cut one rope, left Oni Saud dangling by one arm until he could cut the other rope. Then Oni Saud fell in a heap on the dirt, a grunting noise coming out of him, as if he had trouble breathing.

'Put him into his cell,' Colonel Mustafa said to the guards. 'Put the manacles on him.' The guards dragged Oni Saud into the barred enclosure, propped him up on a low three-legged stool, a slop bucket nearby for his wastes. Clements saw the streaks of blood in the stubble of beard on his forlorn face, his body hunched forward with his elbows resting on his knees and his arms flopping down in front of him as a soldier clamped the heavy iron manacles on his thin wrists.

Colonel Mustafa ordered a soldier to put two chairs close to the iron bars and to bring a lamp closer to the cell. The soldier scrambled to do as he was told. Mustafa offered the ambassador and Kemper a seat and then kicked one of the bars with the leather heel of his boot. It made a ringing sound. Oni Saud did not look up.

'You will pay attention,' Mustafa said in Indonesian to Oni Saud. 'You will answer questions.'

Oni Saud's head made a slight shuddering response. His eyes moved to the two men who sat outside the bars, then up to the colonel and back to the two men again. Clements could see the bruises on the side of the face, the dark hollows that almost looked like makeup beneath the cheekbones. There was a cut on the forehead above the right eyebrow, a line caked with blood. There was a jerkiness to his responses. He was barely conscious, as if he had scurried off somewhere inside himself to escape the pain.

Kemper looked to Clements. 'I have agreed that all

questions to the prisoner will be relayed through Colonel Mustafa,' he said.

'The ambassador shouldn't be limited by such rules,' Mustafa said, a slight mocking edge to his voice. 'If he thinks he can obtain information by his own means then he's free to do so.'

Clements studied the man in the cell. He was aware that Kemper had clicked on a tape recorder of his own. 'Can you hear me, Oni Saud?' he said in Indonesian. 'Do you understand when I speak to you?'

Oni Saud nodded.

Clements held up three fingers. 'How many fingers do you see, Oni Saud?'

Oni Saud squinted in the lamplight. 'Three,' he said.

'I understand you speak English,' Clements said.

'I will speak nothing but Indonesian,' Oni Saud said. 'It is the national language.'

Kemper looked to Clements. 'May I question him, Mr Ambassador?' Clements gave his assent without moving his head. Kemper moved his recorder closer to the bars. 'Why did you shoot at the ambassador?'

'I wanted to kill him.'

'For what reason?'

'For the corrupt oppression of the American imperialist presence,' Oni Saud said in a dry voice. 'Because American imperialists will drain the money from the people of Indonesia to whom it rightfully belongs.' He was reciting cant and Clements knew it. The voice was too singsong; this was a memorized speech just waiting to be made.

'Then you are a dedicated member of the PKI, the Indonesian Communist Party,' Kemper said.

'Yes.'

'A faction known as the Red Brigade.'

'Yes.'

'I understood that the members of the PKI are true believers in Karl Marx and Mao. That would mean that your Red Brigade is Chinese-inspired, is it not? Not Soviet in origin.'

'I am against the American imperialist presence.'

Kemper scratched his chin, boring in. 'If you are a good

party member, then you can tell me the name of the top man in China.'

Oni Saud looked away, said nothing.

'I am willing to give you a cigarette if you can tell me anything to demonstrate that you're telling the truth.'

'I'm not afraid of you.' Oni Saud grimaced up at Colonel Mustafa, then back to Kemper. 'If I can stand the pain he causes, why should I answer you?'

'Because I'm not questioning your bravery or condemning your beliefs. I just want to understand you, Oni Saud. You worked for Pertamina Oil at one time?'

'Yes.'

'Doing what?'

'I was a translator.'

'I see. Which languages do you speak?'

'English. Indonesian. Some dialects. Javanese. Sudanese. Others.'

'Were you ordered by your group to do this thing, Oni Saud?'

'What thing?'

'To shoot the ambassador.'

'No.' The lamp flickered, threatened to go out. A soldier turned up the wick. Clements heard the portable generators working outside for the banks of watchtower lights. No electricity in here. Another soldier was firing up a kerosene cookstove next to an open window.

'Then shooting the ambassador was your own idea?'

'I did it for my country.'

'Your rifle. A twenty-two caliber semiautomatic Ruger. The magazine carries fourteen rounds.'

'I don't know.'

'Surely you must know that. You were on a competition rifle team while you were with Pertamina Oil. You were rated as an expert marksman, I believe. But then you didn't use the Ruger in competition, I suppose.'

'No.'

'Does the Ruger belong to you?'

'Yes.'

'Where did you get it?'

'I bought it. A long time ago.'

'Not *that* long. This particular model was introduced two years ago.'

'I bought it from an American who was going home.'

'Name?'

Oni Saud shrugged. 'I don't know.'

'How much did you pay for it?'

'I don't remember.'

'It must have been expensive.'

'I make money from time to time.'

'Doing what?'

'Sometimes writing letters and documents for people who can't write.'

'You make a lot of money?'

'Not a lot. No.'

'But enough for your wife to have a new motorcycle.'

Oni Saud said nothing.

'It cost the equivalent of a thousand dollars American,' Kemper said. 'That's a fortune in rupiahs. Where did it come from?'

'A relative who died,' Oni Saud said, his face half concealed in darkness.

'A very rich relative, then,' Kemper said.

'A relative of my wife. I don't know her people that well. They live in Central Java. She went to visit and she came home with the money.'

Clements was fascinated with Kemper's technique, the questions designed to elicit specific answers, asked with no sense of prejudgement whatsoever. And a vague suspicion began to form in Clements's mind.

'Would you like a cigarette?' Kemper said.

'Yes.'

'Clove or American?'

'American.'

The cigarette was supplied. Oni Saud sucked on it. Clements wondered how he was dealing with the pain he had to be feeling. 'Now, we have you placed on that roof for one hour and forty minutes total,' Kemper went on. 'That's the period from when the helicopter observed you until you were apprehended beside the warehouse, the rifle still in your hand.' He recreated the scene in some detail, Oni Saud settling in behind the lip of a brick parapet, waiting for the ambassadorial party. He was exactly forty-three feet from the spot where the ambassador would be hit. There was no wind. So Oni Saud would not have to make any kind of hurried shot at long distances, nothing difficult. At the right moment, just up with the rifle and pull the trigger. 'That is correct, isn't it? Not a difficult shot?'

'Not difficult, no.' Oni Saud's face was lost in a pall of blue cigarette smoke.

'Not a bad down angle,' Kemper said. 'You were shooting for the head, I assume?'

'Yes.'

'And you missed the target by a foot, shot the wrong man. At forty-three feet. An unhurried shot.'

'I was nervous.' A deep intake of breath, lungs filling with blue smoke, exhaled like a volcanic fume. 'All the confusion,' he said.

'When you missed the first shot, why didn't you shoot again?'

'I was afraid. I wanted to get away.'

Kemper leaned back in his chair. And now Clements took over, the suspicion alive within him, real. He leaned forward until his face was close to the bars.

'Do you know me, Oni Saud?' he said in a low voice.

Oni Saud looked away, sucked on the cigarette.

'Look at me,' Clements insisted.

Slowly, Oni Saud turned his face toward him. The tiny prick of fire from the cigarette as he inhaled was reflected in his eyes. He was wary, not knowing what to expect.

'I ask you again,' Clements said. 'Do you know me? Have you ever seen me before?'

'I don't have to answer your questions.'

'Then you don't know who I am.'

'I refuse to answer.'

'I'm the American ambassador, you dumb son of a bitch. I was supposed to be your target. You must have observed me, studied my photograph so you wouldn't make a mistake, and you don't remember? On which side of me was the man you shot by mistake? What did he look like?'

'I will answer no more questions.'

Kemper had picked up the meaning now. 'Do you want to know what I think, Oni Saud?' Kemper said.

'About what?'

'About your story.'

'About the truth.'

'Not the truth,' Kemper said, pleasantly. 'We will come to the truth sooner or later, when you are ready to give us the details. But I don't believe you are political at all. You don't know anything about the Communist Party, much less this Red Brigade of yours. You don't belong to any cell. There's not a single political publication in your apartment. I don't think you shot anybody but I think you were hired to take the blame for it. Your wife has a new motorcycle and you'll have money stashed away somewhere. Believe me, we'll find it. We'll find it and you won't get to keep any of it. But then, how did you hope to save yourself at the end of all this? You know how Indonesian law works. You know Muslim justice.'

Oni Saud's jaw began to twitch, hesitancy within him. 'I am willing to die for what I believe.'

'But that's just it, isn't it?' Kemper said, coolly. 'A true believer has a passion to die for the cause, to become a martyr. But I don't hear that from you, Oni Saud.' He rubbed his chin, thoughtfully. 'No, my guess is that whoever hired you in the first place is powerful enough—or at least you believe them to be powerful enough—that they can save you when the time for trial comes. They've probably already proposed a strategy, worked it out with Indonesian lawyers. But my ambassador is willing to give you a deal here and now, with the colonel's permission, of course. You tell us who hired you to take the blame, you give me details, and I guarantee that you will save your miserable hide. Furthermore, if you agree to work for me, you'll not only stay alive, but you can double your money and live to spend it.'

On the mark. Clements could feel it. Kemper wasn't getting any more declamations of political belief out of Oni Saud, only a thoughtful silence, face turned away, screwed up against the last centimeter of cigarette. Kemper stood up. 'With the colonel's kind permission, we will allow you twenty-four hours to think about it. At the end of that time, I can guarantee you absolutely nothing.'

Oni Saud flipped the cigarette butt away, retreated into the darkness. Clements stood up. Even when he was outside in the fresh night air, he could still smell the odor of scorched flesh.

Colonel Mustafa lit a cigarette. 'You gentlemen are wasting your time,' he said, breathing smoke into the warm night air. 'We can be sure of nothing he says. And I don't think he is going to tell us anything.'

'He will, eventually,' Kemper said. 'Can you keep him untouched for a couple of days?'

'Certainly,' Colonel Mustafa said. 'We are friends. We do each other favors.' He looked at the ambassador. 'I have a large understanding so I even forgive your ambassador's bad manners. So this means you will owe me one.'

'Yes,' Kemper said. 'I will owe you one.'

Clements had the most unusual feeling, sitting in the car, looking out over the compound, that he was in terrible danger, but he did not give in to his desire to flee. If a man was afraid in this part of the world, his enemies could smell it. 'Oni Saud didn't fire the rifle,' he said.

'No, sir,' Kemper said.

'Then that means the assassin is still on the streets.'

'The odds are he'll try again.'

'Do you have any idea who he is, who he really represents?'

'This is a crazy part of the world, Mr Ambassador, but I don't have to tell you that. I've dealt with suicide squads, religious fanatics, nuts of every persuasion. I don't suppose there's a chance I can talk you into calling off your scheduled events outside the embassy for a week or two.'

'The Indonesians would interpret that as cowardice.'

'Nobody who knows you would believe that for a moment.'

'There are a hell of a lot of people who don't know me,' Clements said. 'To them, I *am* the United States. And the United States doesn't back down.' He looked around the camp in the darkness, and he could not shake the feeling that the man who had tried to kill him was watching him. He felt like opening the car door and yelling into the darkness.

Come out into the light, you son of a bitch. You shot a young man from ambush. Let me see your face.

81

'You can't give me any guarantees, Harry. Nobody can. So I'll take my chances.' He saw that Kemper had rolled down his window, was listening to the night sounds. 'You feel it too, don't you?' Clements said. 'He's out there, isn't he?'

'I don't believe in any sixth sense,' Kemper said. 'But it occurs to me that he could very well be military.' He nodded. 'He could be here, yes. And if he is, I was hoping he'd make a move, have another try, but under such poor lighting conditions he wouldn't have a chance of succeeding.' He sighed. 'I think we both have active imaginations, Mr Ambassador. So now I suggest we get the hell out of here, if you're ready.'

'I'm more than ready,' Clements said.

5

Kemper had been through all the information before, many times, but now he undertook to review it all once again. He had the most profound of beliefs in human fallibility, especially his own, and so he opened the dossier on the ambassador and slowly worked his way through it, line by line, in the hope of picking up some helpful detail he had missed before. He sat in the darkness of his office with a single reading lamp over the leather chair and he prowled through Clements's past.

Clements was in his forties, had certainly been born with a silver spoon, for his father had accumulated a great deal of oilfield wealth, primarily from the East Texas fields, and when he died the money had gone to Clements, his mother having died some years before. He had gone to the University of Texas and had married before graduation a shy and lovely girl named Alice Adams, who, according to the investigators, had influenced his life heavily. He had specialized in management, graduated *magna cum laude*, shown an interest in political science, done further work at Yale and the Foreign Service Institute, had been in the Navy and was sent to Vietnam on a fact-finding mission. There was a long list of the posts he had held, all with excellent annual reports, everything leading to the rank of ambassador, which he now held, but Kemper did not doubt for a moment that the vast fortune now held in blind trust and the right political connections had aided him up the ladder.

Five years ago his wife had been killed in an automobile accident in Africa. The funeral had been held in Texas and Clements assigned to Washington for a year, during which time his performance record had diminished, but as his grief subsided he had been assigned to a post in the United Nations. He had been involved in a couple of discreet liaisons with spectacular women and finally had been assigned to Indonesia as ambassador. There was nothing in his service record to indicate that he had ever been admonished against the possibility of political compromise.

Kemper sighed. Nothing here to tie in with what had happened. So much for the ambassador. Noblesse oblige.

But Madeleine Rooseno was another cup of tea. There were a couple of versions of her life which had been forwarded to him from the general files in Bangkok, but Kemper was not surprised at the disparities, for very often researchers out here in never-never land were given the information that the respondents thought they wanted to hear. In any event he was able to piece together enough of Madeleine's life to have a rather detailed overview.

She had been born in Saigon, Chinese mother, Indonesian father who was on a diplomatic mission there. Her father had died when she was quite young and her mother had been a good manager of the funds which had been left to her. Madeleine had received her name because her mother had made good friends in the French, who dominated Vietnam at the time of the girl's birth. Later, when the mother had seen that the French were not coming back and the Americans were about to desert the country, she sent Madeleine to live with her Chinese and Indonesian relatives in Jakarta.

Here the reports varied. Either Madeleine had taken on a succession of very powerful lovers who had made her a wealthy woman in her own right, or she had shown fantastic business acumen and the ability to cash in on her contacts. But she owned a good bit of property, was known to be tough in any business transaction and was now a powerful deputy director in the Finance Ministry, no mean feat for a woman of mixed ancestry.

He lit a cigarette, blew smoke toward the ceiling. No great insights to be gained here. Rich man, rich woman. Luxurious love affair. She would have nothing to gain by conspiring against him. To have the American ambassador as a lover would be a coup for any woman in Jakarta, and a faithful lover he was, no other women in the offing.

He closed the folder and then wandered off in search of company, not certain of his reception. He found Tommi sitting in the darkness in her quarters in the compound, the air conditioner off, Mozart playing softly on her record player. She was drinking wine.

'You mind having company?' he said.

'That depends,' she said. 'What did you have in mind?'

'Just talk,' he said.

'In that case, okay,' she said. She rummaged around until she found him a glass without turning the lights on. He sipped the wine, a little sweet for his taste, but he realized how much he had come to depend on her companionship in the late evenings, their conversations as much as the lovemaking, before he could sleep.

'Have I ever told you I don't like classical music?' he said. He could see only the shape of her in the darkness as she refilled her own glass, then her shape blended with that of an overstuffed sofa.

'I guessed that a long time ago,' she said. She sipped her wine. 'Strange, but we've never talked about music.'

'The business has always taken precedence.'

'I like Mozart, but there comes a point when I don't really hear the music. It just gives my mind an inner order. How was your day?'

'I need a listening ear,' he said.

'Does the music bother you?'

'No.'

'What happened with Oni Saud and the ambassador?'

He told her the whole thing, leaving out nothing, even the most commonplace bits of conversation, and he could feel the force of her listening in the darkness as if she were expending energy to assemble the facts as he gave them to her. He finished his recitation and waited. He heard her pouring more wine into her glass. 'Well,' he said. 'What do you think?'

'All I can give you is intuition,' she said. 'And it can be wrong by a hundred and eighty degrees.'

'You have a theory, then.'

'All the facts go against it.'

'Give it to me anyway.'

'First, this is being played small, but I think it's big.'

'Specify.'

She cleared her throat. 'It's all so small-time corny, don't you think? A little banana-republic-type operation. As if two or three radicals get together and play a little drama, give themselves a name like the Radical Brigade or the Red Watch or the Red Brigade. And one of them messes up a shot at the ambassador but kills poor sweet young Lang, and then another calls and claims credit for a very foolish operation. Now, a little immorality play like this has two possible endings. The other men in the conspiracy can follow the foolish example of the first and get themselves killed in the process, or they can get frightened off and leave the first poor bastard, your Oni Saud, to go all the way through to the firing squad. But when you find out that Oni Saud didn't pull the trigger, then that changes everything, because the poor dumb man is taking the rap and he really hasn't been sufficiently prepared for the role. But if he's taking the rap, I think we can interpret that to mean that somebody brought a professional hit man in, a contract player. Are you with me so far?'

'I'm tracking perfectly.'

He heard her drinking in the darkness. 'Now, if a professional was doing the job, we have another problem. Late this afternoon I had the Indonesian television send their tapes around and I saw one that showed Rooseno speaking, and in the background, Lang came up and sat down beside the ambassador. He looked terrible, a drowned rat, bless his heart, and he held a short conversation with the ambassador, who leaned over to hear better. And then the shot came. Pow. It tore off part of Lang's skull, top right side, but the ambassador was on his left. To me, the meaning is simple. If you have a professional high-powered enough that somebody is being paid to take the rap for him, he's not going to miss by that much. He might not hit exactly the right spot on the ambassador's skull but he would not miss it altogether.'

'He meant to hit Lang, then,' Kemper said, a musing, not a question.

'That's my opinion. Lang knew something, was

determined to pass it on to the ambassador, so the hit man intercepted him.'

'That's your hunch, is it?'

'Oh, there's more,' she said. 'The ambassador is now in very grave danger, I think.'

'Why? If Lang's been cut off.'

'Two reasons,' she said. 'First, Lang may have passed the key information to the ambassador, who doesn't know yet what he has. In that case he'll be killed to keep him from finding out. And even if he doesn't have the information, it would make great sense to have him killed, just to perpetuate the story that everybody's supposed to believe now, that Oni Saud tried to kill him and missed, and that one of the other comic-opera villains has followed through. Then it would be complete and nobody would ever follow up on what Lang found that made him so dangerous.'

'That makes great sense,' Kemper said. 'But who's behind it?'

'The Russians,' she said, flatly.

'Why the Russians?'

'That's just a hunch,' she said. 'But you can't go wrong by blaming the Russians. If they did it you're right on the mark. If they didn't do it you can always say it's the kind of thing the Russians *usually* do.' There was a pause. No sound.

Her logic was quite faultless. Buf if indeed she was right, then they were up against big money, good organization.

'You're very tight, Harry,' she said. 'Why don't you slow down? You can't crash-course this one.'

'I worry about you and your safety,' he said, leaning his head back against the softness of the couch. 'And I know damn well that if Jim Lang can have his head blown off that I'm not immune either.' He finished his wine. 'And I want us to have a life together.'

She kicked off her shoes and came and sat by him. He could feel her warmth in the darkness. 'I'm barefoot, Harry,' she said with a smile. 'But I don't want to be pregnant right now.'

He took her in his arms, laughing, and then he kissed her. 'Let's go to bed.'

'Yes,' she said. 'Let's go to bed.'

By the middle of the next morning Kemper felt as if he had been living right, because some of the nets he had cast out came back with information. The first to report in was boyish Houghton himself, all full of charm, who came into the safe room at the embassy and immediately popped a Coke out of the soft-drink machine and took his own sweet time about getting down to business. 'What does Baja California mean to you?' he said. 'I mean, what does it bring to mind when you hear the name?'

'Desert,' Kemper said, going along.

'Competition,' Houghton said, plopping himself down in a chair. 'I have a month's vacation coming next month, and I've bought a dune buggy with a buddy of mine. We've entered the race all the way from Tijuana to the town at the tip of the peninsular. Hell, I can't even remember the name of the town.' He tilted the bottle back, drank. 'You want in on a good deal? We're selling shares. A hundred bucks and you get a cut of the prize money we win.'

'Give me good news and I'll take a couple of shares.'

'No problem,' Houghton said with the supreme confidence of the young. 'I hit the jackpot.'

'Spill.'

Houghton spilled. He had done some tracking of his own in the part of town where Oni Saud lived, and everything fell into place. It seemed that Oni Saud was basically a decent man who was down on his luck. He had been laid off at Pertamina Oil through no fault of his own, simply because one of the Indonesian generals had a son who had been away in California at school and had come home and his father had put him on Oni Saud's slot as an excuse to pay him a considerable amount of money.

No explanation was made to Oni Saud and none was necessary. He had not been born to the ruling class, had no formal education, had taught himself languages on his own because he was a very bright man. He had married late, in a Muslim ceremony, a girl who was literally that, sixteen years old, who, according to Houghton's investigation, managed to make life pretty miserable for the older Oni

Saud, especially when he lost his job and the money stopped. She went out with other men and Oni Saud could have killed her and not been prosecuted, because adultery was a crime punishable by death, but Oni Saud truly loved her.

'I was told he wept a lot,' Houghton said, putting more money in the machine, giving it a whack with the palm of his hand to get it to disgorge another bottle. 'There was a bar he frequented, not a very classy place, but the owner of the bar is a friend of Oni Saud's and he urged Oni Saud to take a chair leg to his adulteress. I had a look at this girl in question who is now twenty-one, going on forty-five, and why anyone would bother one way or another, I wouldn't know.'

'You have the romanticism of a rock,' Kemper said. 'Get on with it.'

'Well, suddenly the miracle happened, according to the man who ran the bar, and the wife was back with Oni Saud, this time with a new motorcycle. That was about a week ago. The owner of the bar had some idea that Oni Saud was engaged in some monkey business because he began to hang out with another man at the bar who paid for all the drinks and generally was quite loose with his money. The man was smooth, wealthy.'

'Paying for a few drinks makes him wealthy?'

'I'll come to that. Oni Saud wouldn't talk about the man at all and the owner got the idea that the stranger was a criminal and that there might be a reward out for him. Sometimes the police pay very well for tips. So one evening, just before dark, the proprietor saw the man coming and snapped a picture of him which he was going to have developed and shown to the police. But the man saw him, threw him to the ground, cursed him soundly and broke the camera. Later, Oni Saud came to the bar owner, paid him a hundred dollars American not to report anything to the police and said there would be more money later. Oni Saud said the man was rich.'

'For God's sake, Houghton, make your connections.'

'I'm coming to that. Yes, I am. I deserve a promotion at the very least. First, because I know what happened. The scoundrel who resembled Oni Saud had a limp and a mean disposition and apparently he had entered into an arrangement where he was going to do something for which Oni Saud would take the blame and for which Oni would be well paid.'

'Jesus,' Kemper said. 'It fits.'

'It more than fits. It dovetails exactly, perfectly, not a seam showing. Oni Saud took his rap all right, was paid the motorcycle and ten thousand American dollars by a gentleman upon whose visage you will shortly gaze.' He took a photograph out of his pocket, flipped it across the table. It spun on the polished surface in front of Kemper, who snatched it up.

Bingo, Kemper thought, and the snarly bastard in this snapshot, steaming toward the cameraman, was indeed very close in appearance to Oni Saud.

'He broke the camera all right,' Houghton said. 'But the picture wasn't ruined. So it is my suggestion, Chief of Station Kemper, sir, that you run this man through ID in the Bangkok Station and you'll have your assassin.'

'Good work,' Kemper said. 'Damn good work as a matter of fact. Now, how do you know that it was ten thousand dollars?'

'The owner of the bar ended up holding the money for Oni Saud, minus a small commission, of course. He is to dole it out to the young wife to make her behave until Oni Saud is released from prison and comes home.'

'And how did a fair-skinned infidel like you find out about all this?'

'I told the barkeep I owed Oni Saud money and asked where I should pay it. The barkeep said he was Oni Saud's banker and before I would pay the hundred dollars American I insisted on seeing the bankroll, which he kept in his safe. He offered to sell me the picture itself, providing I would split the reward if the man was wanted. He also said that he would provide information as to how the scoundrel could be found, for considerable money, of course, if I happened to represent authority.'

'You've done a damn good job,' Kemper said.

'I've always considered myself a born winner, sir. And

unofficially as well as officially, I like to share my abilities. Anytime between now and the end of the month will be fine, talking about the two hundred dollars, I mean.'

'I'll want to know how many shares you're selling,' Kemper said. 'And how much prize money there is.'

'I'll be frank with you, sir. I wouldn't consider this an investment. It's more in the nature of investing in an adventure. But I'll get the specifics together this week.'

Once Houghton was gone, Kemper realized that Houghton would always do well in this world because he had an infectious zest for living, an enthusiasm which could not be dampened by any culture or any language. Kemper put the photograph on a facsimile machine and sent it to the Bangkok Embassy, where they had an expert named Squires who kept up on assassins and terrorist organizations in this part of the world, and sent a coded cable with it, carrying all the information he had, and made an urgent request, top security, for an ID and any information on a terrorist group known as the Red Brigade.

For the rest of the morning Kemper prowled around the offices, and Tommi put fresh coffee on his desk without a word, knowing how waiting affected him. She asked no questions as he slammed doors and pawed through folders in the file drawers until the red light flashed, which meant that a coded telex was coming through. Then he hovered over the machine, watching the printout, the groups of five letters that formed a perfectly symmetrical page. And once it had been printed he retired to his private office and ignored the computer terminal, which would have cut the time for his task by ten, but he did not trust the machines. He was convinced that the Soviets had tapped into the embassy so thoroughly that they would pick up his decoding as quickly as he did.

So he did it the hard way, using the book and the template, blocking out Squires's message with a soft-leaded pencil. The man was known, certainly.

YOUR CLIENT HAS ENOUGH NAMES
TO FILL A GOOD-SIZED TELEPHONE BOOK.

He leaned back in his chair, studied the material. According to Squires, the assassin had been a part of Libyan terrorist groups, German and Cambodian as well, but he was primarily a money man, one of the best hit men in the business, and rumor had it that he was heavy into dope, often psychotic. He never used the same name twice and the last name attributed to him had been Fox. He was credited with the killing of Italian businessmen who had been held for ransom as well as a variety of political figures in Africa and Southeast Asia, men of every political persuasion. Squires had received information on Lang's killing and the subsequent arrest of Oni Saud and it followed in a general way this assassin's method of operation. He had been hired in Chile in the early 1970s to kill a political candidate and was paid by the opposition party for the act, but a part of the deal was the provision of a man of the assassin's general build to take the blame. The assassin had used a handgun at short range, ducked into an alley, passed the gun to the confederate, who took two weeks to admit that he had not pulled the trigger. Fox was long gone by then.

Fox spoke many languages and it was obvious from the picture that he could pass as a native in most of the tropical countries. He was a careful man in his methods but certainly not overly cautious, and he killed in a variety of ways, the same skill displayed in each of them. From the variety of aliases, it was probable that this assassin could pass as English or American.

Now, as to the Red Brigade, Squires had just begun to pick up information about them. It seemed that they were primarily composed of nationalists in a variety of Southeast Asian countries who had allied themselves under a Marxist banner and taken a familiar name. Squires knew practically nothing about them, except that they would have to be bankrolled quite heavily to hire a man like this assassin.

The final piece of information: 'Six Ravens' meant absolutely nothing to Squires. He would not even hazard a guess, but he would keep his ears open.

Kemper ran the coded transmission and the translation

through the shredder, then rang Houghton again and told him to open negotiations with the barman as to the whereabouts of this limping man, authorizing him to put out no more than five hundred dollars in good-faith money, but authorizing ten thousand dollars if the barman gave information leading to an arrest.

He was about to go for a long walk through the malodorous city, for he thought better when he was walking and there was a lot to be thought out and pieced together now. Oni Saud would be a tough nut to crack but Kemper would see him in pieces, if necessary, for Oni Saud had a lot of vital information locked in his head. It would take a bit of doing.

He stopped at Tommi's desk. She was chain-smoking cigarettes, going through sheafs of financial reports.

'I'm going for a walk,' he said. 'I should be back in an hour.'

'Not yet,' she said, glancing up at him over half-moon reading glasses, all business now as she had been all loving last night. 'The ambassador's secretary called. He wants to see you right away.'

'What's up?' he said, curious.

'The ambassador's temper, I believe,' she said. 'He just received his own obituary in the mail.'

The note had caused a good bit of consternation already. It had come through the mail room, been routinely screened for size, which precluded the possibility that this small envelope could contain a letter bomb. It had gone directly from the mail room to Lucy's desk, where she had given it no more than a cursory examination. It was a regular letter-sized envelope made of a cheap paper used in Southeast Asia and there was a return address in the upper-left-hand corner written in ballpoint pen. It was addressed to His Excellency Charles C. Clements, United States Ambassador to Indonesia. She slid a letter opener beneath the flap and sliced through the upper edge. The envelope carried a regular textbook correct address and she was sure it was from a student appealing for financial aid, despite the fact that it was marked PERSONAL AND

CONFIDENTIAL. She took out the typed letter and the printed newspaper clipping. She stamped both of them with the date and added them to the ambassador's stack and was about to move on to the next letter when something caught her eye and she suddenly felt light-headed, sick to her stomach. She called Kemper's office first and then buzzed the ambassador in his office, told him there was something he should see immediately and then took the clipping, the letter and the envelope to him.

He could tell from the expression on her face that something was terribly awry and he was immediately alarmed. 'Are you all right, Lucy?' he said.

She handed him the papers and he sat down in his leather chair to read them.

He scanned the letter first, written on a typewriter. There was no date.

My dear Ambassador,

I find it distressing to have to write you this letter, but you can see from the enclosed that we are quite serious and the policies followed by you and your country have left us little choice. We will no longer tolerate your presence in Indonesia, and ask your country to close down your mission here and go home. We have nothing against you personally, but you are perhaps the foremost symbol of the American presence, and your leaving would satisfy us for the moment as to the larger intentions of your government to pull out from areas of the world where you are not welcome.

You have twenty-four hours from your receipt of this message to leave the country.

The Red Brigade

He examined the clipping. It was printed in regular news type on newsprint paper, with a short headline: AMBASSADOR DIES. And beneath it: '(AP) Jakarta: Doctors at Priok Hospital Number Two revealed this morning that American Ambassador Charles C. Clements died at 0200 hours following futile efforts by surgeons to save his life following the attack by an assassin yesterday evening. According to an embassy spokesman, Ambassador Clements had ignored repeated warnings from a newly organized left-wing faction of the Indonesian Communist Party, the Red Brigade.'

Beneath it was a summary of his career, all accurate.

He felt chilled to the bone.

There was a knock on the door and Kemper stuck his head in.

'I called for him,' Lucy said. 'I hope it's all right.'

'It's exactly what you should have done,' Clements said, forcing a reassuring smile. 'Would you tell my driver I'll be a few minutes?'

'Yes, sir,' she said.

When she was gone Kemper picked up the letter and the clipping, sat down in a chair opposite the ambassador, went over everything very carefully, including the envelope, a puzzled expression on his face. Then he laid them back on his desk and laced his fingers, deep in thought.

'Well?' Clements said.

Kemper shrugged. 'I think in this case that discretion is the better part of valor, Mr Ambassador.' He told him briefly of the information concerning the assassin.

'What name is he working under here?' Clements said.

'I'm working on that. But whatever we call him, it's foolish not to take this threat seriously. I think you should get out of here for a while. You could be called back to Washington for consultation. You could go on a well-earned vacation. I happen to know that you've been on station for over a year.'

'What advantage would that give you?' Clements said. 'If I leave, they apply pressure at another point.'

'But not for a while. It might give us a week or two. It would certainly buy us time to track down this Fox and to see if we can get the dimensions of this Red Brigade, find out exactly what they're after.'

Clements poured coffee from his carafe. 'What do you know of my meetings with the Soviet ambassador here?' he said.

'Not a great deal,' Kemper said. 'I asked for permission in Washington to bug the meetings, was turned down.'

'Then you don't know what I'm doing.'

'No.'

'I have been given permission to back-channel,' Clements said. 'Just as Sergei has received permission from his superiors to do the same. It's unofficial negotiation, disarmament talks without the presence of aides, interpreters, protocol or bullshit. We are old friends, and I use that term loosely, old colleagues would be a better term, and the information we trade is quite useful to both governments in Geneva. I'm telling you this for a couple of reasons. Is there any chance that the Red Brigade could be connected with a disruption of these talks?'

'I can't think why they would be,' Kemper said. 'I'd have to give that a lot more thought.'

'I'm also telling you this to let you know why I can't leave here for any prolonged period. These talks come first, despite the risks.' He sipped the coffee. 'Now, after my meeting with Sergei today, I can rearrange my schedule to be gone for a week, if that will do you any good.'

'That will do fine,' Kemper said. 'Perhaps you could have your secretary give me your itinerary and I'll have it published in the press. It won't hurt if the Red Brigade thinks we agree to their terms. But there's one cautionary note.'

'Go ahead.'

'I'm a cautious son of a bitch because I've learned to be,' Kemper said. 'The odds are that the message they're conveying here is authentic, that they're stating what they want. There's also a small chance that this is designed to lull us into a false sense of security for the next twenty-four hours. So we accept the message but we don't let down our guard.'

'Agreed,' Clements said.

He took the bulletproof limousine this time with a quiet escort of police cars front and rear, but for the first time in months he was apprehensive as his Indonesian driver drove him to the Borobodur Hotel, a lush compound of swimming pools and green lawns near the new mosque, walled off from the city so that the foreign visitor could stay overnight in Jakarta undisturbed by the physical actuality of the city, no intrusions at all except for the amplified wail of the muezzin's call to prayer from the gleaming white minaret of the mosque down the street.

But since Lang's death he had been able to take nothing for granted, for the bullet had come out of nowhere, at a time when it was least expected. Unless something was resolved shortly he decided he would arm himself. He had been an officer on temporary duty in Vietnam and he had grown used to the weight of a sidearm and the feeling that he could protect himself against attack.

The precautions taken today were more than adequate. For as the limousine pulled up in front of the Borobodur he saw the security men already in place, and he knew the lobby of the hotel would have been covered without the guests being aware of what was happening. He took his normal amount of time departing the limousine in case he was being observed. In this country appearances were vitally important. He went into the cool sanctuary of the hotel lobby and then left his escort as he went down the corridor to the private dining room where the Soviet ambassador was waiting for him.

Clements had known Sergei Ludov for many years, having met him in Moscow. Clements had been fairly new to the foreign service then, and he had met Sergei at a reception, a great hulk of a man, peasant stock, with a ruddy round face and an excellent command of colloquial English. They became personal adversaries and there had been many stormy arguments in those days when the Cold War was at its peak. Clements had viewed Sergei as a barbarian whose ignorance was disguised by his command of English, and Sergei had seen him as a capitalist warmonger intent on destroying the political system of the U.S.S.R.

But over the years they had followed parallel tracks and the stormy sessions had been repeated in Singapore and Hong Kong, where both were stationed for a while with roughly equal positions. When their paths crossed in any part of the world they sought each other out to have another sortie in the incessant verbal battle. And once when Clements was suffering from pneumonia and was lying in Bethesda, recuperating, staring out the window at a snowstorm, who should come clomping in to visit him but old Sergei himself, six years since their last set-to, the Russian mellower, black hair graying, mussed, heavily bearded now, the eyes no longer alight with young fire.

'Ah, you Bolshevik son of a bitch,' Clements said with a smile, genuinely glad to see him. 'You had to wait until now to catch me at a disadvantage. But it won't do you any good. You've been wrong for twenty-five years and nothing's happened to make you right.'

'We argue some other time,' Sergei said. 'I heard you almost came to the embrace of the Big Black Bear.'

'Is that your euphemism for dying?' Clements said. 'Another goddamned Mother Russia proverb?'

'No, I made that up,' Sergei said, grinning. 'People expect us to talk that way.'

'Aren't you running a hell of a risk coming here? Visiting a military hospital, an American foreign service officer in the enemy camp?'

Sergei sat down by the bed, face twitching with his little joke, breath smelling of schnapps, voice lowering automatically as if the whole world were bugged. 'I'll send a map of the elevator system to Moscow,' he said, chortling. 'No, I have been allowed to come because I persuaded the ambassador that since you were so sick, you might be willing to defect and come to Russia for medical treatment.'

'Jesus,' Clements had said. 'He believed that bullshit?'

'If the positions were reversed, would your superiors believe it?' Sergei said, touching the sausage of an index finger to the side of his nose.

'Yes,' Clements said. 'Of course.'

'The same on both sides,' Sergei said. 'The whole world runs on such bullshit.'

Now that they were both in Jakarta, neither had missed a meeting since they had stumbled onto the subject of disarmament and found themselves encouraged by both governments.

The private dining room was decorated in an Indonesian version of Versailles, with mirrors in ornate frames and a mural of bewigged French aristocracy at play in a dream pastoral which had never existed. Marie Antoinette in a swing. Sergei was already at the table, his black suit coat draped over the back of an ormolu chair as he stood up, a sober expression on his face, extending a paw of a hand. 'I was very sorry to hear about the murder of your aide.'

'He was a fine young man.'

'Is it against your policy to discuss this with me?' Sergei said.

Clements shook his head. 'I'm sure you know almost as much about it as we do.'

'We were in constant touch with the hospital during the operation on Lang. But our people are frankly puzzled. Was the bullet intended for Lang or was it you the assassin was after?'

'What do your people think?'

Sergei shrugged. 'You,' he said. 'We also think it was the work of a professional.'

'Oni Saud?'

'Not good enough for this job, I think.'

Clements looked directly into his eyes. 'Does this assassin, whoever he is, have anything to do with your embassy or your government?'

'Do you really have to ask that question?' Sergei said, his eyes unblinking.

'Yes,' Clements said.

'I suppose you do,' Sergei said. 'If it were in the best interests of my country to have you killed, or to kill your aide, then I'm sure it would be done, despite any feelings I might have. But I can guarantee you that there is no reason why we would do such a thing. It was not of our doing.'

'And your KGB? Can you answer for them?'

'Certainly,' Sergei said, with just a hint of irony in his eyes. 'I am a KGB colonel myself. There is scarcely anyone with this residence who is not KGB.'

'Have you heard of an operation called "Six Ravens"?'

Sergei considered a moment. 'No.' he said. 'We have very little imagination anymore when it comes to naming operations. We might use alphabetic designations.' He put a hand on Clements's shoulder. 'Now, if you believe me, then we continue. If you don't believe me, and I will understand if you do not, then tell me and we discontinue.'

'We continue,' Clements said.

Sergei rang a bell for the waiter. 'You were not hurt in the attack?'

'No. How's your arthritis?'

Sergei shrugged philosophically. 'I'm fifty-nine years old. I can live with it.' The door opened and the three Indonesian waiters in crisp white uniforms entered with great ceremony, one of them pushing a serving cart glittering with silver food covers. 'Sit down. I hope you have an appetite.'

'What are we having?'

Sergei nodded to the waiters, who uncovered the bowls of spicy rice and chunks of meat from an indefinable source soaking in a red sauce. The waiters poured tea, departed.

Clements picked up his fork. 'I enjoy Indonesian food,' he said.

Sergei ate automatically. 'It does not always agree with me. Perhaps it's the sauce.' He poured himself a glass of wine. 'I want you to know that I have assigned a couple of men to find out who attacked you and why.'

'Altruism?' Clements said, wryly. 'Friendship?'

'Hardly,' Sergei said. 'We have people in our country who would be against the talks we are having. And I'm sure that there are also people in your country who would be equally against it. Either group could be acting outside our knowledge.'

'You do know what the group is calling itself?'

'There have been many Red Brigades not connected with the Soviet Union.' Sergei speared a piece of meat with his fork. 'But I remember in your history, radical groups calling themselves after the heroes of your country. The Abraham Lincoln Brigade in the Spanish Civil War. Your government had no more to do with that brigade than we do with this one.' His solid jaws chewed heavily beneath the beard.

'The hazards of the profession,' Clements said, helping

himself to more rice. He looked out the window at the brilliant sunshine on a flower bed, the view filtered by gossamer drapes which softened the intensity of the light and the colors. They finished their meal in silence and then Sergei pushed the dishes to one side, clearing a space on the white linen tablecloth large enough for the map of Europe and the western U.S.S.R. 'Now, to business,' he said, unfolding his tortoise-rimmed spectacles which lay heavily across the thick bridge of his nose. 'I have been giving this some thought. From East Germany, if we were to mount an offensive here, we would move through the Haf Corridor and the Fulda Gap. Here.' His heavy fingertip smeared across the border, past Nuremberg, toward Stuttgart. 'You have nuclear missiles here. So the objective of this strike would be to take them out.'

'You'd never make it before they were launched,' Clements said, leaning forward, frowning at the map. 'In the first place, you'd have to depend on Polish troops. In the second place, your military commanders would be making a terrible mistake. These are not offensive missile batteries.'

'The hell they're not.'

They went at their gaming for the better part of an hour, negotiating the reduction of missiles on the Soviet side against America's plan to deploy even more missiles into the NATO countries, and Sergei jotted down specific figures in his notebook, wrangling over concessions, gave on the Netherlands, refused to budge on England and the cruise missiles, making notes in Cyrillic script, thinking in English, writing in Russian. Clements leaned back in his chair, tired, and Sergei seemed mentally winded, words exhausted as he filled the two wineglasses and contemplated the mural of the French princess, Marie, in a swing, forever caught just as she was about to begin her descending arc, her face turned to the side, a coy smile of anticipation, not one hair of her wig out of place. Sergei raised his glass.

'To a simpler time,' he said.

'Her time was not a hell of a lot simpler. The Big Black Bear got her within a year.' He picked up his glass of wine, regarded the map a last time. 'It's nonsense,' he said. 'Tell me the truth. Do your people really want arms reduction?'

'Only if we're sure we are not cheated,' Sergei said. 'We don't trust you. I don't believe your Pentagon wants to go out of business.'

'We both have our hawks,' Clements said. 'Well, I guess we've done all we can for one day. I'll have my notes transcribed, one copy to you, one copy to my government. You do the same and we'll both make our changes and inch along. We'll talk again.'

'Soon.' Sergei folded the map. 'I'll let you know what we find out about the man who shot your aide,' he said. 'Please assure your government that we had no hand in it.'

'I will.'

Ordinarily, Houghton would have taken a more cautious route for he had been thoroughly trained in covert operations, and the first caveat he could remember was 'Don't take the chance yourself when you have a local agent who can do it for you.' But back at Langley, where they covered every possible contingency, they seemed to have forgotten one:

What do you do when a local agent develops a toothache so severe that it knocks him out of action?

Actually, Houghton said to himself as he sat in the Jakarta fronton, the immense bank of seats with the jai alai playing area down below him, this was not that difficult an assignment and he did not need a go-between. It was going to be a game of give and take, of negotiation in the Indonesian language, and when it came to bargaining, he was pretty damn good at it. No great risks here, as a matter of fact. All that could be lost was money and there was a great deal to be gained. He would bargain with Mochtar for the identity of the man who had paid Oni Saud to take the rap, the man in the photograph who had been identified as the assassin. It was just a matter of the offer being high enough to overcome the genuine fear that the barkeep must be feeling.

The players had filed out onto the court and the public address system had introduced them in three languages and now the singles had begun, a Basque in red with the long basket, the *cesta* on his hand, was making fantastic shots, scooping up the ball and caroming it off two walls before it spun back into the playing area to be caught by a Spaniard in blue who shot it back toward the wall again.

'Good evening,' the voice said beside him in Indonesian and he knew it was the barkeep without even looking at him. Mochtar chewed betel nut and his breath stank of the light narcotic. 'Have you picked any favorites?'

'I'm not much of a jai alai fan,' Houghton said. 'Are you ready to do business?'

'Soon,' Mochtar said. 'I have a bet on Sanchez.'

'Who?'

'The Spaniard. The one dressed in blue.'

It was a long rally which ended when Blue, Mochtar's Sanchez, slipped and fell and missed his shot and brought down upon himself the curses of the crowd. Mochtar tore up his ticket. 'The games are fixed,' he said. 'It's all decided in advance. But sometimes you hear the truth and sometimes you hear the lie.'

He followed Houghton outside the fronton into the warm night air. There was a street stall down the wall where espresso was being served at small sidewalk tables, and Houghton plotted his strategy even as he asked Mochtar to sit down. He ordered two of the mild little coffees the Indonesians served up.

Mochtar sipped it, making a loud slurping noise. 'I saw Oni Saud's wife today,' he said, wiping his mouth with the back of his hand. 'She knows I have her husband's money so she comes to try to talk me out of it. She would fuck me for it if I let her, but I'm an honest man. I wouldn't even consider that.'

Mochtar was wearing an Indonesian cap tonight. He had waxed his mustache and his beard and he smelled of lemon. *Not true*, Houghton thought. *You'll take whatever you can get, whether it's ass or money.* 'I'm pleased to hear that you're an honorable man,' Houghton said. 'But do you consider it honorable to protect the man who has sent your friend to prison? Do you consider it honorable to take money for delivering such an assassin to justice?'

'Who decides about justice?' Mochtar said. 'Allah decides about justice, whether this is right or that is wrong. But all

I know is that this man himself is very dangerous, and if he knew I was even talking about him, he would not hesitate to kill me. So if I am to take such great risks, then I must have a lot of money.'

'How much money?' Houghton said, taking another sip of the coffee, knowing he was going to have trouble sleeping tonight with this distilled caffeine shooting through him.

'I want twenty-five hundred American dollars.'

Houghton laughed. He ran a handkerchief over his perspiring bald head. 'So do I,' he said. 'I'd like to have two thousand American dollars.' He watched a girl go past. 'If the price is going to be that high, then I think I'll pass. The official reward is only the equivalent of a thousand American dollars.'

'But maybe you want him for some other reason,' Mochtar said. 'I am just a poor man who doesn't know much about such things, but perhaps you want him so much you will pay more than the Indonesian government would. They are notorious for paying such little money when they have all that graft.'

'I'll pay five hundred dollars,' Houghton said. 'I'm the one who has to catch him and turn him in to collect the thousand. I'm being pretty damned generous, I think.'

'My life is worth more than that.'

'I don't think we can do business,' Houghton said with a yawn. 'I'll pay for the coffee and then I think I'll find me a girl for the night.'

He started to stand up, but Mochtar touched his arm with his right hand. 'Nine hundred, if you pay tonight. Then I'll show you where to find him.'

Houghton sat down again. 'Two hundred in advance,' he said. 'Then two hundred more when you show me. And the final five hundred when I catch him.'

Mochtar looked grieved, pained. 'But what if you *fail* to catch him?'

'Then you have four hundred dollars and you can find some way to cash him in for yourself.'

Mochtar heaved a sigh beneath his white cotton shirt. 'All right,' he said, 'Give me two hundred dollars.'

'Not here,' Houghton paid the bill and walked back toward the shadows of the fronton palace and an outdoor telephone.

Then he reached into his pocket and separated the bills before he drew out two of them, both hundreds. 'Now I have to make a telephone call,' he said.

He dialed. Kemper answered. No identification. 'Yes?'

'I have a deal. Side of the fronton palace.'

'Has he given you a location?'

'Not yet.'

'When you get it, stay put.'

'Right.' Houghton put the telephone back on the hook. Mochtar appeared to be very uncomfortable. 'What's the matter?' Houghton said.

'This man has the evil eye. I want the business over with. I'll show you where he lives and then I'm going home.'

'He lives near here?'

'You can see the house from the canal.'

Ah, the stinks of this place, Houghton thought, and in his letters to his relatives he often tried to describe what a canal smelled like, but there was no exact word or combination of words that fit it. They walked along a narrow embankment on the edge of the canal, past a stack of fifty-five gallon barrels. *It is as if the black water in that canal is truly corrupt,* Houghton thought, *and it holds five hundred years of putrefaction.*

Mochtar lowered his voice. 'Now, off there, the other side of the canal. Do you see the old Dutch house?'

'I see three old Dutch houses,' Houghton said, craning his neck to look, not certain that Mochtar wasn't trying to con him. After all, four hundred dollars for a look at a fake house was pretty good money.

'It's the first one.'

'All right.'

'Bottom floor. He has a room there.'

'You're telling the truth?'

'I wouldn't lie. Oni Saud trusts me. Now, the other two hundred dollars.'

Houghton put his hand in his pocket, began to sort out another two hundred-dollar bills and that moment knew he had made a terrible mistake, for his hand was not free to defend himself, to go for the small pistol in his shoulder holster, to break in any way the hold of the wiry arm that came out of the darkness and grabbed him just below the neck, pulled him off balance. And then he found he could not breathe and he panicked and tried to yell. But only a bubbling sound came out of him. The knife had sliced across his throat and he could not move at all, only fall away into death.

Sangre held him up with one hand and with the other went through his pockets while Mochtar stood by, terrified, literally wringing his hands in fright at the strength of the killer who peeled the money out of the clothing and snatched the pistol out of the shoulder holster before he let the body go. It fell on the edge of the canal and Sangre touched it lightly with the sole of his shoe. It rolled and sank into the black water without a sound.

'You will keep your word,' Mochtar said in a low voice.

'Sure,' Sangre said. He peeled off his shirt, wiped the blood off his hands, then threw the cloth on the ground. 'I want your shirt,' he said.

'Why should you have mine?' Mochtar said.

'Because I'm giving you half the American's money.'

Mochtar shrugged, peeled off his shirt. Sangre handled it gingerly, laid it on the top of an oil drum for the moment. He counted the money. 'He had three thousand dollars.'

'The pig,' Mochtar said. 'He tried to buy you cheap.'

'So you have fifteen hundred coming,' Sangre said, and as he looked at the sheaf of bills in his left hand, the knife in his right hand seemed to dart out, quite on its own, plunging into the middle of Mochtar's lean chest, one quick motion, in and out. Mochtar looked surprised, mystified, completely baffled, as if a terrible accident had befallen him. He sank to his knees, clutching his bare chest, then toppled into the water.

Sangre used an unbloodied spot on his own shirt to clean the knife, then he washed his hands in the canal water and shook them dry before he put on the fresh shirt. He put the money and the knife away and then moved off, away from the canal, toward the light.

6

Kemper was filled with a cold fury. He moved with a deadly evenness around the side of the canal that had been blocked off by the Indonesian police, wearing an expression on his face that said, *Fuck around with me and I'll rip your head off.* Colonel Mustafa had done the best job he could under the circumstances. He had thrown a police cordon around the side of the canal where the two bodies had been found, but there was no such thing as a cleared area, for the press of so many curious people was too great. There were a dozen small boats in the canal full of curious street people and children swimming in the water just beyond the lines on the bank marked with yellow Mylar tape. A commercial boat chugged down the canal through the heavy traffic, saturating the night air with diesel fumes, air horn blasting.

Kemper was sick to his stomach as he examined Houghton's body, which had been dragged from the water by street people before the police had arrived. The shoes had been stripped off, because they would be worth a few rupiahs even if there were specks of blood on them, and his pocket had been turned inside out, wallet gone, pen, handkerchief, small change, wristwatch, everything. The pistol could have been taken by the killer or by one of the human vultures who had swarmed over the body before the authorities came. Houghton's dead face was pale, the body drained of blood through the slashed arteries of the neck.

Kemper was filled with an illogical fury. *You couldn't watch what you were doing, could you, you son of a bitch? You had to grandstand it, do it by yourself, and now who's going to run your goddamn race?*

Finally, Kemper turned away, found Colonel Mustafa waiting patiently for him.

'I want Houghton's body taken to the mortuary, where our doctors will conduct a post.'

'And the Indonesian?' Mustafa said wryly, looking toward the other body, which had been covered by a thin cotton blanket. 'Do you think he's worth the same kind of examination?'

'That's your goddamned business, not mine. What did your technicians get off the telephone?'

Mustafa lit a cigarette against the stench of the canal. 'Perhaps a hundred partial prints, all different. There are no private phones around here. So the public phones are in constant use. One of the people who found the bodies used the telephone to call the local headman.'

'I want to talk to him,' Kemper said, moving away from the bodies as the ambulances backed into position, lights flashing, and the attendants unfurled their canvas stretchers.

'Certainly,' Colonel Mustafa said. The crowds parted in front of him as he led Kemper toward the side of the fronton palace where a middle-aged Indonesian sat in a wheelchair, his broken leg in a cast. Kemper made a gesture of respect, for if he was to get any information it would be from this neighborhood headman, known as an RT, whose prestige depended on knowing everything that transpired in his district. He shook hands with Kemper, waved a hand to have one of his men materialize from the darkness a chair, on which Kemper was invited to sit.

When the bodies had been found in the canal the RT was notified at the same moment the police were summoned, and he had immediately spread the word that he wanted any information about these two men in his district tonight.

'And what did you find?' Kemper said in his polite Indonesian.

'The American came to the jai alai games and sat for about fifteen minutes by himself,' the RT said. 'Then the poor unfortunate Indonesian who was to be killed as well appeared and sat next to him. They were engaged in earnest conversation. They left the fronton palace very soon after they met and went down the street where they drank coffee together. Some money exchanged hands, the American giving to the Indonesian, but we do not know the amount. Then both went to the telephone and afterward walked down along the canal.'

The RT fell silent, jaws working. Kemper smelled the betel nut he was chewing.

'What then?' Kemper said.

'An evil spirit came from the canal and killed both of them.'

Christ, Kemper thought. He had to hold his temper in check. 'Did anyone in your neighborhood observe the evil spirit, sir?' he said with forced respect. 'Could anyone describe the shape of this evil spirit, his size, the color of his hair?'

The RT shook his head, spat onto the stones of the street. 'That is the nature of an evil spirit, that it cannot be seen, that it can materialize at will and make itself invisible.'

Kemper took a half-dozen copies of the photographs of Sangre out of his pocket and handed them to the RT. 'I would be very grateful to you if you would circulate these in your neighborhood, sir, and see if this man was observed here tonight.'

The RT examined one of the photographs with a flashlight, then squinted over toward Kemper. 'Did this man attend the fronton?'

'I don't know. I doubt it.'

'I will circulate the pictures,' the RT said.

'You have my thanks,' Kemper said. He stood up, walked with Colonel Mustafa toward the official cars.

'I think you have all the information you're going to get from the RT,' Mustafa said. 'He was proud to be able to give you all the information about your man, but he knew only because your man was American and he stuck out in this district and people noticed him and were curious about him. But the Indonesians who pass through are known only if they take a room here or if they're engaged in any kind of business. And this man of yours in the photograph could pass for Indonesian. Unless the killer did anything to make himself noticed, there will be no information about him. In the RT's own official account of the happening here tonight, he will put down "Two men killed by evil spirits" unless a religious person in the district brings him the name of the evil incarnation, and then he would be more specific.'

'Son of a bitch,' Kemper said. 'He's going to get rid of anyone who can identify him and, if we're not careful, he's going to get away with it.' They got into the car and Colonel Mustafa told his driver to move on. With the horn blaring, the car inched forward, gained speed while Kemper sorted through his options. 'I need to speak frankly and candidly, Colonel, and I don't have time to go through the usual courtesies and cultural ceremonies. I apologize for that in advance.'

'You may speak as freely as you like,' Colonel Mustafa said. 'I may however be limited in the accommodations I can make for you.'

'I'll give it to you in a nutshell. We have an assassin on the loose and Oni Saud is the only man who knows him well.'

'So?'

'I want Oni Saud brought in from the jungle compound, turned over to us. I want photographs of the assassin circulated among every security force you have. I want every employee at every airport to know what he looks like, every bus driver, every RT in all the districts of Jakarta. In other words, I want the most intensive search effort you've ever mounted. And I'm willing to pay.'

Colonel Mustafa rubbed his fingers against his chin. 'These are sensitive issues. It might appear to look as if the whole of Indonesia has suddenly come under American command, so that the American CIA can determine which prisoners are detained and which are set free and what kind of manhunts are to be instigated. It is a matter of sovereignty.'

'Don't fuck with me,' Kemper said, his controls suddenly gone. 'You know goddamn well that you can make it look any way you want it to look. You can hand over Oni Saud on technical grounds, for a day's examination. You can set up the travel surveillance because Indonesia is dedicated to stamping out terrorists. And if you're not dedicated to that, then you had better get with it.' He lowered his voice, brought himself in check. 'Ten thousand dollars,' he said.

'That will not even begin to cover the costs of what you propose,' Colonel Mustafa said.

'The money's going into your pocket, not to the government,' Kemper said. 'Name your amount.'

Colonel Mustafa sighed. 'Fifty thousand,' he said.

'Done. How do you want it?'

'A Swiss bank account,' Mustafa said. 'In Swiss francs.'

'Agreed.'

Tommi had set up a command post in her office, diverting seven of the lines from the chancery switchboard to her own, feeding the calls one at a time to Kemper. He had mounted a blackboard on the wall of his office, listing all of the information he needed to know, checking the items off one by one. She could see him through the half-opened door, prowling the room with the energy of a restless lion, exuding a power and an intensity which was almost sexual in nature. But there was anger here now as well, and guilt that this had happened to one of his men, grief, and a desire for revenge, and she had no doubt that if Houghton's killer were to be put in a room with Kemper her gentle lover would rip the man to pieces with bare hands.

Kemper did not even know she existed at the moment, except to feed him the calls, and he stood at the blackboard, the telephone clutched between his chin and his shoulder as he checked off items with a piece of chalk. Both airports had now been covered. Mustafa had placed men at the docks and the major bus terminals, but Clements knew that the odds of catching the assassin were minuscule at best. For there were too many ways he could get into the interior, especially if he had his own transportation.

And then a combination of luck and the fear of the police who had combed the city with a specific threat that any man who withheld information and was discovered to have done so would lose his business and be subject to government prosecution. Otherwise, the owner of a *losmen* near Merdeka Square would never have come forward with his story of a foul-tempered man who struck fear into the hearts of everybody he touched and who matched the photograph of the assassin. This devil incarnate, this evil spirit in the form of a man had written his name on a registration card. Sangre, the Spanish word for blood. First initial an unrecognizable hen track. Kemper checked it against the list of aliases but it had never been used before, probably would not be used again. The information from the *losmen* was all academic. Sangre had been in the place a week and then checked out on the morning of the shooting. The owner of the *losmen* cataloged Sangre as European, despite Sangre's command of the Indonesian language.

A forensic team was going over the room that Sangre had occupied, but they weren't going to find one goddamned thing. That room had swarmed with transients, before and after Sangre's stay, and it was never cleaned. *One smart son of a bitch*, Kemper thought. And even with the police covering the regular means of egress from Jakarta, Sangre could be counted on to have a variety of disguises, passports and visas at his disposal.

A call from Oberlin, coldly enraged. Houghton had been his friend as well as his colleague. 'Oni Saud's wife is a slut,' Oberlin said.

'Are you with her now?'

'Yes. She doesn't speak English. And she never knew the man her husband was doing business with, never saw him. She never gave a damn how he got the money as long as he got it. She doesn't care that her husband's in prison. She offered to suck me off for ten dollars. She said her husband referred to the other man as "Sangre."'

'The name's right. Have you talked with the RT in the neighborhood?'

'He's an old man and half blind but he's savvy. He knows Oni Saud and Mochtar but he didn't know anything about the other man. I found a couple of men at the bar who saw Sangre knock Mochtar down and break his camera, but none of them can add anything to what we already have. They just say he was average size and had a mean expression.'

'You at a dead end, then?'

'I think so. Sangre didn't stay overnight in this neighborhood or the RT would have known it.'

'Do you know the police barracks off Merdeka Square?'

'Sure.'

'Get over there. Oni Saud's being brought in from the country. Pick him up and bring him here. He's due there any minute.'

'Will do.'

A call from Wiznoski, on a track of a different sort. He had been at a lab at the university analyzing the documents and the envelope sent to the ambassador. 'Cheap pulp paper, no rag content,' he said. 'Manufactured on Java and sold at exorbitant prices to government offices and large businesses. Parenthetical remarks. Large-scale scandal. Wife of a prominent politician getting rich off it.'

'Not interested in scandals.'

'No trace on the paper or the envelope. It was dropped in a slot at the central post office the day before the ambassador received it. No prints, no results from the saliva test, nothing. Now, the wording of the letter. Computer comparison with Squires's samples in Bangkok. Nothing similar. Linguistic analysis, good English, probably written by a Westerner, perhaps European, because of the salutation, 'My dear Ambassador.' Definitely not out of a phrase book.'

'The clipping.'

'Local press, sometime in the past three days. Something to do with the ink's bonding to the paper.'

'Can you trace it?'

'Hardly. Hundreds, maybe thousands of home presses capable of this kind of work.'

'Hundreds?'

'Political science professor here says that in any country where there are unstable politics there are lots of home presses for turning out thousands of pamphlets overnight, if they're needed. Very subtle terrorist technique, the printed obituary. Never heard of it before. Neither had Squires. We're querying Langley.'

He terminated the conversation and suddenly there were no more calls and the light buttons on Tommi's switchboard stayed unlit as he wandered into her office. He stretched, powerful muscles beneath the shirt, and she could tell that he was hurting.

'It's not your fault,' she said.

'Houghton didn't go by the goddamn rules. He got cocky and careless. And it's the duty of a chief of station to make goddamn sure that his people take care of themselves. So *that's* my fault.' He yawned, his fatigue getting to him.

'Did Houghton suffer?'

'No,' he lied, instantly, automatically.

'Thank God for that.'

Kemper sat down in an overstuffed chair, lit a cigarette. 'Oni Saud's our last chance. I'm going to arrange to have him sprung free from any charge of conspiracy if he'll spill everything about Sangre. A part of me wants to grab the son of a bitch,' he said. 'Another part hopes to hell that he's through with whatever his mission was supposed to be and that he's found a way out of Jakarta.'

The phone lit up and he was on his feet again and back in his office instantly, snatching up the telephone. She heard his voice, the beginning inquiry, the exuberance, and then the silence, the exhalation of breath as if something had ended, something which could not be undone.

The light on her telephone went out. Kemper came back into her office, sank down in the chair again, leaned his head back against the leather. 'You might as well shut things down,' he said.

'What happened?'

He sucked on the cigarette as if there might be comfort within it. 'Oni Saud,' he said. 'The Indonesian police were bringing him back in from the country. They had him in the back of a truck and they even took the manacles off him, gave him a smoke. He didn't know what the hell was going on and they told him that the truth had been discovered, that he hadn't killed the American after all. In other words, they gave him a deal. Talk to the Americans and tell the truth about the real killer and he wouldn't have to die.' He was silent a moment. One by one she closed down the lights, returned the lines to chancery.

'And?' she said.

'Oni Saud said that Sangre had theatened to dismember Oni Saud's wife if he opened his mouth. The Indonesian guards thought they were playing it smart, said that they'd cut up his wife if he *didn't* talk. So Oni Saud threw himself out of the back of the truck. It was traveling about sixty miles an hour, followed by another truck full of soldiers. The second and third trucks ran over him before they could stop.'

'So where do we go from here?'

He studied her for a long time. 'I want you to go home,' he said.

'Home meaning where? My apartment? The States? Where?'

'None of this goddamn business is worth it,' he said, closing his eyes, inhaling the smoke. 'I love you and I can't stand the thought that you could end up in some fucking canal just because you made a mistake in the field or I made a mistake in not giving you a proper backup.' He shook his head. 'I want you to go back to the States. I have influence. I'll get you a supergrade slot at Langley.'

'You can't resist it, can you?' she said, without rancor.

'Resist what?'

'Making my decisions for me, just because we happen to be in love. We don't have a traditional love affair. No masculine dominance here. This is my business too, remember? *I* chose the profession and I chose the risks. And I have to live every day with the same fears that you do.'

'And suppose you were COS here? Suppose you had let this happen?'

'You didn't *let* this happen. You couldn't have stopped it. Neither could I,' she said. 'But we don't play hypothetical games. I stay. You stay. That's our business. And now, if you'll take the advice of a loving subordinate, go to bed. Get some sleep.'

'I'm too wired up to sleep,' he said. 'I think I'll stay here awhile.'

She turned down the lamp on the desk, then locked the door and flipped the telephone to an off position. She came over to him and leaned over him, her hair falling about his face. 'Then I'll keep you company,' she said. She kissed him.

115

And they made love in the dim light of the room, an affirmation of life in the midst of death.

The net that had been thrown over the city caught nothing. Within three days Kemper informed Clements that Sangre had successfully negotiated an escape or burrowed so deeply within the city itself that he was not going to be found.

On the third morning after Houghton's death Clements received an envelope hand-carried by an Indonesian Government messenger with the initials M.R. inscribed in the upper-left-hand corner, beneath a bureaucratic seal, and he retired to his office with coffee and a closed door to have a look at what Madeleine had been able to turn up.

There was a report on official stationery, which he ignored for the moment, turning his attention to the scented sheet that bore her elegant, almost calligraphic handwriting.

Darling,
Please don't tell anyone where you got this information. It could be terribly embarrassing to my Chinese uncles. And please plan to spend a night with me before you go to Bali. Relations with the central government are every bit as important as some minor speech out in the provinces. And much more exciting.

He put the note to one side and got down to the report, which was a Xerox of one that Madeleine had obtained from the bank in Singapore, with the name of the official who had provided it typed in at the bottom, Tom Li, then signed in Chinese, and finally, as if to give it the final seal of authenticity, Li's chop mark in spidery red ink.

He scanned the honorifics and the apologies and managed to extract the very simple explanation from the mass of verbiage. The United States Government Foreign Aid transaction was listed under designated number 11076 and came to a total of four million dollars. Number 11077 designated the account of Autowerks, Ltd. of Munich,

Germany. Inadvertently, the two numbers being separated by but a single digit, a clerk had dispatched both together. The error had been caught in Indonesia almost instantly and the funds separated and credited to the proper accounts.

The other six million dollars had been destined for Brisbane, Australia, and was sent to Jakarta by mistake, according to the bank. Clements also found a Xerox of a receipt from the Bank of Australia showing that six million dollars was indeed deposited there to the account of Autowerks, Ltd., on the date it was supposed to be. The report also contained a letter from Mr Li of the bank in Singapore, a formal apology for the harsh things he said to Mr Lang in the lobby of his bank and an explanation that when Mr Lang had persuaded one of the bank clerks to access an account the wrong one must have been punched up, because Mr Lang had been upset by a distinctly erroneous perception which could not have come from either of the original computer files.

There was more, an incredible richness of detail, everything complete. Final culmination of a simple incident. One little error, all perfectly logical, and undoubtedly to Madeleine it would all make perfect sense and bring an end to a potentially embarrassing situation. He appreciated what she had done, but he was still troubled. He leaned back in the chair and sipped the coffee, which had grown lukewarm from neglect.

There was only one problem here. If the two files had been combined and Lang had seen both or either on the computer screen, there would have been nothing that could have possibly aroused such paranoia within him. He punched the intercom, reached Lucy. 'Lucy, see if you can get G.D. for me in Bangkok. If he's not at home or at his office, ask his secretary to have him call me as soon as he gets in.'

But G.D. was on the telephone within five minutes, perfectly relaxed and obviously delighted to hear from Clements. 'You're calling to tell me you're on the way up,' G.D. said. 'Hell, I'll even send a private jet down there to get you.'

'I wish that were the case,' Clements said. 'How much clout do you have in the Singapore banking community?'

'If you want to borrow money, let me get it for you out of Hong Kong instead of going through the Singapore pirates.'

'I don't need money,' Clements said with a smile. 'I need information.'

'That's a snap,' G.D. said. 'I'll spread a little baksheesh money like manure on the strawberry plants and get you anything you want to know.'

Clements gave him the details of the bank and the account numbers. 'See if you get the Chinese records. They're bound to have been written down somewhere, even if the computer data is missing. There has to be something there that set Lang off.'

'You know the Chinese accounting practices,' G.D. said. 'I've been thinking about hiring a couple of slant-eyed fiscal magicians to handle my corporate taxes. You any closer to jumping into the middle of things with me?'

'As a matter of fact, yes,' Clements said, realizing that he was using G.D. as a sounding board. 'I'm thinking about getting married again.'

'No shit,' G.D. said. 'Now you're talking sense, buddy. It's Madeleine, right?'

'We haven't talked about it yet,' Clements said. 'And it's nothing immediate, not within the next six months. But send me some reports on Stateside prospects. We might as well start getting things lined up.'

'Will do. And I'll get back to you. I'll bet you a hundred bucks I can not only get the stuff from the bank but give you the scoop on what spooked your boy.'

Showing off, Clements thought. Lang dead from the very business that G.D. was using as material for a bet, but G.D. thought nothing of it, meant no harm. 'All right,' he said. 'A hundred dollars.'

'Your call has made my day, buddy. I'll get back to you.'

He had no sooner ended the call to G.D. than Kemper showed up, looking bedraggled and ill tempered from lack of sleep. Kemper sat down, accepted the coffee that Clements poured for him. Clements sat down and without a word pushed the official sheets of explanation across the table. Kemper read them, frowning. 'Autowerks?' he said, when he was finished. 'Christ, do they really expect us to believe that?'

'Yes,' Clements said with a sign of resignation. 'And if you follow up, put a man on it, you'll find that there is indeed a company named Autowerks in Australia that received six million on the same day we received four. When people set out to deceive in this part of the world, they go to extraordinary lengths.'

'Then you don't believe this bullshit any more than I do.'

'No.'

'I want a copy of the report. I'm going to put teams on the Australian end and the Singapore bank. If I have to, I'm going to rip this whole paper trail apart.'

'Not for a few days,' Clements said.

'Why the wait?'

'This report came to me in confidence.' He was aware that Kemper had seen the initials above the seal on the envelope. 'I've initiated another inquiry on my own. If it does nothing else, it will protect the source of this one.'

'What kind of inquiry?'

'I won't tell you that either. Let's just say that I have excellent sources.'

'Maybe you don't understand the process, Mr Ambassador,' Kemper said, frustrated. 'But with every hour that passes, every day, the trail grows that much colder. I know you don't want to compromise your personal relationship here but I fished one of my boys out of a stinking canal and that entitles me to step on toes if I have to.'

'I know how you feel, Harry.'

'I don't need any empathy and I don't need any permission,' Kemper said.

'Then do what you have to,' Clements said, a warning in his voice. 'But remember one thing. We've lost Lang and Houghton and that makes a hell of a difference in what we want out of this. But you offend the Singapore Government or the Indonesian hierarchy and you'll find your ass back in the States faster than you can blink.'

'Washington can't ignore what's happening here.'

119

Clements leaned back in his chair. 'And what is happening here, Harry? What can you prove? What demonstrable facts do you have?'

'Two murders, an attempted assassination, a possible coup or terrorist operation in the making.'

'Facts,' Clements said, pushing. 'Imagine yourself sitting at the Asia desk. Make a goddamn case that's going to move the massive machinery of the State Department. Hell, they lose men all the time to thieves and thugs and car accidents. Threatened assassinations are a dime a dozen. Do you think for one fraction of a second that they're going to allow international relations with any of the Southeast Asian countries to wobble as much as a centimeter on the strength of what we have?'

Ah, Kemper thought, *right on the nose, the message coming through, the old goddamned bureaucratic scale of values which was reappraised daily and transmitted around the world by State and the Agency as well.* And Clements was right. Where was the proof? He could visualize the conversation that his immediate superior would have with him, should he go full-scale on this one.

Smooth voice. An 'our team' conversation, advice between friends. 'You're forgetting the first rule, Harry. Learn from past mistakes but don't dwell on them, for Christ's sake. Houghton made the mistake that killed him, not you. Houghton should have used an agent for the negotiation, for the tracking, but he took a shortcut and he got bumped. Hell, in the future, increase the available cash if you haven't already. Money buys the locals. If Houghton hadn't tried to do it himself, he'd still be alive.'

'All right,' Kemper said, quietly. He lit a cigarette. 'Nothing large-scale. Everything quiet and intensive until we hit the hard facts. But suppose that we don't find anything, Mr Ambassador. Suppose time passes and everybody's ass gets covered and we can't do one goddamn thing about what's happened?'

Ah, that was always the significant question, Clements thought, *what to do about a rampant injustice, how to rectify a situation,* and he remembered a time during the Vietnamese War when he had been assigned to debrief

120

Marines who had been held as prisoners of war under the control of a North Vietnamese they called 'the Toad.' An incredible man. He had forced the prisoners to eat their own shit. He had ripped arms out of sockets, castrated one man who got on his nerves. Then after the war Clements had been assigned by State to go back and talk to the North Vietnamese about MIA's, and he remembered the first session in a hut, the three former North Vietnamese officers who had been assigned to work with him, one of them a short, squat man, always smiling, an ugly little grin on his face, even when he was reciting all the evil things he had done to the prisoners under his control. It was the Toad, that mean little son of a bitch, and Clements remembered how grown Marines had wept when they talked about this torturer, the embodiment of evil who was now sitting across a table from him.

Clements could feel the remembered hate, the boiling of his blood every time he was in the Toad's presence. Then one night there had been a session that lasted until midnight and afterward the jeep dropped off the Toad at his house in Hanoi before Clements was taken to his hotel a few blocks away. And Clements couldn't sleep. Because he was going to be leaving the next day and he was haunted by the fact that the Toad would continue to live and prosper, beyond retribution. So Clements decided that if anything was to be done, it was up to him. He avoided the patrols, walked back down the streets until he found his house and then he set fire to it. The old house was dry wood and it burned like kindling. And when the flames shot up, the Toad came running out, half dressed, carrying his shirt wadded up against his grotesque belly. And Clements took careful aim, holding the pistol in both hands, and shot him in the head. The Toad dropped like a stone and Clements turned and walked back to the hotel, expecting to be stopped and arrested at any moment. But no one had seen him leave or come back.

He sipped his coffee again. 'Oh, I'll take action,' he said. 'I don't forget, Harry. Never.' Kemper was surprised at the conviction in his voice. 'And if we can't come up with hard evidence that will make Washington move, then I'll damn well take matters into my own hands. You can count on that.'

'Then let's make a deal,' Kemper said, impressed. 'Officially, I hold off. I don't do one goddamn thing to upset the applecart. But I'm going to collect information. And when the time comes, there will be two of us.'

'You've got a deal,' Clements said.

Madeleine knew she was dreaming, caught up in terror, but she could not bring herself awake. She could hear her mother screaming and she heard the punch of a solid object against flesh, the splattering sound of blood flying, and she huddled in the dark until she could stand it no longer, and then she looked around her bedroom in Saigon until she found a brass candlestick and she threw open the door and there her mother was kneeling on the antique Chinese rug, stained with her own blood. Two members of the local Communist committee were standing over her, and one of them was a man who had been her lover, and he was chewing betel nut, breathing heavily, holding a stick with which he had been beating her mother, the end of it streaked with red, and with a scream Madeleine charged at him, swinging the candlestick, the metal catching his head with a glancing blow and knocking him down before the other man was on her, pinning her arms, holding her against the wall. She saw the knife in his hand, knew she had gone too far, knew that she was going to die. . . .

She came awake with a gasp, sat upright in bed, terrified, her heart pounding, but Clements slept on beside her. She climbed out of bed, went to the window, silently talking to herself. *Only a dream. Nothing to be afraid of in a dream.* She lit a cigarette with a gold lighter in her trembling fingers, stared down upon the moonlit garden without seeing it. Not a dream, no, an exact memory which had shaped itself into a recurrent dream. All true. It had all happened, and as she drew the smoke into her lungs, she forced herself to remember the rest of it, her mother screaming in Vietnamese at the man who was about to kill Madeleine until the knife withdrew from Madeleine's throat. Only then did Madeleine see her mother full-face, the bleeding mouth, the front teeth knocked out, the right eye puffed almost closed, and slowly she raised herself from the floor and caught herself against the back of a chair before she could fall and made her way to the wall where she removed a small section of baseboard which covered the hiding place.

Madeleine's former lover shoved her aside, shoved his fingers into the recess, came out with the taels of gold, the small square shapes, individually wrapped, and he divided them up with the second man, put his share in a small pouch, then winked at Madeleine and smiled and put his hand over his own genitals with a vigorous shake. 'Later,' he said.

When the men had gone, Madeleine rushed to her mother, reached down with both arms to lift her, but the older woman lashed out with her right arm and struck Madeleine on the side of the face with such force that Madeleine was stunned and fell back against the wall. Her mother pounced on her, cupping her face with one hand and striking her with the other, yelling at her in a spray of blood. All in Chinese.

'You told him we had gold.'

'I told him you were sending me away.'

'That's the same as telling him.' The hand, already red with blood, struck her cheek. 'That meant we had money.' Another blow. Another. And then the older woman hobbled over to a table. Madeleine started to sit down, but her mother fixed her in place with a glare. 'You stay there or I'll kill you. I mean it. You stay there. You listen.' And she lit a cigarette and put it in the corner of her battered mouth. 'All men are dogs. You remember that. You turn your back and they'll eat your food. They sniff you out in heat and then they fuck you and steal your money and prowl off in the street. But you remember this night.' The blood from her mouth drenched the cigarette, put it out. She lit a fresh one. 'You protect yourself against the dogs.' She drew in the smoke and then, painfully, slowly, went to another corner of the room where she lifted up another piece of baseboard. 'If the dogs kill me, the bulk of the money is here. You remember this. Always divide what you have. Let them beat you until you're almost dead and then give them the small part.'

She sat at the window, remembering the bitterness of that night when the last shred of her innocence had disappeared. But the memory was always there, coming unwilled into her mind when she began to lose her perspective, when she began to trust a man too much. She looked at Clements on the bed, the form of him indistinct in the moonlight. She came as close to loving him as was possible for her, but in the end, her mother would be right, for Clements would be required to move on and he would leave her behind and take with him something that belonged to her which was far more precious than gold and would cause more pain than if he stole her money. She had vowed never to give a man her true affection, and yet it had gone to Clements without her bidding, almost as if it were beyond her control.

He came awake. 'What are you doing out of bed?' he said, instantly alert.

'I had a bad dream.'

'Come here to me.'

'Yes,' she said. She snuffed out the cigarette and came back to the bed, putting her arms around him, feeling the roughness of fresh beard on his cheeks and she knew him well enough to know that there was passion within him when he was half awake, and with her fingertips she traced the outline of him in the semidarkness, felt his maleness become hard at her touch. All the while she kissed him lightly on the mouth, breathing in the smell of his sleep, until finally he had been kindled by her and his hands pressed against the small of her back, fingers splayed to encompass a buttock. *Make me forget*, she thought. *Catch me up and bring me to the point of the little death*. He stroked her until she felt the heat spread upward from the honey sleekness between her thighs and the insistence of his whole body which pressed upon her as she opened to receive him. She tried to remember her mother's face but could not, the true test, as the feelings rose from her loins and engulfed her thoughts. She clutched him to her, wrapped her legs around him, no artifice here, swept along in a passion which rose until she thought that she was indeed dying, with an inner tightness which stretched so insistently within her that there was no further tolerance and then burst in a great pushing, rising to meet him, again and again, until all the energy was released with a sudden rush, and then another and another, until she was both drained and filled at the same time and lay quiet with her head on his chest.

'I love you,' he said, quietly.

'Please, no words.'

'There have to be words.'

All words were temporary, false, and she did not want them now, but she could not stop them, because she so wanted to believe. 'I am pleased that you love me,' she said.

'I want more than that,' he said, running his hand over her hair. 'I'm not going to stay at this post forever. The Russian talks aren't really going anywhere.'

'I don't want to talk about your leaving.'

'I'm thinking about going into private business in the States. I want you to marry me when the time comes, go back with me.'

She put her fingertips on his lips. 'No more,' she said. 'You don't have to say that.'

'I've learned to speak up for what I want. I know what you have going for yourself here, how hard it might be for you, but I want you to promise me that you'll at least think about it.'

She was quiet a long time, and her mother's face became distinct in her mind. *They'll leave you in the end. Without anything.* She moved up until she could kiss him on the mouth and her expert hands began their artifice on him. She felt no need this time except to still the voice that rang in her ears and the outline of that sneer on her mother's bloodied face, and when she had sufficiently aroused him she rode on his feeling, and gradually her mother became a phantom at the edge of her mind, but even in the quickened heat the image was not altogether obliterated this time but stayed in her thoughts, whispering. *Careful, careful. The dogs will fuck you and then prowl away.*

Aboard the Garuda flight to Bali, Clements thought about the Toad. He had never told a soul of that killing in Hanoi but it often haunted him. He was never sure why he had done it, for as a diplomat it was expected that he remain dispassionate, with no show of his emotions except when the diplomatic situation required him to display anger or demonstrate indignation whether he really felt it or not, but it was as if for that single moment in time he was able to right a horrendous wrong through one simple, direct action.

He had something of the same feeling now about the situation in Indonesia, because Kemper was indeed right, and the blood which had been spilled here thus far was only a small foretaste of the bloodbath to come. And again he was going to have to take some action, as yet beyond his knowledge, for the situation here would not be solved by a committee in Washington.

Somebody was going to pay for Lang. Somebody was going to pay for Houghton.

He ordered a drink from the stewardess.

'Do you mind if I sit with you, Mr Ambassador?'

He looked up to see Minister Rooseno standing in the aisle.

'Not at all, Minister,' Clements said. 'Have a drink with me.'

The minister sank into the aisle seat and the stewardess was at his side instantly. He asked her for fruit juice. 'When I am in your country, I occasionally have a glass of wine,' Rooseno said. 'But when I am at home, I follow the Muslim customs very closely.'

Not quite true, Clements thought. For there was the smell of alcohol on Rooseno's breath, a few drinks before he came onto the plane, followed by a minty mouthwash which had not done its job.

Rooseno folded down the table from the back of the seat in front of him. When he had been served the fruit juice he tasted it and he set it down. 'I sent my message of condolence concerning your aide, did I not?' he said.

'You did, Minister. It was most appreciated. I forwarded it to Lang's mother in the States.'

Rooseno's eyes were rheumy, melancholy. 'There are so many things in politics I do not like,' he said. 'But they have had to be done.'

'What, for instance?' Clements said, but he knew that Rooseno was not likely to get much more specific on this particular subject. Rooseno was setting an emotional tone to the conversation because there was something he wanted to know but he did not want to ask a straight question.

'The violence, for one,' Rooseno said with a sigh. 'If there is not present violence, then there is always the hint of violence in the future.'

'The United States is interested in stabilizing Southeast Asia,' Clements said. 'We, too, deplore the violence.'

'I'm sorry to say that I believe only part of that,' Rooseno said. 'I am sure you've had your fill of violence in Vietnam. But now your government is primarily interested in protecting your businesses which would strip us clean.'

'Which companies?'

'Your petroleum companies.'

The old refrain, Clements thought. *Justification for any action the Indonesian Government wanted to take.* 'I don't think you want to pursue the same conversation all over again, do you, Minister?'

'We wish to be fair,' Rooseno said. 'Have you given any more thought to the meeting I propose?'

'No. Frankly, I haven't.'

'How do you think your government would interpret such a meeting of the regional oil-producing countries?'

'The same way I would,' Clements said. 'I would guess that you intend to form your own regional OPEC. Is that true, Minister?'

'If it were true, what would be the reaction of your government?'

'That would depend on what comes out of the meeting,' Clements said.

Rooseno was suffering. He summoned the stewardess again, ordered a gin and tonic. 'I am not as fervent in my religion as I was at one time,' he said. 'My parents were very strict, but my father did not have to face the things I face. He acted as a middleman in the export trade, sending out a shipload of goods to be sold in Africa and bringing back a shipload of goods to be sold here. It was a gift from Allah, the ability to make a great deal of money. But unfortunately I never had it. So I have many rich relatives who have the gift and I must do the best I can in a political life.'

The drink was served. He downed it even as the stewardess stood there and then ordered another. And Clements began to get an inkling of what Rooseno wanted from this conversation. 'It's my understanding that there is very good money to be made in Indonesian politics,' Clements said.

'I've heard all the jokes,' Rooseno said, nursing the second drink which was served to him. 'Even the President's wife is accused. Some people call her Madame Tien-percent.' He sipped the gin, seemed to be more confident, bolder, since the glass was in his hand. 'How far will your government go to back your oil companies?'

'It's not our mission to protect their business interests,' Clements said. 'They're Americans and we will protect their civil rights, their persons. But they're quite capable of taking care of themselves in the negotiations they conduct.' *That was grossly oversimplified*, Clements thought, but with every additional ounce of alcohol Rooseno consumed, a complex conversation was even further out of the question.

Rooseno finished the drink, ordered another. This one he let sit for a while as if it represented his reserve, at ready when needed.

'Your aide was making an investigation,' he said.

'Correct.'

'And exactly what did he find, Mr Ambassador, if I may be so bold as to ask?'

'A great many things,' Clements said, with purposeful vagueness. 'Concerning money. We also learned something of the Six Ravens.'

Rooseno sighed. When he spoke his voice was fearful. 'The pressures are very great on a man in my position,' he said. 'I love my country but it is also necessary for me to look out for my wife. So at times I have learned to keep my eyes closed and my ears shut because I don't want to know everything that's happening.' He patted his lean cheeks with his hands. 'I will be direct. What do you know about me?'

'In candor?'

'Yes.'

'For one thing we know that you personally received two hundred and fifty thousand American dollars in the past six months from the refugee funds our country appropriated for Timor.'

'You can prove that?'

'Certainly.'

'And what will you do with this information?'

'We assume that your superiors know that you are taking a share of the foreign-aid funds.'

'Of course, they know,' Rooseno said, defensively. 'How long have you known this about me?'

'Some months now, Minister.'

'And you've been waiting for the right time to use it against me,' Rooseno said defensively, the alcohol affecting him. 'But if your country makes an issue of it now, if you decide to punish my country for its petroleum policy by using the money I take as an excuse for cutting off foreign aid, then *I* will end up being the scapegoat. I will be the only one to suffer. Me, and my family, my *entire* family, we will all be thoroughly investigated.'

Clements laughed sharply. Rooseno was not so drunk as to lack subtlety. 'And your family would also include your niece.'

'Alas, yes,' Rooseno said mournfully. 'Madeleine would not escape.'

'I'm quite sure Madeleine can take care of herself, Minister,' Clements said, easily. 'If I were you, I'd be worried about myself and my immediate family.' He ground out his cigarette. 'But there are ways you can avoid any difficulty whatsoever.'

'How?'

'By cooperating with me.'

'In what way?'

'The Six Ravens, for instance. And the extra six million dollars which was piggybacked on the United States funds.

It was time for the reserve drink. Rooseno picked it up. 'I know nothing about that.' His eyes were on the liquid in his glass.

'I think you know a good deal about both.'

Rooseno shrugged, rattled the ice in his glass. 'My health is not as it should be,' he said. 'I have been told by my doctors that the air in my own country is not beneficial to my lungs. So in a week I shall go to a clinic in Scandinavia for a month. My wife has never seen snow. Is there any snow on the ground there in the summer-time?'

'In the Norwegian mountains,' Clements said. 'There are snow plains there the year-round.'

Rooseno held the cold glass against his forehead. 'My wife would like that. And on the other matter . . .'

'Yes?'

'I will give it some thought. It is not always easy to know what's best to do.'

'In this case,' Clements said. 'I would do what's best for myself if I were you, Minister. As you say, you will be the first one sacrificed when this scandal breaks.'

Too short a time, Clements thought, no time at all to take advantage of a mistake in judgment on Rooseno's part. For there had been a thorough discussion of Indonesian skimming at State and a decision not to make an issue of it, and Rooseno should have known that if he was to be blown away for graft it would have happened months ago. But there was no reason to disavow Rooseno's protests, his attempts to evade, and Clements would continue the pressure when he had the chance. But not now. For the jet began its descent and out the window he could see the ground rushing up as the 707 made its precipitous drop toward the runway which had been carved in the jungle to end at a barrier just short of the ocean. His stomach was always in his throat on a Garuda landing, especially on Bali, for the sirens would be screaming to get the natives off the tarmac. They lived in the jungle on either side of the runway and used it as a connecting road. Once, Clements had watched a jet overshoot the runway and plop into the shallow waters with no loss of life, no injuries, no great furor among people who maintained a fatalistic view of life.

The time for dying had already been written; it was foolish to worry about it.

But Rooseno was clearly worried about a problem connected with living. The stewardess approached to take his glass and he emptied it first in a single draft and then white-knuckled the armrests until the jet shallowed out and made a perfect landing, stopping well short of the barrier at the end of the runway. It taxied to the terminal, which resembled a concrete fortification, a bunker.

As the jet came to a stop the portable steps were rolled into place. Rooseno unbuckled his seat belt. 'It has been enlightening talking with you, Mr Ambassador.'

'A pleasure as always, Minister. We'll talk again, soon.'

'Yes,' Rooseno said. 'Very soon.'

When Rooseno reached his hotel he put in a call to Jakarta almost immediately. His stomach was paining him. He was sure he had an ulcer as well as lung trouble. He lay down on the bed, fully dressed, while he was waiting for the call to be completed, and then sat up when it was answered.

'He knows,' Rooseno said, and then listened to the voice, the words carefully picked so no one would understand the subject matter if the call was being recorded.

'I'm certain he knows,' Rooseno insisted. 'And I think he's available for a compromise. After all, if he didn't want something, he wouldn't have discussed it.'

The voice told him to wait for further instructions. Then the line went dead. Rooseno put the telephone back on the cradle, then lay back in the direct blast of the air conditioner, letting the cold air cut through him. He put his troubles out of his mind, thought of Norway and the snow.

Sangre had no respect for the money. Hell, it was handy for the pills and the weed but now he could always be more than himself, and that was the real reason he enjoyed it so. For he could be anybody he chose to be, with any background, and he could be crazy or non-crazy as he chose, and he could assume a variety of shapes and histories which were just automatically there when he needed them, without his having to think them through. He was certain he had been born with an infinite number of personalities inhabiting his body, all of them distinct and separate, only he was not a psycho who got caught in any of them, swept away by forces beyond his control. He controlled all of *them*, not the other way around.

And one part of himself was an excellent businessman. He had not really discovered that until once in Cambodia when he had a whole jeepload of stolen M-16's and he ran across a real crook of a mountain guerrilla leader who ran opium and could have stolen them from him with a wave of his hand which would have seen Sangre sliced up or blown away by the ragtag gooks that surrounded the jeep. But Sangre never showed the fear that wanted to make him throw up. Instead, he bargained for the rifles, rejecting the offer of ten grams of uncut heroin for each weapon, bartering until he made a fortune from the very rifles which they could have taken from him. But in that transaction he learned the first rule of negotiation, the use of something which didn't exist for anybody.

The future.

The guerrilla leader traded with him because he thought Sangre could deliver more rifles in the future. Hell, you didn't cut the throat of somebody who might have something you wanted down the line.

So he had learned the art of business, and for now on this job had taken the identity of Mr Lomax, and he liked being Lomax because Lomax was a snappy dresser who wore circular wire-rimmed spectacles and a slight line of a mustache which so changed his appearance that even his mother would not have known him. Lomax lived high on the hog. Lomax stayed at the luxury hotels, and tipped like there was no tomorrow, and liked to be massaged by lovely girls who rubbed oils into his body. The wounded leg became a badge of heroism, the hunting of a wild boar in the Philippines which had turned on Lomax's host, and only through Lomax's intervention and a gun that jammed and a knife which found its way to the heart of the beast was a man's life saved, even as the tusks ripped Lomax's leg to the bone.

And now Lomax was on Bali, with a whole strategy to be

worked out in less than eighteen hours and a hundred thousand hard cash to be gained from this one, above expenses. He hired a car with an interpreter from the hotel and immediately set out for the back country, armed with enough forged documents to give him complete freedom of action.

The first item on his shopping list was a truck. Not incongruous, of course, that a man in a white linen suit, carrying a cane, wearing a white panama hat, should be out shopping for industrial equipment, for among his many papers was a bogus surveying permit from one of the minor mineral ministries. Denpasar was a foul city, fetid smells, open sewage. He rolled his windows up and had the driver turn up the air conditioner. He made the comment that such smells gave him a headache. For Lomax was like that, so used to first class that even the mention of compromise, even the thought of less than perfect surroundings would be enough to upset him. When the car finally turned into an industrial yard full of official government trucks in various states of disrepair, Lomax would not even get out of the car. He insisted that the driver locate the headman, the supervisor, and bring him to Lomax.

Only when the bowlegged little man came out of a tin maintenance hut did Lomax open the back door of the car and pivot around so he sat with his legs extended, using the cane as a pointer.

'Ask him which of these trucks are in the best condition,' he told his interpreter, who spoke to the supervisor in Balinese and then retranslated.

'There are only two trucks which are in first-class condition, sir,' he said, his expression mystified. 'But he says these trucks belong to the government and are not for sale.'

'Tell him I wouldn't have one of his pieces of junk if it was given to me as a present,' Lomax said with disdain. He fished through his briefcase, came up with a false document which required any government agency in the field to cooperate with Mr A. P. Lomax to any degree that Mr A. P. Lomax required. The bowlegged man studied the document while Lomax came out with a sheaf of brand-new thousand-rupiah notes, the paper bank band still around them. He riffled the edge of them with his thumb, then passed them to the bowlegged man while he relayed a message through the interpreter. 'You may also tell him that this money is his, a convenience fee for disturbing his schedule. But I need a truck, fully gassed, within five hours. And I will need a driver in that truck for approximately two hours in the morning, to make a delivery.'

'Yes, sir,' the translator said, and Lomax could see the greed on his face at the sight of all that money. He could not be sure when the translator relayed the message that he was not building in a kickback for himself. It really made no difference. The gooks were all alike. Sooner or later they would all be eradicated.

The deal was made. Lomax himself would pick up the truck this evening and return for a government driver in the morning.

Now, of course, came the tricky part, the most dangerous area, and Lomax felt flushed with excitement because he hated gook soldiers with a passion and yet now he had to deal with them and bring this off without alarming anyone. He had the driver take him to the main barracks for the island, a compound with a drill field and a motor pool near the barracks and the offices, everything spic-and-span today, grass all neatly trimmed because of the official ceremony which would take place on the island in the morning.

Lomax left the translator in the car and slipped a pair of sunglasses over his eyes before he left the coolness of the air conditioner and strolled across the lawn to the headquarters building. He controlled his limp quite well, because Lomax did not limp. Even if his leg had pained him to the point of agony, Lomax would refuse to yield to any outward signs of distress.

He asked the clerk in the headquarters anteroom if he spoke English, met a blank but subservient look, then was ushered into the commandant's office. The commandant was a short, brown, middle-aged man who held himself ramrod straight and had a great dignity to him. He also had a command of English.

Immediately, Lomax sat down by the commandant's desk and put a business card on the polished wood, a card with raised lettering. The commandant picked it up, looked at it, put it back on the desk. Lomax exhibited a paper from the Defense Ministry which proclaimed that Mr Lomax had been retained by the Indonesian Government as a soil expert to make density tests of various shore areas in the north part of the island for possible future defense installations.

'I shall require the following explosives,' Lomax said, producing a sheet countersigned by himself in the name of a well known general who Lomax knew was on vacation in Malaysia and could not be reached. 'And here is the voucher which shows that the explosives in question have already been requisitioned, and here, sir, is the customary convenience money, I believe.' And he pulled another stack of thousand-rupiah notes from the briefcase. 'How long will it take you to assemble the items?'

'A very short time, Mr Lomax,' the commandant said. 'Perhaps fifteen or twenty minutes.'

'I believe that it can all be put into a box which will fit into the trunk of my hired car,' Lomax said. 'It will save me time in the morning.'

'I believe so, yes,' the commandant said, picking up the stack of money as if it were nothing, placing it in the top drawer of his desk, which he locked before he pocketed the key. 'What kind of fortifications are you building on the north coast of the island, sir? I've heard nothing about them.'

'I'm not in the business of *building* anything,' Lomax said. 'I merely test soil and rock and blast a few holes. Then I draw up a report telling the government how much weight a particular soil area will carry. If you don't mind, I would appreciate a glass of cold bottled water, Commandant. I come from a temperate climate and I must admit I find the tropics terribly uncomfortable.'

'Certainly, Mr Lomax.' And he sent one aide scurrying for the water and another enlisted man to put together the explosives. 'If you require the services of my men . . .' he began, but Lomax cut him off.

'You're most helpful but I've had considerable experience in this field. And I work much better by myself.'

He drank his water, took a couple of pills, a yellow and a red, for he felt as if his head was going to split into two parts. He stayed in the office, under a slow-moving ceiling fan which stirred the air, and he watched through the window as the wooden box was loaded into the trunk of the car. Then he sauntered out to face a very uncomfortable driver-translator. 'They tell me, sir, that the box contains explosives.'

'All perfectly safe,' Lomax said, deprecatingly. 'They require detonation. You could drop them, have a car ram into the trunk of yours, and they would be quite safe.'

'I have no permit to haul explosives.'

Lomax grinned. 'Ah, you do have me there, don't you?' he said in a nonthreatening voice. 'But I don't take offense, my friend, because I understand how difficult it is to make a living on this island. I know what your expenses must be. The cost of gasoline would eat you alive, and all the fees you must pay to hotel employees and the police and the government and even the priests, just to permit you to operate.' He looked around, to make certain he was not being overheard. 'I will trust you, my friend, if you will trust me. I am being paid an enormous amount to handle these explosives because of the very thing that frightens you. I am willing to pay you a very hefty fee, a great deal of money, if you will help me.' He smiled disarmingly. 'Besides, would I ride in the same car with the explosives if I thought there was the least danger?'

'How much?' the guide said.

'A hundred dollars, American.'

'I don't know.'

'A hundred and fifty then.' Important not to go too high or the man would become suspicious enough to ask around, seeking reassurance. 'I don't want to talk you into anything. I'll be glad to pay you what I owe you now and hire another car, if that's the way you want it.'

With the possibility of losing the money, the man was convinced. 'All right,' he said. 'I'll do it.'

'Very good,' Lomax said. 'You've made the right decision.'

He signed the necessary forms in the commandant's office, shook the little brown hand, and once he was in the car and the car was under way, he took out his handkerchief and carefully rubbed the commandant's sweat off each finger in turn. It was so goddamned easy to catch diseases out here. He had had a buddy once whose hand had become infected from germs crawling into a slight scratch, and the hand puffed up like a balloon, and the skin turned greenish black and he had lost four fingers and damn near died before the medicines could take hold. And Lomax would have cleaned his hands anyway, fastidious as he was.

He directed the driver to follow the road past the hotels on the beach, through a heavy grove of trees in which stood the ruins of an ancient temple, so far gone that now it was little more than a pile of rubble and a few walls. Lomax had the guide turn the car toward the beach, pulling in far enough that it could not be seen from the highway. Then he directed him to stop.

'Perhaps you do not know the customs here,' the guide said, looking around at the piles of stones which were covered with the green fungus of centuries. 'The hotels are not allowed to build here because nothing is permitted to disturb the spirits which remain in every old temple.'

'Ah,' Lomax said with a broad grin. 'I admire your zeal and respect your religious persuasion. But I certainly don't intend to conduct any soil tests here. I'll be working on the *north* coast.' He got out of the car and walked along a short path to a position overlooking the beach. Nobody in sight here but one old fisherman who waded in the mild surf and with a smooth arc of his hand cast a wide net over the water, then let it settle before he began to gather it in. It came back empty as he folded it into sections and moved on down the beach, seeking better waters.

The guide was still waiting in the ruins and Lomax smiled. 'No more beautiful or more peaceful spot on earth,' he said. 'I would very much like to take your picture, standing against the ruins. The old and the new, so to speak.' And holding his two thumbs, tip to tip, he formed a framing square with his hands, then stopped short, as if a cautionary thought had just occurred to him. 'I won't be breaking any religious rules if I take a picture of you here, will I?'

'No,' the guide said. 'Pictures are permitted.'

'Very good. Now, if you would just stand right here.'

The guide shrugged. 'How will you take a picture without a camera?'

'I have a small pocket camera.'

'And it gives you good pictures?'

'Superb,' Lomax said. And he posed the guide at the edge of a low wall which fronted a shallow excavation. 'I will certainly want you to smile for me. This is Bali, after all, land of the perpetual enchantment, the enduring smile. That's what all the advertisements say.'

The guide managed a smile and Lomax reached into his pocket. His hand came out with the small pistol and he pulled the trigger before the smile had a chance to change. The bullet entered the narrow face right between the junction of descending eyebrows above the nose, the explosion caught by the silencer like a sneeze. And the guide went over backward, just as Lomax had calculated, backs of the ankles catching on the low stone wall, the body laying itself into the excavation perfectly. Then Lomax went to the trouble of getting his camera from his briefcase because this was one of those absolutely perfect shots and the body lay face up, arms at the side, everything so symmetrical it would appear that the body had been laid out.

He took an entire series of pictures.

He went back to the taxi, opened the trunk, then took a stroll around the ruins again, making sure there were no side paths along which tourists might come and discover him by surprise. When he was certain he was alone he pried the cover off the wooden box, and then, working with the tools from his briefcase, he began the wiring of the timer and the detonator. He checked his nine-volt batteries, found both of them fully charged. In less than fifteen minutes everything was assembled and back in the wooden box.

He took off his coat and, folding it carefully, laid it across the backseat of the car. He removed an aerosol can of white lacquer-based spray paint from his briefcase and carefully covered the exposed sides of the box, waiting until they were dry before he turned the box on its side and sprayed the bottom. He smoked a cigarette until he was sure the paint was completely dry. Then he took the stencil from the briefcase and taped it in place on one surface of the box and with an aerosol can of red covered the cutout spaces on the stencil. Again a wait and then he removed the stencil. There was a perfect Red Cross insignia on the box with the Indonesian writing that spelled out 'Medical Supplies.'

He still had a little time to kill, so he took the can of red lacquer and, stepping over the low wall into the slight depression, he sprayed the head and the hands of the dead guide a brilliant red, then stood back to survey the effect. It was not quite right, no, not a sufficient contrast against the dirt and the stones, so he took the can of white and sprayed a halo around the head and an aura around the hands. It was a vastly superior effect, that glaring red against the electric white. Lomax had a highly developed sense of art composition, and he took another series of pictures. And down the line, perhaps ten years away, he would have an exhibition of photographs, perhaps at the Pompidou in Paris, a wave of new art, *arte morte*, like Warhol and his stencils maybe, a whole series of repetitive figures, different-colored corpses against white. *Dead Gooks*, he might call the series, except that his assignments might not be centered in Southeast Asia much longer. He could not call the series *Dead People*, there wasn't any shock value to that.

He went back to check the box, found it dry. He closed the trunk, then went over the area to make sure he was leaving nothing of himself behind, no footprints on mossy stones, no cigarette butts, no fingerprints, no threads pulled loose from his clothing. He paused for one look down at the body. Red and white. Goddamn, maybe the press would come out here and cover this and a photographer would recognize the Pop Art element here and give it magazine coverage.

He drove back to the truck depot where the bowlegged man did not even question the absence of the guide. But

Lomax could see that he was going to have difficulty. 'Do you speak English?' Lomax said.

'Very good,' the bowlegged man said with a broad, uncomprehending smile.

'You don't speak a goddamn word of English, you son of a bitch,' Lomax said, keeping his voice even and pleasant, his smile unbroken. 'I could slice off your balls and you'd still pretend to understand English, wouldn't you?'

'Very good,' the bowlegged man said.

Lomax tried to decide whether it would be in character for him to speak Indonesian. It seemed pretty logical that Lomax would know the language if he spent much time here. He decided Lomax would indeed speak Indonesian. 'Do you speak Bahasa Indonesian?' Lomax said, and the bowlegged man responded instantly.

'Of course. Yes sir, I do. My English isn't very good.'

'*Au contraire,*' Lomax said.

'Pardon?'

'I was saying I found your English very good.' And now he got down to business. He directed the bowlegged man to have the rather sizable box transferred from the trunk of the car to the open bed of the truck where a single strap held it down without covering any part of the Red Cross insignia.

'You are with the Red Cross?' the bowlegged man asked.

'No. I'm a medical doctor,' Lomax said. 'I've come down to take care of anyone who might accidentally be injured at the ceremony tomorrow, the opening of the bridge. You would be amazed at the number of people who are affected by sunstroke or develop allergies to insect bites. The ceremony is scheduled for nine in the morning, so I would like to have your driver ready at seven-thirty.'

'You don't need the truck overnight then.'

'No,' Lomax said. 'I thought I would but I was able to rent other transportation. But I shall want the driver promptly at seven-thirty.'

'Certainly, Doctor,' the bowlegged man said. 'Everything will be ready for you.'

Clements had scarcely had time to settle into his suite before the calls began to come in from Jakarta and the chancery.

They were intercepted, of course, by the small staff which had arrived in Bali a day early to get everything set up. The summaries and the memos were already waiting for him, stacked in neat piles on his coffee table. He took the time to write out a coded message concerning the technique he was using with Rooseno. He would have it sent right away, knowing full well that there would be no time for State to rule yes or no before he was finished.

He put in a call to Madeleine's house and in a few minutes she was on the line. She laughed when she heard his voice.

'Don't you know my telephone is tapped?' she said. 'But you don't really care, do you?'

'Not at all,' he said. 'I just wanted to hear your voice.'

'What would you like me to say?'

'That you'll go away for a few days with me when I get back,' he said. 'I'm due some vacation.'

'Do you realize the scandal that would cause?' she said. 'Can you see the newspapers? I'd love to.'

'I'll call you the day after tomorrow, unless you can come to Bali.'

'As much as I love you, I don't like Bali. Take care of yourself.'

The minute he put the telephone on the cradle it rang again and this time it was G. D. Majors. 'Jesus, Charlie,' he said. 'Trying to get through your staff is like trying to get into Fort Knox.'

'Where the hell are you?'

'Here in the hotel. I bribed a telephone operator to ring your room.'

'What are you doing here?'

'I came here to see you,' G. D. said. 'Well, half and half. You asked for information and I got that, but I found something else we need to talk about.'

'Come on up.'

'I think you better come down. It's possible your room is bugged and I know damn well mine isn't. It could be bullshit but you'd better hear it and make up your own mind.'

'What's your room number?'

'Ten twenty-one.'

'Five minutes,' Clements said.

G. D. was lining up a putt on the thick carpet in his suite when Clements arrived, and he ignored him for the moment until he edged the putter back and nudged the ball toward a metal contraption which simulated a hole. The ball missed by a foot, rolled under the couch. G. D. shrugged, poured a stiff bourbon and water, put a cube of ice in it and handed it to Clements.

'You giving me a drink or an anesthetic?' Clements said.

'If you don't like the way I mix drinks, then fix your own, buddy. You going to have time for a round of golf while you're here?'

'Is that your urgent priority?' Clements said. He sat down facing the view of the ocean, the sky beginning to darken. 'You afraid that somebody's going to eavesdrop on a conversation about golf?'

'Hell, no,' G. D. said. He propped the putter against the arm of the divan and then opened an attaché case and removed two sets of papers. 'We'll start with the simple stuff. I think these are what you wanted me to get for you. The first is a Xerox of the Chinese and the second's a translation.'

'From the bank in Singapore.'

'Right.'

Clements sat down and studied the papers while G. D. fixed himself a drink. There were no surprises. The information was exactly the same that Madeleine's cousin had provided, right down to Autowerks and Australia. G. D. tasted his drink, added more bourbon. 'Is that what you were looking for?'

'The same dead end,' Clements said. 'It just confirms what I already knew.'

'Do you trust me?' G. D. said.

'Why the request for a profession of faith?' Clements said with a smile. 'Of course, I trust you.'

'You know I'm not the kind of guy to get spooked, right?'

'What are you trying to tell me?' Clements said.

'I made a bet with you. A hundred bucks I could find out what spooked Lang.'

'Did you find out?'

'Hell, I don't know if I really found out anything,' G. D. said, a strange, uncomfortable expression on his face. 'I don't know whether the information I got is true or false, but I'd feel a hell of a lot better if you passed the word that you don't feel well and have decided not to make any public appearances here. Then we can get on my jet and go find a decent golf course and ride this damn thing out.'

'What damn thing? You're not making any sense.'

'I spread some money around Singapore,' G. D. said, stirring the ice in his glass with a spatulate finger, perfectly manicured. 'You know how stubborn I can get. I'd spend a couple thousand just to win a hundred off you. So I sent out a man named John Hesse. You know him?'

'No.'

'He's a good man. I use him once in a while. He got evidence on my third wife for a countersuit. Anyway, Hesse talked to some of the people at the bank, not officials, the Chinese caretakers, janitors, and the story is going around that what Lang uncovered was something regarding a payment to terrorists.'

'Then you're saying that the material you brought me is not what Lang saw.'

'Not if the other story is true,' G. D. said. 'But Hesse also picked up some other stuff. He hangs around the bars and he buys drinks and information. And he also heard that whatever this terrorist organization is, they have an assassin on Bali this week. No information as to why he's here, just that he is. It might be the same man who was in Jakarta and then again it might not. But I put two and two together. Hell, you're here, so I figured you might be the possible target.'

To hell with it, Clements thought wearily. First the threats against his life and now a crazy story like this coming out of Singapore that was just offbeat enough to be true. He drank his bourbon in silence. 'All right, give me the rest of it.'

'That's all there is,' G. D. said.

'That's it? Was the name of the terrorist group "The Red Brigade"?'

'I don't know,' G. D. said, flatly. 'That's all that Hesse got.'

'Can somebody from the Singapore consulate talk to Hesse?'

'You mean some of your intelligence people?'

'Yes.'

'Sure. Hesse's aboveboard. I guarantee it. I'm sure he can provide the name of the bar, descriptions, things like that. But that's all the information he got. If it had been anybody else, I might have discounted what he said by half, but Hesse's reliable.'

He drained his glass, filled it again. 'I don't think you should take the chance. We'll fly up to my place in Bangkok for a few days.'

'Hell, I'm not going anywhere,' Clements said, a little less comfortable than he cared to reveal. 'Suppose that the rumor you have is true. It's so goddamned vague, it's not even actionable. Even if he's here, there's no indication that I'm his target.'

'Give me one good reason why you have to take the chance that you are.'

'I'm the American ambassador and I'm scheduled to appear.'

'Who cares?'

'*I* care. I won't run. I've lived with threats before. It goes with the territory for anyone who has a foreign assignment. The friendly world is shrinking. Any assignment is in the middle of an enemy camp now.' He suddenly wished for the presence of Kemper, to whom he would simply hand all this business and then follow his advice. But Kemper was back in Jakarta.

'Well,' G. D. said, hunched forward, patting the heels of his hands together, soundlessly. 'If you won't leave, you won't leave. What's your schedule for your stay here? What do you have to do tomorrow?'

'There's a bridge that was built with American donations, primarily from a missionary organization. It's the usual ceremony, a few speeches, entertainment from a gamelan orchestra, maybe some Balinese dancing. Then back here to the hotel for a luncheon. And I fly out at two o'clock.'

144

'At least let the Indonesians know it's possible that the man is on the island,' G. D. said.

'I will. But government security's going to have enough troops here to mount a small invasion,' Clements said. 'They're already spooked enough over what happened in Jakarta. They won't make any mistakes.'

'Let's hope you're right,' G. D. said.

'You'll be my guest at the luncheon tomorrow, of course.'

'If I can't talk you into changing your mind.'

'Not this time,' Clements said.

'All right, buddy. You call the shots.'

Before he went to bed that night Clements was finally able to reach Kemper in Jakarta, aware even as he did so that his line might be tapped and that it would give him an advantage if it were. For he would be passing the message to the other side that he was not unaware of what was going on here.

Kemper did not seem to be greatly disturbed. 'You can hear a rumor about anything if you listen hard enough,' he said. 'And who's the source on this one?'

'I'll tell you when I see you.'

'All right, I'll push for extra precautions from this end. I would also advise you to do the same there, Mr Ambassador. I've been over their security plans though, and I can't see that they've missed a trick.'

After the call Clements wrote an *aide mémoire* in longhand, detailing everything that G. D. had told him and including the names of G. D. and Hesse. He put it in an envelope and gave it to his protocol officer to be delivered to Mr Kemper in case of accident or other acts of God. He also put in a call to General Suhud, head of Kopkamtib, the Command for the Restoration of Security and Order on the island. General Suhud was not available. Clements identified himself to the junior officer, passed the message that the man known as Sangre was said to be on Bali. The junior officer responded politely.

Clements had a message typed to General Suhud and a true copy kept on file. The message was hand-delivered to Kopkamtib Headquarters in Denpasar and signed for. It was a foolish bit of business, Clements realized, but if tomorrow the assassin got to him, he wanted it on record that the authorities had been forewarned.

Lomax was up early, at the crack of dawn, and he wondered while he took his shower why they would call it the 'crack' of dawn. Perhaps there were places in the world where the darkness was solid, and when the light touched it there was a break in the darkness, a cracking sound which was beyond the hearing range of humans. He had laid out fresh clothing on the bed, all white, clean cotton underwear and a T-shirt to absorb the perspiration, white shirt, white suit, white socks and shoes and, finally, a white tie with a silken texture to it.

He also armed himself as meticulously as he dressed himself, because weapons were a part of the clothing after all, and for years he had never been in public without at least two weapons capable of killing an attacker or an enemy, a pistol with a range of at least ten yards, for killing at a distance, and a knife, generally fixed in a scabbard bound to his shin, in case he was attacked at close quarters. At one time he had considered his body a killing machine until his leg had been injured and let him down. Because one needed sound underpinnings for the martial arts in order to provide the leverage for the work of the arms or the deadly swing of feet.

But there were advantages to the methods that had been forced upon him. He would never have discovered the artistic side to it had he stayed with the deadly power of hands and feet. He had broken a man's neck once, during his early days, just by a simple blow with the toughened side of one hand. But the man just dropped like a rock, a lump of dead meat, absolutely no color to the act whatsoever, no sound. There was no more satisfaction in that than there would have been in watching a man die of natural causes.

His telephone rang as he expected it would and he picked it up and simply said, 'Yes?' and then listened. The voice from the other end spoke in jargon, delivery dates and merchandise, but he knew precisely what was being said, and when the voice emphasized that they wanted what had been ordered and no more, Lomax chuckled. 'In the first place, it's impossible,' he said. 'In the second place, you'll be getting the bargain of a lifetime. Two for one. Think it over. You'll find it makes sense.' He severed the connection.

He checked his camera equipment and then went downstairs to the dining room and the buffet breakfast, but refused to stand in line. Instead he instructed a waitress to bring him a fruit plate and croissants along with a cup of hot, black coffee. He studied the shape of the fruit on his plate a long time before he touched it, absorbed in the textures and the colors, strawberries, kiwi, mangoes and a half-dozen strange fruits he could not identify. His nose was assailed by the rich yeasty smell of the croissant and the bitter marvel of the black coffee. He ate carefully and sparingly so as not to allow a single stain to reach the fabric of his suit, then he stopped at the desk and had the clerk confirm his reservations on the noon Qantas flight to Perth.

And as he stood there his stomach tightened because he saw the three Indonesian officers come into the hotel and he knew from the way they walked they were on business because they were such officious little bastards. He also knew that they were looking for Sangre, and despite his temptation to get out of there, he stayed rooted to the spot. For he was not Sangre after all. He was Lomax, Dr Lomax, and Dr Lomax always cooperated with authorities because Dr Lomax *was* an authority, in his own right.

He stood and went over his airline ticket and he heard the officers talking to the room clerk in Indonesian, even showing him the picture they had received overnight from Jakarta. And Lomax could not resist tempting fate, playing his own kind of roulette, to prove that he was immune.

He moved down the counter to the officers. 'I beg your pardon,' he said in English. 'But I couldn't help overhearing. I am Dr Lomax. Is there any way I might be of service?'

'English?' one of the officers said.

'Canadian, actually. A specialist in tropical diseases.'

'How long have you been on this island?'

Lomax's eyes rolled toward the ceiling. 'About a week, I should say.'

The picture was placed in front of him, the black and white photograph from the broken camera, and his heart jumped. It was a perfect likeness. It was him, all right, but of course at the same time it was not him at all, because he was standing here now in a dazzling white suit, being of aid, polite and politic, and the man in the photograph was scuz. Lomax frowned at the picture, then nodded. 'Yes, of course.'

'You've seen him?' one of the officers said.

'On Kuta Beach, about three days ago, I believe. I was looking for fungus infections and he allowed me to examine his leg. It was in pretty bad shape. Definitely an infection. I told him he should get to a hospital and he said he would stop in Jogjakarta.'

'He was going back to Java?'

'That was my impression.'

'You're sure it's the same person?'

'He has a distinctive look about him. I'm sure it's the same man.'

'Did you get his name, sir?'

'No. He was not a part of my official research project, you see. I was much more interested in the natural immunity of the indigenous population. He overheard me talking to a Balinese gentleman and asked me to take a look at his fungus condition.'

'Did he have an accent? Could you guess his nationality?'

'No, I can't say that I could. He spoke English very well, but then he might not have been English at all.'

'And do you know if he went to Jogjakarta?'

'He *said* he was going to Jogjakarta, but then, one never knows if a person actually intends to follow through, does one?'

'Thank you, sir, for the information.'

'You're welcome, I'm sure. Sorry I couldn't do more.'

He watched the officers leave. He rooted around in his mind, trying to come up with a way of asking if they had found the body, red skin, white aura, and what they thought of it if they had, but obviously he could ask no such thing. And he felt that if the body had been discovered there would be an undercurrent of excitement all over the hotel this morning, because there was always a keen interest in the bizarre.

He sat in the lobby a few minutes and pretended to show interest in a local tourist paper, but he was secretly watching the counter where the guides gathered to pick up assignments or to wait for tourists. If one of their number had been found dead, there would certainly be a buzz of interest there. But there was no such interest, and the dispatcher (if that's what the locals called him) leaned on the counter and yawned. The two guides who had shown up so early in the morning sat on a padded bench against a pillar, smoking cigarettes, chatting about nothing in particular.

Finally, Lomax wandered out into the early morning air, already warm, rich with the oxygen from the trees. He could smell the odor of rice straw burning in the fields. He walked down a path and across a minor road, a full two miles to where he had left the guide's automobile tucked away in some trees. And when he was close to it he passed it by, sniffing the air, alert for any signs that the car had been found and that there were watchers waiting for someone to display interest in the car. But he could detect no such interest. A group of Balinese women in sarongs walked by on the edge of the highway carrying bundles atop their heads. He waited until they had rounded a bend in the road and then examined the car from a closer angle. He had left a twig leaning against the front door of the car so that if anybody opened it the twig would fall. But the twig was still in place.

He opened the door, picked the key out from under the mat, then climbed in. The engine came alive on the first try and he drove out the highway toward the Monkey Forest until he came to the bluff overlooking the bridge that was to be dedicated later that morning. He parked in the shade of a banyan tree a half mile from the wooden bridge, which spanned a wide, clear river flowing in the canyon a hundred feet below. On the opposite side of the river he counted the army trucks, three of them, with perhaps twenty-five soldiers currently cooking over small fires, another platoon

149

striking the small tents where they had spent the night and policing the area. There were also soldiers on this side of the bridge, a couple of officers fussing over the height of a ribbon which would be tied in place later and then cut by the dignitaries to signal the opening.

He smoked a cigarette while he studied possible angles and assessed the potential impact if the truck were placed in different positions. But there were aesthetic values to be considered here as well. Two tall trees rose immediately to the left of the bridge on the bank of the river and he did not want to see them toppled. So he would place the truck to the right, angled toward the entrance to the bridge and the spot where the two men would stand to cut the ribbon and have their pictures taken. Unless he was wrong, a small platform would be built to the right where the gamelan orchestra would sit and there would be a row of chairs.

The television crews and the news photographers would have to take their pictures from the center of the road, facing the bridge, and even with the use of wide-angle lenses they would have to be back at least fifteen feet to get the whole scene. He did not want the explosion to take out the photographers because he wanted the scene preserved on videotape. The explosion would turn the truck bed into shrapnel and there would be a ball of fire which would rise straight up, in a direct line with the pine trees. Frozen on film, the composition would resemble a Motherwell painting.

He began to get the shakes. He took a couple of pills to bring him down just a hair, enough to get rid of the tremors without killing the high. He had to be sharp today. He turned the car around and drove toward the government garage, a full half hour drive away.

At the government motor pool he found his truck to one side of the fenced compound, the bowlegged man already on duty in the headquarters shack. The bowlegged man apologized that the driver was not yet here but Lomax assured him that there was plenty of time, that he himself was early, and he needed the time to check the medical supplies. So, in comparative privacy, he changed the detonation system. He realized that there was no way he could know precisely in advance exactly when the principals would be in position. He would have to set the device off by remote control and then hope to have enough time to catch his Qantas flight.

The driver showed up at eight, a young man with bad teeth. Lomax led the way in his car, parked it in the trees overlooking the bridge, his scrotum tight as he moved over to the truck. The vehicle rattled down the road toward the bridge and the large assortment of soldiers supervising the last-minute preparations. The gamelan orchestra was beginning to assemble on the low platform with their gongs and drums, their flutes and xylophones, and the soldiers were lining up a row of six chairs. A truck from Indonesian television was already in place, cameramen setting up equipment on a roof platform. But there was also a roadblock fifty yards this side of the television truck. A soldier waved Lomax to a stop with a carbine.

The soldier asked the driver for a pass in Indonesian. Every vehicle had to have a pass. Every individual had to have a pass. Anything that crawled or flew or slithered could not pass this line without authorization.

The driver was upset, being a country boy with no experience with police or military officials, so Lomax whipped out his sheaf of bogus papers affixed with seals and signatures and proper letterheads and thrust them past the driver and toward the soldier. 'I am Dr Lomax and this is official Red Cross business,' he said, imperiously. 'It is part of the precautions that your superiors in Jakarta considered to be absolutely necessary in case of any trouble.'

'These papers are no good,' the soldier said. 'You have to have local authorization.'

'Get your superior officer over here,' Lomax said. The soldier waved and a lieutenant left the television crew and came up to the truck, thumbing through the papers.

'I speak English,' the lieutenant said. 'The guard is correct, sir. You do not have local authorization.'

'That's fine with me,' Lomax said, without rancor. 'Considering the high rate of violence lately, I'd just as soon be elsewhere. If you will kindly write a note on the authorization from General Suharto's office explaining that

151

I have been refused admittance, then date it and sign your name, I'll go back to Jakarta.'

That always did it, Lomax thought, the signed name which implied the acceptance of responsibility for countermanding an order from higher up. The lieutenant looked uncomfortable. He glanced at the crate on the truck bed, the Red Cross insignia. 'All right,' he said. 'You can pass, but please park your truck to one side, out of the way.'

'We certainly will,' Lomax said. He told the driver where he wanted the truck and then took fifteeen minutes getting it in exactly the right position, at precisely the right angle. 'I want you to wait in the truck until the ceremonies are over,' he said to the driver. 'Then we'll go back to the motor depot. Do you have plenty of cigarettes, everything you need?'

'Yes, sir. Thank you, sir.'

'Then I think I'll walk up to a place where I can see the ceremony better.'

He walked down the road, pausing every once in a while to frame the scene with his hands, and if a soldier stopped him, he would say that he was going to take pictures as well as be the medical supervisor, but no one interfered. He walked all the way to the top of the hill and then sat in the car and checked the film in his camera and tested the remote-control detonator. Yes, everything live, a small red light glowing. Only a matter of time now.

Clements had not slept well. He felt as if he were coming down with a tropical fever, which caught up with him from time to time. It affected him in minor ways, a tendency to chill, an occasional light-headedness, and it could be controlled by Atabrine, a medicine which he did not like to take because it sometimes made him dizzy. Today he would bluff it through, get past the ceremony, fly back to Jakarta and spend twenty-four hours in bed.

He met with his staff early, went over the remarks with the protocol officer, decided that in this instance he should make his talk in the Indonesian language and, above all, keep it short. There were no special messages to be woven into the texture of this short speech for the Indonesians to unravel, no attitudes to be revealed, nothing except a straightforward and standard friendship speech.

He saw Rooseno at breakfast, and if he himself did not feel well, the minister looked even worse, a grayish cast to his complexion, heavy pouches beneath his eyes. He sat with his staff, occasionally glancing toward Clements's table as if he could not make up his mind whether to approach the ambassador or not. He was dressed in a fresh short-sleeved suit, khaki, with a row of civilian medals above the left breast pocket. While he had his croissants and coffee, he listened to his advisers and made notes on a small pad. Clements hoped that this was not going to be another long-winded speech.

He knew that it was not when, following breakfast, Minister Rooseno approached him in the hotel lobby, his face heavily lined, troubled.

'I wonder, Ambassador, if we might not share the same car out to the bridge this morning.'

'Certainly, Minister,' Clements said. 'Either limousine you like.'

'Mine, then, I think, if that's satisfactory with you.'

'Certainly.'

The limousine stood under the portico, white, with the seal of government stenciled on the side, but not as elaborate as the one in Jakarta. Clements informed Wilkins, his protocol officer, that he would be riding out with the minister but that the American limousine was to be brought along nonetheless. Because the American limousine had its own communications system and Clements had the feeling he would be contacting Jakarta before the morning was out.

As usual the procession was preceded by police cars and an entourage of army personnel, without sirens this time. The minister was thoughtful, reflective as the cars pulled away. He studied the back of his chauffeur's head, the hair black as a raven's wing. 'Do you mind if we speak in English?' Rooseno said. 'I know this driver and I know he speaks nothing except Indonesian.'

'Not at all, Minister.'

Rooseno looked out the window at the fields, the smoke

drifting straight up into a cloudless sky from the stacks of burning rice straw. 'I am very fond of Bali,' he said. 'I was here once a long time ago at a working meeting which Sukarno held at a vacation house which he had built for himself.'

'I've seen it.'

'He was heavily criticized by many for having it built,' Rooseno said. 'But on the whole, political careers are much shorter here than they are in your country. It was a miracle that Sukarno lasted as long as he did, and it is more than a miracle that I have held my post for as long as I have.'

'Are you making a point, Minister?'

'Of course,' Rooseno said. 'I am not angry with you, by the way. If I had the same information about you that you have about me, I would certainly consider all my options.'

'I'm sure you would.'

Rooseno occupied himself with the lighting of a cigarette. 'And I must consider the options that I have as well. Ordinarily, I would use the services of a Chinese go-between who would approach you in an oblique fashion and negotiate with you in such a way that you would know exactly what I was suggesting, but my name would never be mentioned.'

'It was my impression that the Chinese go-between would be used only in matters of financial negotiation,' Clements said.

Rooseno smiled. 'True.'

'Then what you are to suggest involves money.'

'Yes,' Rooseno said.

'I imagine, Minister, that if we know you received an illegal quarter of a million dollars from American funds last year, then we could uncover three times that much if we decided to look.'

'You could do that,' Rooseno said, tapping the cigarette against an ashtray. 'But what would you gain?'

'Very little,' Clements said. 'But I'm just pointing out how much you stand to lose.'

'Indeed. So I am proposing something which you may consider bold, Ambassador. I want your country to pay me three quarters of a million dollars. I did not sleep last night but instead I spent the time thinking this through. The money is to be deposited in Switzerland for me, within four days. Then, on the fifth day, my wife and children will leave here to go on holiday. My wife will have the authority to pick up the money from the Swiss account and then they will proceed to Oslo. And as of next week I shall meet them there.'

'You want to move very quickly, I see.'

'As you will discover, time is of the essence.'

'And what will the United States receive for this money?'

'Information that will give you the power to shape all of Southeast Asia as you want it,' Rooseno said, lowering his voice, despite his driver's inability to understand. 'You raise your hand and it goes one way. You lower your hand and it moves another. You do nothing and it moves in even another direction. If your country is interested in the money end, it will mean billions of dollars. Money and power. Those are the only two things that matter.'

'And I take it you will emigrate?'

'Oh, yes,' Rooseno said. 'For my health. I will stay in Norway and your country will make an official request of the Norwegians that this be allowed.'

Clements rubbed his hands together. He was chilling slightly, feeling feverish. 'I'll need more information before I can approach my government.'

'I'm not sure there will be time for that,' Rooseno said.

'Even if I'm convinced, it will take some time to have three quarters of a million dollars moved to a Swiss bank.'

Rooseno gave him a skeptical look. He was not a member of the upper political circles, Clements realized, not a part of the financial aristocracy or he would know better. He would know that even at its expeditious best, the bureaucracy would not part with that much money without a preordained accounting, a rationale.

'We'll take first things first,' Clements said. 'I don't doubt your word, Minister, that you have valuable information. But I have to give my government something more tangible than that.'

'There is a conspiracy of such magnitude that it will change history.'

'A conspiracy that extends beyond Indonesian borders?'

'Yes.'

'Do you know who hired the assassin?'

'Yes.'

'Is that same assassin on Bali?'

'I was informed that you reported this to the authorities last night.'

'You didn't answer my question.'

'I don't control the assassin.'

'So you don't know whether he's here or not.'

'That's true.'

'And if he is here, am I his assignment?'

'I don't know.'

Minister Rooseno was decidedly uncomfortable, and in that moment Clements could see why. 'I don't wish to insult you, Minister,' Clements said. 'But it's possible that whatever this conspiracy, you are on the edges of it, not at the center, not at the decision-making level.'

'That's true,' Rooseno said. And then, abruptly: 'I can give you the Six Ravens.'

'How much information?'

'Everything.'

'Then suppose I stay over this afternoon. We can talk later on this evening, and when I'm convinced that it would be in the best interests of the United States to pay you a large sum of money, I'll put it in the works.'

Rooseno sucked on his cigarette. 'I am willing to gamble that what I have is so startling that you will be authorized to pay any amount for the full information.'

'Suppose you give me a sample.'

Rooseno nodded. 'Within the next month there is going to be a terrorist attack on the Straits of Malacca. It is the major shipping route between the Indian Ocean and the South China Sea.' The big oil tankers from the Persian Gulf moved through these straits between Malaysia and Sumatra to Singapore at the southern tip of Malaysia and then into open water. 'The terrorists will operate out of the town of Medan in Sumatra and the port that opens into the straits.'

'Who runs the terrorists?'

'Religious radicals.'

'The Red Brigade?'

'Yes. The strike against the tankers in the straits will punish the Indonesians for splitting from OPEC. The Americans are going to be shown as weaklings in Southeast Asia. And if everything is successful, then the Red Brigade will take power in Indonesia and make the whole country Muslim.' Rooseno fell silent. The procession was approaching the bridge now, moving down the slope. 'That is all the information I will give you for nothing. Does it intrigue you?'

'Yes,' Clements said. 'I think we have something to negotiate.'

The car stopped and the door was opened. Rooseno was out first, Clements following, knowing as he put one foot on the ground that he was in difficulty. For the chilling was worse and his stomach had begun to cramp. He could already feel the sweat pouring down his face. The gamelan orchestra was playing, the musicians sitting on a low platform, and Clements forced himself to smile as he was being introduced to the local dignitaries, the headmen of the villages, dressed in sarongs. He knew that the cameras were live, recording everything. He could not show weakness until he was through the line and approaching the chairs, and then his protocol officer caught up with him.

'You look like hell,' Wilkins said, under his breath.

'I feel like hell.'

'Our security wants you to limit yourself to the area immediately close to the chairs and the ribbon-cutting section of the bridge,' Wilkins said. 'They've made a sweep for three hundred meters.'

'Look around and see if you can find me some Atabrine,' Clements said.

'Yes, sir. And remember, if you're not well, we'll speed up the ceremony and schedule you before the village headmen and the Balinese. Then we announce that you have a tight schedule and make the apologies. I worked out that protocol with my counterpart in their Foreign Ministry. They won't take offence.'

'We may have to do that,' Clements said. He sat down in the chair, waited, trying to rise above the level of his physical discomfort. He stood up again to return the greeting of a local general.

In less than a minute, Wilkins was back, ashen-faced but trying to pretend that everything was normal. 'I want you to follow me, Ambassador. Our car is parked over there, on the other side of the television trucks.'

'What's wrong?'

'Just do it, sir. Please. No questions. Your life is going to depend upon it.'

Clements put a hand on Wilkin's shoulder to steady himself, began to walk.

Shit, things were awry and Lomax could feel it even before he began to see the evidence of it. He watched from the grove through a pair of binoculars as the American ambassador and the Indonesian minister arrived. Even from this distance it appeared to him that Clements was unsteady on his feet. After he had shaken hands with the locals, he was mopping the back of his neck with a handkerchief. And then Clements was talking with one of his men who wandered over toward the Red Cross truck even as Clements sat down.

Christ, Lomax should have told the gook driver what to say, given him some lines in case anything was asked of him, for now the American was asking questions and the driver was climbing out of the truck and walking back toward the truck bed where the large crate was fixed. And as the gook fumbled with the lock, the American went back to Clements and they were engaged in conversation. Lomax squinted through the binoculars, trying to see the expressions on their faces, to read their attitudes through their body positions.

And quite suddenly there was no doubt of their intentions in Lomax's mind, none at all, for the ambassador was moving toward the American limousine and two or three soldiers were moving toward the truck. Lomax couldn't believe his lousy luck, as if somebody had read his mind, and all thoughts of aesthetics fled from his mind as he dashed toward the car and fumbled with the briefcase, grabbing up the remote-control device. He pushed the button just as a soldier was trying to insert a crowbar beneath the locked hasp on the box.

And suddenly there was an explosion, a magnificent ball of fire that blew the soldiers and the truck all to pieces and enveloped the gooks in the orchestra in flames. He grabbed up his camera as the concussion knocked the cameramen from atop the truck, rolled upward in smoke and debris and threw the television truck over on its side. The wooden bridge was burning and there was so much dust and smoke he really could not see how much damage he had done, but he knew goddamn well that Lomax had better haul ass. He clicked away with the camera for another ten seconds, then he started the car and spun around in the grove and shot back down the highway toward Denpasar and the airport.

7

Outwardly it was business as usual at the American Embassy in Jakarta, and the same number of students lined up each day at the chancery waiting to apply for study visas, and the businessmen sat in the waiting room, all very patient, for the clerks were always behind and the wait was bound to be a long one. There were a few outward changes, more Marines at the public gates, a new metal-detecting booth through which everybody entering the chancery was required to pass, another contingent of Marine observers on the roof, watching the traffic, both motorized and pedestrian, on the boulevard. At the delivery gates a pattern of emergency concrete pylons had been installed, so that any delivery driver had to make a pattern of right and left turns before he approached any building. There would be no suicide drivers here with their trucks full of explosives.

But beneath the placid surface the embassy was locked in a quiet crisis and Kemper had shifted to an emergency status. Three days had passed since the explosion in Bali and he had invoked a contingency plan which saw the ambassador's meetings and conferences outside the compound all but canceled until Kemper could discover what was happening and how to protect him.

He sat in the ambassador's office, briefing papers spread over the ambassador's desk, going over everything with Clements for the twelfth time in the certain knowledge that there were still pieces missing here. In any investigation there was more truth at hand than could be instantly perceived. Clements did not look well. The explosion had thrown him down the slope and he had suffered minor abrasions, but the doctor was of the opinion that Clements was more drained from the minor malarial attack than from the effects of the explosion itself, and that Clements was certainly outspoken enough to tell Kemper if he was tired of the questioning process.

But Clements was holding up surprisingly well, in Kemper's opinion. It had been Kemper's experience that the rich and the powerful were generally the most intolerant when it came to discomfort, but Clements drank tea, roved around the office, looked out the window at his garden and sat in thoughtful contemplation as Kemper asked him the same questions again and again, varying the form of the question each time as if to evoke a different perspective.

'You're sure that G.D. Majors didn't give you any more information than you've told me,' Kemper said, doodling on a piece of paper.

'Positive. I wrote it all down within an hour of the conversation. What he told me was limited to what his man picked up.'

'And Rooseno confirmed that the assassin was on Bali?'

'No. If he knew, he wouldn't admit it.'

Kemper shrugged. 'I don't think he knew any more than he told you. Or he wouldn't have been caught in the explosion. Now, about the attack on the Straits of Malacca. He said it was to come out of Medan?'

'Yes.'

Kemper looked thoughtful, preoccupied. 'It's possible, I suppose. They could be getting their financing out of Iran.'

'Have you talked to G.D.'s man, Hesse?'

Kemper nodded. 'Typical old Asian hand. The Asians tend to forget he's not one of them. And we couldn't track his story to any specific source. A rumor gets started and it spreads around, and it takes only the money for a few drinks to get as many versions of the story you want. But the rumor was right on the money this time. He made his try.'

'I want to attend Rooseno's funeral,' Clements said.

'When is it?'

'The day after tomorrow.'

'You are free, of course, to do as you please, sir. But if I were you, I'd hold off making any appearances until we have a line on the assassin.'

Clements touched his chin. 'You're not going to get him, are you?'

'Probably not,' Kemper said.

'And he's going to try again.'

'I'd say there's a ninety percent chance he will. Yes, sir.'

'I think the rest of the embassy personnel are safe.'

'I'd agree with that,' Kemper said. 'We have a hell of a lot of American personnel who live outside the compound. He could have picked off a half dozen of them anytime.'

Clements nodded. 'I won't make up my mind about the funeral until tomorrow. I'll let you know.'

'Fine,' Kemper said.

Kemper studied the videotape again and again, took the call from Wiznoski on Bali as he unraveled the pattern of movements of the man who called himself 'Dr A. Lomax.' Wiznoski had tracked him from the hotel to a guide who called himself by the English name of Sam, thence to a municipal motor pool and an army camp. And Sam had been found dead only yesterday by women who smelled the stink of decomposition from the road. Wiznoski had gone with the police and taken his own pictures of what he considered to be a ritual killing. Why else would a murderer paint a man's face and hands red and then spray in a white background?

'Ritual killing, my ass,' Kemper said, impatiently, to Wiznoski over the telephone. 'We have us one assassin who's crazy as hell. And where did he go after the explosion?'

'He drove to the airport, caught the first plane out, which happened to be Jakarta.'

'Did the police then dust the car?'

'They're not bad technicians,' Wiznoski said. 'They picked up some print but absolutely nothing on the driver's side. Our Dr Lomax was pretty goddamned tidy. Everything wiped clean. A filter vacuum picked up a couple of hair specimens which could be his, a white cotton fiber, but then we know he was dressed in a white suit. I've gone over his hotel room myself. There's nothing to show that he was ever there.' Wiznoski paused. 'I think we have to proceed on the assumption that this man is not necessarily Sangre.'

'Why?'

'Sangre's very crude. People at the dock described him as one mean-looking son of a bitch. But Lomax was refined, not pretend, but *really* refined. The desk clerk, the waitresses, all of the officials who dealt with him, they all say so.'

'I believe it's the same man. He goes under aliases.'

'But does he undergo personality changes?'

'I'd bet on it. He may be polite in one place and an absolute asshole in another, but he's an expert killer. He's tidy, clean and he doesn't make many mistakes.'

'Then why didn't he push the button when he had the ambassador within range?'

'Malfunction, maybe.'

'I checked out his remote control. It's perfect.'

'What about the long-distance call he got at his hotel?' Kemper said.

'No record of the number. Just that it came from Jakarta.'

'Somebody's moving him around.'

'No doubt.'

'Keep on it. I'll feed this information on into Washington and see what we get back.'

He hung up the telephone, leaned back in his chair, pressed the remote-control button and the tape cassette began to play on the television monitor again. Most of the footage was random as the cameraman tested his equipment, some of it shot with sound, some of it silent. But Kemper was most fascinated by the placement of the bogus Red Cross truck. If you took the straight road and the bridge as a north-south axis, bisected it with the river as an east-west line, then the truck was exactly on a forty-five-degree angle, the back end of it pointing toward the center of the bridge and the ribbon which was to have been cut in the ceremony. He held a frame on the tape, observed the driver, who sat in the truck as he thrust his hand out the open window. Was he giving a signal? No.

Kemper could see the cigarette in his hand. He was just flicking ashes.

He let the tape roll on, saw Clements and Rooseno arriving, Clements shaking hands, then Clements sitting down, talking with Wilkins, the camera moving with Wilkins to the Red Cross truck, his talking with the driver, the driver getting out of the truck and the two of them standing by the box on the truck bed, then Wilkins moving back to Clements, a hurried conversation and then Clements moving away, out of frame, as a couple of soldiers headed toward the truck.

Kemper ran the tape back, then forward, timed it with a stopwatch. At least three seconds, perhaps as long as five, and at any point the button could have been pushed and Clements would have been ripped apart.

Where in the hell were you for those five seconds, you son of a bitch, Sangre or Lomax, or whatever you want to call yourself? Why in the hell did you wait?

He let the tape roll all the way through to the end. The camera was on a wide-angle, the cameraman setting his focus on the ribbon when the bomb went off, and the angle was wide enough to show the Red Cross truck at one side, the gamelan orchestra to the left of center, the whole of the bridge opening and a pair of trees rising at the side of the frame. When the bomb went off the truck disintegrated, the soldiers next to the box simply disappearing, the driver vaporized, and a wall of flame swept the orchestra away, set them on fire, scattered pieces of bodies. And the tape caught Rooseno in the act of turning just as the blast smashed him into a side of the bridge and literally pulped him. Then the truck turned over and the picture spun away with it, camera still turning, miraculously, still after it hit the dirt, lens pointed skyward, picking up a bloom of black smoke in the top left quadrant of the frame, a black pattern against a cerulean blue sky, almost like an abstract painting.

He shut it down, went to Tommi's apartment after leaving word with communications where he was going to be. She was dressed in shorts, a cotton blouse, sitting cross-legged and barefooted in the middle of the floor, wearing her horn-rimmed glasses, chewing on the eraser end of a pencil as she studied the map on the floor in front of her.

'As long as you're up, pour me a glass of wine from the fridge,' she said, not looking up. 'And help yourself while you're at it.'

'Thanks,' he said, wryly. He poured a glass for her and one for himself and then sat down in a chair where he could see the map over her shoulder. She used a compass to draw a circle out from Medan at the center. 'He did say "Medan," didn't he?'

'Who?'

'The ambassador.'

'Yes.' The wine was sweet, heady, and Kemper realized how tired he was.

'It won't wash,' she said, shaking her head, running a hand through her blond hair, absently.

'If you're going to talk to me, you're going to have to be more specific,' he said. 'What won't wash?'

She stood up and he was aware of her long brown legs and the softness of her. He was also aware that she was in a thinking mode and the expression on her face told him she was onto something.

'If you were going to bottleneck the straits, how would you do it?'

He forced himself to concentrate. 'Unlimited resources?'

'Within reason. Unlimited money, but you have to take into consideration all the patrol boats, the security in the straits as it exists.'

'I don't know,' he said. 'That would take some doing.'

'Then I'll ask you the same question in another way to make my point. Would you use Medan as a rendezvous point for your attack forces, whatever they're going to consist of?'

'No,' he said. 'Whatever attack I planned wouldn't call for any rendezvous point at all. I wouldn't even need a large force for that matter. I could take a truck overland and set up on either side of the straits, depending on which lane of traffic I wanted to hit. It wouldn't take much to set one of the tankers afire, disable it, cause an explosion, even a chain effect. I'd use a hand-held heat-seeking missile if I could get one. Otherwise, I'd set up a simple mortar. That would do the trick.' He drank the wine halfway down, onto it now, almost as if all of the multiple viewings of the tape were finding an outlet in a horrific scenario. 'Or better yet, I could put two private planes at Singapore, load up with napalm, explosives of any sort, and make my own bombing run on the straits. There would be absolutely nothing to stop me.'

'Could you get past the Singapore airport authority?'

'Of course. I could get an export license for explosives.' He shook his head. 'Christ, I could load a plane at Kuala Lumpur or Penang or a thousand air strips.' The whole thing was leaky as a sieve, too many possibilities, and no way to cover even a tenth of them. He finished the wine, and then seized on the slight hope. 'Now, suppose that there isn't any rendezvous, for God's sake, because we don't need that many operatives to run this one. And we wouldn't run our operation by boat anyway, because there are only two ends to the straits and they'd be able to flush us out. So let's assume that the information is accurate, that Medan is going to be our center. In that case I'd pick the airport there. I might even fly in with my explosives, stop only long enough to refuel, give me plenty of time for a hit-and-run with a destination at another airfield, probably in Malaysia.'

'Then what say we send one of our Indonesian recruits up there to monitor traffic coming in and out. They're not going to do this one cold, not without a few practice runs to get acquainted with the territory.'

'Houghton had up-country,' he said with a trace of sadness. 'We haven't assigned that yet, have we?'

'No. I have his list. Mostly planters. He always had a way with the Indonesian gentry.'

He glanced at her, looked away. 'Would you like to run them?' he said.

'Are you serious?'

'I wouldn't have mentioned it otherwise. It wouldn't hurt, you know, not if you really want a COS slot. The more diversity you have on your record, the better off you are. And while you're at it, I'd like you to have a crack at the computer in Singapore. I would like to uncover what Lang found out.'

'Do we have permission from the Singapore COS?'

'They've gone through the motions,' Kemper said. 'But sometimes I think Langley assigns only cautious types to Singapore. You might just have an informal look around the place, if you don't mind.'

'Why would I mind? I'm delighted.' She smiled at the thought, hugged herself, terribly pleased, her pleasure quite obvious. Then she frowned. 'But who would you get for backup here?'

'I'll have a new communications chief moved in from Bangkok.'

'Do you really think I could handle it?'

'Come on, you know damn well you can handle it. You could do my job if you had the chance, but I'm not ready to vacate.'

She kissed him impulsively. 'Then I'll start making arrangements in the morning,' she said. 'Now, how about a bite to eat? Have you had anything today?'

'I don't know,' he said.

'I'll cook you a steak, then,' she said. 'It'll only take a jif.'

As she went to her small kitchen she stopped short and turned back to him. 'One thing I have to know,' she said.

'Shoot.'

'You're not giving me this break only because you love me.'

'If I didn't think you were the right person for it, I wouldn't give you the assignment for any reason.'

'I didn't think you would, but I had to be sure.'

He listened to her humming to herself with joy in the kitchen and he realized that he was not being truly fair with her. For he did not believe for a moment that an attack on the straits would come out of Medan. That was a little piece of what he called 'soft information,' somebody's conjecture. The assignment would look good on her record, but he was indeed sending her there only because he loved her, determined to get her out of harm's way. He wondered, drowsily, if he was not making a terrible mistake, mixing sentiment with business, something he had sworn he would never do. But for better or worse, the decision had been made and he would stick to it.

Five days. Quite enough, Clements thought. He had conducted all his business from the protection of the embassy while he waited for specific instructions from Washington. He had forwarded all of the same information to State that Kemper had sent to Langley. He needed to know specifically whether Washington wanted him to notify the Indonesian Government of the rumored attack and the evidence of Rooseno's involvement.

But Washington was damned slow to respond. There was nothing more than a routine message from the Indonesian desk which in official language said the equivalent of 'Hold on and everybody will get around to you presently. And in the interim it might be a good idea if you took a vacation and left the area for a while to give the United States a distinctly low profile in the area. We'd like you to find a pleasant nonpolitical area where the reporters won't have access to you. Blend into the landscape. If that's not convenient, then come back to Washington on the pretext of a briefing.'

A trip to Washington was definitely out, he decided, because it would be a total waste of time. Nobody knew what in the hell was going on. There would be innumerable meetings at Foggy Bottom and at Langley and circular cables would be making their rounds of the ambassadors and chiefs of stations in all Asian and Middle East posts concerning the possibility of an attack on the Malaccan Straits, with recommendations as to how to handle it if it happened.

Considering the inclination to precipitous action by the current American President, Clements was not at all sure what would happen if the straits were attacked. Had the resolution of the problem been left to Clements, he would have had tea with the Foreign Minister, a very understanding gentleman who was also known to take direct action. Clements would simply have informed him that there was a possibility that there was going to be a military action coming out of Sumatra which might or might not amount to anything. And the Foreign Minister, without any fuss, would have dispatched troops to Sumatra in quantity to have a good hard look at that part of their territory to see if anything was afoot.

The American President was a rather surprising man, however, and Clements would not be surprised if he decided to ship the Marines into the straits for war games at the request of the Malaysian Government. If the President decided on such a display of force, Clements would welcome it. It was all conjecture. Clements was instructed by State to enter into no discussions with the Indonesian Government concerning this projected attack until the American Government had had more time to study it.

On Friday afternoon, following the Muslim example of working only until noon, the Jakarta bureaucracy closed down and on impulse Clements decided to leave the embassy compound alone, without the usual escort of guards and Indonesian police. There was always the possibility that Sangre-Lomax would be watching for just such a lapse of good sense but Clements doubted it, because the Indonesian Government had gone through a furor of breast-beating and official apologies for allowing such violence to happen not once, but twice, and they had made a great show of sending troops and police into the neighborhoods around the American Embassy, house by house, to make certain that the assassin, if he was still in Jakarta, had no effective vantage point overlooking the American Embassy.

Clements had the advantage of rain, the protective cover of a black umbrella, which he held low over his head against the monsoon downpour as he went through the gates and out onto the street. He hailed a motorized *betjak*, furled his umbrella as he ducked under the arced canopy which covered the passenger's compartment and he requested the driver to take him through the less-crowded boulevards to Madeleine's house. He felt more relaxed than he had in days, sheltered by the curtain from the downpour, sitting back against canvas cushions as his driver threaded his way between trucks and limousines until the streets became too narrow and crooked for heavy traffic and they entered the old Dutch quarter with the restored houses which reminded him of Amsterdam. He stopped the driver down a lane from Madeleine's house, paid him and then unfurled his umbrella again and waded through the rapidly rising water, aware that his feet were getting soaked. He came upon her perfect house around a corner on one of the few canals that had been cleaned up, the street people forcibly moved away. A concrete foundation had been poured which someday perhaps would hold a wrought-iron fence to surround these historic houses as a cultural site and at the same time control the environs for the few rich Indonesians who occupied the houses.

He did not go up either of the flights of stairs to the landing and the main door. He took out his key and opened the door to a small room which had at one time been a tradesmen's entrance but which now represented what Madeleine referred to as Clements's hideaway, a place where he could come at any time and be alone or in her company, as he preferred.

The original heavy teak beams still supported the ceiling above a stained-glass window which filtered the light streaming in from the street and shattered it into a shower of colors. He locked the door behind him and slipped off his raincoat, putting it in a small closet before he went into the main room, fitted with sofas and European antiques, cooled by an air conditioner which purred softly in the distance.

He fixed himself a bourbon and water at the bar, then sat down and picked up a copy of the Asian edition of *The Wall Street Journal* and pressed the button which would let her know, if she was in the house, that he was here. The bourbon was warm in his stomach and the stories in the *Journal* were bland, one article out of Jakarta quoting the general's comment that he was 'outraged' by the acts of terrorism in his country and that every effort would be taken to prohibit any more acts of 'radical vandalism.'

Radical vandalism.

Ah, now there was a phrasemaker, Clements thought with a smile. A professional assassin was on the loose. He had killed ten people on Bali and severely wounded another half dozen, but with the well-bred dodging of the

170

professional politician, the general would lump the incidents under 'radical vandalism.'

There was another article on the forthcoming oil meeting in Bangkok that had been planned by Minister Rooseno. The Philippines Foreign Minister had suggested that the meeting be delayed out of respect for the recently departed. But the *Journal*, clearheaded as always, found another spokesman from Thailand who ventured an opinion that Minister Rooseno would want his work to come to fruition without delay and suggested that the meeting be held as scheduled.

Clements put the newspaper down just as the door burst open and Madeleine came in, wearing an afternoon tea gown and an enchanting smile. He started to get up, but she leaned over and kissed him and then sat down beside him and began to examine his face, running her delicate fingertips over his lean cheeks. 'The papers said you were injured,' she said.

'Abrasions,' he said. 'Scratches. Nothing more.'

'A terrible thing,' she said. 'You could have been killed.'

'I'm sorry I wasn't able to go to your uncle's funeral,' he said.

'He was not an orthodox Muslim,' she said, momentarily distracted, rising to pour herself a glass of wine. 'Many of his relatives are not Muslim at all, at least not on the surface, because the generals are suspicious of Muslims and his relatives wish to rise in the government. But I don't want to talk about gloomy things. How are you feeling, truly?'

'Battered,' he said. 'I feel as if I'm caught in the middle of something I don't know anything about. My government is suggesting that I take a vacation.'

'Could we go to Europe together?' she said.

'Not now. I have to avoid reporters.'

'Then someplace quiet. I will arrange things.'

'I don't want you to arrange things, dear,' Clements said with a smile. 'That's my profession. I'm very good at it.'

She pressed a button to summon a maid. 'You mistake allowing yourself to be pampered for weakness,' she said. 'What's the good of power and money if you still do everything for yourself.' There was a tap on the door and a maid came in, dressed in a uniform. Madeleine spoke to her in Chinese and the girl immediately knelt at Clements's feet and removed his wet shoes and socks. She brought a heated towel to dry his feet and put slippers on them before she bowed and left the room.

'The servants will dry your shoes within a half hour,' she said. 'Do you wish to change your clothes?'

'No,' he said. He patted the damask covering of the sofa beside him. 'Bring your wine and come sit by me. I want to talk to you.'

'We can talk in the upper bedroom if you wish,' she said, settling in beside him. He was continually amazed at how delicate and fine-boned she was and yet how substantial as he put his arm around her.

'We can go to the upper bedroom later,' he said. 'But now I need some information.'

'What do you wish to know?'

'More about your Uncle Rooseno.'

'In what way?'

'I don't know any delicate way to put this. But was he the type of man who could sell out his country? Could he betray the current government to the extent that he would be willing to aid a revolution?'

'Do you think that's what he did?' she said, a half-smile on her face as she snuggled in against him.

'I can't tell you the details,' he said.

'Then suppose I tell them to you,' she said. She drank the rest of her wine and put the crystal glass on the end table. 'I won't tell you the exact details, because I don't know them. But see if I don't come close. There is to be some sort of very large-scale military action in a remote part of Indonesia and there is a chance that it may grow to topple the current government. And you will tell me that my uncle was being paid a large sum of money to aid this scheme.' She looked up at him with knowing, innocent eyes. 'Am I close?'

'Damn close,' he said.

She ran a delicate hand over the front of his shirt, slipped her fingers into the opening between the buttons to caress his chest. Her fingers were light, warm, incredibly smooth against his skin. 'There is not a general in the government who wouldn't take money for the same purpose. There's always some group that wants to overthrow the government, some foreign power with lots of money. Any clever general would take the money, knowing, as my uncle knew, that whatever the scheme, it would come to nothing.'

He shook his head in the negative. 'This one is real. There is an assassin attached to this one.'

'*All* of them are real. There have been assassins before.' She kissed him on the neck and he began to catch the rising scent of her and he turned her head to meet her mouth with his. And suddenly he was tired of thinking, of figuring out. And everything about her said that she had missed him for too long, not just the words, but the feel of him, and her hand traced over the flatness of his stomach. Without another word she led him to the old-fashioned elevator with the folding doors and once they were inside, rising toward the loft, she pressed herself against him and did not move away even as the elevator stopped. He opened the door into the bedroom with the mirrored walls and the canopy bed and gossamer drapes that covered the massive loft window that led onto a terrace with a paradise of tropical plants. The bed she had brought from Shanghai, where it had belonged to a famous courtesan of the last century, and the legend that surrounded it said that it had never been used for sleeping, only for lovemaking. Clements undressed her, filled with an unbearable wanting. And then he made love to her and she wrapped herself around him, possessing him until the moment of release, when she uttered a sharp cry and went limp.

He continued to hold her in his arms and she lay against him, only momentarily depleted. 'My Chinese uncle has a villa at Padang,' she said, when her breath came back. 'We could go there for a few days. It's on the beach. When the sun is out, we can swim. And when the rains come, we can make love.'

'I'd like that,' he said.

She kissed his arm. 'I have so many things to teach you.'

'About what?'

'The art of lovemaking.'

'Do I hear a complaint?'

She smiled. 'None at all. But there are many things the Chinese do that Westerners know nothing about. I would love to show you. But they take much time. And patience.'

'Then Padang it is,' he said.

'Yes,' she said. 'We'll have to find my Chinese uncle tonight to make arrangements. This is his evening of pleasure and he never uses the telephone when he has his good times.' She glanced toward the window. The rain was still pouring down on the tropical forest on her terrace. 'I will have my bath now,' she said. 'I will have the servants dry your trousers and press your suit. In the meantime it might be very good for you to sleep. Knowing my Chinese uncle, you will want to be fully alert around him.'

He watched her walk away in the rainy twilight of the room, exquisite in her nakedness, a pale golden form. And then he closed his eyes and in a few minutes was asleep.

At eight o'clock Madeleine had a light dinner served in a formal dining room furnished with Dutch antiques from the age of the Dutch East Indies. She had the servants set only two places at the end of the long table before she dismissed them. The place settings were gold, the plates old and rich, the crystal antique and hand-cut, with the facets catching fire from the candle flames.

'You make a perfect setting,' Clements said. 'Probably the most elegant setting possible for what we have to talk about.'

'And what's that?' she said, refilling her wineglass.

'You can't avoid the question. I want you to marry me.'

'I don't want to give you an answer now,' she said, her face troubled. 'I don't want to spoil things.'

'Then you're going to turn me down.'

'I didn't say that.'

'That's the only way you could spoil things. I've loved you for a long time. And I know you love me. If you have reservations, I want to know about them.'

She shifted her salad with a golden fork, not daring to raise her eyes, for she was certain that if she looked, she would see her mother's face in the shadows of the room, glaring at her, telling her what a fool she was even to consider what this dog of a man was telling her. 'If we married, you'd want to live in the States?'

'Yes.'

'Where?'

'Anyplace you like.'

'I don't know much about the States. I've never been there.'

'I think you'd enjoy San Francisco.'

'What would I do there?'

He smiled, cut a piece of steak. 'Shop, go to the theater, the ballet, the galleries.'

'While you worked.'

'Of course. But not all the time.'

She looked at him, and she saw his face by candlelight, the only man she had ever truly come to love, and yet she could not have him and she knew it, for everything had already gone too far, and even as she knew that she was trying to find a way to change things, to make what he suggested possible. But her spirit mother was still in the room, and there was no way to make her disappear.

'I couldn't live like that,' Madeleine said. 'I have to work. It's very important to me.'

'You can work there. You can do anything you like.'

'There's no reason why you can't stay in Indonesia,' she said. 'There's no reason why everything can't go on as it is now.'

She was afraid, he thought, and it was going to take a long time to reassure her, time which he didn't have. 'There's every reason I can't stay here,' he said. 'Even if all the trouble was resolved and I stayed on as ambassador, I would be rotated in the normal course of things. And as an oilman in private business, I wouldn't stand a chance in the current climate here.'

'I could make extra concessions for you,' she said.

'Which I couldn't take.'

'Do you know how much money I make in my position here?' she said.

'Money's never going to be a problem.'

'How can I make you understand?' she said, and she

raised her eyes slightly and did not see her spirit mother in the shadows near the carved screen, but she could still feel her presence. 'I'm very rich here, and I have many Chinese relatives. It's not the same as having an American family. And if I leave here . . .' Ah, there was the point beyond which her mother would not let her go, for if she left here, she would be dependent upon this man, and despite any precautions she might take to protect herself, she would be subject to his penury or his generosity. She sipped her wine. 'If I leave here, I'll become a stranger somewhere else.'

'Not as my wife.'

But people die, she wanted to say. *You've lost a wife and she cost you nothing except grief, but I lost a father, and all my protection went, and I could not keep my mother from being beaten by thieves and a man I loved and trusted. And perhaps I might trust you as long as you were with me, and perhaps I might help prolong your life, but people die anyway.* She put her hand over his, felt the strength of him. 'Let me have more time to think,' she said. 'I love you. You know that. But I'm at home here and I know how to take care of myself. And I don't know how I'd do in America. So let me have a few days and you'll have your answer.'

'Fair enough,' he said. 'But if you let loose of the past, we can have a fine life together. I promise you that.'

Madeleine listened closely, thought she heard the voice of her spirit mother laughing, derisively.

Clements had never experienced another night quite like it. From the moment he left Madeleine's house in her small sports car, with Madeleine behind the wheel, he moved into a world which he had heard about but never seen. The rain still plummeted down in torrents, and most of the time it seemed to him she was driving blind at exorbitant speeds through streets running curb-deep, leaving a wake of water which washed over the sidewalks and sprayed the bicyclers. She drove into the Chinese quarter of the city, a subdued area with bland walled exteriors and signs written in Indonesian, no Chinese characters, nothing to indicate that a different culture inhabited these houses and these buildings.

Clements was aware how much the Chinese were hated, not just the Chinese Communists but the people who had been here for generations, for they seemed to hold themselves apart from the mainstream of Indonesian life, profiting from the struggles which carried the country in any direction, acting as middlemen in any large-scale graft involving Indonesian officials. The Chinese were considered to be the best businessmen, able to strike the shrewdest bargains. But during the war for independence from the Dutch, the Chinese had remained aloof, not identifying themselves with the national cause. For that they would never be forgiven. They were not even allowed to use their Chinese names on official government documents, only among themselves.

Madeleine pulled into a narrow lane, parked beneath a portico, then let herself out and waited for Clements before they entered a building through a narrow hallway. Deep within the building Clements could hear the roar of a crowd and the shrill flute rising above the low monotony of a gamelan orchestra. Off the hallway were kitchens, dirty, cluttered with boxes and pans and cooks who chopped meat into tiny cubes with cleavers and chattered with each other, spraying ashes from the omnipresent cigarette held tightly in the corner of the mouth.

Up a long flight of narrow stairs and then through a door and into an office where a group of Chinese men in Western business suits were examining two naked and muscular young men, occasionally feeling the shoulder muscles or the stringy calves, then arguing among themselves. The room was large enough that Clements and Madeleine were ignored, and she went to a bar near a teak desk at the back of the room and poured a straight bourbon for Clements and a glass of champagne for herself.

'What are they doing?' Clements said, sipping the bourbon.

'Having a marvelous time and making money in the bargain,' Madeleine said. 'At least my Uncle Wong is. He's the man standing back, making notes.' Of all the men in the room, Wong was perhaps the most unobtrusive, and yet looking at him Clements could tell that the power lay in

177

this man, an aura of supreme confidence and a smile that conveyed that he was enjoying himself immensely. 'My uncle owns the young man on the right. I don't know who owns the other one. But they are looking them over because they will not be placing their private bets, but they will be setting the odds on the floor.'

'Fighters, then,' Clements said.

'*Pencak silat* fighters.'

'Not ceremonial then.'

'No,' she said. 'They fight like they did hundreds of years ago. Sometimes they will just injure each other and at other times there will be fatalities.'

Finally the fighters had been sufficiently examined and the loose brocaded robes and turbans were brought into the room, the curved knives glittering in the light. There were arguments and counterarguments, polite arguments but serious nonetheless. Finally Wong spoke, a quiet authoritative voice yet very mild, and one or two questions were asked in Chinese. Wong answered, and then the other men wrote figures on small square pieces of paper and threw them down on the desk.

'Did you follow the arguments?' Madeleine said.

'Not all of them,' Clements admitted.

'My uncle has offered odds of five to one on his fighter,' Madeleine said in a soft voice. 'The others only wanted even odds because my uncle's fighter is not the favorite. The other man is said to have hypnotic powers so he can snatch his enemy's weapon away while the enemy is powerless. He goes into a trance, you see, and that gives him supernatural powers. So my uncle has unsettled them by giving them far more than they want.'

Clever, Clements thought, for the pronouncement of the odds had not been made for the gamblers at all but for the young man who was the favorite. His eyes reflected the bewilderment that a man should not only be betting so much money against him but offering such ruinous odds as well. The fighters were ushered out through another door to be dressed and the other businessmen went with them. Only then did Wong realize that he had guests and he bowed in apology.

'Uncle,' Madeleine said. 'This is my friend, Charles Clements, the American ambassador.'

'Of course,' Wong said, shaking his hand, genuinely warm. 'I should have recognized you. I am honored to have you here.'

'It is my honor,' Clements said. 'I hoped that we might have a chance to talk.'

'We will,' Wong said. 'But if your schedule permits, Excellency, you might enjoy the contest which is about to take place.'

'I've plenty of time,' Clements said.

Wong proceeded to gather up the slips of paper from the table. He was perfectly groomed, from the expensive Western business suit, immaculately tailored, to the unblemished shoes, the trimmed black hair, the manicured hands, as if behind this man there existed a phalanx of support personnel to keep him in such excellent physical shape. 'I need to advise you, Ambassador, that what you are about to see may not be to your taste. But there exists in the Indonesians a great strain which needs release, a split that demands resolution. With each other they may never raise their voices or they lose face. They may not stand with hands on hips because that is the traditional puppet stance of confrontation. So I offer them here a chance to release these feelings in a legitimate way. They identify with the fighter they support and come to hate an artificial enemy. The form of fighting is a very old one, and at one time only a man of royal blood could learn it but now it is universal, with many variations. This is a very rough style of *pencak silat* but it also moves very quickly. A man may win or lose his money just as fast. They do not have to work for it or intrigue for it. They simply place money on the ability of one man to do all the things which they are forbidden to do.'

Clements was aware of the roar of the crowd again, closer now, and Wong pulled up a bamboo screen which covered a large wall window overlooking a ring and a large room bisected by a stratum of blue cigarette smoke, packed with men. Wong seated Clements and Madeleine in chairs by the window, preferring to stand himself, watching the musicians beside the ring. The music became louder and more strident as the fighters appeared, bizarre in their ceremonial robes, going through brief ceremonies in the ring during which they were armed with short knives with curved blades. They made a tour around the ring and only now did Clements see the blood staining the canvas from the last fight.

The appearance of the fighters led to a flurry of betting, men standing, raising fists clenched with money, yelling to the brokers while the drums increased their tempo and the gongs clashed. Not the old days, Clements thought, not the martial arts as mental discipline. These men would be out to kill each other, a blood sport. He had been too close to death lately. He had no desire to see it as a commercial enterprise. From this vantage point, looking at both of the men in the ring, he could see the scars on the faces, and on the neck of Wong's fighter a long slash on which the red marks of the sutures were still in evidence. But he began to see the logic of what Wong was doing. His fighter ·was dressed in robes that were predominantly white, a color of ill fortune and bad luck.

'You picked the colors, I take it,' Clements said.

'Yes,' Wong said.

'You see, Uncle,' Madeleine said with a knowing smile. 'I told you that Charles knows the customs here.'

'I know that white is bad luck,' Clements said. 'You're going to make certain that people bet against him.'

Wong said nothing.

With a clash of cymbals and the piping of flutes, the fight began, the two young men circling each other like two animals in the jungle, almost regally, and Clements moved his mind away from here, for what was happening here would end in blood and he could not get the picture of the wounded Lang out of his mind, the side of the skull blown away, the uncontrolled rolling of his eyes as if he knew that death was close and yet could not be seen. The men in the ring were acting out an ancient ritual, far older than man himself, and one of them crouched like a monkey and then with a ferocious cry sprang up and smashed the side of his opponent's face with the callused heel of his right foot, and then as he spun around raked the side of his opponent's face

180

with the curved blade of the knife, a shallow incision that ran across one cheek and started blood pouring down onto the white robe and the sash.

Houghton, Clements thought, and he had identified Houghton's body, with the slash across the neck, the flesh a bloodless white. He lit a cigarette and looked at the crowd instead of the fighters, the men who yelled and moaned and exhorted and reflexively aped the movements of the fighters. And Clements studied Madeleine, who was excited by what was happening below her in the ring, and Wong, whose face was impassive, as if none of this mattered at all in the end. *Perhaps we're all the same after all*, Clements thought. The whole world was hooked by violence, paid money to witness it in the most serene of times. There was a roar from the crowd and Clements looked at the fighters again and realized that the battle was close to the finish, for the fighter in white had now been cut on the opposite side of the face as well, and his forearm had been slashed, and his tunic was literally drenched with blood. He was still on his feet, the knife held tightly in his hand, but his opponent moved around him like a whirling dervish, bringing another foot up to smash against the neck, unwounded, the only blood on him the blood of the sliced-up fighter.

Go down, goddammit, Clements thought, and now Wong's fighter was cut on the forehead with the blood forming a curtain over his eyes, blinding him, and he was vulnerable now. The next slash of the knife could half sever his head from his body but the gods were with him, for the next blow of his opponent's heel caught him on the temple, knocking the turban loose, sending it across the ring in a long spiral of cloth. Mercifully, the man went down and the crowd went wild. The doctors moved into the ring. Clements looked away. Wong drew the curtain, then sat down himself and said something in Chinese to Madeleine, who went to the bar to bring him a drink.

'Do you speak Chinese, Excellency?' he said to Clements.

'To some extent,' Clements said, trying to dispel the sight of blood from his mind, remembering the explosion on Bali, the blast which had literally ripped people in two. He could not afford to show what would be taken as weakness in the presence of this man.

'We are forbidden to speak Chinese in public,' Wong said. 'If the authorities had their way we would cease to be Chinese altogether and become immediately transformed into something more to their liking.' He accepted the wine from Madeleine, raised his glass to Clements. 'To your health, Mr Ambassador.'

Clements drank the toast. 'Explain something to me, if you will,' he said.

'Certainly, Excellency.'

'The fight. You gave outlandish odds on your man, who was obviously the weaker of the two. You dressed your man in a bad-luck color. At first I thought it was to make his opponent uneasy, but if that was the point, it didn't work.'

Wong smiled happily. 'It was my gift to the people who came here tonight to bet, but it is also good business. I own the building. I charge heavily for the right to come here and for the food and drink. I collect a percentage of all the bets regardless of how they are made. So tonight the men down there think "Wong has lost his mind. He has given us odds of five to one on a man who lost." But they will not have bet heavily against me because they know I don't like to lose money. They will have made small bets to test me out, and next week, if I have an entry, then they will bet against him very heavily, and I will make all the money back that I may have lost tonight.' He drank the rest of his wine, held out the glass to Madeleine to refill. 'Is not the principle of business the same in the United States?'

'In a strictly cynical sense, it would be,' Clements said, without judgment. 'But according to law, this would be classified as a confidence game.'

'A very good phrase,' Wong said. 'To manipulate confidence is to manipulate money and power.'

'I don't want to talk business,' Madeleine said. 'We came to find you, dear Uncle, to borrow your villa at Padang.'

'It is yours without asking, of course,' Wong said. 'But I don't believe the ambassador has come here just for that.'

'I had hoped for a frank conversation,' Clements said.

182

'That would suit me very well,' Wong said. He glanced at Madeleine. 'Do you wish her to stay or leave?'

'I have no objection to her staying.'

'If we are talking business, money to be made, then I will exclude her,' Wong said, without malice. 'She would think nothing of striking the deal before me, if she could.'

'Uncle,' she said, chiding.

'It's true,' he said. 'You know it is. Your mother was the same way. But if the ambassador wishes for you to stay, then you stay.'

'I want to talk about Minister Rooseno.'

'He's dead. It will do no harm.'

'He was skimming large sums of money from foreign aid, and other sources. No man is allowed to skim unless he is being bribed.'

'True.'

'But he was very fearful. He was planning to leave Indonesia even before I talked with him. So whoever had supported him had now become a threat. Do you know what kind of scheme he was involved in?'

'No.'

'Was there a middleman in the Chinese community who was handling Rooseno's deal, whatever it was?'

'No,' Wong said. He inserted a cigarette into an ivory holder. 'If there had been a middleman, then I could not talk about it.' He lit the cigarette, eyes narrowed against the sting of smoke. 'He would have been wise to use a middleman because then he would have been protected. But he was getting money from a source unknown to me and he received it directly, so there was no one to stand between him and his enemies.'

'Do you know what group is out to kill me?'

'No.'

'Not even rumors?'

'It's no secret that some of the ultranationalists would not be displeased if the American ambassador were to be killed. But I have heard nothing of any groups devoted to bringing that about.'

'Have you heard of "The Six Ravens"?'

Wong shrugged. 'Only vague rumors, nothing solid at all.

A company name, I've heard. But what they sell or deal in, I don't know.'

'One final question. What do you know of an attack on the Straits of Malacca?'

'By whom?'

'A terrorist group that calls itself "The Red Brigade".'

For a moment Wong's face lost its impassivity. 'Is this definite or a rumor?'

'Certain authorities believe it's definite.'

'Then you've done me a service by telling me about it,' Wong said. 'If there is an attack it will most certainly be disruptive and it will most certainly be blamed on the Chinese. There will be reprisals, new taxes and I may have to restructure some of my businesses. When will the attack take place?'

'I don't know. Soon, I would think.'

'Then I wish to show you something if you have an extra hour, Mr Ambassador.'

'Certainly,' Clements said.

'Am I to be excluded?' Madeleine said.

'No,' Wong said with a smile. 'You are my favorite niece. You may be of help here.' He picked up the telephone, spoke in Chinese. 'I have ordered a car brought around,' he said. 'I have driven with my niece behind the wheel before and I realize that life is very precious to me.'

The car was a Mercedes limousine with windows tinted to such a degree that no one could see in. Wong seated himself in the middle, the better to talk with Clements during the ride.

'You lay yourself open to misinterpretation by coming to see me,' he said.

'You're not dedicated to the overthrow of the Indonesian Government,' Clements said. 'You aren't listed on any collection of seditious organizations.'

'We Chinese abroad are like the Jews in many ways,' Wong said. 'It really makes no difference which government is in power. It is helpful to have a minority race in the country to serve as a scapegoat. Sometimes I think we are well paid just to take that role. It is curious to me sometimes that we should be the middlemen for the

Indonesians, who are notoriously poor at arranging their own financial grafts. They have the will and the avarice for it, but not the competence.'

'And it truly makes no difference to you who's in power?'

'No,' Wong said. He leaned forward, gave instructions to his driver, who turned off a main boulevard into a network of smaller streets, then he leaned back and lit another cigarette in his ivory holder. He sucked on the cigarette, deep in thought. 'Is the assassin Chinese, Excellency?'

'No.' Clements said.

'I thought not,' Wong said. 'The Chinese families here are like the ivory spheres which the carver makes to nest inside each other. They are all together and yet they are independent and can turn separately. I think I would have known, but there are outsiders working here now as well.'

They were in the dock area. Despite the heavy rain, Clements could smell saltwater and the sourness of bilges being pumped. The limousine pulled up to a warehouse next to the pier and the driver sounded his horn. A door swung open and the limousine pulled inside.

Clements was surprised at the size of the operation taking place here, for through one end of the dry-dock warehouse powerboats were being brought from the hold of a merchant ship, metal parts coated with Cosmoline, interior fittings packed in paper and cloth. And in a makeshift assembly line they were being cleaned up, outfitted with what looked like tripods on the fore and aft decks, being painted gray. Three boats were on stands, their twin diesels being tested, roaring away, filling the top half of the warehouse with dense black smoke. *Hatteras 48's*, Clements thought. A yacht for the upper middle class.

'You may wonder why I have brought you here,' Wong said.

'I am curious, yes,' Clements said.

'These powerboats were bought by me in Japan on a contract with the Indonesian Government,' Wong said. 'I paid a large amount in American dollars for each of them, including transportation from Yokohama. I have been hired to assemble, paint and fit each of them with bases for net mounts on the front and rear.' His voice was filled with irony. 'I am to be paid triple my money for each of these boats.'

'That's a nice profit, Mr Wong.'

'If you ever see a penny of it, Uncle,' Madeleine said.

'You are very bright for a woman.'

'And what would keep you from collecting?' Clements said.

'Any excuse at all would be enough,' Wong said. 'The official who ordered these boats doesn't intend to deliver them to the Indonesian Government. He will resell them one by one to fishermen in the islands farthest away from Java. But the Indonesian Government will pay for them. But suppose there is an incident in the Straits of Malacca. Then these boats would be confiscated, any deal wiped out, because I am Chinese. And I would face the loss of all my money.'

'There must be a way you can protect yourself,' Clements said.

Wong nodded. 'I offer you a business deal, Mr Ambassador. In return for one million dollars, you have a half interest in these boats. Within seven days, you get your money back, with an additional million and a half dollars.'

'And what would be your advantage in that?'

'Your name,' Wong said. 'It would be known that you had invested in a consortium to sell these boats to the Indonesian Government. In that fashion the boats would then be protected from confiscation.'

True, Clements thought sadly, and Wong's scheme would work perfectly were Clements to go along with it, for corruption was considered to be an integral part of life here and he would even gain esteem among the Indonesians if they knew he had made a deal which had increased his investment by one hundred and fifty percent. 'I'm sorry,' he said. 'I appreciate your position, Mr Wong, and I hope you appreciate mine. I have to go by the rules of my office here.'

'Certainly,' Wong said.

Madeleine squeezed Clements's arm, then turned to her uncle. 'May we talk in private, Uncle? I'm sure we will be excused.'

'Surely,' Clements said.

He watched the two of them walk away, toward the strip of black water under cover of the warehouse where a good-sized ship could be raised from the water. Madeleine was very animated, laying her hand on her uncle's arm, obviously wheedling. And at first Wong seemed to resist but gradually came around. She brushed her hair away from her face with the back of her hand. They returned to him.

'I'll have my car take you back to Madeleine's car,' Wong said. 'It has been a great privilege to meet you. I hope that you enjoy the house at Padang and I guarantee that you will not be bothered by anyone while you are there.'

'Thank you,' Clements said. 'I'm sorry I couldn't be of more help.'

Once they had reclaimed Madeleine's car from where they had left it, she drove through the waterlogged streets again, back toward her house, but she drove much more slowly than she had before. 'You're judging him,' she said. 'I don't like that.'

'I'm not judging anybody.'

'Then why didn't you allow him protection?'

'I don't know what you're talking about.'

'If you had given him even the slightest permission to use your name, even in conversation, his whole investment would be perfectly safe.'

'He may use my name anyway.'

'No, he's an honorable man.'

'So we're finally having our first argument,' he said. 'It was bound to come, sooner or later. Do you have the slightest idea what my government would do if I became a part of this?'

'If you're using what your country does as an example . . .'

'I took an oath when I accepted this post. There's no way I can get involved in making money out of representing the United States. And what's more important, there's no way I *want* to profit from it.'

'Because you can afford it.'

'Come off it. Your uncle is one of the richest men in Indonesia. You have your own fortune.'

'But he would put himself at risk in your behalf if you asked him to. Out of respect.'

187

'Only because I'm an ambassador,' Clements said. 'He's a private citizen, for God's sake. I can't back him personally without implying that the backing of the United States goes right along with it.'

'It's done in Indonesia all the time.'

'Because this is never-never land,' he said, angrily. 'Because here it's every man for himself, whether he's in or out of government. I don't see one ounce of loyalty that's not based on cash.'

'And I suppose that applies to me as well?'

He shook his head in the negative. 'No, that doesn't apply to you as well,' he said, his voice softer.

'And suppose I were in the same position. Would you back me?'

'Personally, yes,' he said. 'But there's no way I could give you the backing of the United States.'

'All right,' she said, as if suddenly she had reached a point where she did not want to talk about it anymore. She often did that, he realized, tracking along in a conversation until she reached some point in her mind when she was through with a subject and then she dropped it immediately. 'When do you want to go to Padang?'

'In the morning, I think.'

'Will you spend the night with me?'

'Yes.'

But there was now a breach between them, not on her part, he realized, for she had the facility of closing off an unhappiness through an act of will and moving on as if it had never happened. She was doing exactly that with him now. At her house she gave him a kiss and went to take a bath while he went downstairs to the room that had been arranged for him where he could make his telephone calls.

He needed the time to himself to reconcile the difference between what he professed to be and what he had actually become. He poured himself a drink, sat down in a leather chair next to the telephone in the darkness, listened to the purr of the air conditioner and the heavy drumming of the rain. He considered himself to be a humane man and yet he had stood in Wong's office and tolerated as fierce a display of savagery as he had ever witnessed as if he condoned it.

188

And of course Madeleine could not understand the position he had taken with her uncle because she saw things from a totally different perspective and could not understand why he refused to use his personal status as ambassador to help her uncle or make further money for himself. He finished the first drink, poured himself another and was suddenly struck by the force of his own naîveté, the distortion of reality by his own idealism.

He clicked on the lamp above the table, dialed the embassy and asked to be put through to Kemper. He gave Kemper the number he was speaking from, asked to be called back on the scrambler.

He picked up the telephone again at the first ring. 'What's up?' Kemper said.

'I'm not sure,' Clements said. 'I'm going to Padang first thing in the morning.'

'I think that's an excellent idea. Can I have somebody pack for you?'

'No need,' Clements said. 'but I need to talk to you tonight.'

'Do you want me to come by there?'

'You know where I am, then?'

'Of course. Yes, sir.'

'Even the special door, I suppose.'

'It's my business to know these things.'

'How long?'

'Say, fifteen minutes.'

'I'll be waiting for you.'

It was twenty minutes before Kemper arrived, tapping lightly on the wood of the door with his knuckles. Clements turned out the lamp before he opened the door and Kemper slipped inside, then stood in the darkened room and looked back out through a crack in the door at the curtain of rain, which made it almost impossible to see anything in the darkness except an abstract smear of lights as cars and trucks edged through the rising water. Finally he closed the door and Clements clicked on the lamp.

Kemper was soaked through, despite the raincoat which he removed and hung on a rack near the door. Clements went into the bathroom, came out to toss him a towel, then poured two stiff drinks.

'Were you followed?' Clements said.

Kemper toweled his hair, wiped his face and hands dry, then picked up the glass. 'I picked up a tail at the embassy but I think I lost him a long time back.' He drank half the glass. 'It's an excellent plan for you to be leaving now,' he said. 'Our friend Sangre-Lomax is still in town.'

'How can you be sure?'

'The police staked out the *losmen* near the train station where he was staying when he shot Lang in the vague hope that he would come back again. I personally didn't think he'd show because he had switched to Lomax, not the type of character for a place like that. The police finally gave up, and then yesterday afternoon they got a call from the proprietor. Some abusive son of a bitch who claimed to be Australian wanted to register and the proprietor and his wife both named the man as Sangre. They rented the room all right and the minute Sangre-Lomax was out of sight they called the police. But by the time the police arrived S-L had realized what had happened and had left again. He didn't come back.'

'Tell me something,' Clements said. 'I'm no longer a logical target for him. Anything I know is bound to be passed on by now.'

'If you try to get logical in a matter like this, you'll get screwed up,' Kemper said. 'There's a code with people like Sangre-Lomax. If he took a contract to kill you, he missed it. Now, even if there's no practical reason for continuing the chase, he would have to do it to preserve his reputation.'

'I'm willing to stay if you think we can bag him,' Clements said.

'Use yourself as bait?' Kemper said, startled.

'Something like that.'

'No,' Kemper said. 'This man's a real pro, crazy as they come, but he knows his business. You set yourself up as bait for him and he'll blow you away without a blink of an eyelid.'

'All right. Then have the press secretary make a statement that I'm on vacation in Australia.'

'New Zealand,' Kemper said. 'I gave him a ring before I came over. I will need to tell him how long you're going to be gone.'

'Make it two weeks,' Clements said. 'As of the first of next week, I'm going to show up at the oil meeting in Bangkok.'

'Fine,' Kemper said, finishing his drink, declining another. 'Now, what's this urgent business you wanted to talk about?'

'The Straits of Malacca,' Clements said. 'How much credence do you give that story?'

'I'd rate it as a strong possible,' he said. 'Why?'

'It may be nothing,' Clements said. 'But I think you should check it out.' He told Kemper about the evening with Wong, the warehouse and the boats. 'They're supposed to be one big scam by somebody in the Indonesian Government who's going to sell them off as fishing boats.'

'Then what's the problem?'

'The welders were putting up superstructures fore and aft,' Clements said. 'It didn't occur to me until I called you that these appurtenances had nothing to do with nets. I believe they were gun mounts.'

'You're familiar with gun mounts?'

'I saw them in Vietnam. These would take fifty-caliber machine guns.'

Kemper grimaced thoughtfully. 'Wouldn't Wong know the difference between a gun mount and a net hoist?'

'If he knew they were gun mounts, he sure as hell wouldn't have shown them to me.'

'And where was this dry dock?'

Clements told him. 'I want you to check it out without causing any difficulties for Wong.'

Kemper shrugged. 'They may be illegal as hell and they may be an attack force, but I don't think they're headed for the straits. They wouldn't be worth a damn up there. They'd be visible as hell.'

'But you'll check it out?'

'Sure.'

'Then I'll let you get back to a dry place. I'm sorry to have hauled you out on a night like this.'

'Perfectly all right. One further item. The Russian ambassador.'

'Please have Lucy call his office. Let him know I had to make a run to New Zealand but that I'll see him in Bangkok. He'll be at the oil meeting.'

Kemper put on his raincoat. 'Good night, then,' he said, shaking the ambassador's hand. 'Have a safe trip.'

'Thank you.'

Bullshit, Kemper thought as he slogged out into the rain. He climbed into his car, feeling disgruntled. He could not help but compare his situation with that of the ambassador, who had called him out in the middle of the night to a cozy suite of rooms furnished with antiques that a lifetime of Kemper's salary could never buy. He felt a little guilty that this comparison should cross his mind at all. Clements was ambassador, after all, and Clements had the money and the clout. And at any time that Clements wished, he could simply opt out of the whole situation and go home, leaving Kemper to deal with the crazies of the world.

He drove back to the embassy very carefully so his engine would not be drowned out, keeping an eye on the rearview mirror for any sign that he was being tailed. But he saw nothing out of line. He made it safely through the gates and back to his quarters, where he stripped down and dried off before he poured himself a cup of coffee and set out to work.

The naval attaché was a Commander Rhymes. Kemper occasionally played golf with him and knew full well that this physically trim and land-locked sailor was working naval intelligence and trying to pump Kemper for any information he could feed back to his superiors in Washington. For that reason Kemper had no hesitation about ringing Rhymes in the middle of the night. But Rhymes was not asleep. And he seemed pleased to hear Kemper's voice.

'I need some information,' Kemper said.

'Anything.'

'What kind of patrol boats does the Indonesian Navy use?'

'Standard cutters,' Rhymes said. 'I think, as a matter of

fact, they buy cutters from us, the same kind that our Coast Guard uses.'

'How about harbor patrol?'

'They don't have any harbor patrols as such. It's all a part of their Navy.'

'Any particular kind of boat?'

'Runabouts, I believe. Nothing in particular.'

'And how are they armed?'

'Nothing heavy,' Rhymes said. 'The Navy's going in for helicopters for any harbor enforcement. But if you ask me, they wouldn't have much need for harbor patrol as such. Smuggling is endemic and smugglers pay off the locals. There doesn't seem to be any enforceable traffic rule except watch your own ass because no other skipper will.' His voice was heavy with curiosity. 'What's going on?'

'I'll make a trade with you,' Kemper said. 'I need some information and I realize that you have to send it back to the DOD. But I'll need a lead time of twenty-four hours in case there's a leak from your end or a feedback.'

'All right,' Rhymes said. 'You have your twenty-four.'

'I want to know if any agency of the Indonesian Government has ordered any forty-eight-foot Hatteras twin-diesel pleasure craft to be converted to harbor or river patrol work.'

'Hold on,' Rhymes said. 'I'm taking notes.' Kemper could hear the whisper of pen against paper. 'Twin diesels. All right.'

'If not, I want to know if an Indonesian official has made such an order on official requisition with a view to selling them privately.'

'That'll take a little longer to find out. When are these boats due to be delivered?'

'Soon.'

'Give me an hour for preliminaries,' Rhymes said. 'Who knows? I just might get lucky.'

He severed the connection just as the telephone buzzed again. It was Oberlin, a puzzled Oberlin. 'Are you out of your tree?' Oberlin said. 'Did you really send Girl Friday to Singapore and Medan?'

'That's correct.'

'She signaled from Singapore. Said to let you know she found some special computer material.'

'My God. She leave a number?'

'No. She'll check in from Medan in the morning. What's that all about?'

'I'll brief you later. Right now, I want some digging.'

'At two in the morning?'

'That will make it a convenient time in the States. Get the Indonesian desk at Langley. I want simulations on an attack on the Straits of Malacca. I want to know if a bevy of Hatteras forty-eights, properly armed, would constitute an effective force.'

'I can give you a negative on that right now,' Oberlin said. 'Indonesia has added a half-dozen attack helicopters to their patrol fleet in Sumatra. That gives them seventeen in total with enough firepower, rockets, heavy stuff to blow your forty-eights out of the water.'

'Check it anyway.'

'All right. But who's going to handle coordination since Girl Friday's out roaming?'

'I have a personnel request in to Bangkok. Until then, clear everything through me.'

'All right.'

Oberlin checked back first. By some miracle he had been put right through to Operations and found the one man who had done most of the simulations on the Straits of Malacca. 'A wasted call,' Oberlin said. 'He confirms everything I told you. He's run computer simulations a dozen times with the small-boat option. It doesn't make any difference where they're launched. They are spotted within five minutes and it takes the Indonesians no more than seven minutes to get all their gunship helicopters into the air. Now, even if all of the Indonesian gunships were on the wrong side of the island, they would still blow your forty-eights out of the water long before any concerted attack could be put together.'

'Thank you,' Kemper said.

He dozed in his chair until dawn. He did not dream. He was awakened by Commander Rhymes calling back. 'I've gotten lucky,' Rhymes said. 'It seems that there is consternation and confusion in the Indonesian ranks.'

'What else is new?'

'There were some boats ordered but no one knows why. The Navy's not phasing them in.'

'Why not ask the man who ordered them?'

'It would take a good psychic to do that. Minister Rooseno ordered them. A source in the military says there's some bickering going on about who will get possession when they come in.'

'*When* they come in,' Kemper said. 'Did your source have a delivery date?'

'No.'

'Many thanks.'

'Wait a minute. We had a deal. What's going on?'

'A false alarm,' Kemper said. 'I thought those boats were being assembled for an attack on shipping going through the Straits of Malacca.'

'You're putting me on.'

'Nope. That was the story. Is it still raining outside?'

'It stopped about an hour ago. It's due to start again anytime.'

He stood up, stretched. He would have to go out to the docks to examine this shipment for himself, this collection of small craft ordered by a man who had become no more than disassembled particles on the island of Bali, quite dead. Kemper was stiff from sleeping in the chair.

It was raining again by the time he reached his car and pulled out of the embassy gates onto the boulevard, but the temporary respite during the night had been enough to allow the water level in the streets to subside. And he thought as he faced the suicidal traffic of the early morning, the heavy trucks hurtling at breakneck speeds with drivers unable to see any better than he could, that as chief of station he should have somebody he could send out on a mission like this. Were his job even remotely similar to what Langley considered it to be, he would not be doing this himself.

But his only alternative was to assign Oberlin or Wiznoski to contact one of the locals in their net and have *them* infiltrate this dry dock-warehouse and make a report, and ten would bring you dog shit that the report they turned in would be totally useless, because they wouldn't know a damn thing about powerboats and armaments. No, it was far simpler to do it himself, to drive straight up to the building and have a look-see, because a white man in a business suit might represent money which could be pried loose under the right circumstances. He also represented power, and he wanted to look at the bills of lading for the boats and a little chat with the headman of the crew that was making modifications on them.

He was more alert by the time he reached the harbor. He threaded his way through the swarm of trucks coming in to load up at the fish market where a part of the fishing fleet had just pulled in.

He wondered about Tommi's discovery, certainly something of significance or she wouldn't have described the computer material as 'special.' That could wait. He was pleased to have her out of it for a while. As he was looking for a parking place he made up his mind that he was going to request a senior analyst position back at Langley right away and go home. And to hell with Tommi's ambitions in the field. He would talk her out of that nonsense, get her a spot where her brain power could be utilized. He would take her with him and marry her and have a house in Virginia. If he played the political scene right (and that would happen by not playing politics at all) they could both put in regular hours and leave the shit work in the field to some poor bastard who fancied that there would be romance or drama inherent in sitting up all night and then slogging out to have a look at boats that were not going to fit into any logical part of the scheme of things.

He spotted the dry dock-warehouse but could not find a parking place anywhere close, so finally he squeezed his car in between two trucks a couple of hundred yards down the way. He locked the door and sloshed through the standing water to the warehouse, soaking his feet. He found a side door, let himself in. He blinked in consternation. He patted his pockets until he found the sheet on which he had written the information gleaned from Clements. This was the address all right, the right building, for there were not two such buildings in this area, but there were no powerboats, no assembly line, no great bustle of activity, only a junk-type fishing boat with a broken mast which sat in the middle of the cavernous space, its hull still wet from being pulled out of the water, undergoing the scrutiny of perhaps six workers who were examining leaky seams in the wooden planking.

Kemper walked across the warehouse, heels clicking on the floor. The men saw him coming, fell into silence. 'I want to speak to the headman,' Kemper said in Indonesian. A spare man with a sarong wrapped around his waist stepped out, bowed.

'How may I help you?'

'Where are the boats that were in this place last night?'

The headman looked thoughtful, confused, befuddled. Kemper had to control his temper, which would cause any sense of cooperation, however minor, to shrivel immediately into nothing. *The Indonesians must study this goddamned expression of innocent bewilderment*, Kemper thought. *So many of them are expert at it.*

'This was the only boat that was here last night,' the headman said.

'And what time did you lift it out of the water?'

'Quite early, sir. My workers are for the most part Muslim, and they were at worship, so it was necessary for me to bring in other workers.'

'None of whom are here this morning, I take it.'

'True, sir. Since my regular Muslims are at work today.'

Kemper looked around the floor. He touched a section of heavy metal tubing about six inches in diameter with his foot. He shifted scraps of metal. There had been an assembly line here last night, he was sure of that. He looked up toward the tall ceiling, at the haze.

'What kind of engine does the junk have?' he said.

'A wretched diesel, sir.'

'Why wretched?'

'It has not worked for the owner in a week. He had been operating under sail only, and now he has a split mast as well as a leaky hull. So we will repair his engine while his boat is here.'

'I see. And you haven't tried the engine since you've had it in here?'

'There would be no sense in that, since the owner took the engine apart while he was at sea.'

He turned his back on the man, began to go through the pieces of scrap discarded by the welders. A cold chill passed through his blood. Jesus, he had been blind. He should have remembered from the short time he had spent studying warfare in Southeast Asia. This was a red herring on a grand scale.

He stood by the door and lit a cigarette, thinking it through, looking out at the street. He was certain now that he was being watched. That would have to be a part of it so they could gauge his acceptance of what they wanted him to believe. But how would they work it? That was the important question. How could he reassure them that he did indeed believe that the boats that were here last night were to be used in the Malacca Straits? He could afford no missteps now. He would have to put himself in their minds, think as *they* thought.

Urgency. Yes. Since the boats were gone, he was supposed to assume that the boats were on their way north. So he would use a telephone, the closest available. There was one at the fish market down the street and he walked at a brisk pace, past the piles of lifeless fish with marble eyes. There was a man already standing at the telephone, talking about the price of shark. Kemper finished his cigarette, feigned impatience which had reached the breaking point. He fished a thousand-rupiah note from his pocket, folded it and held it in front of the man's face. 'Official business,' Kemper said. 'I need the telephone.'

The man nodded, accepted the money without hesitancy and backed away, leaving Kemper with the phone. Kemper severed the connection. He put his money in and dialed the embassy and asked to talk with Commander Rhymes.

'Commander Rhymes here.'

'This is Kemper. Don't say anything. Just listen. I'm making this call for the sake of appearances. I'll talk to you later.'

He severed the connection before Rhymes had a chance to

utter one question, then he fumbled through his cigarettes until he found a dry one and lit it. The question now was how he was going to prove a hunch which might turn out to be of the wildhair variety. If he was wrong, the wags at Langley would make this another of those deadly little anecdotes about the fuck-ups in the field who dealt with nonexistent ghosts under the bed while the live crooks were stealing the silver.

He walked back to his car. He yanked the door open with the distinct feeling that something was awry, but he did not know what. It was only when he turned the key in the ignition that he knew what it was that disturbed him. For he had left the car locked and now it was unlocked. Only a brief flash of realization before the bomb went off beneath the car and he felt himself being hurled through the door, which was blown off by the blast, and in the shock, in the craziness of the fireball and the knowledge that his own flesh was burning, there was one small kernel of sanity within him that remained intact, one clear bit of information that clung to what was left of his mind. *Gasoline was burning his skin and water would not quench it*. He stumbled down the street, toward the pile of fish, a blazing human torch, until an Indonesian fisherman threw a tarp over him. Kemper struggled to be free of it and fought so wildly that it took three men to wrap him up and extinguish the flames. And then, lying in the water, looking up, he thought he saw the face of the man in the photograph, Sangre-Lomax, a blur as the face looked down at him and moved on. And then Kemper closed his eyes and surrendered himself to what he thought was death.

Right up my alley, Oberlin thought with mixed feelings as he set up a small office in the hospital right down the corridor from where Kemper lay close to death. He had been trained in technical work in the beginning and his mind functioned best on those small finite problems which required analysis. Now he sat with diagrams and photographs and police reports spread in order across the desk, recreating the bomb which had demolished Kemper's car. It was not the usual kind of booby trap at all, the sticks

199

of dynamite which were bundled together and affixed to the chassis below the driver's seat so that when the ignition key was turned the spark set the bomb off. In that case, considering the clearance of the chassis from the cement, the ground itself tended to act as a resonant base to amplify the explosive waves upward and the person who turned the key was literally blown to pieces.

But this bomb was different. It was a combination of plastic explosives and napalm which had been placed at the very front of the trunk compartment, inside the car itself. Then a hole had been drilled to allow the exit of the wire, which ran beneath the chassis and up to the ignition. It was almost as if this bomber had done twice the work of an ordinary demolitions man in the hope of accomplishing some strange result that eluded Oberlin altogether. The bomb had no logic to it. It exploded the gas tank and set the interior of the car ablaze with a mixture of napalm and gasoline, blew all four doors out and tossed Kemper out as well. But at least a third of the bomb's energy was directed downward into the flooded parking lot with such a searing blast of heat that the water was vaporized and turned into a cloud of steam.

It was as if Kemper's destruction was a secondary goal.

He waited at the hospital to see if there was anything he could do. Finally, when the doctors told him that the odds were fifty-fifty and there was no point in his being there, he checked to make sure that a Marine sentry was on duty and then went back to the embassy. He sat down at a typewriter and drafted a full report, keeping one ear out for the sounds of movement in the hallway which would announce the arrival of someone from Communications with the answer to the coded question he had sent to Bangkok:

COS WOUNDED IN BOMBING ATTACK.
PROGNOSIS FOR RECOVERY IS ABOUT FIFTY-FIFTY.
WHO WILL TAKE CHARGE THIS STATION?

There was sound in the hallway and the door opened, but it was not Communications at all. Tommi stood there, ashen-faced, drawn, weary beyond redemption. She put her purse down, poured herself a cup of coffee, put on her reading glasses.

'I just got in from Medan,' she said. 'I haven't been to the hospital yet. Is he still alive?'

'Yes.'

'Then brief me.' She fumbled through her bag for a cigarette, lit it as she sat down and took the typed sheet which he handed her. She shifted into a numb objectivity as she read about thermal units and firing angles. There was no passion in these reports. Kemper was not called Kemper, he was referred to as 'subject.' 'When subject turned the ignition key . . .' 'Subject was hurled through the left front door . . .'

She put the paper down. 'What was Kemper doing?'

He was about to explain when Wiznoski came into the room, looking damp and dour, taking off his wet coat and hanging it on a rack, his expression temporarily blank as he wiped the moisture off his glasses with a handkerchief and then put them back in place. He looked to Oberlin, pulled a paper from his pocket. 'I passed by Communications and they asked me to give you this.'

Oberlin looked at it, the cable from Bangkok.

It had one word on it:

WIZNOSKI.

Oberlin handed it back to him. 'I asked them for a new chain of command,' he said with relief. 'It seems that you're it.'

'Command of what?' Wiznoski said, more a rhetorical question than an actual one. 'Well, we had better sort this out. I've been with the police, such as they are.'

'And?' Tommi said.

'They watched the man wire the car, as a matter of fact. He unlocked the trunk with a key, they believed, and then a local foot patrolman came over as he was fumbling through the trunk and drilling a hole. The constable asked what he was doing and the man smiled and said he was fixing his car so it wouldn't drown out in the high water. The policeman asked if he could help and the man thanked him profusely but said not, even whistled while he worked.'

'Sangre-Lomax?' Oberlin said.

'Undoubtedly. Although the description was that of an American in his thirties, well-dressed, speaking faultless Indonesian. Introduced himself to the constable, as a matter of fact. The constable believes he gave the name Jackson.'

'And what happened to this "Jackson"?' Tommi said, with a little too much force, as if it took everything she had to hold herself in control.

'He wandered around taking pictures,' Wiznoski said. 'By the time the explosion happened, he had disappeared.'

'I repeat,' Tommi said to Oberlin, 'what was Kemper doing?'

And Oberlin made his report, the business of all the scenarios of an attack on the straits involving small craft. Wiznoski shook his head. 'He was at a dry dock looking for a fleet of small craft,' Wiznoski said. 'There weren't any goddamned small craft.'

Tommi stood up, took off her glasses and put them back in her purse. 'I'm going to the hospital to be with him,' she said.

'Not for long,' Wiznoski said. 'I'll have an assignment for you just as soon as I can get things organized.'

'I'll be at the hospital, Wiznoski,' she said without passion. 'That's my post.'

And she left the room.

He drifted, mind not spinning, no, no spiral motion, no whorl, but a gentle undulation like a sea swell. Occasionally he knew that he was in a room and that there were doctors hovering over him, one doctor's face that he should recognize, did not, and wanted to apologize for not knowing, except that for the time being he was beyond the place where he had the power to make words or to receive them, and then he was caught up in the surge of his own bloodstream again. Somebody was beside him, somebody he did indeed recognize, Tommi, and they sat on the bank of a lake, on the grass, an Indian summer day, with the sunlight so intense on the water that it hurt his eyes, and the trees beginning to turn color with the approach of winter, and he could feel her fingers interlaced with his own. But there was something awry, something he had to say to her but could not bring into focus, some message to pass. He closed his eyes and tried to communicate it to her without words, but when he looked at her again, she still had the dreamy look on her face. She could not read his mind. And the surface of the lake indeed caught fire and the trees were really burning with a sudden heat so intense he flashed with it, fled from it into a dark part of himself where it was cool and where he felt nothing.

She was allowed into the room, wearing a gauze mask, and despite the sterile atmosphere, the faint smell of antiseptic, she was sickened by the odor of scorched flesh as he lay naked on the bed, his body covered with war zones where the flames had turned him to cooked meat with strips of flesh and skin hanging to be cleansed away. His face itself was charred on one side. His hair had been burned away, as if a blowtorch had swept over him. She was aware that the doctor was speaking to her, an American named Phillips who had spent his whole life in Indonesia and served the English-speaking embassies.

'It's going to be touch and go,' he said. 'On the one hand, he suffered a trauma which would have been a mortal blow to most people. But he's one tough cookie.'

And just how many times have you rehearsed this one-tough-cookie speech to do it so perfectly?

It was not the doctor's fault that Kemper lay here hooked up to IV's and catheters and oxygen tubes. Nobody's fault except the son of a bitch who was still wandering around Jakarta. And she would like to have that bastard for a while, just her, no backup, and she would show him what true savagery was, the great blood-thirsty wanting of true revenge.

'I want to sit with him,' she said to the doctor. 'In case he says anything, I want to be there to hear it.'

'He's not going to say anything.'

'Just in case . . .'

'I don't think . . .' the doctor began, but she cut him off with the unanswerable dictum:

'He is Central Intelligence Chief of Station here, Doctor. I am on his staff. If you want to get into chapter and verse of the regulations, then we'll do it. But I don't think either of us has the energy to fight that particular battle.'

The doctor shrugged. 'It won't do any harm, I guess,' he said.

'Thank you,' she said. And she proceeded to pull a metal chair with a stiff plastic cushion up next to the head of the bed where she talked into the ear that was not burned, a low, soothing voice. 'All right, darling,' she said. 'I'm here to keep you company and whether you can hear me or not is beside the point. Because someplace inside you, you're going to know that I'm here and that I'm talking to you, and that you're not going to give up. I don't even know whether you can swim, you know that? I don't even know whether you can keep yourself on top of the water but you are sure as hell going to float now. You are not going to go under because if you did you would miss a fine life with me. I'm not your common, ordinary person, you know, because when I decided to love you, then you really didn't have a chance. And I found out what scared Lang. Oh, you would have been proud of me, the way I worked it. I pretended to be a government employee in Singapore, making a survey, and I tracked down the Chinese girl who was operating the computer that day. She wasn't fired – they were much too shrewd for that – they promoted her and moved her to a branch bank at Kranji, on the southern bank of the Johore Straits.'

She proceeded to give him all the details, keeping up a stream of words, of sounds, emotions, silent only when the nurses came to change dressings or bottles or give him another shot.

'The girl's name was Mary Toh, a pretty young Chinese girl with straight hair and a round face, the most anxious eyes I think I've ever seen. I told her I was making a survey of malfunctioning computers and she broke into tears. She was apologizing because she had caused so much trouble, but when she stopped crying, she remembered that last day at the bank and told me about it in elaborate detail.

'Photographic memory, dear. Talk about luck. When I asked her what file she had accessed, she *knew*. Instantly. It was an Austrian firm with a name in German that she could pronounce but couldn't translate. So she asked one of her fellow workers who happened to speak German what the name meant.

"'The Six Ravens,'" Tommi said into Kemper's ear. 'An export company located in Vienna. Mary Toh rattled off the contents of the screen, including most of the names and numbers. The payment of specific sums to Indonesian bureaucrats, Rooseno among them, cargo fees, the payment for munitions, explosives. There was a mention of some American oil companies, targets, I suppose, maybe owners of the tankers, I don't know, and she hadn't bothered to make sense out of any of it. All just names and figures to her, but poor Lang made sense out of it. No wonder he got hysterical. The funding of a terrorist revolution, and Americans would be high on the enemies list.'

She stopped talking abruptly. She imagined that he had spoken. She sat upright, listening, and she saw his lips move, a coming together as if he were thirsty, but it was not a random movement, nothing automatic. He was forming a word.

'Yes,' she whispered into his ear, watching his tortured mouth. 'I'm here. If you have a word for me, then give it to me and I'll do my damnedest to understand.'

'F-f-f-f.' Lower lip brushing the edge of the upper teeth, an exhalation of breath. She waited, her own breath suspended for fear that the word would be so faint that her breathing would override it. 'Fiiind,' he said.

'Yes,' she whispered. 'Find. I understand what you said. Find what?'

'Clem,' he said, then sucked in air as if he had used up all he had.

'Do you mean "Clements"? Do you want me to find the ambassador?'

No acknowledgement of yes or no. 'Me . . .'

'Yes. You what?'

'Melong,' he said.

'I don't understand,' she said, trying not to become frantic, but he was slipping away from her, she could feel it. 'Did you say "Melong"? Is that a place? Is that what you want me to tell him?'

But he had fled again, scurried away into the darkness from the great belching of flames which covered the earth.

She panicked, pressed the button for the nurse, jabbed it savagely and a nurse came scurrying into the room. 'He's dying, goddammit,' Tommi said. 'Do something. I don't want him to die.'

And the calm brown face was unperturbed as the stethoscope sought an unburned place on which to land and listen. 'No, missy,' the nurse said. 'Not dead. Sleeping well. He be all right.'

'Yes,' Tommi said, and she nodded and contained her own hysteria. She was torn now. She knew the ambassador had left the country, New Zealand she'd heard, and it would take time to track him down, and in the meantime Kemper could die, just slip away when she was not here with him. And she could spend the time to get a message to the ambassador which would mean absolutely nothing, the ravings of a man who was not cognizant enough to know his own name.

She stood up, legs stiff, mind tired. She had no choice. He had told her to find the ambassador. She would do it.

8

Wong's villa on Sumatra reminded Clements of the villas he knew in the South of France, built with cool marble terraces and splendid rooms overlooking the sea. Where the Chinese businessman had found the white marble, how he had shipped it here to this rocky jungle coast south of Padang and built this palace was something of an engineering marvel. But Clements was grateful for it. Here, in this temporary respite, he had time to think, to follow the path down a steep cliff to a virgin beach of white sand and sit watching the sea birds. Or if he was so inclined he could hike another trail to the east of the villa which, after a short stretch of garden, became the densest jungle he had ever seen, replete with screeching monkeys, rare tropical flowers and an atmosphere of pure oxygen.

He was aware of Wong's security force, of the men he rarely saw who patrolled the edges of the jungle and maintained the spur road off the main highway which led to this retreat. There was no telephone here, no television, and his only link with the outside world came from the telegraph office at Padang where any message directed to Mr Wolfe was picked up by one of Wong's men and brought down by jeep. And Clements sent out his messages in the same way, coding them himself first. He could not cut himself off completely, for there were parts of his duties which continued wherever he happened to be.

For the most part Madeleine understood. And while he sat at a table with a portable typewriter, laboriously pounding out a position paper, she sat in her bikini on the open terrace, in his direct line of vision, a broad-brimmed hat on her head while she painted a seascape with little talent but much enjoyment. At other times, when she felt too ignored, she sunned herself on the terrace wearing nothing at all, and he realized with some amusement that she was posing.

But he had to be prepared for the meeting in Bangkok at which he would be an unofficial delegate, along with the ambassadors from the Soviet Union, the United Kingdom, Australia and Canada. They would all serve, Clements reasoned, as witnesses to the planned robbery that the Southeast Asian countries would perpetrate on the foreign oil companies. Inviting the ambassadors was a shrewd move on the part of these countries, because their presence would add a certain legitimacy to the proceedings.

The whole conference was to be held at the Empress Hotel, that grand doyen of hotels in Bangkok, right on the Chao Phraya river, where there would be fireworks and the tribute of the priests, a grand dinner with champagne flowing like water. By the time it was over, the whole complexion of the oil business in Southeast Asia would have changed.

He did not plan to attend many of the meetings in Bangkok. Instead, it would be the perfect spot for what would probably be the last of his intensive talks with Sergei on neutral territory, at least three days when the press would be interested in the financial drama taking place in the hotel's meeting rooms and leave him to have his conferences with Sergei undisturbed. The subject this time would be the position of their two countries in Southeast Asia following the realignment of the oil-producing countries here.

He spent a whole morning coding his dispatch, which would be sent by the noon runner from the telegraph office in Padang to Jakarta and thence to Washington. He attached a rider to the document requiring that it be sent from Jakarta without being decoded, so that Washington would reply straight to the Empress Hotel in Bangkok, where his staff had already booked a half floor of rooms overlooking the river. He would probably not be staying there. He had decided to hold his meetings with the Russian ambassador at G. D.'s estate, which had the advantage of strict privacy.

At noon the Chinese dispatch carrier came crunching up the graveled driveway on his motorcycle and delivered a sheaf of coded messages. He managed a half-military salute to Clements as he took the envelope with the Jakarta dispatch and was off again in a cloud of dust.

Clements walked back into the house, into the coolness of the marble dining room with filigreed walls that allowed the sea breezes access to all sections of the villa. Madeleine was arranging flowers in the middle of the dining table, which had already been set for two.

'Would you like a drink before luncheon?' she said.

'I'm sorry,' he said. 'I'm really not hungry and I need to get these dispatches decoded.'

She put her arms around his neck, kissed him lightly. 'You don't want to ruin my surprise, do you?'

'What surprise?'

'I can't tell you that or it wouldn't be a surprise at all, now would it? Sit down at the table.' She pulled out his chair. 'Humor me. It's something very rare and you must have it at precisely the right time or it's not any good.'

'All right,' he said, smiling. 'Does anybody ever refuse you anything?'

'Not often.' And as he sat, she rang a silver bell and a line of servants moved in from the kitchen, bearing a platter of fruits and a pot of black tea, and a large silver platter of a substance which looked terrible, like an island of overdone meat in a sea of gravy. It smelled delicious. 'It's *rendang padang*,' she said, 'a roast of buffalo meat which has to cook for days in coconut milk. I had them begin this when I learned we were coming up here.' She directed the waiters to serve the master of the house, and as the meat was carved and put on his plate, Clements discovered a ravenous appetite.

'It's actually quite good,' he said, after he had tasted it. 'I'll have to arrange to have this served to the Russian ambassador sometime.'

She picked at her food, finally abandoned it altogether and rested her chin on her laced fingers, studying him. The time had come and she knew it, and she concealed her nervousness. For her spirit mother had not come with her to

Padang, leaving her to handle this situation herself, and she fell back on the example of her Uncle Wong, who at one time, when Madeleine had just come to Indonesia, had so provoked a younger cousin that the boy finally exploded and cursed Uncle Wong, coming back the next day to apologize, abjectly touching his forehead to the floor. And Uncle Wong had forgiven him but he had never favored the younger cousin again or put him in a position of power. For the younger cousin, under pressure, had shown the truth of what he was. And now Madeleine was about to provoke Clements and she was afraid of what he might do.

'Would you answer a question for me?' she said.

'If I can.' The buffalo meat was spicy, hot, and the black tea with a hint of citrus in it cooled his mouth. He knew her well enough to know that this was not a random conversation, that she had planned the meal as an excuse to get his full attention for a while. 'Now, what's on your mind?' He blotted his mouth with a linen napkin, settled back with his cup of tea.

'It's more of a situation than a question.' She took a cigarette from her purse and no sooner had she raised it to her lips than a servant was there with a light. 'I want to make a trade with you,' she said. 'I've done something you won't like at all. It may make you angry. But at the same time I can tell you something you don't know, information you couldn't get any other way except through me. I'll give you the information on the condition that you don't get angry.'

'I can't promise you that,' he said. 'You'll just have to risk it.'

She tapped ashes into a tray. 'Would you like to know who ordered the boats, what they're to be used for?'

'How do you know? Where did you get the information?'

'From my Chinese family. It's never been said in so many words. But we all *know* such things.'

He looked at her evenly. 'If your family is involved, I'm not sure that I want you to tell me,' he said. 'If I have to take any action, I don't want to see your family hurt.'

'I have to take that chance,' she said, her eyes watching his face for any change of expression. 'In my Chinese family it is said that my Indonesian Uncle Rooseno was actively involved in the smuggling trade. He is supposed to have made money off bringing things into Bali and other tourist centers that the government didn't know about. Mostly American cigarettes, some marijuana, other things like that. But he didn't manage it by himself. There were a number of men in the government who were involved with him. They planned to use the boats to pick up goods from ships at sea and run them ashore. But when my Uncle Rooseno was killed, then my Uncle Wong got very nervous. Because there could be a fight over who now owned the boats and they might take them from him without paying him.'

'Then your Uncle Wong knew all along.'

'Yes.'

'Is that what I'm supposed to be angry about, that he lied to me?'

'Let's just say he didn't tell you everything he knew,' she said.

'Let's just say he led me to believe certain things,' Clements said. And as he sat across from her it suddenly occurred to him that he had become a victim of his own presumptions and that he should have known better. For as intimate as he had been with Madeleine, as long as he had spent in native cultures, he had made the basic mistake of assuming he knew how she thought, her mental processes, and by projection, the way her uncle functioned.

She puffed on the cigarette, stalling, for now she felt the presence of her spirit mother, goading her, pointing out the signs of beginning anger in this man, the slight flush beneath the skin of his face, the way he placed his fork down on the plate. But she could not stop short. 'Do you remember when he offered you the boats and you turned him down?'

'Of course.'

'I drew him to one side and I offered him half a million for a share of the boats. He accepted it immediately, of course.'

'What does that have to do with me?'

'There's another question that comes first. If I were to marry you, I would carry your name.'

'That's customary, yes.'

'So, indirectly, whenever you made a decision you would be making it for both of us. And when I made a decision it would also represent us.'

'What are you getting at?'

'Everyone who matters in Jakarta knows that I am your mistress,' she said, inhaling the smoke. 'So my Uncle Wong will let the members of the government who might try to take advantage of him know that the American ambassador's mistress shares in this deal. And they will assume that you are acting through me.'

'My God,' he said, stupefied. 'You can't be serious.'

'Never more serious.'

'How in the hell could you do that?' he said, the anger sweeping over him.

'You're angry then.'

'Of course I'm angry.'

'Because I saved my Uncle Wong from ruin and doubled my money?' she said, her own temper rising, knowing that her spirit mother was gloating because she had been right all along. 'I would have dishonored my uncle if I hadn't offered to help him.'

'You don't give a damn about your uncle,' he said. 'You saw a chance to double your money and you took it. You used my position to dishonor me.'

She stood up, snubbed out the cigarette, suddenly withdrawing into a place where she could not be touched, behind a wall. 'You don't set the rules for me and you never will,' she said. 'I didn't even have to tell you what I'd done.'

'You told me because you knew damn well I'd find out, sooner or later. And if somebody suddenly popped up with this to discredit me, you knew exactly how I'd feel about being screwed.'

'If you can't accept the way I am,' she said, 'then go to hell.' She turned and stalked off and he could hear the receding tattoo of her high heels against the marble floors as she went down a long corridor.

He did not see her for the rest of the day, but the sense of betrayal he felt did not diminish. It took him most of the afternoon to decipher cables that merely confirmed what he expected. Sergei had communicated with the political affairs officer to confirm the arrangements for the meeting in Bangkok, to agree to discuss the ramifications of the meeting of the oil ministers. It took him three hours to decipher the text of a long communiqué from State that suggested the attitude he should take toward each of the countries represented at the meeting. He wadded that one up, dropped it in the wastebasket.

A final text had been garbled in transmission, and despite his efforts to make sense of it, he only managed to retrieve a partial message which had something to do with some member of the embassy being attacked and in the hospital. His first thought was that Sangre-Lomax had gone into action again, but he could not be sure. He would simply have to wait until he was in Bangkok and have the message verified.

He walked down to the beach at sunset but did not stay long. The fair skies were beginning to disappear as a thunderhead moved in from the west. Beneath the massive storm he could see the bolts of lightning. It was raining by the time he made it back to the villa, great dumps of water that sent the servants scurrying through the rooms to lower the bamboo blinds on the windward side.

He had dinner by himself, then a solitary drink and went to bed at ten o'clock, after listening to BBC Worldwide on the radio. The storm continued to rage outside, the lightning flashes illuminating the room, and in one of the brief flares he was startled to see Madeleine standing in the open doorway of his bedroom, and it took him a moment to realize that the sound he heard over the roar of the storm was her weeping. She came and sat beside his bed and when she talked into the darkness her voice was very ashamed. 'I want to talk to you,' she said.

'We'll talk in the morning.'

'I want to talk about me,' she said, trying to control the tremor in her voice.

'It's late, Madeleine,' he said. 'Go back to bed.'

'I want you to understand,' she said. 'When I was a small girl, my mother was very poor. She was Chinese in Vietnam and if the Chinese were persecuted elsewhere, they were hated in the village where we lived. She did many things that she wasn't proud of because she had to live. And then she met an Indonesian named Rooseno. The brother of the man who became the minister. And she married him just to keep from being Chinese. He was an ugly man. I never saw him but once or twice when I was small. My mother hated him. He promised to take her to Indonesia, but he never did. And my mother was always trying to force him to send me to my relatives in Jakarta so I wouldn't starve. But there was never enough money. And then my mother began to steal, to whore, to manipulate the markets, to lie, to do anything to bring herself money. And when she had enough she bribed the officials to allow me to move to Jakarta.'

The lightning flashed. There was a rumble of thunder. The storm was moving on. But in the brief light he had seen her face, pale, desperate with a story she had to tell. He said nothing.

'My father didn't want me because I was a *peranakan*, half Chinese and half Indonesian,' she said. 'The word literally means "child of the Indies" but I would have been a great drawback to my father, who wished to make a life in politics.'

'What happened to him?' Clements said.

'Fortunately, he died. He had no other wives, so my mother got what money he had and added to her wealth. So I was finally sent to my Chinese relatives here, most of whom disapproved of me because I wouldn't follow their ways any more than I would take the example of my father. My mother always wanted to come here but the Vietnamese authorities knew she had a great amount of money and couldn't find it, so they wouldn't let her go. They would beat her. God, how they would beat her.'

'Is she still alive?'

Madeleine stood up, began to walk around the room, restlessly. The night was very warm and with the passing of the storm the air was saturated with moisture. She lit a cigarette. 'No,' she said, her face briefly illuminated by the glow of the cigarette. 'She died of a fever. But she lives with me as a spirit mother.' She paused, her voice filled with sadness. 'Because they wouldn't let her go, she converted her money into diamonds because they were easier to smuggle out. One of my Chinese relatives put them in a plastic bag to properly protect his innards and then swallowed them. He passed through Vietnam before the diamonds passed through him. I sold most of them, of course, invested in real estate.'

'Why are you telling me all this?' he said.

'It's very necessary,' she said. 'I knew I was dishonoring you when I made the deal with my Uncle Wong. Ordinarily I wouldn't have cared because I really don't like men very much. My spirit mother hates all men just as she hated men when she was alive. But for the first time I felt guilty about it. So I had to tell you. Telling you, I believe, is an honorable act.'

'We have different rules of honor, Madeleine . . .' he began, but she stopped him.

'Wait. Before you go on, it is necessary to tell you one more thing, while it's dark and I can't see your face, and I will say it only one time and then I won't mention it again.' She inhaled the cigarette, stared at the ceiling. 'You would be very wise not to trust me. Because sometimes I think of my father and I am very angry and since I can't get even with him, I take my revenge on other men. And sometimes, even though I have a lot of money, I get very frightened because I remember what it was to be poor and I think what it would be like if suddenly the authorities took everything I had and I became poor again. And at times like that I would sell my best friend if the profit was large enough. Which brings me to one more thing,' she said in the darkness. 'I can make love with you. I can be very fond of you sometimes, but I can never be *in* love with you or anyone. Can you understand?'

'I think I always have,' he said.

'Then everything has been said. All the words have been spoken.' With that, quietly and with great dignity, she left the room, and waiting for her in the shadows was her spirit mother, looking pleased, and with sadness Madeleine wondered why she felt that something within her was lost forever.

The next day at noon Clements heard the sound of the motorcycle and watched the Chinese dispatch rider come up the gravel road, leaving a trail of black smoke pluming off behind him. There was the usual ceremony of delivering the cables from the telegraph office, the salute, and then the Chinese stood by as if waiting for a reply.

Clements left him in the driveway and went indoors, out of the sun. He heard the sounds of Madeleine directing the servants in the packing of her wardrobe, for they would be leaving for Bangkok sometime in the late afternoon. He settled in the study, thumbed through the pile. There was an envelope in the stack of coded dispatches with his name scrawled on the front in a great hurry, feminine hand-writing, H. E. (for His Excellency) Ambassador Charles C. Clements. He slit the flap with a letter opener and took out the pair of sheets.

Dear Ambassador Clements,

I don't know whether this will reach you or not because my Indonesian is of the *bahasa pasar* kind and the gentleman here at the telegraph office speaks no English at all. I have bribed the Chinese rider who carries your cable traffic to bring you this letter. I have gone through literal hell to get up here and track you down because even though the matters I have to discuss with you are of critical importance, your loyal embassy retainers are still insisting you are in New Zealand and even the men in Communications insist that when an ambassador is on vacation he is to be considered to be totally un-available until he signals to the contrary. This may be a wild-goose chase for me, because Kemper is still out of his head and the doctors say that his chances of living are about fifty-fifty. But I am here to deliver the information anyway. I will be at the Hotel Machudum on Jl. Hilagoo, down from the market, until four o'clock this afternoon, after which time I will be on my way back to Jakarta.

Sincerely,
Thomasina Mims

Christ, he thought, *and that was the garbled signal from yesterday, the wounding of Kemper.* He did not know Thomasina Mims well, but it took a good deal of spunk for her to move counter to established protocol and come all the way up here, and he would not leave her wondering whether he would respond a moment longer than was necessary.

He shuffled through the rest of the coded dispatches, recognized that they were long communiqués from Washington, for the most part concerning negotiations with Sergei. They could wait.

He rang the silver bell, summoned a servant and told him to have a car made ready. Then he bundled his official papers into his attaché case. Madeleine had heard the bell and she came into the study just in time to see him grooming himself in the mirror for his ride into town.

'I'm going into town on business,' he said. 'What time does the plane leave?'

'Six-thirty.'

'Then there will be plenty of time. Have my things packed, if you will.'

'I'll arrange the car,' she said.

'I already have.'

'I'll double-check the arrangements then.' And she was down the corridor and gone instantaneously. He put on his hat and his sunglasses, checked his wallet to make sure he had cash and then went out into the front courtyard to find that Madeleine had indeed made arrangements, as if he were going into battle. For the Chinese motorcyclist was already positioned in front of the car and he was wearing two conspicuous pistols. And there were three bodyguards, Chinese men in fatigues, armed with carbines and semiautomatic weapons ready to go with him into Padang.

'Your escort is ready,' Madeleine said.

Clements looked to the driver, a middle-aged man who appeared to be very muscular. 'Do you have a pistol?'

'Yes, sir.'

'I don't need the escort, Madeleine,' Clements said. 'The driver will be enough. I should be back in a couple of hours.'

'It may not be safe for you,' Madeleine said. 'My uncle's people will protect you.'

'I'll be fine,' he said. 'Don't worry.'

'Would you like high tea when you return?' Madeleine said, finally accepting.

'That's a good idea. The food on the jet will be abysmal.' He marveled at her ability to go on as if nothing had been said.

He climbed into the backseat of the car and told the driver to move out, leaving the small army behind him, less certain of himself than he had led Madeleine to believe. For it was possible that Sangre-Lomax had followed Thomasina Mims from Jakarta, but then it was equally possible that Sangre-Lomax had known all along exactly where he had gone to prepare himself for the Bangkok conference and was simply waiting somewhere in the cover of the jungle along the road, or in the city itself. He could attack at any time, a rifle bullet from the jungle undergrowth or as they neared the congested city, which resembled a massive sprawling compound of low buildings and poor houses. Sangre-Lomax could simply step out of the dense crowds as the car inched along and with one deft motion of his hand bring a sawed-off shotgun out from beneath his coat and press it against the window glass and blow Clements away with a slight pressure on a trigger.

Clements told the driver where he wanted to go and, with the aid of a horn which blasted pedestrians out of the way and spooked the horses which pulled tourist sightseeing carts and slowed traffic miserably, they finally stopped in front of the hotel at two o'clock.

Clements surveyed the crowds on the street from the car. No Europeans or Westerners at all as far as he could see. Padang had a heavy Muslim population and no tourist would want to come here at all except as a stop on the way to someplace else.

'Do you want me to go into the hotel first?' the driver said.

And what would you look for if you did? Clements thought, but he did not say it. 'No,' he said. 'Find yourself a place and have something cool to drink. Come back in an hour.'

'I'm a very good shot.'

'I'm sure you are. But it's not going to be necessary.' He

got out of the car, unprepared for the heat, which engulfed him like a furnace between the coolness of the air-conditioned car and the moderate temperature in the lobby of the hotel.

He saw Thomasina immediately and thought he had never seen a more woeful-looking creature, a very pretty girl who at the moment was rumpled from too many hours of flying and getting transport in and out of cities and, above all, the strain of doing something she really thought was against reason. And from the look in her eyes as she stood up on his approach, that mixture of despair and anger, he suddenly realized that this woman was in love with Kemper.

He offered her his hand and she took it, but there was to be no easy forgiveness here. 'I wasn't sure you'd come,' she said.

'Of course I'd come,' he said. 'In the first place, I didn't know about Kemper.'

'A dispatch was sent to you.' An accusation.

'Garbled in transmission. Let's go to the bar and have a drink. You look like you've been through it.' And he took her elbow and led her into the dark coolness of the bar, just enough music from a piano player to keep the conversation in their booth private. She ordered a double martini and he a bourbon and water. From the look of the way she sat in the booth, he could tell that she was highly trained, disciplined and she would not fall apart. The drinks were served. 'Now,' he said. 'What happened?'

And she told him while she drank the martini, a flat report, her discovery of the Six Ravens, then Kemper's visit to the dry dock, the discovery of a junk there, no small boats. Then the booby-trapped car, the explosion which had burned Kemper so terribly. Then the time at the hospital and finally the whispered message which he wanted delivered to the ambassador.

'Melong,' she said, flatly.

'Melong?'

'Yes.'

'Are you sure it wasn't "Mekong," as in the Mekong River?'

219

'I'm quite sure.'

'Go on. What was the rest of it?'

'That's all of it. Just "Melong." Nothing else. My God, it took every ounce of concentration just to get that one word out.' Her eyes burned into his face. 'Does it mean anything to you?'

He shook his head, unhappily. 'I'm afraid not.'

'I knew it,' she said, looking away. 'I should have known he was rambling, that he didn't know what he was saying. But I have been so desperate to do *something*, anything for God's sake. I wanted that goddamned word to count, to make it worthwhile for me to go through hell.' She raised her hand, ordered another drink.

'What can I do for you?' he said.

'Can you keep him from dying?'

'No.'

'Then there's nothing you can do for me.'

'He's stayed alive this long,' Clements said. 'When you get back to Jakarta, you have the best burn doctor brought in from the Burn Center in Sydney. Get air force transportation from the Philippines if you have to. Tell them that I have authorized whatever you think is best and I'll back you up.'

'He's really the finest man I've ever known,' she said, and he could tell the first drink had taken hold now, and her hostility toward him was disappearing with his demonstration of caring and now she just wanted to talk about Kemper to someone who knew him. 'I've had a lot of time to think, since he's been in the hospital, to sort things out. Do you know what I mean? I think I was trying to impress him from the first day I met him, to let him know how bright, how ambitious I was. I told him I didn't want to get involved because I was determined to be chief of station before I was through, to prove myself.' She smiled. 'And it was only after he sent me to Medan and I set up an office near the airfield that I realized what he was doing. He was getting me out of the line of fire and giving me something that would look good on my yearly evaluations at the same time. And then, when I found out he was hurt, all of the professional ambition I'd built up just droppd away. It's a terrible confession, really, but I didn't give a damn what happened to the station out here. There could be revolutions and realignments and all I wanted was for Harry to be alive, just for him to be breathing.'

'Yet you left him to come up here.'

'Not in the name of duty,' she said. 'I love him. He asked me to get the message to you, and even if I had known in advance that it didn't mean anything, I would have done it for him. I know that I'm not making a great deal of sense.'

'You're making perfect sense,' he said.

'Anyway, if he lives, and I'll force him to live, if I can, then somebody's going to have to take care of him. What happened to him was inhuman and it's going to take a lot of doing to make things right. I suppose what I'm saying is that I'm resigning but not resigning. Wiznoski is a good man, but he doesn't have the grasp of things that Harry does, the background in security that Harry has. I'd suggest that you shift him to Political for cover and bring in a separate security chief. I'll be available until Harry can be moved and then I'll go back to the States with him. But I want it made clear that what happened to him was no error on his part. There was nothing he could have done to have prevented it. I would appreciate a letter from you to the Agency, Mr Ambassador, to that effect, that you've investigated and find him blameless.'

'He'll have it,' Clements said.

'I have to go,' she said, standing up. 'I have an hour to get to the airport and the taxis are fitful at best.'

'I'll take you,' he said.

'I don't want to impose.'

'No imposition.'

At the airport he saw her luggage aboard the plane and then she leaned forward and pressed her cheek against his. 'God bless,' she said.

'Take care of Harry. He's a good man.'

'I will.'

She went up the loading steps. He stayed until the plane lifted off the tarmac and realized that he was feeling a slight envy as well as a sense of loss. For Alice would have had the same devotion to him that Tommi had for the wounded Kemper, but Alice was a part of the past, and now he was faced with the problem of a woman who had betrayed him, a woman who believed in spirits, a woman he happened to love. But he would make no decisions now, not until he had had ample time to think it through.

He climbed into the car and told the driver he was ready to go.

It was only halfway back to the villa before he began to realize what Kemper had been trying to tell him. Melong. A village in Vietnam. An analogy. The equivalent of hell. But all he had was an unsubstantiated theory, with a possible knowledge of *what* was going to happen and absolutely no idea why. Being almost sure was not good enough, certainly not enough to persuade anyone else to take action.

When he reached the villa he said nothing to Madeleine about it. While she was making final arrangements for departure he went into the cool study, with the ceiling fan making slow circles above him. He thought the whole business through. The meetings were to begin tomorrow in Bangkok and were scheduled to last three days, culminating with an outdoor party on the grassy lawns of the hotel flanking the river.

Three days.

With any luck that would give him time enough to get in touch with the ambassador and the chief of station in Bangkok and hand the problem over to them. Sitting alone in the room, with a gentle breeze filtering in from the sea, he began to feel peaceful. In another twenty-four hours the responsibility for what was happening would be in the hands of others.

He did write a cable to the ambassador in Bangkok, a man named Thorenson, with whom he had had some small disagreements in the past, and another to Squires, the CIA Chief of Station, asking for a meeting tonight, the moment he arrived in Bangkok. They would confirm by having someone at the Bangkok airport to meet him. He coded the messages, then added a final cable to G. D.'s people asking that transportation be provided for Madeleine. He summoned the Chinese motorcycle courier and sent him scurrying into the telegraph office to have the messages dispatched forthwith.

The flight to Bangkok was strained, with little, but polite conversation from Madeleine, always the good hostess. It was dark by the time the jet landed in Bangkok and Clements was relieved to see Squires waiting for him, a pleasant man who combined a genial disposition with his sharp grasp of the true state of affairs in Bangkok. Squires was a supergrade CIA employee, a part of a new stratification of the Agency which saw him in charge not only of the Bangkok station but responsible for an overview of all the stations in Southeast Asia. He greeted Clements with a smile and a handshake, ushered him and his party through the airport to the platform where two limousines were waiting, the first to take Madeleine and the luggage to G. D.'s estate and the second to act as transportation for what Clements hoped would be a meeting with Thorenson.

But no sooner was Clements alone with Squires in the car heading into the city itself than he learned that his conversation with Ambassador Thorenson was bound to be a brief one, because the ambassador was hosting a cocktail party for some of the delegates who had arrived early for the meetings.

'Did he get my cable?' Clements said. 'He must have. You got the one I sent to you.'

'You know Thorenson, Mr Ambassador. I'll give you his exact reaction to your cable, if I can remember it,' Squires said. 'He summoned me to his office and pushed your cable across the desk at me and said. "What is this? What do you know about it?" I told him I knew nothing more than he did except that all hell had been breaking loose in your bailiwick and that there might be a terrorist action brewing at the least and a revolution at the worst. And he said to me, in that harrumphing way of his, "Clements is always dramatizing. I hope he doesn't think that we're going to play his game up here. Remind him that we have our own business to look after."'

Clements smiled despite himself at the accuracy of the imitation, refusing to take offence. Thorenson had been a businessman with years spent at the United States Chamber of Commerce before he came to Bangkok, and he believed that the answer to any problem lay in straight business negotiations with money changing hands at the end. 'And do you agree with Ambassador Thorenson?' Clements said.

'Not necessarily,' Squires said. He lit a cigarette, obviously stalling any serious conversation until they began to approach the center of the city and the limousine pulled up in front of the Empress Hotel. 'The ambassador has taken a hospitality suite here,' Squires said, leading the way into the ornate lobby to the elevator, pressing a button for the third floor.

The suite was on the river side, with a large balcony that overlooked the dining terraces below, the candles glowing like fireflies, and beyond the lawn which sloped to the water the lights of a string of barges. Thorenson was dressed in formal attire, engaged in vigorous conversation with a Filipino minister and his wife, and his eyes acknowledged Clements's presence while he continued his story without missing a beat. There was another group at the makeshift bar, a group from Thailand with Thorenson's wife, a statuesque woman, guiding the conversation.

'What will it be?' Squires said.

'Bourbon and water,' Clements said, and he wandered out onto the balcony, leaning on the balustrade, studying the river and the lights of the section of the city across the Chao Phraya. In a few minutes Squires joined him, handed him his drink. 'I want you to know how goddamn sorry I was to hear about Houghton and then Kemper,' he said. 'I didn't know Houghton but Kemper and I were buddies. I just got late word from the hospital, by the way. He's still holding his own, maybe a little better. You have one vicious son of a bitch running loose down there.'

He was interrupted as Thorenson came out onto the balcony, operating under a code of good manners while his eyes revealed his impatience. 'Ah, there you are, Clements,' he said. 'I'm so glad you could make it.'

'You received my cable.'

'Yes. I think we had better understand each other. I don't

mean to sound harsh, but some very delicate business will be taking place here in the next couple of days. And I've been instructed to keep everything on an even keel, if I can.'

'I understand that perfectly.'

'Now, what's this brand of violence that you mentioned in your cable that so upset our COS here?'

'You know about the boats?' Clements said to Squires.

'Almost too much about the boats,' Squires said. 'I've made so many investigations through Langley, run so many scenarios, as a matter of fact, that they've begun to kid me about them. I got a coded dispatch from one of our jokers in Hong Kong today letting me know he had seen three new speedboats in Aberdeen and asking what action he should take.'

'And the Straits of Malacca.'

'That, too,' Squires said. 'I can't give you the details, Ambassador Clements, but we have more people watching the straits every day than go to the Super Bowl. A canoe couldn't get into the straits without a picture of it hitting my desk within fifteen minutes.'

Thorenson glanced back inside. His impatience glowed. 'I think we had better get directly to the point, Charlie.'

'You know what's been happening in Jakarta.'

'Of course. I've been meaning to give you a ring, see what we might be able to do for you.'

'And you know about my COS.'

'Yes.'

'Kemper sent me a message,' Clements said. 'After he had seen the boats, after he had been burned, he still considered what he had to tell me so important that he sent one of his staff all the way to Sumatra.' He sipped the bourbon, tired from the day's travel. 'We were trying to figure out how those boats could be used in an attack on the Straits of Malacca and we couldn't do it. Because they couldn't be used there. They would be useless in an action of that sort. But the message he sent me was a single word. Melong. Were either of you in Vietnam?'

'The highlands, briefly,' Squires said.

'I was stationed in Canada,' Thorenson said.

Clements looked to Squires. 'Were you ever down on the rivers?'

'No.'

'There was an episode there. Quite unique. It happened only once, probably because the Vietcong couldn't get any more private boats. But they confiscated the boats of some planters quite early on and then spent a long time rigging them. They welded pipes to either side of the speedboats and adapted their own homemade torpedoes to fit them. They built in gun mounts, fore and aft. There was a pacified river village that was being used as an officer's retreat, a swimming pool, bar, the whole works, protected by our gunboats. And then one day these speedboats came out of nowhere, just a couple of them, and they got past all the defenses because they were so quick and because they looked so goddamned ridiculous. And when they swooped in, a bunch of the officers just stood at the end of the swimming pool and watched them and wondered if the river was clean enough for waterskiing. Then the boats launched their torpedoes, sluggish damned cylinders aimed to take advantage of the river current so they would arc right into the docks. And the poor bastards at the officers' club never knew what hit them. The torpedoes were filled with high explosives and nails and scrap metal. And those who tried to run were mowed down by the fifty-caliber machine guns mounted on the decks.'

Squires cradled his drink in his hands, an appraising expression on his face.

'You were there?'

'No. I was following up MIA reports after the war. I had read about Melong. It became a classic textbook example of innovative warfare. One of the North Korean officers I interviewed was very proud of that makeshift attack.'

'That's all very well and good . . .' Thorenson said.

'Kemper's message had to refer to that day at Melong,' Clements said. 'I think the boats I saw being outfitted in Jakarta are headed here, Ambassador.' He looked out at the water. 'They'll wait until the lawn party and then they'll come out of the canals like bats out of hell. I don't have any objective proof, but they're going to attack the lawn party on the final night. They're going to wipe out oil ministers from all the countries represented here and take out a number of assorted ambassadors and dignitaries at the same time.'

'So that's your theory,' Thorenson said.

'Lang knew it was going to happen. He saw the proof on the computer screen and it got him killed. He saw enough to put it all together. He was scheduled to come to those meetings with me. They tried to kill me in Bali because they were afraid I would figure it out, killed Rooseno instead. They killed Houghton because he was getting too close to it. They tried to kill Kemper when he found out about the boats. What other answer can you give me? What other scenario can you invent that will tie everything together so well?'

'And what do you want me to do?' Thorenson said.

'Take adequate precautions.'

'I know you believe this is going to happen,' Thorenson said. 'I know that's true or you wouldn't be here. But there are thousands of rivers in the Far East where such boats could be used, if they're going to be used at all. And who is this "they" you're talking about, for God's sake?'

'I don't know,' Clements said. 'But I don't think you can afford to take the risk of doing nothing.'

Thorenson looked out at the river. 'I have the reputation of being a very levelheaded man,' he said. 'Not particularly excitable, not inclined to go off half-cocked, and that's where my value to my country lies. I never act on hunches. I'm as good as my word.'

'Then do me a favor,' Clements said. 'Use your influence to take one precaution which will make all the rest unnecessary.'

'And what's that?'

'Move all the festivities indoors. The Empress Hotel has a ballroom large enough for the convention.'

Thorenson scratched his chin. 'I'll give it some thought,' he said. 'In the meantime, we'll follow up. Now, if you'll excuse me.'

And he went back inside the suite, leaving Clements with a burning frustration. 'Just like that,' he said.

'You do know how to strike nerves, don't you?' Squires said. 'Ambassador Thorenson is well known for his firework displays. They're very popular. And you want to move everyone inside so they can't get a full view.'

'Somebody is going to take action,' Clements said. 'I won't stand by and see a slaughter take place just because of some goddamn capricious vanity.'

Squires nodded. 'I'll tell you what I'll do, Ambassador. On a strictly unofficial level, I can suggest that it might be a good idea if the Thai Navy enhances their security from the river side. That's highly unlikely, since the Thai Navy force on the river consists of some old wooden gunboats that are ancient enough that they could be used as props for filming *Terry and the Pirates*. They don't have enough helicopter gunships for proper patrol. I can alert the Navy to the possibility that these boats may be in Thai waters, but the odds of spotting one of them would be astronomical.'

'And that's your bottom line, then.'

'I'll put my people on this,' Squires said. 'And I'll see how much of what you say can be verified. I'll go further than that. I'll feed it to my people and if any one of them picks up on it and says, "Hey, wait a minute, that ties in with what I'm working on." If I pick up anything, and I mean even the smallest connection, then I'll go straight to Thorenson and tell him to cover his ass because if he's been warned and does nothing and something like this happens, he's dead politically, even if the bullets don't get him.'

Clements finished his drink. 'Fair enough,' he said. 'And I give you the same warning, Mr Squires. If you let this happen, your career goes with it as well as Thorenson's. Now, if you'll call a car for me, I'm going across the river.'

There were dozens of apocryphal stories about the size of G. D.'s estate in the countryside west of Thonburi, across the river from Bangkok, but Clements realized that G. D. encouraged such tales and liked to have people think of him as an eccentric American determined to live on a scale just below that of the royal family. Clements believed that G. D. would like to have topped the King of Thailand in conspicuous consumption and gracious living except that the Thais might consider it impolite. Ordinarily, Clements would have been in good spirits as the car carried him through the massively ornate wrought-iron gates, because G. D.'s house (a cross between a rambling Texas mansion and a Thai palace) was always full of movie stars on location or visiting dignitaries from around the world, stimulating company to say the least. Too, it was the one place where he and Madeleine could stay under the same roof without the least hint of scandal leaking through the diplomatic community.

But tonight he was not hopeful. For Squires, in his own way, had spelled out the weakness in Clements's position. He had but the most tenuous of connections to suggest that what he feared was really going to happen here. Presented with hard facts and the evidence of a clear and present danger, Ambassador Thorenson would certainly act responsibly, but he would not change any of his plans based on theoretical predictions.

The car let Clements off at the main house, a massive structure with a roof that resembled the long sweep of a bird's wing, which by daylight glittered with golden tiles that sparkled in the sun. And no sooner had he stepped out of the car than the servants came out of the house to greet him, smiling, bowing, bringing their hands together as if in an attitude of prayer, the *wai*, the traditional greeting of respect. The majordomo was an ancient and dignified Thai houseman who went by the name of Horace. He bowed to Clements with great solemnity.

'Please come in, Ambassador,' he said in a deep voice. 'It is much too long since we have seen you.'

'Thank you, Horace,' Clements said. 'I take it my baggage has arrived.'

'Quite so, sir, and in your rooms. And the lady, sir.'

'Very good. Where's G. D.?'

'In town. But he says that I should get you very drunk and make you feel very welcome.' And Horace opened the door to the entryway, where there were cages of exotic birds in the greenery and a tile step down into the main room with its high, peaked ceiling. And Clements was surprised to see that there was only one person in the room, a tall man in an elegant silk suit with a scarf cravat wrapped around his neck and wearing the first monocle that Clements had seen in years.

'May I have the honor, Mr Ambassador,' Horace said, 'to introduce to you Lord Powell-Owenby.'

'I'm very pleased to meet you, sir,' Powell-Owenby said, regarding him with one eyebrow arched over the silver rim of the monocle. 'G. D. told me I would have the pleasure of seeing you and, I must say, I'm frankly delighted. I believe we've met before.'

'I'm sorry to say I don't remember where, Lord Powell-Owenby,' Clements said.

'It was at a reception at the court of St James's. We just shook hands, I believe. But that was years ago when you were a commercial secretary, I believe, and we had a general conversation about English architecture. I was just considering opening my castle to the public at the time. Taxes were positively confiscatory.'

Horace appeared with a silver tray containing a bourbon and water for Clements and a gin for Powell-Owenby. Powell-Owenby lifted his with a delicate pincerlike movement of thumb and forefinger. 'I was just admiring G. D.'s library,' he said, glancing up at the shelves which covered one wall of the room, complete with a wheeled ladder on rails to allow inspection of the upper reaches. 'He must have collected every book ever written on the Far East.'

'Where did you meet him?' Clements said, sitting down on a leather sofa.

'We were on an oil project together in the North Sea. And afterwards we went hunting for grouse in Scotland. He's a terrible shot, I'm afraid, but a marvelous human being.'

And as if on cue, G. D. came sweeping into the room, a broad smile on his face, partially sloshed, arms extended. And Clements stood up for the embrace, G. D. patting him on the back, grinning at him. 'Damn, it's good to see you, Charlie. Have you met his lordship?'

'Yes,' Clements said.

Horace appeared at the door to the dining room. G. D. checked his watch and then looked to Clements. 'Okay,' he said. 'Serious question, so listen up. How many seconds would you say it was from the time you came through the front door until Horace had a drink in your hand?'

'Hell, I wasn't counting.'

'An estimate. One minute? A minute and a half?'

'Less than that. Maybe thirty seconds.'

Horace beamed. G. D. grunted with mock disapproval. 'You just cost me a hundred dollars, friend,' he said, taking out his wallet. 'I told old Horace he was slowing down. So we bet a hundred bucks that it would take him at least ninety seconds to get a drink in your hand. He thinks he's some kind of speed-king Gunga Din.' He flipped a hundred-dollar bill out of his wallet, handed it to the delighted Horace, who bowed and touched his fingertips to his forehead in respect.

'And what is your pleasure, sir?'

'Nothing. Hell, I've had a drink with every oilman in the whole goddamned world in the past four hours. But you can get me those cigars that just came in from Hong Kong.'

'Yes, sir.'

The cigars were passed around but only G. D. took one from the box, rolling it between thumb and forefinger close to his ear as if to listen to its expensive crackle. Then he passed it back to Horace, who snipped off the end and provided a light for G. D.'s ritual of turning the cigar so that the tip would be evenly lit. He puffed and the cigar was going and then he dismissed Horace for the night. 'If we want anything, I figure that the three of us should be able to handle it.'

'The two of you, I'm afraid,' Powell-Owenby said, stifling a yawn. 'I know that it's frightfully bad manners, but the jet lag has laid me low, G. D.'

'You can crap out tonight, Morris,' G. D. said, pleasantly. 'But you pull any more of this early-to-bed business on me and I'll take offense.'

'I do hope you'll forgive me, Ambassador,' Powell-Owenby said. 'I look forward to a long conversation while we're here.'

'Good night,' Clements said. And Powell-Owenby left the room, an impeccably correct man with a slight rolling gait to his walk. G. D. grinned after him. 'I do believe he's drunk,' he said. 'Well, sit down, for God's sake, and let me know what's going on. How's your drink?'

'Brand new.'

'Your lady's here, I believe. Checked in a couple of hours ago. I called to tell you to come on down to the Empress. Damnedest parties going on there you've ever seen. Reminds me of the old days in the frat house.' G. D. studied his face while he puffed on the cigar. 'You were always a lousy actor,' he said. 'Something's wrong, isn't it?'

'I'm faced with a dilemma,' Clements said. 'There's going to be a disaster here, G. D.'

G. D. raised his glass, smiled. 'Join the club, good buddy. You're damn right there's going to be a disaster. They're going to clean my plow,' G. D. said. 'And that's for certain.'

'What are you talking about?'

'You haven't heard? I'm going to have to sell my house here, the whole thing. You know how long it took me to build up this place? Twelve years. I've got my own goddamned zoo that's better than the King's private collection. I've even got my own canal with a water purification system in it. My only trouble is that I didn't pull out of this part of the world in time. Hell, I thought it would hold another couple of years.'

'I'm talking about a different kind of disaster.'

'If there's anything worse than losing twenty, thirty million dollars, I'll put in with you.'

Clements stood up, carried his drink to the massive stone fireplace which G. D. occasionally used by turning the air-conditioning down to frigid before he ignited the logs. Clements looked at the wall of photographs which decorated the wall above the massive mantel, pictures of a smiling G. D. posing with every type of celebrity in existence, G. D. and prime ministers, G. D. and presidents, G. D. and American generals. 'I want your advice,' he said. 'I don't know that there's a damn thing you can do about it, but maybe you have contacts in the Thai Government.'

G. D. smiled. 'I've paid enough money over the years to own *half* of the Thai Government.'

'What would you say if I told you there was going to be an armed attack on the oil ministers?'

G. D. grinned, downed his drink and got up to pour himself another one. 'I'd say hallelujah and where do I stand in line to sign up.'

232

'I'm serious, G. D.'

'So am I. There's nothing I'd like to see more than for somebody to knock these officious little bastards on their collective asses.' He settled back in his chair. 'Are you sure about this? What's your source?'

'Rooseno, originally. Only he thought there was going to be an attack in northern Sumatra. He was wrong. The strike's going to be here, on this meeting.'

G. D. looked suddenly tired, drained, and Clements could see the deep lines in his face. Occasionally, G. D. dramatized a situation to make it far worse than it was, but Clements could tell that was not the case this time. He was indeed about to lose everything, and it was hard for him to maintain his perpetual good humor. 'I'm tired of wars,' he said. 'Just bone tired of wars and intrigues and people blowing up things. And now, another goddamned river attack. Is there anything I can do?'

'Maybe. Can you force the Thai Navy to take some kind of action?'

G. D. pressed his cold glass against his forehead as if he had a headache. 'I don't know,' he said, truthfully. 'I can spread some money around. They might be willing to set up patrols on the river. And then again, they might refuse to take it seriously. I never know what they're going to do.'

'What do you think would happen if I take this to the media?'

'The combined delegates from all these goddamned little countries would say it was an American threat to disrupt their meeting,' G. D. said.

'But would they take precautions?'

'That's a point. They might.'

'Then I'll hit the media with it in the morning. I don't care about appearances. I frankly don't give a damn if they condemn the United States as long as the attack is forestalled.'

G. D. yawned. 'I'm sorry. I'ts been a long day, buddy. I suggest we call it a night. And I'll give all this a hell of a lot of thought. I wouldn't mind throwing a scare into the little fuckers whether the attack is real or not. What time you want Horace to get you up?'

'By nine at the latest.'

'I've put you and your lady in the guesthouse by the pool. I took it for granted that you'd want it that way, but if you want privacy, say so.'

'No, the arrangement's fine.'

G. D. stood up, patted him on the arm. 'It's great to have you here. I mean that. There's nothing that I'd like better than for us to get our business off the ground while you're here.'

'Maybe we can,' Clements said. 'We'll talk in the morning.'

'You know your way.'

'Of course. Good night.'

He went out the back of the house, onto a terrace in the bright moonlight with the waters of the swimming pool immediately below, the guesthouse that G. D. had called 'The Tree House' off in a grove to the left, the other guesthouses to the right. From off in the forested compound he could hear the gibbons chattering and hooting at the moon.

There was a light in the veranda room and he was pleased to find that Madeleine was still up, lying on a chaise longue with a magazine propped up on her bare knee, the windows open to the night breeze, the air-conditioning shut down. She looked up at him. 'I was waiting for you,' she said.

'I'm pleased you're still up.'

'It's too beautiful a night for sleeping. I thought you would be very late coming to bed. We have so much to talk about.'

'It's all been said,' he said.

'I don't see any reason why we can't go on as before,' she said. 'As long as you're in this part of the world.'

He sat down in a chair, lit a cigarette, blew the smoke toward the ceiling. Something was awry. He could feel it even if he could not define it, not with Madeleine, no, because what she was saying was expected. The trouble lay with G. D., something about the conversation. And suddenly the suspicion was there, based on something G. D. had known about when there was no way for him to know.

234

'Did you have a conversation with anyone here when you arrived?' he said.

'I met the Englishman.'

'Did you talk to him?'

'Only "Good evening," "How do you do?" . . . that sort of thing.'

'And you're absolutely sure you didn't talk about anything else.'

'Like what?'

'The boats.'

She was perplexed. 'Of course not. There was no reason to talk about the boats.'

He smoked in silence for a moment, thinking it through, not wanting to alarm her unduly. 'Christ,' he said, quietly. 'G. D. mentioned the boats. There's been nothing in the news about them, not a whisper, but he knows the attack is coming from the river.'

'He's an American, after all. Maybe somebody with the American Embassy here let him know.'

'No. I just talked to the chief of station. He's handled the whole thing on a top-secret basis.' He stood up, walked to the telephone on a wicker table, picked it up. It rang on the other end without his dialing any number.

'Yes, sir?' A man's voice.

'Horace? Is that you?'

'Yes, sir, Mr Ambassador. Is there something I can get for you?'

'Can you get me an outside line?'

'I'm terribly sorry, sir. But the telephones are very unreliable in this place. I have been told that outside service should be restored by morning. If you wish anything, I will bring it to you.'

'No, thank you.'

'Then good night, sir.'

'Good night, Horace.'

Madeleine was alarmed by the expression on his face. 'You're frightening me,' she said.

'There's nothing for you to be afraid of,' he said. 'But I want you to do something for me. First, get dressed.'

'Where are we going?'

'I'll explain when you're dressed.'

He sat down at a table, pulled out Squires's card and then looked through the drawers until he found a sheet of writing paper. He wrote a brief note detailing his suspicions, asking Squires to look into it. Then he folded the paper, attached the card to it with a paper clip. That should do it. Because all he would need to do was backtrack G. D. a short distance and the connections would begin to appear.

Madeleine came back into the room dressed in a batik dress with long sleeves to protect her arms from the mosquitoes. 'Now,' she said. 'I want you to explain to me exactly what you're doing.'

He took out his wallet, gave her a couple hundred dollars in small American bills. 'Listen to me carefully,' he said. 'I want to get you out the front gate without anybody being aware that you're gone.'

'Why?'

'I'll explain that in a minute. When you're out the gate, you go straight down the private road. It makes a bend and then there's a public thoroughfare and there's a police station on the corner. You give them a couple of dollars and they'll let you use the telephone.' He handed her the card and the note. 'You call this number and regardless of who answers you tell them you have a message for Squires from Clements. You stay in the police station until they send a car for you.'

'And then what?'

'When you've given Squires the message, have him take you to the Siam Intercontinental and take a room. Wait there until you hear from me.'

'There's no reason why both of us can't go.'

'The minute I try to go through the gate, I force his hand. He couldn't let me out at this point because he knows I'm going to the media. And that leaves only you.'

'No, if there's going to be trouble, I want to be with you. I don't want you hurt.'

'I won't be hurt,' he said, rather sadly. 'That's part of how he gave himself away. But you have to do exactly as I say. I don't want him to know that you're gone, not until sometime tomorrow.'

'I'll try,' she said.

'I know you will. I'm counting on you.'

He turned off the light and looked out at the pale moonlight in the trees. 'If we're stopped between here and the trees, we're just taking a walk because it's a lovely night. Have you got that?'

'Yes.'

They walked out into the night and followed a circular path that looped around the main house and toward the gardens near the front gate. When they were within viewing distance of the gate, Clements paused, studying the layout, amazed that he had been here so many times and had passed through the gate without ever noting precisely how it worked. There was a small guardhouse right next to the tall, wrought-iron auto gates, which could be opened only by an electric switch. But to the right of the massive gate was a narrow pedestrian gate that allowed people to pass up a narrow sidewalk bounded by a fence, which let the guard have a look at them before he permitted them passage into the grounds.

The guard was sitting in the small building with the lights on, reading a book. He was a small Thai in uniform. He was armed with a carbine.

Madeleine held on to Clements's arm. 'I don't think I can do this,' she said.

'Of course you can,' he said. 'I'm going to distract him, get him out of that guardhouse, and you're going out through that pedestrian gate. Five seconds and you should be in the shadows of the trees. And remember, the police station is right on the main thoroughfare. Now, are you ready?'

'As ready as I'm going to be.'

'You stay here until he leaves the guardhouse.'

'Yes.'

He moved in the shadows to the other side of the guardhouse and perhaps a hundred feet beyond. He could see Madeleine no longer. His heart was trip-hammering against his rib cage. There was always the chance that this guard might be easily spooked and decide to fire first. He took a deep breath to calm himself. Then he called out, 'Hey, I need help. Hey somebody!' The uniformed man peered out through the open side of the guardhouse in his direction. Clements ran toward the guardhouse and now the Thai came out, carbine held at ready, and there was a brief moment when Clements could feel the strength of his indecision whether to fire or not. Clements waved his hands and then that moment passed as Clements came closer and the guard could see he wasn't a threat.

'Do you speak English?' Clements said.

'Yes, sir,' the guard said.

'One of the gibbons is loose. He came by the guesthouse and scared the hell out of me.'

The guard looked off into the darkness. 'Very harmless, sir. Sometimes get loose and around. But go back to cages for feeding in the morning.'

'Then you don't need to notify anyone?'

'If you disturbed again, you pick up telephone and say, "I disturbed." Very simple, eh?'

'Of course,' Clements said. 'I was startled, that's all.'

'You wish escort to your abide place?'

'No, thanks,' Clements said with an expression which he hoped would approximate sheepishness. 'I imagine I startled the gibbon quite as much as he startled me. Good night.'

'Good night, sir.'

He went back down the driveway, paused once to look at the gate, the shadows beyond. Plenty of time and he was sure she had made it. He went back to the cottage, went through the bar until he found a bottle of bourbon. He poured himself one more drink, more melancholy than alarmed, for a whole era seemed to have come to an end, and tomorrow he would start to pick up the pieces.

9

He was gripped by a bad dream, on Bali again, with people
all around him, a party, yes, the pleasant babble of voices,
and he knew that momentarily a bomb would explode and
cover them all with fire and he opened his mouth to warn
them but no sound would come out. And he tried to run, but
his feet were frozen to the floor. Then there was a flash of
fire and he knew it was happening, beyond his warning or
control, and he came awake and sat upright in bed, gasping
for air.

Christ.

He heard the birds in the trees outside the guesthouse
and he realized where he was and what was happening. He
glanced at his watch. Eight-fifteen. He rolled out of bed and
sought the bathroom and the shower to come alive, shaved,
brushed his teeth. His nerves were on edge. He didn't know
what was happening, *couldn't* know, but Squires should
have his boys hot on the trail this morning and Madeleine
should be safe in the Siam Intercontinental and that was
what counted.

He stepped outside the guesthouse, into the blinding
sunlight of the early morning and the pervasive heat, which
seemed to hang in the air around the clock. The confrontation lay ahead of him and he was filled with mixed
and conflicting feelings, that a man who had been his friend
had caused the deaths of so many people and yet at the
same time tried to spare his life.

He found G. D. having breakfast in the shaded part of the
terrace overlooking the pool and the cabana dressing rooms.
G. D. looked up at him, managed a grin without conviction.
The son of a bitch knows that I know, Clements thought. *He*

*can read it on my face. How long do you think you can bluff it
through?* 'You sleep well?'

'Not particularly.'

G. D. rang a bell and Horace appeared. 'Get the
ambassador here a Bloody Mary,' he said.

'Hold it,' Clements said to Horace. 'Just black coffee.'

'Yes, sir,' Horace said, and went back into the house.

'This whole goddamn thing is getting to you, isn't it?'
Clements said to G. D. 'Bags under the eyes. Drinking your
breakfast.'

G. D. looked at him, and Clements could see him trying to
interpret the ambiguity. *God, he knows, he can't help but
know, but he's going to delay it as long as possible.*

'It keeps the juices flowing when I'm tired,' G. D. said. He
stirred his drink, absently. 'Where's your little lady this
morning? Still asleep?'

'Yes.'

'You always did have good taste, Charlie,' G. D. said,
watching a brightly colored parrot flying between trees. 'My
God, this is a beautiful part of the world. I don't think the
Garden of Eden could have been any prettier than this.'

'How long can you keep this up?' Clements said.

'Keep what up?'

'You know goddamn well what I mean.'

'Maybe you better let me in on it.'

'I didn't remember where I heard about Melong until I was
walking down the path this morning. It wasn't a part of any
investigation I conducted over there. Shit, *you* were the one
who first told me about it. You were stationed there when it
happened.'

G. D. slid down in his chair, looked up at the sky, his
callused hands holding the Bloody Mary glass on his
stomach. 'You must think you know something,' G. D. said.

'You mentioned the river attack last night. There's no way
you could have known about those goddamned boats unless
you had something to do with them.'

'I was afraid of that,' G. D. said. 'I knew I'd made a mistake
the second the words came out. But I'd been drinking.'

'You've had a lot of good people killed,' Clements said.
'Lang, Houghton, even Oni Saud, in his own way.'

'That's what comes of having a killer on retainer.' G. D. shook his head. 'That wasn't my idea, by the way. But from the second he stumbled across the material in Singapore, I knew it was just a matter of time before he was taken out. I liked Lang, you know that? I thought he was a bright young man. I know it doesn't matter a damn, but I'm having a scholarship set up in his name at the University of Texas.'

'For the love of God, why?' Clements said, quietly.

'Why what?'

'You've always been an oilman, not some fucking re-volutionary, some international conspirator.'

'Hell, there's not that much difference,' G. D. said. 'If I produce oil in the U.S. I have to get around the government with loopholes and flimflammery, new oil substituted for old oil, bribes, payoffs, business through the back door. And over here, it's even worse.' He drank from the glass. 'I had my bookkeepers total up the number of people I've had to bribe in Indonesia and Thailand in the past year, not the number of bribes, mind you, because some of these bozos get paid off every week, but the number of people. Five hundred and sixty-four. Can you imagine that? Five hundred and sixty-four goddamned people who're on the take, and I haven't got my money's worth. They've upped the ante. Now, maybe if I was Union Oil with resources in the billions, I could handle it, all the double crosses, the backstabbings. But I don't have billions. If I'm lucky, I can sell all my holdings and have enough to slink back to Texas with my tail between my legs and retire. And I lose this place.' He looked around him. 'You ever see such a para-dise?'

'No,' Clements said.

'Neither have I.'

'So how do you plan to save yourself?'

'You really think I'm going to tell you?'

'Yes.'

G. D. held his glass up, over his head. 'Horace,' he said, 'keep it full.'

'Yes, sir,' Horace said, materializing out of the shadows with a pitcher. He filled the glass, retreated.

G. D. drank again. 'I'm not the only one,' he said. 'Not the only sucker who's decided to take action. There are a number of us. I get two million clear for acting as coordinator, for taking the risks.' He snorted with derision. 'Hell, two million used to be pocket money, and now I need it to stay afloat.'

'Your plan?' Clements repeated.

'Shit,' G. D. said. 'I knew you were going to make the connections, sure as hell.' G. D. waved his glass in the air and described the brilliant plan which he had come up with. 'I didn't start this, buddy, but I made my feelings known and there were some other oil operators felt the same way. I was having a drink at Raffles in Singapore and a go-between asked me if I was interested in setting something up, I mean, one big bang of a protest against the Southeast Asian countries. I was a little sloshed at the time, I admit that. But my CPA's just told me that my cash flow was down to a trickle. All because of these bureaucratic sons of bitches down here who were picking me clean.'

'So you remembered the raid on Melong.'

'Hell,' he said. 'I was one of those officers standing on the bank when those goddamn little boats opened up. They fooled us all and it was a miracle I didn't get killed. I passed on the suggestion and the boats got ordered through Wong and Rooseno. I made arrangements for all the accouterments, the gun mounts, the makeshift torpedo tubes put on the boats at a dry dock in Jakarta.'

It was a good plan, but there were hitches from the beginning. The actual cost would run about six million dollars and the financing had to be done sub rosa from the Jakarta end. So a dummy company had to be formed, and six million piggybacked into Jakarta on a transfer of American relief funds. Rooseno and an officer in the Bank of Indonesia had been hired to take care of it from that end, and the bank in Singapore would forward explicit directions on how the money was to be utilized, about who was to get what.

'Did Rooseno know what you had in mind?'

'Sure.'

'And Wong?'

'Hell, no. It was just a business deal with him.'

'You have a great act,' Clements said. 'But why did you come all the way to Bali to try to get me out of it?'

G. D. shrugged. 'We all knew Rooseno had to go. He was getting too greedy. By the way, Rooseno was to be killed on the platform in Jakarta but Lang became more urgent. Things haven't always gone according to plan, but then, hell, nothing does, does it, not in this part of the world.' He took another drink. 'But once I talked to you, I knew Rooseno hadn't tipped you off. So there was no reason that you should get the same treatment. Hell, I really wanted you out of the whole thing. That's the reason I was pushing the business. And that's still true, buddy. A hell of a lot of things have gone on that I don't like and I know how you feel. But if you can look at it in a different way . . .'

'You make it all sound inevitable. Run into a little trouble, trot out your hired killer and erase it.'

'Hell, I lost control of it,' G. D. said. 'The whole thing got too big. Pretty soon, it just became easier to order a hit than to try to hide one more move. I thought it was pretty ironic that you were approached to help finance the deal on the boats.'

'So this is what it all comes down to,' Clements said. 'One big slaughter, Vietnam style.'

'I'm going to wipe out some of the most corrupt bastards on the face of the earth,' G. D. said. 'The very goddamn people who will finish me off in a different way if I don't get them first. On the night of the fireworks I'll have three boats on the river. They're souped up, manned by mercenaries. They'll sweep in and blow hell out of that lawn party, massacre the combined oil ministries of all the Southeast Asian countries.'

'My God,' Clements said. 'What's the point?'

'That's the beauty of it. The groundwork's been laid. It's going to look like it's the work of one big terrorist group, out to overthrow the Indonesian Government, bankrupt the country, cause the current government to lose face. And now our American group comes in, shocked by all the bloodshed, willing to protect all the oil operations, to guarantee with a cash bond that we'll do the job. Hell, there's a good chance we can get the backing of the American Government, Marines to guard the rigs.'

'And you don't think these people will know?' Clements

said. 'They're bureaucrats but they're not stupid, for God's sake.'

'They simply get some of their own back,' G. D. said. 'They may *suspect* but they won't know for sure. They give us concessions and we go back in business with a larger share and the American Government provides protection and everybody comes out okay. We'll even include the British and the Australians to give the whole damn thing an international flavor.' He snapped his fingers. 'Horace,' he said. 'The ambassador's coffee is bound to be cold.'

'Yes, sir,' Horace said.

'I don't want any more goddamned coffee,' Clements said. He shook his head. 'It's not going to work, you son of a bitch. Don't you know that?'

'I can't see any reason why not.'

'What's all this Six Ravens business?'

'I didn't pick that name. But it fits. It's a dummy corporation in Austria and a good code name for the operations and there are six of us involved. I am Raven Six. Raven Five was Oni Saud and Raven Four was the assassin. Raven Three was Rooseno.' He stopped, drank again. 'You remember the arguments we used to have in college? I believed that money could buy anything and that's the reason I wanted to corner the market on cash. You never agreed with that, did you?'

'And Raven number two?'

'The banker in Jakarta. But I'd really pick an honorary Raven number two.' G. D. inserted two fingers into his shirt pocket, extracted a business card and a folded piece of paper, flipped them onto the table. 'Hell, it's the first time I've ever been described as "an instigator."'

Squires's card. Folded down the middle, along with his note to Squires. And at that moment a movement caught his eye and he saw a woman come out of the cabana by the pool, dressed in a bikini. She sat down on a webbed chaise longue, began to cover herself with tanning lotion, starting with the shoulders. Sunglasses covered her eyes. She did not look in the direction of the house.

'What did you do to her?' Clements said. *The wrong question, and he remembered her face when she was telling him about herself, warning him against this moment, which she knew would come, sooner or later.* 'You bought her off,' he said. 'She didn't leave last night.'

'No. She waited until you had gone through the gibbon routine – hell, the guard didn't believe you; by the way, he had instructions to go along with anything that didn't let you walk out of here – and then she came up to the house and had a drink. But you ought to be pleased to know that she insisted that you not be hurt.'

And now Clements saw Lord Powell-Owenby coming up the path toward the pool from the guesthouse to the right and in that moment saw the rolling gait again and realized the Englishman was favoring his leg. No, not a real Englishman, and a chill ran down the bones of his spine despite the heat of the morning. 'Raven number four,' he said. 'Your assassin. Sangre-Lomax.'

G. D. shook his head in the negative. 'Don't fuck with him, Charles,' he said. 'He's really crazy. He knows that he's been assigned to guard you but sometimes I don't think he knows who he really is.'

Powell-Owenby had stopped to chat with Madeleine at the pool, lots of smiles, a pleasant tone to the conversation even if the words were lost from this distance.

'It won't work,' Clements said. 'The CIA knows that I'm here. I've told them what's going to happen.'

'You can't con a con man,' G. D. said. 'And you can't bluff somebody who's known you as long as I have. The CIA didn't believe you or there would have been some shifts in the defenses for the meetings. And there haven't been. Hell, Thorenson is one man who's dedicated to the status quo, and Squires isn't going to move until he has something real strong to go on. And he doesn't have it.'

'I won't let you get away with this,' Clements said.

'I admire your guts, but I think you'll change your mind,' G. D. said. 'If you want to get yourself killed' – he nodded toward Powell-Owenby – 'then you can count on him to do it if you give him the slightest excuse. He'll kill you and I'll be the first one at the mourner's bench, because we've been friends a long time, but I'll figure you've made that choice.'

And now Powell-Owenby was at the terrace. He carried a

cane which he used as a swagger stick, nestled under his left arm at the moment, sunglasses in place against the glare, impeccably dressed in a tropical lightweight suit and polished boots. 'Good morning to you, G. D.,' he said. 'And I hope you rested well, Mr Ambassador.'

'Yes,' Clements said.

'Are you ready for breakfast?' G. D. said.

'Quite so. I'm famished.' He looked up to Horace, who hovered over him. 'I would appreciate some best back bacon, if you have it, and two eggs, poached, and toast, of course. Orange marmalade. And coffee, the coffee first, I believe.'

'Yes, sir.'

Ah, crazy indeed, Clements thought, *the whole situation in general and the fake English lord in particular.* For out in the pure waters of the pool, picking up blue from the sky and the color of the tiles, the woman who had betrayed him was swimming, gliding through the water, and his friend of a lifetime was slowly trickling alcohol through his system and getting ready for mass murder, and the bogus Englishman was expressing delight at the stimulating effects of caffeine and admiring the day in such perfect English that Clements would think him real if he did not know otherwise.

Powell-Owenby poured hot milk into his coffee, stirred in sugar with a silver spoon. 'I understand that I will have the pleasure of entertaining you for the next couple of days,' he said, a fixed smile on his face, so rigid it seemed that it might shatter and break away at any moment.

'To a degree,' Clements said. 'I have a good bit of paperwork to do. So I'll be in my cottage most of the time.'

'I do hope you'll find time for me to show you my photography collection,' Powell-Owenby said. 'I do have some rather unusual items.'

'If you'll excuse me,' Clements said. He walked past the pool without looking in Madeleine's direction. Once he reached the cottage he examined the doors. He was not surprised to find that there were no locks.

He sat down in the living room, listening to the birds outside in the trees. An involuntary trembling seized him as he realized the odds were great that he would not leave here alive. And his threats had been so much bravado. G. D. was right about the ambassador. Thorenson would be only too delighted to have Clements absent from the meetings and Squires would be found eternally on the side of caution. When the time came, as it surely would, that Clements's presence was missed in Bangkok and the question was put, G. D. would cover it easily, delivering the big lie in a halting voice as if he were giving thought to his answer.

Hell, he was here a couple of days and then he said he had business to take care of. He had a hell of a good time at my place, I can tell you that.

And where did he go, Mr Majors?

Let me think. Features contorted, fingernail scratching the bridge between the eyebrows, lips pursed. *Yeah, I remember now. I had my pilot fly him to Hong Kong. Yeah, it's logged in my flight book.*

So easy to disappear in Southeast Asia, so many things that could happen to anybody. He went through the small kitchen, found no knives except dull-tipped blades with serrated edges which could be used for slicing but not for attack.

The whole thing seemed incredible, that this mild-mannered Englishman who seemed so delicate and precise in his movements could have sent the bullet smashing into Lang's skull, could have ripped Houghton's throat, could have rigged a bomb that had killed Rooseno and so many people who were not even remotely connected with any scheme that G. D. Majors was out to protect. And eventually, despite G. D.'s sentimentality and the over-simplification of the choices he offered Clements, Powell-Owenby, Sangre-Lomax, whatever he wished to call himself, would be assigned to dispose of Clements. G. D. could not afford to keep him alive.

The only question, therefore, was how long G. D. intended to let him live. That grace period, however truncated it might turn out to be, was his only hope of salvation. For he had now but two choices, to get himself out of this compound or to bring help to him, and for the moment the former seemed impossible. He would have to get a message to Squires, or to Thorenson himself, a simple call for help would do at the moment, and the Thai police would come rolling in (no firepower to stop them at the gates) and he would be taken away from the present danger.

He took a writing pad and a ballpoint pen from his attaché case and then he sat facing up the path toward the pool. He blocked out the message carefully, presenting the facts in a straightforward manner, trying to phrase it in language which would not seem hysterical. Once he finished the letter he folded it around one of his ambassadorial cards and sealed it in a letter-sized envelope. He addressed it to Ambassador Thorenson at the Empress Hotel. He folded it and put it in an inside pocket. Then he made his way down the path to the swimming pool, putting his sunglasses in place against the glare as he sat in the bright sunshine on a webbed deck chair immediately next to Madeleine's towel. She was still swimming, quietly lapping the pool, very much at home in the water, and she made her turn at the far end of the pool almost professionally, a flipping turn and a push off underwater, and then the almost silent strokes of her arms brought her to the end of the pool where he was.

She pulled herself out of the pool, stood dripping beside him, almost steaming as the sun struck the water on her flesh. She dried her hair with the towel, canting her head to one side. 'I'm sorry,' she said. 'I tried to tell you a hundred times, but I couldn't do it. I really didn't know about the boats and the attack. My Uncle Wong didn't either. I really believed my Uncle Rooseno was into smuggling. And I didn't know it would come this far. G. D. has promised me that you'll be released at the end of the week.'

'My God, you can't believe that,' he said. 'Don't you know who the Englishman is?'

She continued to towel her hair. 'A very delightful man.'

'He killed your Uncle Rooseno, Lang, Houghton, a dozen others in the Bali explosion. He's our psychopath.'

'I don't believe you. At this point, you'd say anything.'

'Then let's talk a language you can trust,' he said, aware that time was slipping away and that he had very little of it left. 'We'll talk money. How much do you want?'

'For what?'

'To take a letter to Ambassador Thorenson for me.'

She smiled ruefully. 'I don't think G. D. would trust me that far. I'm surprised that you would, after last night.'

'I was operating on faith then. Now I'm operating on currency. You're a clever woman,' he said. 'For enough money, I have the feeling you'd be willing to try.'

She sat down on the chaise longue next to him, stretched out as if offering herself to the sun. 'Put some lotion on my shoulders.'

'No,' he said.

'Why not?'

'If I touch you, I can't think of anything that would stop me from killing you.'

She turned her eyes toward him, narrowed against the sun, looked at him long enough to see that he meant what he was saying. 'How much are you offering then?'

No bargaining. The figure would have to be high enough to snag her instantly, without question. 'I have fifty thousand in a reserve account in a bank here. I'll give you a check for the entire amount. You can go to the bank and cash it before you deliver the letter.'

She shook her head in wonderment. 'You'll be wasting your money. You're in no danger here. I believe G. D.'

'And what about all the people who will be killed at the Empress Hotel?'

'They're none of my business. Politics is a dangerous profession.'

'Then you won't take the money.'

She thought about it a moment. 'You knew I'd take it when you made the offer.'

He went back to his cottage and made out a check on the Thai bank. But before he went back to the swimming pool, he took the turn toward the main gate and from the shelter of the bushes surveyed it by daylight. And he could see why G. D. had been operating with such sublime confidence that he would stay put. For there were three armed guards at the gate now and a crew of workmen was erecting heavy floodlights that would illuminate the entire gate area. Through the foliage he could see the beginning of the metal fence that circled the vast compound and the electric transformer that was connected to the top wires. Anyone who attempted to go in or out by scaling the fence would be electrocuted.

He doubled back to the pool and found that Madeleine was sitting on the chaise longue, her perfect legs extended in front of her. She had put on a pair of harlequin sunglasses that came to a rising feline point on either side of her eyes. She was smoking a cigarette. She glanced in his direction as he approached and then looked straight ahead.

He handed the check to her. She examined it carefully. 'And where's the letter?' she said, once she had found the check satisfactory. He handed her the envelope and she frowned at it. 'You just might be angry enough to have included a paragraph telling them to arrest me for fraud.'

'That's easily solved,' he said. 'Once you're out of here, open the letter and read it.'

She nodded, took the letter. 'You know I can't resist the money,' she said.

She walked toward the main house and he watched her go with mixed feelings. *Christ, the anger was there all right, burning brightly, and the hurt as well at the betrayal, but money blinded her, took precedence over all else. She had told him that and he had not paid attention.* He heard a voice hail him from the shadows of the terrace, and there was Powell-Owenby, dressed in a white shirt and slacks, white shoes, a natty white cap. And around his neck was a Leica camera suspended from a leather strap, a long lens making it look very heavy.

'I say,' Powell-Owenby said, through his fixed smile. 'Can I interest you in a drink, Mr Ambassador? I'm having a gin and tonic myself.'

Clements could feel the craziness in the charade which the bogus Englishman seemed to regard as real and Clements went along with it, not knowing what it would take to set the man off. For Powell-Owenby had a webbed belt around his middle, and on the webbed belt a leather holster, and in the holster, a snubnosed thirty-eight caliber pistol.

'Yes,' Clements said. 'Thank you.'

'A gin and tonic then, is it?'

'Yes, please.'

'A very civilized drink. I understand that from time to time you suffer a mild malaria.'

'That's correct.'

Powell-Owenby put the camera on the table, picked up a glass and held it even with his eyes while he poured the gin. Then he put down the gin bottle and repeated the same pattern while he poured in a dash of tonic. 'I'm not adding any ice, you see. This is an old, old remedy for malaria among members of the English colonials in the tropics, gin and tonic without ice, in precisely the right proportions. Preventive medicine, as well.' He slid the glass across the table to Clements, then raised his own. 'Cheers,' he said.

Clements lifted his glass, drank.

'Please do have a seat,' Powell-Owenby said. 'I do miss good conversation.'

'I'm in no mood for conversation.'

'Ah, but you should be.' The smile took on a crazy shine to it. 'Such a delicious little drama you were playing out with her. I was trying to send you my thought waves, to let you know what she was doing.'

'And what was she doing?'

'She has an agreement with G. D. He's agreed to pay her double any amount you give her. So how much did you give her?'

'Fifty thousand American dollars.'

'By check.'

'Yes.'

'Then that makes her one up, doesn't it? Fifty thousand that she can convert into a hundred. And I was all prepared with my camera because I thought there was a strong chance you would kill her.' He sipped his drink, eyes glittering. 'Tell me, if you *had* killed her, how would you have done it?'

'I wasn't going to kill her.'

'For the sake of conversation,' Powell-Owenby said, pronouncing each word distinctly. 'If you had, how would you have done it? That's not such a difficult question now, is it? You certainly have the physical strength. You have very large hands. You could have strangled her, for instance.

251

Thumbs in front, of course, parallel, vertical, to crush the larynx. Or you could have toppled her into the pool and held her under. In either case she would have died from asphyxiation, from loss of breath.' He poured himself another drink, his face contorted with the seriousness of the thought. 'Now, the question is, where does that last breath go?'

'I don't follow you,' Clements said. He eyed the pistol on the webbed belt, wondered what the odds would be if he went for it. Not good, he realized. For this was the man who was swift enough to slit Houghton's throat without a struggle, and Houghton was professionally trained.

'Just consider,' Powell-Owenby said. 'You reach for her and she takes an instinctive gulp of breath. Believe me, she would have. I know because I have experience in these matters. And when your fingers went around her throat, they would have trapped the air inside her. So the question is obvious, isn't it? If she had died, would the breath have been expelled? And I do mean "expelled" in the true sense of the word, sent out because the body had no further use of it.' He scratched the tip of his nose. 'I was rather hoping you'd do exactly that. I heard a theory from one of the African tribes that when that last breath goes, the soul goes with it, rides it out, so to speak, and I hoped that if I took a rapid succession of pictures as she died, one of the frames just might happen to catch a depiction of her soul. Would it be gray, I wonder? Would the soul of a woman like that, with absolutely no scruples at all, vary in color from the soul of a virginal woman who had done harm to no one? But then that leads to another question, doesn't it? For if a woman were truly virtuous, then it wouldn't be likely that anyone would want to kill her. Am I right? Would you care for another drink?'

'What do you want with me?' Clements said, cutting through the wandering maze of words.

'At the moment, a conversation.' Powell-Owenby smiled. 'And it seems to me a most stimulating one. Were you ever in the military?'

'Yes.'

'In a combat unit?'

'No.'

'Killing can be an exhilarating experience, you know, not only physically but aesthetically as well. There is a beauty in dying. The modern psychologists have only just now begun to come around to that way of thinking, because if death is a part of the life experience and life itself is beautiful, the process, of course, not the circumstances, which can be quite dismal, then it follows, *quod erat demonstrandum*, that killing can be a beautiful act as well. I know what you're thinking.' The eyes glistened with a smile. 'You think you have found a flaw in my logic and you relish my mistake, but I didn't say *is*, no, I said *can be*, all the difference in the world between the two. You do agree?'

'What do you want with me?'

'I'm a specialist, you know. An artist.' He picked up the camera in one hand. 'I would prefer to paint in oils. I have had lessons at the Royal Academy of Design and the Sorbonne, but that which I specialize in changes much too quickly. The moment of death is far too transient. I calculate that death occurs in a nanosecond. It is not precisely measurable, of course, but it happens too quickly, alas, for a brush to capture it. Even a camera is much too slow. There's no way it can be caught, as a matter of fact, unless it wishes to be caught. And properly, it should be done in a composition. A framework, so to speak.' And Powell-Owenby picked up the gin bottle again and held his glass at eye level to pour an exact measure. In that moment the rage which had been bottled up in Clements broke loose, beyond words, and he hurled himself at Powell-Owenby, caught him by surprise, grabbed him around the middle and threw him against one of the stone pilasters, and in that second grabbed the thirty-eight from the holster and moved away, breathing heavily. He was ready to squeeze the trigger and kill him on the spot only to find that Powell-Owenby was not even breathing heavily. The smile remained on his face, unperturbed.

'You see?' he said, picking up another glass, the first having been smashed on the marble terrace. 'You do have the proper reflexes, after all, wouldn't you say?' He squinted at the level on the glass which he had drawn in his mind,

253

past which the gin should not be poured. 'You couldn't kill the woman because you were not sufficiently threatened by her. You were angered, but that's not the same thing at all, now is it?' He poured in a thin trickle from the bottle. 'But with myself, the experience was different, because I *did* have the pistol, after all, and considering the frail grasp I have on reality, according to the way you think' – he smiled at Clements, winked as if sharing a joke – 'then you had to take a try at the pistol. But now, of course, you're faced with the other side of the problem. You didn't want to be killed and now you don't want to kill, do you?'

'I'll blow your head off unless you do exactly as I say,' Clements said.

Powell-Owenby tasted the gin, then carefully added just a dash of tonic, nodded to himself as if the proportions were now correct. 'You still don't grasp what I'm talking about, do you? It's all either/or with you. Either I do something or you shoot me, when you don't understand that I'm not afraid of being killed any more than I am afraid of killing. That's the essence of bullfighting, you know, the moment of truth, when the bullfighter risks being killed by the animal, when he takes the sword in over the horns and risks being gored.'

'You're going to get me out of here,' Clements said.

'How?'

'You're going to call for a car and then you're going to talk your way past the guards.'

'Taking you with me, of course.'

'Yes.'

'Wrong way,' Powell-Owenby said. He sat down, studied the glass and the mixture of gin and tonic. 'If you took this in the right spirit, old man, you'd take on the guards at the gate. After all, they don't have your intelligence, your wit or your grace. They would hesitate to kill you, because there might be penalties involved. That isn't to say that they wouldn't kill you, but they would hesitate, and in that hesitation give you the advantage.'

'Off your ass,' Clements said.

Powell-Owenby just smiled his crazy, humorless smile and drank his gin and tonic. 'I was off just a bit in shooting your aide. I was really aiming for the one spot right in the middle of the forehead, but then he leaned over to talk to you, just as I squeezed the trigger. The bullet went awry and disintegrated part of the skull. It was definitely a bad shot, no beauty to it at all. The photographs are definitely second rate.'

Clements brought the pistol up, steadied it in both hands until the muzzle was right in the center of Powell-Owenby's face. He remembered quite vividly the moment of Lang's death, that second when the young man ceased to be. He pulled the trigger.

The gun clicked.

He pulled the trigger again and again.

More clicks. Empty.

And with a roar he leaped toward Powell-Owenby and swung the pistol at his head. Powell-Owenby shifted to one side, like smoke in a draft of air, and grabbed his wrist with a hand of steel and flipped him over so that Clements fell hard against the marble, the useless pistol bouncing from his hand and skittering away into a flower bed. Clements was stunned by the fall and the striking of his head against the terrace, dizzy. He raised up to see that Powell-Owenby had taken a switchblade knife from his pocket and with a flick of a button the blade sprang out as if it were alive.

'I would ask you, sir,' he said, 'not to be afraid that I'm going to use the knife on you just because you aimed at me and pulled the trigger. Because you see, I'm truly pleased that you did that. It shows you have spirit. Do get up and sit down and finish your drink.'

Clements stood up. 'I don't want your goddamned drink. Obviously, G. D. has hired you to kill me. So do whatever you're going to do, but I won't have a fucking drink with you.'

'You don't understand me at all,' Powell-Owenby said. 'I get paid, of course, because the workman is worth his hire, and I do have to make a living. But no artist can work without patrons.'

Clements turned around and began to walk back toward his cottage. He expected Powell-Owenby to stop him at any moment, but the man's voice was quite pleasant. 'I would suggest that you cooperate with me, old chap, because it is a matter of choice now, isn't it? I mean, you're convinced that I'm crazy and I haven't disabused you of that conviction. And if I am crazy, then I may do the exact opposite of what you expect me to do, that is to say, that even if I were being paid to kill you, I might very well decide not to, if you get my meaning. So stop by my cottage this evening and see my pictures. About seven would be convenient. We'll have dinner. Something light, of course. And please don't try anything foolish or precipitate. We can really have some quite good times together. Quite.'

When Clements reached his cottage he was sick to his stomach from the blow on the head. He threw up in the toilet, then washed his face with cold water and caught a glimpse of his face in the mirror, pale, ashen, a slight cut on the right temple. And he talked to himself without speaking. *Ah, you've fooled yourself for years because you've believed that simply because you represented the United States that the whole damn country was there to protect you, and that if you went down the Marines would come marching in. Spoiled rotten.* And now he was up against it with a madman (*and how would he diagnose from what he knew of mental illness, schizophrenic, certainly, psychotic, a sociopath with a sense of reasoning that took nonsense and gave it meaning*), a madman who was not influenced by his position or the power that lay behind him.

Unless you do something, he's going to kill you.

He poured himself a shot of bourbon and then picked up the serrated knife without a point that he had examined and discarded before. He went through the house, looked out of all the windows. He could see no sign of Powell-Owenby or any of the guards. He found a radio, turned it on, raised the Thai music to such a level that the sound of what he was going to do would be covered by it. Then he opened the door and sat on the threshold, running the end of the knife blade back and forth on the cement. He despaired at first, for it seemed that the metal would wear a groove in the stone without being affected, but as he held the blade up to examine it, he could see that he was beginning to wear it down. Given enough time, two hours, perhaps three, he could work a point on the end of this knife, and then

Powell-Owenby, also known as Sangre-Lomax and a dozen other names, would have his chance to make an acquaintance with dying. Firsthand.

It took three and a half hours to bring the blade to a stiletto point, almost a needle tip, slightly unbalanced, because the blade did not grind down to a perfect symmetry. He carried it into the guesthouse, then found a broom and swept the bright metallic filings off the cement of the sidewalk.

He had never killed a man with a knife, yet all he had to do was to keep the image of Lang in his mind, the image of Lang dead, the conversation with Lang's mother, and when the time came he would have no trouble plunging the blade into Powell-Owenby's body. He took a sheet off the bed and tore it into narrow strips. First he wound a strip around the shin of his left leg, then laid the knife flat against the skin and took another turn or two of the cloth to hold it in place before he tied it off. And then he practiced.

He placed a pillow in the dining-room chair to represent Powell-Owenby, tying it at an appropriate height to approximate the position of his torso. And then he sat down in a chair across the table and pretended to be engaged in conversation. He leaned down to scratch his leg and in that moment grabbed at the knife. But the serrated edges stuck in the cloth and it took him a full fifteen seconds to pull the blade free.

That would never do.

He found the slick heavy paper of a magazine cover, cut it to the right length, doubled it over to serve as a sheath for the knife blade, allowing room for the blade to slide freely before he wrapped the rest of the cloth strip over it and tied it off. He took off his wristwatch and laid it on the table. He waited until the second hand rose to twelve and then grabbed for the knife. This time it came free instantly. He lunged across the table and plunged the homemade stiletto into the pillow. Only five seconds this time, but his aim had been off. The blade had plunged into the edge of the pillow. Not a vital spot.

Laboriously, he found a pen and drew a circle in the center of the pillow, at a position approximating the heart, and then tried again. It was awkward to raise the trouser leg and draw the knife. It required his full attention and was difficult to do

257

automatically. To bring the arm up and lunge across the table threw him off balance, so that he missed the target area again.

He tried twice more, either improved his aim at the cost of his timing or the timing at the cost of his aim, but neither was good enough. He rested, thought it through. When he sat down at the table he would have to pull the trouser leg high enough to clear the handle of the knife, eliminating one step in the chain of actions he had to take. He tried it. He sat down at the table, adjusted his trouser leg, quite normally, until he could feel the knife handle come free of the hem of the trousers. Then he timed himself once more, a series of movements reduced to one fluid motion, the hand grabbing the knife and coming up even as he had pushed himself across the table, placing his free hand flat on the tabletop to steady himself while the knife arm straightened like a pointer, lunged. This time the point of the blade pierced the exact center of the target area.

He was elated. He tried it again. Not so accurate this time, but the second time was perfect, the third was good, the fourth was more than adequate. After a half hour he stopped, close to a state of exhaustion, realizing that the odds were good that, with a little luck, he could bring it off.

There remained, of course, the problem of what he would do once he had killed Powell-Owenby. He would have to handle that most carefully. From Powell-Owenby he would get the weapons he needed, for he was certain that Powell-Owenby would have a veritable arsenal. If there was an operative telephone in Powell-Owenby's cottage he would not need the weapon. He would simply call out and alert Squires and the Thai police and then relax with the full knowledge that the authorities would take care of everything.

If, on the other hand, there were no operative telephones he would have to risk an attack on the front gate. If necessary he would kill the guards that blocked his way. There was no hope at all of traversing the wilderness behind the house, the branches of filthy klongs that wound their way through rain forest, the pens of animals, the electrified fences, the areas still undeveloped. No, it would have to be the front gate. He did not countenance the thought of

258

killing, especially men who would have no idea why they were dying except that they had been hired to hold ground. It was ironic that he had spent a whole career as a diplomat devoted to the avoidance of bloodshed. Now, with luck, he would have a meeting with Sergei and advance that very concept, and in order to accomplish it he would have to shed blood himself.

About midafternoon he felt the first slight chill and realized that the malaria was back. He took a mild dose of Atabrine to head it off, refused to medicate too much for fear it would dull his senses. He would need all of his resources tonight. Shortly before six he set up another practice session with the knife and the table and the pillow, worked until the movements were almost second nature to him and he could strike the vital zone each time. Then, with a half hour left before he was due at Powell-Owenby's cottage, he shaved and washed his face and combed his hair, feeling the chill waiting at the edge of his consciousness, ready to move in and seize him. Still he refused to take the full dose of medication. Instead he put the pills in a small container in his shirt pocket and then set out down the path toward Powell-Owenby's cottage. It was still some time before sunset, but from the remote reaches of the compound he could hear the cry of the gibbons and the chatter of the monkeys as if they knew that night was coming. This close to the equator there was no twilight, for there was no traverse of the sun across the western horizon and it simply plunged straight ahead and sank like a stone, leaving an instant darkness behind it. He comforted himself with the thought that with any luck he would be out of here tonight, back in a rational world with the reestablishment of sanity.

His heart sank as he neared the cottage, for he heard the sound of voices and realized that Powell-Owenby was not alone. He saw the two of them standing just inside the open French doors, Powell-Owenby in his white linen suit talking to Madeleine, who was wearing a black silk sheath dress. A beautiful woman who wore an orchid in her hair and at one time would have taken his breath away with her presence, but not now. He went through a mental readjustment of his plan. There was still the possibility he could use the knife on Powell-Owenby, that the plan would work, and now he wondered if he could kill Madeleine as well, if his desperation came to that point.

'I'm delighted you could make it, old chap,' Powell-Owenby said. 'It occurred to me that you might not object if I enlarged our dinner party.'

'May I speak to him alone for a moment?' Madeleine said to Powell-Owenby.

'Of course,' Powell-Owenby said, a glint in his eye as he looked at Clements. 'Please do speak with her,' he said. 'Otherwise, she will sulk through the dinner and there's nothing I find more depressing than a sulking woman. I'll speak to the cook. Too, we can't begin until G. D. gets here. So fix him a drink if you will, my dear.'

And automatically, without consulting him, Madeleine turned to the bar and began to pour bourbon into a glass, adding water, lifting ice cubes with silver tongs. She handed him the glass, then sank down in a chair opposite him, lit a cigarette.

'You didn't deliver the letter,' he said.

She looked toward the dining room to make certain they were alone, then lowered her voice. 'I didn't believe they were going to have you killed. I thought you were lying about the Englishman.'

'What happened to change your mind?'

'I asked G. D. He told me the truth. I didn't know or I wouldn't have gone along with it. You have to convince G. D. that you're with him, that you approve of what he's doing. He doesn't want to kill you. He's proven that. If he had wanted you dead he could have done that a long time ago.'

'And what about Powell-Owenby?' Clements said.

'He takes orders from G. D.'

'And if I go along, G. D. calls off the dogs.'

'Yes.'

They were interrupted now as G. D. came through the French doors wearing his tropical suit, looking fit, his skin the consistency of leather from his constant exposure to the sun. He was looking tired this evening, as if the day had been a long and difficult one. 'Well Charlie,' he said. 'How goes it?' And then to Madeleine: 'I'd appreciate a drink, scotch and soda. Two cubes of ice.'

'You look harried, G. D.'

'I sure as hell am,' G. D. said soberly. 'You should be at those meetings, listen to the talks.' G. D. accepted the drink from Madeleine, sat down, tasted the liquor. 'They've whipped themselves into a frenzy against the interference of the Americans and the Brits, and they're looking for a way to get at the Dutch as well. They've passed another resolution stating that there's going to be a freeze on the assets owned by any foreign companies in Southeast Asia. Equipment, financial assets, everything. And these assets will be evaluated and then the foreign companies will be allowed to take the equivalent of those assets in oil, over a protracted period of time.' He finished the drink, held it to Madeleine for another.

'So they really do have you by the short hair,' Clements said.

'No thanks to the goddamned U.S. Government, who's been sitting around with a thumb up their collective asses while all this has been allowed to happen.'

Clements sighed, lit a cigarette for himself. 'You're going to compound the problem,' he said, deciding to try a different tack, to test Madeleine's suggestion.

'How's that?'

'You're not stupid,' Clements said. 'At the final meeting there will be Thai royalty in attendance. That's customary, isn't it?'

'I don't know who the hell is going to be there.'

'Then you had better find out. If you mount your attack and harm Thai royalty, you cut your own throat. They worship the royal family and they carry grudges for a hundred years.'

G. D. studied his face, pushed the ice around in his glass with a callused finger. 'Are you reevaluating, Charlie?' he said.

'Maybe.'

'That's good,' G. D. said. 'Damn good.' He clinked the ice in his glass, then drank again. 'But the conference solved that Thai problem for us. They're going to finish up tomorrow, a day early. So the fireworks go tomorrow night, and the conference received a message from the King himself, expressing regrets that none of the royal family would be able to attend. By the way, Squires asked about you today, wondered whether you were coming to any of the meetings. I told him you were having a touch of malaria, might have to miss the whole thing. He sends his best.'

'So the ambassador has his garden party one day early,' Clements said.

'We all move up one day.'

'And what if I decide to take your offer, G. D.? What if I decide to go along?'

'Well, I think if you dictated a statement tomorrow, lay the attack at the door of the Southeast Asians for causing such political strife, and saying that cooperation with the West is the only answer, then I think that might do it. You'd be showing who your friends are.'

'I'll give it some thought.'

'I think dinner is now ready,' Powell-Owenby said from the dining room.

'Then let's eat,' G. D. said. And to Clements: 'Let me know which way you want it. And soon.'

The dinner was Thai, spicy rice and meat, served by the kitchen staff from the main house. Clements ate sparingly, drank little of the wine, aware of the subcurrents at the table, Powell-Owenby's sprightly manner with an occasional glance at him as if to gauge his mental temperature, G. D.'s inclination to reminisce about the old days at the university and early days in the oil business, and Madeleine's withdrawal into a reserve which was apparent to no one except Clements.

Clements was aware of the knife bound to his leg, and he thought how ironic it was that the way they were seated at the dinner table, with Powell-Owenby at the head of the long, thin table and Clements at the foot, there would have been no possibility of using the techniques in which he had trained himself all afternoon.

After dinner G. D. drew him to one side, lit up a cigar. 'Well?' he said.

'All right,' Clements said. 'You can count me in.'

'Good. It's the only sensible solution,' G. D. said. 'You couldn't have gotten out of here because I've put extra men on the front. And you know about the difficulties out back or you would have tried that during the daylight hours.'

'And what about your Powell-Owenby?'

'I'll have a few words with him,' G. D. said.

'If I make a deal with you, I want him hung by his thumbs.'

'That would be a little difficult,' G. D. said. 'He'll be shipped out of here by the day after tomorrow.'

'All right,' Clements said.

'I'm glad you decided in this direction, buddy,' G. D. said. 'I'll see that you get a typewriter in the morning.' He reached out, shook Clements's hand. 'Now I better go take care of things.'

G. D. walked over to Powell-Owenby, who was standing by the French doors, almost reached out to touch the man's elbow but caught himself in time, because Powell-Owenby had made it clear that he did not like to be touched by anybody. G. D. gestured toward the door and Powell-Owenby followed him outside, into the warm night air on the terrace.

'You should add another European to your kitchen staff,' Powell-Owenby said. 'The Thais rely far too much on spices, to the point that one flavor is canceling another.'

'I've been thinking,' G. D. said. 'About Clements.'

'A word of advice, if you'll permit me,' Powell-Owenby said. 'I think he'll do whatever you ask him, but when the time comes, if he can't stop you, he'll blow the whistle on what you've done. And he does have influence. Let me kill him. That's what I'm paid to do.'

'What the hell difference does it make to you?' G. D. said, bluntly. 'You get paid the full fee whether he lives or not.'

'No difference at all, personally. That's up to you, of course,' Powell-Owenby said. 'My best advice at this point would be for the ambassador to disappear, permanently. Then you don't have to worry about him, one way or the other. Whatever influence he has or doesn't have is simply neutralized.'

G. D. looked away, blew a cloud of blue cigar smoke into the heavy night air, studied the coal. 'He's my friend.'

'So?'

'So I don't want to know what happens to him. I don't want one goddamn word from you about what you've done or how you've done it. As far as I'm concerned, he's cooperated and gone back to the States or to Europe. You understand?'

'That's the way it should be,' Powell-Owenby said. 'It's the age-old concept of somebody departing on a permanent trip.'

'That's the last I want to hear about it.' G. D. nodded to Madeleine. 'It's time to go back to the house.'

'And what about Clements?' she said as she came out the door. 'What happens to him?'

'He's staying here awhile,' Powell-Owenby said. 'I'm showing him pictures. He's a photography buff.'

'You know what I mean,' Madeleine said. 'What happens to him?'

'He's accepted my proposition,' G. D. said. 'Where he goes or doesn't go is up to him, but I imagine he'll be going back to Jakarta tomorrow night.'

She nodded, accepting, walked off through the darkness toward the main house. G. D. paused as if he had something more to say, then decided against it. He waved at Clements once more, fixing in his mind the image of his friend alive and well, before he followed Madeleine to the house.

I can read you like a book, G. D., Clements thought. I've known you too long not to recognize the signs, and I know that underneath it all, you're a cautious bastard. You've told him to go ahead with the execution.

Because for all of his high rolling with money, G. D. didn't take chances on human beings. After his first wife he had insisted on each of the subsequent mates signing prenuptial letters of agreement, because his trust level was so low, and in each case, as he betrayed and then projected that betrayal onto the woman, it only confirmed what he had already set in his mind, that there was nobody on earth he could trust completely.

264

You're right not to trust me, G. D., you son of a bitch, because you're just as responsible for the bloody murders as your madman.

G. D. was doing the only thing he knew how to do. He had no taste for confrontation. He preferred that people who caused him problems should simply disappear, so he could preserve the illusion that he was not responsible for what happened to them. G. D. had shed his last wife by giving an attorney instructions that he did not wish to see the woman again, that she was to walk away with absolutely no fuss. Clements was sure the death sentence had been passed to Powell-Owenby.

In a way Clements was relieved. By that one act all that was past between him and his friend was now dissolved, and there were no debts to be paid. But now Powell-Owenby would require all his energy. The bogus Englishman was a true schizophrenic with wild mood swings and a logic which could not be predicted. Clements would have to take this night minute by minute and wait for his chance, knowing that the knife still lay against his leg, ready to be used. When that moment came he would not hesitate to kill him.

Powell-Owenby lit the candles in the living room of the cottage and squinted at the label on a bottle of liqueur. Powell-Owenby's face was a mask of rigid pleasantness. He saw to the dismissal of the servants, sending them back to the main house, and then he poured two small glasses full of the liqueur and brought out a leather portfolio with handles which he placed on the coffee table and left closed, awaiting the preface he would give before the exhibit.

'This is an Italian liqueur,' he said. 'Corsican, actually. Originally it had something to do with the blood of goats, either actually or symbolically, I'm not sure. Cheers.' He raised his glass, his eyes not leaving Clements's face for a second, studying, assessing, gauging.

Clements tasted the liqueur. It was sweet, heady. He did not drink it. 'That's very good,' he said.

'It's different.'

'Yes.'

Clements remembered another incident with a psychotic who had broken into the embassy in Paris and held a clerk at knife point, constantly talking all the time he roved the office in a lucid babble of French and English. And since the clerk was weeping, and the police were evacuating the building and Clements was the only man left on the floor, he stepped into the room and immediately entered the mind of the lunatic, chatting about de Gaulle and Nixon in exactly the same way the psychotic saw them, agreeing to the wild leaps of logic, the brilliant idiocy until the Marines were able to move close enough to a side door of the office that they could grab the man when his back was turned.

The psychiatrist had commended Clements for his coolness under pressure, for the way he had handled the man. One never disagreed with a dangerous psychotic. One never exploded the illusions, or did anything to set him off, and yet now, as Clements watched Powell-Owenby, he could remember the final remark the psychiatrist had made before he left the embassy.

'Of course, you were also very lucky, Mr Clements. Because there was always a fifty percent chance that regardless of what you said he was going to hear what he wanted to hear and would have killed either you or the clerk anyway.'

Powell-Owenby was leaned back in an overstuffed chair, hands laced over his lean chest, smiling. 'Penny,' he said.

'What?'

'The old expression. A penny for your thoughts.'

'No sale.'

Powell-Owenby laughed. 'So what do you think your American friend and I talked about before he went back to the main house?'

'That's not difficult,' Clements said. 'He waffled a bit and then decided it would be best if you go ahead and dispose of me.'

'Perfect. And what will I do, Mr Clements?'

You'll kill me if you can, he thought. 'I expect you'll follow orders.'

'Would you like another liqueur?' Powell-Owenby said.

'No, thank you.'

Powell-Owenby frowned. 'But you said you liked it.'

'I do. But shortly I'm going to have to take an Atabrine for

266

my malaria. And the combination of the medicine and certain alcohols makes me sick.'

'Then you're excused. But I shall have another.' He poured the small glass full of the red liquid, then held it to his nostrils, enjoyed the smell of it with his eyes half closed. Clements's eyes darted around the room in search of weapons, a pistol, anything, but from the looks of it, Powell-Owenby was either truly defenseless or was trying to lead him into another rash action.

Powell-Owenby drank, very slowly. 'There are some things in life that are like no other things and this drink is one of them. But I would like to get to the pictures. With a preface, of course.' He rubbed his hands together in anticipation. 'Now, as you will be able to guess from the subject matter, I make my own prints. I'm very careful with cropping because I'm a great believer in composition, but I do not retouch the image itself. The image is sacred and should not be altered. Tampering with it would render it meaningless.'

'Do you mind if I smoke?'

'Not at all.' Powell-Owenby slid an ashtray in front of him, a bronze fish. Clements laid his cigarettes and a box of small wooden matches on the table in front of him. As he lit a cigarette he closed down some area of sensibility within him and told himself that he would be looking at pictures, nothing more, flat patterns of black and white and color on emulsified papers. He would refuse to react, in the clear knowledge that Powell-Owenby, a sly expression in his eyes, expected him to react.

The viewing of the pictures began, some of the prints almost abstract in concept, but they were all pictures of death. The first was one of a dog Powell-Owenby had shot, the picture taken just as the animal exploded into an amorphous shape of blood and tissue. 'Frankly experimental,' Powell-Owenby said. 'I mounted a SLR camera on the barrel of the rifle and with the right speed and f-stop managed to catch the moment of impact, and perhaps a fraction of a second following impact, in time for the shape to take form. But here's another.' And the next picture was a human being, just the head, a grainy picture because it had been enlarged, and the eyes had a glazed look about them, the lips drawn back from the teeth in a grimace. It was only when Clements studied the picture that he saw the ragged line across the neck, with the blood seeming to leap away from the slash. This was a picture of Houghton in the process of dying and Powell-Owenby was watching his face very closely, looking for revulsion. Clements would not give him that satisfaction.

Powell-Owenby was leading up to something. The next picture was that of a man who had just been shot in a ruin in Bali and had toppled backward into a stone niche just as if he had been laid out for a funeral.

'That's a freak picture, of course,' Powell-Owenby said. 'A good composition but in reality I had nothing to do with the aesthetics of it, except that I shot him in such a way that he did fall backward in that particular pose. So in that sense the picture reflects an action on my part, but it's more serendipity.'

He flipped the next photograph faceup. At first Clements could make no sense of it and it took a long moment for him to realize that this was the picture that Powell-Owenby had taken of the explosion at the bridge, in color, and the fireball had just formed, a ragged circle on the left of the frame, with musicians scrambling away from the heat that would consume them, and Rooseno standing with his hand raised, his whole body on fire.

'The framing is everything here,' Powell-Owenby said, with rising excitement. He swept a finger along the right side of the picture, at the trees, which were three perfect vertical lines. 'You can see how the lines balance the oval shape of the fireball, and the burning man is in the center. Eventually, of course, I shall exhibit this one. I shall call it "Burning Man," a metaphor for life and death, with the most glorious flame at the moment of dying. One might say that this man encountered the peak experience of life, which in this case happened to be pain, just at the moment of leaving it.'

Ah, Clements thought, sucking on the cigarette, and Powell-Owenby was trying to move him into action with all this talk of art which denied the reality of the pictures themselves. But what Powell-Owenby did not realize was that he was providing Clements here with the one thing that Clements lacked and could not get elsewhere, hard evidence, the pictures prima facie proof of murders, and with every time that Powell-Owenby lifted a print to reveal another, he left his fingerprints on them. And Clements sucked on the cigarette and suddenly realized what Powell-Owenby was going to do.

For there was a camera somewhere in this room, and the lens was trained on Clements, and somewhere on Powell-Owenby's person there would be a remote-control device to operate the camera at the moment he decided to use his pistol.

Curious, and then it became clear. However Powell-Owenby had come by the knowledge, whether he had observed the grooves in the concrete where the metal had been ground down, or whether he had observed the process, *he knew about the knife*, knew that Clements had trained himself and was now offering him the opportunity to use it, even to the point of appearing to be so engrossed in the composition of the pictures that he would not notice if Clements's hand slid down to the handle of the knife.

No, you son of a bitch, you won't have that, Clements thought. He kept both hands on the table, in plain sight. Powell-Owenby could not mistake any of his movements as a threatening gesture. And then came the photograph that Clements knew would come, the one which was supposed to provoke the action. But when Powell-Owenby's hand slowly turned it over, Clements was ready and he made no reaction to the close-up of Lang's agonized face as he was cradled in Clements's arms on the speaker's platform, the head out of proportion, only moments after the shot, the rain streaking straight down as if to provide a veil and soften the details. Clements was sick to his stomach but he did not show it. Instead, he lit a cigarette.

'A shame,' he said.

'What?'

'That you couldn't have taken this about five seconds earlier. It would have been classic.'

'Oh?' Powell-Owenby said, truly startled, not expecting any of this.

'It would have been the exact composition of the Pietà,' Clements said. 'A modern counterpart. Five seconds earlier, his face was more downcast, because he had just been hit. And then he raised his head to speak to me. But then, one can't be lucky all the time.'

'Nonsense,' Powell-Owenby said. 'His head was farther back. It was forced back by the hit.'

Clements shrugged. 'If you say so.'

'Don't patronize me.'

'I told you what I thought.' He ground out his cigarette in the belly of the bronze fish, shook another cigarette free from the pack. 'You're the artist here, after all.'

'If it had even approached the composition of the Pietà, I would have known it.'

'I apologize,' Clements said, knowing that even as he said it Powell-Owenby was becoming more excitable. He leaned over to examine the picture more closely. Clements took another match from the box, lit it, and then, quite casually, dropped it into the open box of matches which whoofed up in a quick ball of flame, directly below Powell-Owenby's chin. He jerked back, reflexively, off guard, just as Clements right hand scooped up the bronze fish and with all his might hit Powell-Owenby in the center of the face with it, knocking him backward, upsetting the chair. Yet even in that second Clements knew he did not have the advantage, for in the act of falling, one of Powell-Owenby's hands was reaching out to break the fall and the other was scooping the pistol from the back waistband of his trousers.

Clements grabbed the handles of the leather portfolio and snapped it shut as he headed for the door. He heard the pistol explode behind him, heard the whine of the bullet against marble, then he was out onto the terrace, plunging immediately toward the darkness of the trees, anticipating, not surprised at all as he plunged into the heavy undergrowth that the lights suddenly flicked on behind him, the floods that bathed the terraces and the pool but could not reach into the trees. He stayed where he was. In another moment Powell-Owenby came out onto the terrace. Clements was amazed at how quickly he had recovered himself.

For he seemed totally unruffled, the automatic weapon held in the crook of his arm as if it had grown there, the camera on a strap around his neck. 'I know you can hear me, Clements,' he said in a casual, conversational voice. 'That was really quite clever of you, old man, the first time that I have been caught off guard since I was a child. But it shan't happen again. So watch yourself, please. I wouldn't want you to make this too easy for me. And should you consider throwing yourself on the mercy of the gate guards, I prefer that you wouldn't.' He stood silent, head pivoting, eyes slowly searching for movement. He saw none. 'I'm going to get some insect repellent,' he said at last. 'The mosquitoes are terrible. So if I were you, I would use the time, old chap.'

He went back into the cottage. Clements faded into the darkness of the path through the trees, aware that his chances were minimal. But he was alive for now, and he had won the first bout, and he would hold on to that life as long as he could.

Powell-Owenby went back into his cottage and examined his face in the mirror. The flare of the matches in the box had singed his left eyebrow and the hair just above his scalp line, turning it wiry and brittle, left a burn akin to severe sunburn on a portion of his forehead. The edge of the bronze fish had caught him on the cheekbone, caused an abrasion which was close to a cut, and it would have been painful except that by force of will he kept it from hurting him.

He had been taken by surprise, because he had been so certain that Clements would choose to use the knife, and he had set the camera on the buffet to capture the action at precisely the right moment, with the lighting so arranged that his own face would have been in shadow and Clements's profile unrecognizable, because he had in mind a picture which would have been breathtaking, one of those classics in which the man with the pistol would have been equally close to death from the knife at the moment of firing. He did wish the blade could have been more substantial instead of being a cheap cutting knife, hand ground against concrete, but he doubted that the end photograph would have been that discriminating in detail.

But now he was faced with a marvelous prospect, for Clements existed out there, and Clements had the photographs which could tie Powell-Owenby (in his other forms of course, Sangre, Lomax, *et al.*) to the killings of so many people, and that made this night all the more exciting, for there was something at stake. But since he was now British, working within the rigors of a code which was far more stringent than he had ever faced before, there were certain concessions which he had to make. The first, of course, was an evening of the odds. He went into the trunk he carried with him and selected a very light twenty-two-caliber rifle. He removed the magazine and slipped one round into the chamber and then went outside again. The night was stuporous with a damp heat. At the edge of the trees he stopped, leaned the rifle against the trunk of a tree and spoke again in a conversational voice.

'Clements, old chap,' he said. 'I'm not giving you even odds of course, because that would be rather stupid of me, but I am giving you a bit more of a chance. Only one round, but you were so clever in the room that you should be able to make full use of it.'

He stood, listening. He heard nothing except the cackle of night birds and the chatter of monkeys, proof that something was aprowl out there in this jungle. He went back to the house and called the main gate, talked with the captain in charge, left orders that if Clements turned himself in, he was to be delivered to Powell-Owenby. Then he called the main house, got Horace on the telephone. He told Horace not to disturb his master but that Clements was loose. The main house should be locked up tight in case Clements decided to come in that direction.

Only then did Powell-Owenby sit down for a moment. He took an upper with a gin and tonic. Despite his powers of concentration, his cheekbone had begun to hurt. The pain was there because the personality of Sangre had begun to leak through from the past. Sangre indulged himself in self-pity and hurt too easily and was always down on the world. In a minute or two, with the gin and the pill working together, Sangre faded away and Powell-Owenby felt a rush, as if caught up in a sudden surge of hopefulness.

A picture popped into his mind, an inspiration, a composition he wanted to capture tonight, not like anything he had done before, but one which would serve as the last image in a volume of images. For there was in the center of G.D.'s godforsaken mini-jungle a crocodile pool, an end of a stagnant canal that had been blocked off from the active canal, which wound its way through the trees to the river. G.D. had undertaken to raise Thai crocodiles for their unique leather, which was most expensive. Powell-Owenby had watched the feeding one afternoon, with servants throwing large chunks of red meat into the water, which already had a greenish cast from crocodile saliva.

He had been most impressed by the reptilian maelstrom, the hurtling of scaly bodies into the muddy water, the flashing of teeth as the giant jaws ripped and tore, the crocodiles rolling to tear meat loose from bone. And Clements would end up in that water tonight. Powell-Owenby formed the image in his mind, one leg extended from the muddy surface of the canal, the shoe in place on the foot, the entire upper half of the torso caught in the grip of the long jaws and teeth, and the picture would symbolize modern man being consumed by the ancient evil and proof that brain power was no match for the power that lay in those vestigial remnants of the days of the dinosaurs.

He finished the drink and waited until the pill had taken full effect. He stood up and tested the leg to see if he could detect even a shred of pain, of discomfort. He sprayed himself with insect repellent, then selected a camera, a Nikon with a variable flash, and finally a weapon, a light submachine gun with a magazine of tracer bullets. He turned out all the lights in the cottage and with a powerful flashlight (he corrected his own thoughts, his American terminology, for Powell-Owenby would call it a 'torch') he swept the edge of the trees. He was delighted to see that the rifle he had propped against the tree trunk was gone.

Fine.

An exciting bit of business that, one bullet out there which could kill him if Clements used it properly.

Powell-Owenby slipped out the back door of the cottage, pulled his shoulders back, the better to inhale the rich night air. Slowly he moved into the protective cover of the trees and froze. He was perfectly willing to take his time, to become a part of the night, to wait, to listen and to see. Clements would be the impatient one, and that impatience would cause him to make a mistake, and the mistake would cost him his life.

Clements grabbed the rifle and retreated into the bush, stopped close enough to the light that he could examine it to make sure it was not a trap of some sort. He took out the cartridge, looked down the barrel, saw light, not blocked so that it would explode in his face. The single bullet was intact, not tampered with, no tricks here. He had not the slightest clue why Powell-Owenby would provide him a weapon, except as a sort of nonverbal boasting that even with this weapon Clements would still have no chance.

He jammed the bullet in the chamber and moved away from the light, down a twisting path, trying to remember how G.D. had laid out his own small jungle which he had intended someday to turn into a nature park until he had gotten so involved in his oil deals that this property was put on hold and left as it was until G.D. could get back to it. He did know that there was a canal snaking through it, that the canal fed a water purification plant in one area and a crocodile pit in another, that there were bridges leading among cages full of tropical birds, monkeys and gibbons toward the back of the property.

Clements smelled the klong before he came to a footbridge leading across it. In the dim light of a half-moon filtering down through the trees he saw a motorboat anchored beneath the bridge, but he also heard the clanking of the chain which held it in place. He made his way down the bank, followed the chain with his hand to the point where it looped around a wooden bridge piling and doubled back upon itself. He fumbled with the padlock, massive, so heavy that one twenty-two-caliber bullet was not going to break it apart. And even if he could have freed the boat he had no idea how to make it operative without the key. And it was likely there was some sort of gate across the klong at the edge of G.D.'s property which would block his escape if the motorboat managed to drift that far.

He took to the path again, through the trees, jumping as

he heard a yowl. He was in front of one of the gibbon cages, the longarmed ape shaking the wires. The lock which held the cage door shut was insubstantial. He knocked it loose with one blow of the rifle butt, then opened the door and moved out of the way as the gibbon came out of the cage, chattering as it took to the trees. There was a platform within the cage, built on a tree trunk stripped of bark and sheltered by a slant roof from the daily rains. Clements put the portfolio of pictures on the board platform, then closed the cage behind him. He realized that he was wandering aimlessly, with no plan, either for his own defense or a possible attack. Unless he came up with something, Powell-Owenby could always outwait him until daylight and then pick him off at his leisure.

Christ, he felt a shiver again, the malarial chill. He would have to deal with that first, facing the possible dulling effects of the pill rather than the certain shakes and fever which would be on him before morning and leave him debilitated and powerless to protect himself. He fished a pill from his pocket and dry-swallowed it. He sat against a tree and with a sinking feeling in his stomach realized that he knew absolutely nothing about self-defense, about hand-to-hand combat. All of his military training had been cerebral, not physical. He sorted through all of the case studies he had read of men who had been captured by the North Vietnamese and was depressed to find he could remember no incident in which an American had escaped.

And then he remembered the fight in the Chinese ring, with Wong looking down at fighters imitating animals, and he tried to remember exactly what it was that Wong had said. Something about illusion, something about bluff, something about the aura of confidence that the one man displayed that made his opponent believe that he had powers which he did not have.

Illusion, deception.

He was up against a deranged mind which had no real grasp of reality anyway. He could not depend upon Powell-Owenby to see an illusion even if Clements were able to create one. And then Clements remembered the photographs again, the objective images which brought

275

back to him his feelings of rage. Fever or fear notwithstanding, he would find a way to kill the son of a bitch who was stalking him out there.

The second pill made Powell-Owenby feel invincible. He stayed against the trunk of the tree while his mind went spinning off in a million directions all at the same time, back and forward in time at the same moment, all in perfect balance, everything within his control. He created an English estate in his mind, with a maze like the one at Hampton Court, and the full knowledge that he now had enough money to buy such a place, and a part of him was interviewing servants (*We shall want to hunt, Henry, for what would an estate mean without the fox and the hounds, eh?*) and Henry had been a man he had known in Cambodia whose last name was Lomax, and he remembered the frantic scramble to get to the detonator before the ambassador got out of range. But the photograph was a good one, nonetheless, a fine composition, the color of fire (orange and yellows) mixed with the color of blood (red, shades of crimson, venous blood near black), and Sangre had been a good name, because it meant 'blood.' Meanings were everything, quite, and he would write essays to go with the pictures in the book, *De Res Moribundus*, was that correct? Did it mean 'Of Morbid Things'? Latin. The chant of a priest. From where? South America, Bolivia. He rooted out the shred of memory. He had killed a man with a knife once in the shadow of a church with the priest's voice droning on in the distance, from somewhere inside the church.

Ah, work to be done, a challenge to be faced with one part of himself while the rest went on about other business. (*Is it possible to buy a title along with an estate, Your Worship? As to my original name, there is none, and it can be proven that my name is whatever I call myself.*) He glided down the path, noiseless, invisible. In his mind's eye he could see the pattern of all the paths and the canal as if there were a luminous map behind his eyes.

Clements, Ambassador, where will you be?
In the tall bushes, high up in a tree?
Wherever you are, death sits with you there,
Waiting to turn your soul into air.

Hummed, tunelessly, set it to music. Felt the melody in his veins. The automatic weightless in one arm, the torch (*Got that word correct this time, Your Lordship*) in the free hand, giving no light.

Time passed.

No sign of Clements. Other signs. Apes turned loose. Clever. Forms in the trees, skittering along the path, and Powell-Owenby was supposed to be confused by them and fire upon them, make his presence and location known.

Much too clever for that, old chap. All of us have contributed to each other, you see, and I am the sum of us all. So I award you a 'C' for an average effort.

He settled near the center of the vast compound, knowing that Clements would stay away from the electrified fences. And finally, near three in the morning, he heard Clements's voice ring out from someplace to the right. 'I have you spotted, you son of a bitch.' A quiet voice, determined. Was there also a touch of fever in that voice?

Powell-Owenby nestled in behind a tree. 'Very good, Mr Ambassador,' he said. 'I rather hoped you would make a stand.'

Silence.

Powell-Owenby laughed. 'I've given you a directional target,' he said. 'What more can you want? Of course, you are at a disadvantage, because you have only one shot. But if I were you, I think I would take the chance, old chap. Fortune just might smile on you.'

He jumped slightly. For to his left a rag tied to a tree had leaped into flame, the gasoline catching in a whomp, far enough away that he could see only a blur of movement as a form he had to assume was Clements moved into the shadows. Clever. Where had he gotten the gasoline? Was it Molotov cocktail time? He did not move. He could see the crocodiles in the muddy water now, from the glare of the

277

burning rag. He stayed tucked in against the tree.

Another whomp. Another rag leaped into flame, this side of the pond, not twenty feet away. He brought the muzzle of the automatic around, soundlessly, instantly alert, on the edge of action, finger on the trigger, thumb edging the safety off. He was ready now, for on the next lighting of a rag, he would cover the area with bullets. There was no way that Clements could outrun a spray of death ripping through the undergrowth.

And then it happened. Clements made his mistake. Miscalculation? Accident? Sheer stupidity, perhaps, with Clements taking the chance of hitting him. The twenty-two barked, the spark of the small explosion visible, ten feet to the left. Powell-Owenby stood up and pulled the trigger, sending an arc of bullets into the trees, spraying the area on both sides of where the rifle had been fired so he could not possibly miss. And then there was silence, no screams, no thrashing through the bush. He flicked on his torch and trained it toward the rifle. He blinked. For the rifle seemed to be suspended in midair, barrel pointed up and to the side as if it were floating, and it took him a moment to realize the rifle had been tied to a vine and there was a stick in the trigger guard with a string on it, and he tried to bring all the pieces of his mind together to deal with the trick.

'You made a mistake, you bloody bastard,' came the voice behind him and he whirled around, and the light caught the one view he had not anticipated, figured, Clements standing there with the hand-honed knife tied with rags to the end of a long straight stick, the point glinting in the light, already heading toward him so he had no time to move, to guard. The point caught him in the center of his chest, beneath the sternum, sliced up into his heart, and he yelled silently to Lomax and Sangre and all the others who skittered away from him and left him alone. *Oh, Christ, don't leave me alone, not now*, and in the moment of dying he looked for the face of the father he had never known, the mother who had been no more to him than a two-dimensional photograph, and he screamed out without sound. *Goddamn you, at least let me know my name*. No answers, nothing, and he tried to hold on to something until he could remember how to die, only to discover that it took no knowledge and no skill. A glimpse of clarity, a peephole into sanity. *Forgive me, Father, for I* . . . His fingers dropped the machine gun and the torch. He grabbed at the pole, trying to draw the knife from him, but there was no strength in him. And his vision began to fade just as he stumbled backward and fell into the muddy waters. He did not even see the low shapes that flopped into the water and headed toward him, jaws agape.

Clements was numb, winded, caught up in shock. Lang's face appeared in his mind and Houghton's and all the faces in the photographs and he turned away. He did not even watch what the crocodiles did to Powell-Owenby in the muddy water. For time was running out and he had only passed the first part of what was to be an ordeal. He picked up the submachine gun and the flashlight and moved back toward the gibbon cage to pick up the photographs.

10

He came onto the house from the side, and from the protection of the trees he spotted the guard who had been posted near the French doors, a young man with a carbine slung over his shoulder and a cigarette drooping from the corner of his mouth. The sky had begun to lighten in the east; the sun would be up shortly, and Clements heard the sputtering of boat engines on distant klongs, the equivalent of morning traffic, and it would have been easy for the guard to have ignored the sound of gunfire off in the jungle compound. The guard yawned, lit a fresh cigarette from the glowing remains of the first, just as Clements stepped in behind him and the butt of the submachine gun whacked against the skull. The man went down, soundlessly except for the clatter of his carbine against the cement.

Clements peered in through the glass pane of a French door, saw no stir of movement in the large room. He was tired now, light-headed from the Atabrine, but they would not stop him now. He would take control of the goddamn house and within a half hour he would put the whole matter in the hands of the authorities and be done with it. He broke the glass pane next to the inner lock, reached in and turned the bolt, then slipped into the house, holding the machine gun at ready, half expecting Horace or some of the servants to come running into the room, but there was no stir inside the house.

Only one guard? He could not believe it. He slipped through the house like a wraith, checked through the windows for the presence of guards outside. There were none. The servants were still asleep. He left the portfolio of pictures on a carved table. Then, wearily, he climbed the curved staircase to the second floor, padded down the carpeted hallway until he reached a pair of doors which were the entrance to the master bedroom. He eased one of them open. In the darkness of the room he made out the figure of G.D. asleep on a king-sized bed. Clements closed the door behind him, then walked over and opened the drapes covering the windows, which looked out over the compound to the west, the trees reflecting the light of the sunrise. He sat down in a chair next to the bed, looking at the sleeping G.D. with his mouth agape and a sonorous snore coming out of it, a stubble of beard on the face, and he remembered the young G.D. in the frat house in Austin who also slept with his mouth open. Times full of promise, now come to this. He felt no pity. He moved the weapon forward, pressed the cold barrel against the slack flesh of the cheek. G.D. snorted, came awake with a grimace, the fear leaping into his eyes when he saw Clements sitting beside his bed. He scooted away, reflexively, sat up in the bed.

'Jesus,' G.D. said, a prayer as much as an expletive of surprise. 'You startled the hell out of me.' He was beginning to recover now, and Clements could almost see his mind trying to assemble a position which would save him. 'What are you doing here so early?'

Always a lousy bluffer,' Clements said. 'Don't try it, G.D.'

'Bluff? I don't know what you're talking about.' He groped on the nightstand for a cigarette, lit one, inhaled. 'We came to an agreement last night, remember? You were going to pitch in with me.'

'He couldn't kill me,' Clements said.

'He wasn't even supposed to try.'

'You had better shut your goddamned mouth,' Clements said. 'I've had a hard night and I'm not in any mood to listen to your bullshit. You told him to kill me and he tried. My God, he tried, but your crocodiles have him now. So you will keep your mouth shut until I ask you a question or I'll blow you away. Nod if you understand. But not one goddamned word.'

G.D. nodded.

'Now, pick up the cigarettes and the lighter from the nightstand. Put them on the bed where I can reach them. But be very careful how you handle them.'

G.D. lifted the pack of cigarettes with great care, placed it on the covers, then put the lighter beside it and withdrew. Clements lit a cigarette. 'Now, you lift the telephone and you say exactly what I tell you to say.'

G.D. bobbed his head.

'You tell Horace that you want him to fix a pot of coffee and bring it up here. And then you tell him to patch your telephone into an outside line because you want to make a call.'

G.D. reached for the telephone, dialed a single digit, listened a moment, then jiggled the cradle. He tried again. 'The goddamn thing's dead.'

'It had better not be.' Clements came around the bed, the weapon trained on G.D. all the way, took the telephone receiver, put it to his ear. Completely dead, lacking even the blank resonance of a telephone left off the hook somewhere in the house. And suddenly it began to occur to him, the larger scheme which had not yet dawned on G.D.

'Get out of bed,' Clements said. 'We're going downstairs. But first, which bedroom is Madeleine in?'

'She's not here. She left last night.'

'Left to go where?'

'Back into the city.'

'For what reason?'

'She wanted to arrange for a flight back to Jakarta.'

Clements smiled, despite himself. 'Shit, G.D., it's no wonder you have yourself in a predicament. You've been had, all the way around.'

'What the hell are you talking about?'

'She's left a sinking ship, run out on you. And I'll bet you a hundred dollars that you don't have one goddamned servant downstairs. You've been left alone in an empty house.'

And now, as if he had forgotten that there was a machine gun trained on him, G.D. threw the covers back and without pausing to put on his slippers ran to the doors and threw them open. 'Horace,' he yelled. 'Get your goddamned ass up here. And I mean now. Horace!'

But his voice rang through the house without a sign of responsive movement. Clements came up behind him. 'We're going downstairs,' he said.

'What's going on here?' G.D. said, eyes almost frantic. 'Where are the servants?' And then, more quietly: 'Did you kill them?'

'No,' Clements said. 'Lead the way to the kitchen.'

G. D. made his way downstairs, muttering to himself, occasionally calling out for Horace again, swearing, making dire threats against the sons of bitches. The large tiled kitchen was empty. Clements sat down on a chair. 'You're going to make coffee,' he said.

'You've done this,' G. D. said, glowering at him before he opened a cupboard and took down a container of coffee. 'I don't know what you're pulling, Charlie, but this is your doing.'

'You're one dumb son of a bitch,' Clements said. 'Or maybe it's not that you're so dumb, but that they are so much more clever. I'll bet you another hundred dollars that you never met your Raven number one, your prime mover in all this.'

'Harvey MacDonald. He's president of Unicon, out of Sydney.'

'You're sure.'

'Hell, yes. I've known him for years.'

'But you didn't see him. You didn't meet with him about this. You told me this was all arranged by a go-between. Hell, you never even talked directly to him, just to one of his aides who was confirming the sending of some money or some arrangements.'

'He sent me a note. I know his handwriting. I can't be fooled. There wouldn't be any reason. He's losing as much as I am. Hell, don't try to jerk me around.' He poured bottled water into a percolator, measured the coffee. 'There wasn't any point in meeting personally.'

'A thousand dollars says he doesn't know one damn thing about any of this. His name was used, but you've been the fall guy all along, the one who would set everything up. It seemed logical and you never questioned it.'

'I don't know what the hell you're talking about,' G. D. said, turning on the heat beneath the pot.

'The one guard on the terrace,' Clements said. 'He wasn't there to protect you, to keep anybody out. He was there to keep you in.'

'Why?'

'I wasn't the last assignment for Powell-Owenby. When he had finished with me, he would have come for you. You wouldn't have been much of a challenge for him since you were alone in the house, unsuspecting. No servants, no telephone. He would have had a fine time inventing an innovative way of killing you.'

'I don't believe you. You're full of bullshit.' He waited on the coffee, stood at the kitchen window, looked up toward the gate, toward the mass of men and machines which were little more than shapes in the dim light of dawn. 'I've got a small army on my side out there.'

'Then you'll be free to test that after a while, if you like. I'm sure they're waiting for Powell-Owenby to get rid of me and come back and dispatch you and then let them know that the job is done. When he doesn't, they'll come in to find out why. I don't know what kind of deadline they're on, but they'll have one. And if they find you alive, then they'll kill you.' He nodded toward the coffee. 'Pour me a cup.' He kept the weapon trained on G. D., even as the cup was set on the table. He sipped the coffee, hot, black, bitter. 'It would make sense for them to loot the house. You have a goddamned museum here. And when they're through, they'll set it on fire, give it a good head start and then call in the totally inadequate fire department. But it will go up in a cloud of smoke and you with it, nothing left behind, no trace of any of this nonsense of the Six Ravens, and there's no chance you can queer up the works.'

G. D. looked as if the wind had been taken out of him, as if there was only a minimal resistance left within him. He poured himself coffee, sat down in his blue silk pajamas, sagged in the chair. 'Harvey knows that if I said one goddamned thing, I'd incriminate myself.'

'Precisely the point. If you said one goddamned thing, the authorities would investigate Harvey and find out he had absolutely nothing to do with this.'

'Then who?'

'I have my ideas. You must also know where the boats are.'

'They've already rendezvoused.'

'Where?'

'On the southern peninsula, south of Hua Hin, in the Gulf of Siam. I don't know where they are now.'

The coffee helped clear Clements's mind. Nothing was what it seemed. The enemy would have to have a contingency plan, something sufficiently strong to block Clements's original warning to Thorenson and Squires, something to make it an absolute impossibility. And even worse was the fact that Clements was going to have to use G. D., simply because he could not bring this off by himself. He wanted to leave G. D. behind, to suffer the agony of waiting for those guards to come up from the main gate, knowing that they were going to cut him to pieces and that he had no place to hide.

'You're going to help me,' Clements said.

'Why in the hell should I help you?'

'Because you really don't have any choice,' Clements said. 'You can cover this entire house and find that your servants took all your weapons before they left.'

'And what sort of deal are you offering me?'

'No deal,' Clements said. 'The chance to live a little longer, maybe.'

'And then?'

'If somebody else doesn't kill you, then I will.'

G. D. sipped his coffee, mulling it over. 'What do you want?'

'You have a motorboat down on the klong. I know it has gasoline in it because I used some of it. Is the klong closed off or does it open into the network of canals?'

'It's open.'

'Then you will get dressed and you'll get the keys, both for the boat and the lock. And you'll be damned quick about it.'

G. D. nodded, went up the stairs, followed by Clements, who watched him dress and then looked around the bedroom until he found the wet bar. He took two unopened bottles of scotch, a couple of packs of cigarettes. Downstairs, he picked up the portfolio of prints, all but useless now that he was beginning to recognize the larger scheme, but he carried them along anyway, making G. D.

carry the liquor as they went down the side path and into the trees, just beginning to come alive with the dawn birds.

They reached the klong, and after the whiskey had been stowed aboard, then G. D. fumbled with the padlock and Clements heard the shouts up at the house. The guards had passed their deadline, discovered what had happened and were spinning off the paths down into the trees. G. D. heard them too, became rattled, dropped the lock in the water as it came free. He climbed behind the wheel, inserted the key in the ignition, turned it. The motor growled, did not catch. Clements heard the voices coming closer. The guards had heard the grinding of the starter and a man was yelling to his companion to catch up. Clements eased the machine gun around, and when the first man appeared at the bend of the trail he pulled the trigger and the foliage hissed as the tracers chewed it to pieces.

The man disappeared and Clements did not know whether he had hit him or not. The motor caught suddenly and the boat leaped forward, throwing him against the seat. G. D. was hunched over the choke and the throttle, his face the color of putty, scared into a deathly silence as he shot up the narrow canal at top speed until it reached the edge of his property and joined the larger canal, which was already congested with market boats and barges and the long Thai needle boats that threaded through the traffic at top speed. G. D. missed a shallow boat full of fish by a scant six inches, eased out into a clear channel.

'All right,' Clements said, over the roar of the engine. 'You can slow down now. Pull off into one of the smaller klongs and stop the boat.

G. D. did as he was told. He pulled the boat in next to a piling at a wood mill, close to collapse, sucking the air into his lungs, a stunned expression on his face as if he could not believe he had been betrayed. 'You were right,' he said. 'They set me up. They would have killed me.' His eyes followed the children swimming in the filthy water, a graceful woman at one of the stilted houses drawing cooking water from the klong.

'Now you know how it feels,' Clements said. 'Open one of the bottles.'

'It's too goddamned early for a drink.'

'Not for you. Open it.'

G. D. opened the bottle. He eyed Clements, then took a long pull and coughed. 'What's the point?'

'Drink some more. I want you to have a pint in you before we go any farther.'

'I'll get sick to my stomach.'

'Drink.'

G. D. drank half of the bottle with great effort, then slouched against the seat behind the wheel. 'You son of a bitch,' he said, words beginning to slur.

'You climb in the back. I'm taking over.'

G. D. managed to make it into the back before the full effect of the whiskey began to grab him. He slouched against the cushions. In another five minutes, he was out cold. And now, Clements thought, the work would begin.

He slid beneath the wheel, started the engines and moved the boat back into the main klong. He put the weapon under the front seat where it could not be seen but where he could grab it up. The word would be out. The same men who had provided guards for the house would be sending out boats to sweep the klongs as soon as possible and he would not have the luxury of time. He followed a tour boat that was stopping at a pier along one of the larger klongs where a baby elephant had been tied to a tree for picture taking, and he tied his boat up at the end of the pier, examined G. D. briefly to make certain he was not faking and then scrambled up onto the teak scaffolding and the platform that supported the souvenir market.

He took a ten-dollar bill out of his pocket, approached an old woman who was selling small dolls. 'I need a telephone,' he said in Thai. At first he thought she did not understand, but then she took his money and led him back to a central office where there was a telephone on the wall. He dialed the number of the American Embassy and asked to speak to the ambassador only to be told that the ambassador was not there. Then he asked for Squires and momentarily Squires was on the line.

'Clements, is that you?' Squires said.

'Yes.'

'You've heard then?'

'Heard what?'

'Ambassador Thorenson tried to call you personally last night to apologize, but the lines are all dead out in that part of Thonburi.'

'What in the hell are you talking about? Apologize for what?'

'I should let the ambassador tell you, but he's already down at the Empress. You were right about the attack. If you hadn't warned us, we would never have known.'

The craziness had begun, Clements thought, and even before Squires began to fill him in, he knew that this was the contingency planned, designed to divert attention from the main assault, to defuse whatever Clements had to say.

'You were a hundred percent right about the boat,' Squires said. 'You just had a few of the details wrong. I took the precaution of informing the Thai police and they discovered a boat matching the description you gave me upriver at Ayutthaya.'

The boat had been full of explosives which were being transferred to a truck which had no license plates, and when the police arrived, the boat took off in one direction and the truck started down the highway toward Bangkok. 'The Thais took the boat on in a gun battle and the damn thing blew sky high. The truck was caught in a roadblock and the police caught the driver who had maps and a detonating device and confessed to the whole goddamned plot. There was to be one attack by the boat, which would blow itself up at the Empress landing, and then, when the people went indoors, the truck was going to break through the barriers and into the underground garage before the suicide driver detonated the explosives and brought the whole building down on top of him.'

Clements felt as if the air had been squeezed out of his body. It took him a moment to catch his breath. 'No,' he said.

'No, what?' Squires said. 'What do you mean?'

'It's all a diversion. The boats are still going to attack the grounds.'

'The Thai police interrogated the man at length. He

admitted being a revolutionary. He confirmed that there were other boats, but they were planned to hit other targets. Why don't you come on in and we'll talk about it. I think we can convince you. One of your own people is here. She can tell you.'

'She?'

'Thomasina Mims.'

Christ, it just might be possible after all. He did not even ask how she came to be in Bangkok. 'Where is she?' he said. 'I want to talk to her.'

'She's here, as a matter of fact. Hold on.'

And then Mims's voice, not only efficient but grateful, prepared to listen. 'Yes, Mr Ambassador.'

'Please listen to me carefully,' Clements said. 'Whatever has happened upriver is a diversion, a very smooth one, but a diversion nonetheless. Are the delegates still going to have dinner on the Empress lawn tonight?'

'No, sir,' she said. 'They're finishing early. They'll be having luncheon al fresco while they read their final communiqué.'

'They're going to be attacked,' Clements said. 'Take my word for it. Do what you can to get those people inside the building. Make sure the Thai gunboats are patrolling the river.'

'You sound like you're on your last legs,' she said, picking up the fatigue in his voice. 'Let me know where you are and I'll have you picked up.'

'I'll be on the river,' he said. 'Do what you can.'

He severed the connection, went back to the boat and cast loose. He started the motor, threaded his way down to the river, the great, sluggish, dirty Chao Phraya, which wound its way through Bangkok and south to empty into the gulf. There were barges on the river, the stench of diesel in the air and garbage in the water. He cruised downstream, beneath the bridges, the Empress Hotel off to his left, the hotel employees busily draping bunting over the platforms and terraces shaded with umbrellas. He passed one wooden Thai gunboat at a dock downriver from the hotel. It was painted light blue. The uniformed naval officers stood at the railing and smoked cigarettes as they watched the river.

One of the boats from Indonesia has been sacrificed for the sake of diversion, Clements thought. *G. D. said there were three up here. So that leaves two to go.* And as he continued to make his way downriver it occurred to him the odds of his finding these two boats was infinitesimal. They could have come upriver under cover of darkness and be anchored in any of the canals or inlets. And they were no longer necessarily gray. They could have been painted any color on the trip up from Indonesia.

So now he decided to take his last chance, using the process of elimination, in the terrible hope that he would be proven to be mistaken, for the possibility of this reality was even more horrible than the thought of a terrorist insurrection. He pulled into an industrial dock and used a telephone again. This time he called the Russian Embassy.

'I wish to speak to Sergei Ludov, please,' he said.

'Who is this?'

'Ambassador Clements.'

The line went dead and at first he thought he had been cut off, then Sergei's voice came on the line, full of concern. 'Where are you? I expected you to call yesterday.'

'I'm disappointed in you, Sergei.'

'What? What disappointment? What are you talking about?'

'I thought you were negotiating in good faith. But I know the whole goddamn thing now. You tried to have me killed.'

'Have you gone crazy?' Sergei said. 'I am here to negotiate with you, nothing more. What kind of game are you playing with me?'

'If you're operating in good faith, I want you to meet me right away,' Clements said. 'I'm at an industrial marine dock down the west side of the river. There's a large yellow sign along the road.'

'What are you doing there?'

'Will you meet me?'

'Of course. Give me half an hour.'

Clements hung up and went back to the boat. And now would come the difficult part. If Sergei indeed knew nothing about this plan, then his car would come driving up directly, and Clements would enlist his aid. But if Sergei and the Russians were behind this, then Sergei would be aware of what had happened at the house and the search that was being made for Clements in the boat. And instead of Sergei's car a powerboat would come sweeping along the edge of the river, and as it drew abreast of the dock the guns would appear and they would blow him out of the water. He went back to the boat, sat behind the wheel, smoked a cigarette, one hand on the stock of the machine gun, listening to G. D.'s raspy snore.

Waiting.

He sat and smoked, the boat rocking in the wake of the passing barges heading downstream toward the open gulf. There was a smell of rain in the hot air, a large white thunderhead off to the northeast, and the dock workers were pumping diesel into a scow down the way. G. D. had begun to come around, mumbling fitfully, opening his eyes, trying to get up off the seat, seemingly startled to find that he could not manage his balance. He fell back against the cushions. His eyes were glazed; he had difficulty remembering where he was.

'What the hell?' he said, looking at Clements. 'What the hell are we doing here?'

'Waiting,' Clements said.

'What for?'

'*Mai pen rai*,' Clements said in Thai. Ah, the marvelous catch-all expressions in every language, and this one meant everything, nothing, *it doesn't matter, come what may, that's the way the cookie crumbles*, a verbal placeholder, and all the time his eyes alternated between the flat brown river and the road that came through the trees toward the landing. Far downriver, just close enough to be visible, he saw the blue shape of another Thai Navy patrol boat, then back to the road that came through the trees toward the landing. He saw the black Mercedes, the Russian limousine, and it stopped at the edge of the dock, the windows tinted so he could not see how many men were inside, but apparently the occupants were having a discussion, because the door was a long time opening. And then it was a tentative Sergei who climbed out and stood at the end of the dock, slightly stooped from his arthritis, more than a little wary.

'Clements?' he said, shading his eyes as he looked toward the boat.

'Yes,' Clements said. 'Come on down the dock.'

'My men advise me not to trust you.'

'Very good advice,' Clements said, taking another drag of his cigarette. 'It's been a long goddamned night, Sergei. I'm edgy, tired, suspicious as hell.'

Sergei made his way down the dock. He was dressed in a dark suit despite the heat of the morning. He stopped just short of the boat, put on sunglasses against the glare as he looked out into the river. And suddenly Clements knew without doubt that it had been Sergei all along, not Sergei as an individual perhaps, but Sergei acting as an instrument of Russian policy. Sergei had betrayed himself when he looked out into the river, put on those sunglasses, for it was apparent that he was here to stall for time, to use it up until the river force could move into place. The dark glasses were meant to conceal the movement of his eyes.

'I expected your call yesterday,' Sergei said. 'I thought we would have dinner last night, talk. I have new instructions from home.'

'Too late,' Clements said. 'I know what you're doing, Sergei.'

And Sergei tried to dissemble. 'How could you know?' he said. 'There's nothing for you to know.'

'Little things gave you away,' Clements said. He flipped the cigarette into the water. '"Six Ravens,"' he said, deprecatingly. 'That's not Australian, for God's sake, not American. We might have used "Eagles" for a code word, but not "Ravens." And to have a cover company in Austria. That should have been a dead giveaway that the funds were coming from your part of the world. If this had been a Western plan, the operating funds would have been shuffled through the Bahamas or the Caymans first, not Austria.'

'Ravens?' G. D. was saying. 'What's this about the goddamn Ravens?'

'This is your number one Raven,' Clements said, drolly. 'Not your unseen Australian friend.'

'A goddamned lie,' G. D. said, and sank down against the cushion once more.

'What can you possibly gain from a massacre at noon?' Clements said.

Sergei shrugged. 'Neither you nor I make policy, Mr Ambassador. Our countries call the tune and we dance accordingly. There will be an attack here. And it will all be laid at the feet of the Americans and the Australians, as if they are interfering with the energy policies of these countries. And we will help these countries prove who their enemies really are. We will provide money for rebuilding. It's all foolishness, of course,' he said, rather sadly. 'We don't have the money to take care of our own, but there are adventurers in every country.' He paused to light a cigarette, looked out to the river again and Clements followed his gaze. The Thai Navy boat was just passing a line of barges in the middle of the river. Evidently Sergei was going to have to stall awhile longer. Sergei exhaled smoke into the heavy morning air. 'It was not my scheme, none of it. I would have preferred that it be handled through another residence, but then, as I say, you and I can't determine what happens to us.'

'And the negotiations?'

'We would have made headway had it not been for the other plan. But I can offer you a chance.'

'For what?'

'To survive,' Sergei said. 'I ask you to leave the boat and come with me, now. No questions asked. The other details can be worked out later.'

Clements picked up the urgency in his voice, the sincerity, and he knew that this was Sergei's way of offering what he could from the position in which he found himself. Clements glanced toward the river, saw the reason for the urgency. The Thai Navy boat had come this side of the barges, picking up speed, and Clements saw the lines of the cruiser, the twin tubes, one to either side of the hull for torpedoes, the gun stand on the bow. Clements raised the submachine gun from below the seat, pointed it at Sergei.

'Into the boat,' he said. 'You're my insurance.'

Sergei shook his head, a sad smile. The men had climbed

out of his limousine and were starting down the pier. He waved them back. 'I would be no insurance for you,' he said. 'I am old, expendable.'

'Goddammit, I'm offering you a chance as well,' Clements said. 'Get in the boat.'

For the Thai gunboat was bearing down straight toward the pier, picking up speed, and then Clements could wait no longer. He kicked the engine alive and shot forward just as the burst from the fifty calibers came from the gunboat and raked the water like punctuation marks and splintered the wood of the docks and raised just enough on the turn to stitch through the midsection of Sergei's dark suit. The bullets spun him around, left him flailing with arthritic hands for support to keep him upright, as if standing could help him stay alive. But there was nothing to prop him up and he fell to the dock.

Clements fell back on a cunning he had not known in years, until last night when he was up against a superior force. He knew he could not outrun the twin diesels of the powerboat, and the firepower against him was too great, so he paralleled the pier and then ran beneath the pilings, with less than an inch of clearance between the top of the windshield and the wooden beams. He emerged into a cul-de-sac on the other side, a maze of smaller wooden boats, and he whipped to starboard to avoid a shallow-draft junk and then in an opposite direction to graze a scow, finally hitting open water again at full throttle. He looked back over his shoulder and up the side of the pier to get his bearings.

The gunboat was there, just making an arc of a turn, men in uniform still searching the pier with binoculars as if they expected him to come shooting out of the pilings at any moment. They had been damn clever, he thought. Gray paint in Indonesia, then royal-blue Thai markings, men in Thai naval uniforms, and who would question the presence of armed Thai gunboats? And unless he was very careful, they were going to wipe him out. For the fifty calibers were too great a force for his single machine gun in an open fight. He decided to gamble, and before the gunboat could make its full turn he opened the throttle and made a run for the line of barges moving down the center of the river. He was spotted. The gunboat came around, the fifties opening up, more an intimidation than a real threat from this distance.

'What the hell are you doing?' G. D. was yelling from the backseat. 'What's going on?'

Clements did not answer. He ran across the bow of the chain of slow barges, ducked in behind so the gunboat could not see him and then he stayed close to the heavy teak hulls, sunk low in the water from the weight of scrap iron, no crew visible, the men too smart to be caught in a cross fire.

Timing was everything now. The gunboat would come roaring around the stern barge, ready to open up on him. He moved to the last barge in line and then cut back on the power until he was barely holding his own against the current. Then he propped his elbows against the wheel to hold the boat steady. He knocked out the glass of the windshield with the muzzle of the machine gun, rested it in front of him, ready to fire, knowing he would have but a single chance. For if he knocked out the gunner on the foredeck, another man would take his place. And he could put a dozen holes in the hull and do little more than slow them down.

His only chance was the round circle of the makeshift torpedo tube, acting on the belief they would not have had time to construct a truly professional projectile and that the nose of the torpedo would be vulnerable.

Steady, God, how long could he keep the boat steady with his elbows on the wheel, and suppose he had guessed wrong and the gunboat swung around the front of the string of barges after all and attacked him from the stern? Then he would have no chance at all. But he was committed, and with the sweat pouring down his face, he waited.

And then the gunboat came around the stern of the last barge, in precisely the right position, close in, not fifty feet away, and Clements led the target, watching the tracers angle across the water, kicking up spray, and he led the bullets and then held, and in a moment the gunboat exploded with such force that it seemed to disintegrate, men hurled into the air, the remains of the hull spun around from the blast, metal plates separating. And Clements kept firing until the machine gun jerked to a stop, the ammunition exhausted. He sank back in the seat, revved up the engine, headed toward the opposite bank and the cover of a canal for the moment, in a state of shock, knowing he would have to get himself together again before he could go on. He looked around. G. D. had passed out on the backseat, was lying in a sprawl, half on the cushion, half on the floor.

Clements checked his watch. Already eleven-thirty. Luncheon al fresco. One bogus gunboat left to go and his ammunition was exhausted. Nothing left to fight with. The delegates would be assembling on the terraces and he would be powerless to do anything about it. He picked up a bottle of scotch, uncapped it and took a long drink, then recapped it and put it in the seat beside him and turned the boat upriver.

Squires had been chief of station in Bangkok for six years and area chief since the new divisional duties had been put in effect two years ago, but he had never found himself in quite the situation which faced him now, with the intense young woman sitting across the desk from him pushing for something which he knew was useless. He offered her a cigarette, which she declined, and then took the time to light one for himself, trying to pick the proper phrases that would pacify her. For he was aware of the feminist movement inside the Agency, especially at Langley, and he could do without a complaint filed against him on the basis of sexual discrimination.

'I understand your point of view,' he said. 'I understand that the ambassador is very upset.'

'My point of view is not based on how Ambassador Clements *feels*,' she said. 'I simply want to know what you're going to do.'

'It's been done,' he said, patiently. 'It's over.'

'And what's your basis for that judgement?'

'The explosion of the boat, the capture of the truck, the confession of the driver,' he said, tapping the ash into a ceramic bowl. 'When you've been here longer, you'll realize that, as a rule, potential coups, rebellions and terrorist

296

attacks are more straight-line in this part of the world. I mean, a monk sets himself on fire in protest or a radical group springs an unplanned and foolish attack on an army barracks or a government building. I've seen them.'

'And what would you do if Kemper asked to continue this investigation?' she said, in what he knew was a rhetorical question. 'It's my understanding that a chief of station would be given that courtesy outside his territory.'

'We both know that Kemper's in no shape to make such a request.'

'You appointed Wiznoski as acting chief of station. I have an official request from him in writing that I be allowed to take whatever steps are necessary to continue our investigation.'

'I've got my hands full,' he said wearily, on the edge of irritation. 'And I'm sure as hell not going to complicate matters by informing the local intelligence community, which I'll tell you now is one of the most macho, anti-female groups in the world, that the United States is not satisfied with the answers they've come up with and have assigned a woman to check things out.'

Ah, a wrong move, he thought. *A wrong move expressed in the wrong language and she seized on it immediately.*

'I'll file a report with that exact language then,' she said. 'That I am being kept from an investigation because I am a woman.'

'That's not what I said.' He shook his head. 'What do you want?'

'I want to interview the driver.'

'And that's all?'

'A quiet interview, no more than an hour.'

'All right,' he said, 'And at the end of that time, you go back to Jakarta, filing no reports. Agreed?'

'You're all heart,' Tommi said.

She dressed in a suit and pulled her hair back to a severe profile, removed her make-up and wore flat heels when she went to the office of the local commander of Thai Intelligence, and she was quite surprised when he made no objections at all, either to the fact that she was a woman or that she wanted to interview the truck driver. He had a man in plainclothes conduct her to a miserably hot interview room without windows where she was seated in a straight-back chair and in a few minutes the miscreant who had driven the truck was dragged in. The man had been thoroughly beaten, of course, his face pulped so that his eyes were almost shut, yet he squatted on his haunches on the floor at the side of the small interrogation room and even managed a makeshift *wai* of respect, pressing his manacled hands together. She gave him a cigarette, lit it for him.

'You are a native of Bangkok?' she said in Thai, lighting a cigarette for herself.

'*Kah,*' the man said, nodding. 'Yes.'

She smiled. 'You have a family here, wife, children, mother, father?'

His swollen eyes darted up to look at her, then shifted away. 'They had nothing to do with this.'

'I'm certain they didn't,' she said. 'I was just curious to know if you are a family man.'

He said nothing, as if he didn't know which way he was supposed to answer. And she began to get the familiar feeling that here was another man who would say anything that the authorities wished him to say. She glanced at the précis of the confession which the Thais had prepared in English for her. 'And you confess to all these things you've been accused of?'

'*Kah.*'

'You're a very brave man. And an explosives expert, I assume?'

'*Mai chai,*' the man said. 'No.'

'But you were willing to blow yourself up. You were going to drive into the delivery basement of . . .' She paused, grimaced, looked at the paper. 'Which building?'

'The hotel.'

'Which hotel?'

'The Empress Hotel.'

'Then your wife would have grieved for no reason,' she said, taking the chance. 'You would have made a mistake, killed yourself for nothing. The hydroelectric engineers were meeting at the Oriental Hotel.'

The man said nothing, seemed to retreat, hunched up inside himself, holding the cigarette in front of his face as if to hide behind the smoke. *I've got you now*, she thought. *Because you didn't know what the hell you were doing and now you're not sure you got it right.* She puffed on the cigarette without inhaling, giving him time to think. 'The confession says you were attacking the hydroelectric engineers in the name of the Communist Party.'

'If that's what the paper says, it must be so.'

She played a hunch. 'You will lose merit with Lord Buddha,' she said.

The man's eyes glinted behind the puffed flesh of his lids.

'The Lord Buddha has never called for the deaths of innocent men,' she said. It was a trick statement, of course, and she had heard it used on hard-core killers, terrorists, and it always brought forth a vehement defense of whatever the man had done, however heinous, because responsibility for the deaths of a dozen people was nothing compared with the giving of offense to Lord Buddha. But this man said nothing. He sucked on the cigarette, stared straight ahead.

'I'm trying to understand you,' she said. 'I can help you if I understand. I don't want your wife to be a widow and all your children to be fatherless and your parents to be disgraced. After all, you didn't kill anybody. You were simply driving a truck filled with explosives. There's only your confession that you were driving a bomb with the intention of blowing up engineers, scientists, whoever. Now, if you can explain to me exactly why you were doing this, for what reason, why these people had so offended you that you wanted them dead, then we can talk about it. If you think that these were evil men you were attacking, then tell me and we'll put it in the newspaper and on television so everybody will know about it. If you did this because you are a part of a group that feels strongly about the terrible things that happen in this world, then I will see that your group gets publicity. But if this is all I have to go on' – she flipped the paper with an index finger – 'you'll go before a firing squad for no reason at all.'

The man shook his head slowly, ground the cigarette out against the floor. 'You won't believe me.'

'Give me a chance to believe you.'

'I am not a political person.' The story came out in a reedy voice that was close to desperation. The man said he had been approached by a man in Bangkok, a foreigner who spoke Thai, and promised a good deal of money to drive a truck. He was to pick up explosives which would be transferred from a boat on the river up at Ayutthaya and carry them by truck to Bangkok, where he would deliver the truck to somebody at Wat Po. If he was intercepted he was to say that he intended to blow up a hotel, but obviously he had not gotten that part of it exactly right, and when the police suggested it was the Empress Hotel, he admitted to that, and when she suggested the Oriental, that sounded correct as well. The man abandoned his air of resignation, began to wail. 'So I will get shot and I never received any money and I never intended to kill anybody. I am a devout follower of Lord Buddha. I won't even kill an insect.'

She stood up. 'I'll see what I can do for you,' she said, and on the way out she chatted for a moment with a captain of the Thai Intelligence and passed on her suspicion that the whole story had been rigged. But the captain just shrugged. '*Mai pen rai.*' What does it matter?

She checked her watch. Close to eleven and she had her driver break all the speed laws to get her to the Empress Hotel, where the tables were being set out on the lawn next to the river. Squires was nowhere in evidence and she borrowed a pair of binoculars from a security man and made a careful sweep of the river, heavy with traffic at this time of day, full of barges and fishing boats and sightseeing craft. Downriver she saw the lumbering old Thai river patrol boat wallowing its way upstream, against the current. And upstream, close to the second bridge, she thought she made out the shape of another Thai naval vessel, but it was too far away, too obscured by haze to determine anything except the color. She also searched the sky, hopeful that there would be a sudden rain which would drive the lunch indoors, but the thunderhead which had been evident earlier was now even farther north, and only the vague outline of the top cloud was evident.

Then she remembered her training at Langley, which

was to take nothing for granted, and she found a public telephone in the lobby and rang Thai Naval Headquarters, only to be frustrated by a lack of specific Thai naval vocabulary to ask the questions of the young officer who had answered the telephone.

'Is there anyone there who speaks English?' she said, finally, in Thai, but the officer responded that there was not. So she did the best she could. 'How many Thai naval boats are on the river?' she said, knowing even as she said it that she would not get a straight answer, for the question was too loose. The officer said he didn't know. She severed the connection and was about to head up to the hospitality suite when she literally bumped into Squires as he was coming out of the elevator. She grabbed his arm. 'Come with me,' she said. 'There isn't time to explain.' She was surprised that he came with her, out onto the terrace, where she borrowed a pair of binoculars from a security man again and handed them to Squires. 'Look by the bridge,' she said. 'The other side of the river, near the first wharf.'

He squinted through the binoculars. 'What am I supposed to be looking for?'

'Do you see the Thai patrol boat?'

'I see it.'

'I could be mistaken but I don't think I am,' she said. 'The last time I attended a briefing on defense forces in Thailand, they didn't have any modern patrol boats.'

He focused the binoculars, frowned. 'They do now.'

'It's a ringer,' she said. 'And so was the truck driver. He was *told* what to say in case he was caught, just like Oni Saud in Jakarta. There's going to be an attack on this hotel, all right, but not from any kamikaze truck.'

'Christ,' he said, and she could see his indecision. 'There's no way we can be sure.'

'If you're willing to take the chance, then don't do anything,' she said.

Abruptly he turned on his heel and, with Tommi in tow, took the elevator to the sixth floor and the hospitality suite. Ambassador Thorenson was there all right, engaged in an earnest conversation with the British ambassador.

'You'd better let me handle it,' Squires said to her. He left

301

her standing by the door. And despite Thorenson's strict instructions that when he was in a conference with another man of equal rank he was never to be disturbed, Squires walked up to him, greeted the British ambassador with a proper nod and then asked Thorenson for a moment of his time.

Thorenson allowed himself to be led away. His face was angry. 'I thought we understood each other . . .' Thorenson began, but Squires cut him off.

'This is important,' Squires said. 'Or I wouldn't have interrupted you. I think we're in danger of imminent attack from the river. And I think the luncheon should be moved indoors.'

'Let me tell you something, Squires,' Thorenson said, glancing around the room to make sure he would not be overheard. 'If these countries go through with what they've planned at this meeting, the United States corporations stand to lose at least a billion a year and the British just somewhat less. And believe me, these goddamn rumors have gotten around, the attack from the river, and everybody breathed a sigh of relief when they caught the bastards upriver. But if the luncheon is moved inside on my recommendation, then we start the rumor mill all over again, and we send signals to them that we don't want to send.'

'What would it take to convince you, Ambassador?'

'You have the Thai Government advise me that it's unsafe for me to host a luncheon party on the lawn and I'll insist that it be moved inside.'

Ah, Squires thought, *the passing of the buck, and if the Thai Government advised against it, then they would lose face*. He gathered up Tommi and took her with him as he went back up on the covered veranda and sought out the Thai police commander. Captain Kruba was in charge, a small and dapper man who wore black boots polished to a mirror gloss and made such a good impression on foreign dignitaries that he had earned himself the command of security at all foreign functions. He was just hanging up the telephone when Squires and Tommi arrived.

'We have interesting news,' Kruba said in English. 'There

has been trouble at the estate of one of your countrymen, a G. D. Majors in Thonburi. His house is burning. Also I have been informed of a shooting downriver which involved the Soviet ambassador and an attack on a Thai patrol boat.'

'You know the patrol boats you have on the river,' Tommi said, with relief. She pointed out the hazy shape of the vessel near the bridge. 'That's not one of yours, is it?'

The captain raised his binoculars, looked, nodded. 'It must be ours,' he said. 'It has the proper look.'

'I would suggest that you check it out with the Navy, Captain,' she said.

'There's no more time,' Squires said, looking out toward the river. 'Captain, I want you to advise that the luncheon be moved indoors, that you have reason to believe there will be an attack and can't be responsible for the safety of the delegates.'

Captain Kruba frowned, rubbed an index finger over his mustache. 'I don't see the connection between these other happenings and the situation here.'

Shit, shit, shit, Squires thought, and of course the good captain wasn't going to cause any difficulty because that might create a complaint which would remove him from this very excellent duty.

'Mr Squires is right,' Tommi said.

Kruba stared down at the lawn. 'I have taken my precautions,' he said. 'Many police cars at the front. Plainclothes in the hotel itself. Some troops down along the water to protect against beggars coming ashore in small boats, or swimmers. That has happened before. But what happens on the water belongs now to the Navy to take care of.'

Too late anyway, Squires thought. Below the terrace the delegates were beginning to make their way out onto the lawn for drinks beneath the canopy of a tent, the political aristocracy of Southeast Asia and their ladies. 'So much for the local security,' he said to Tommi. A United States Marine orchestra had begun to play. 'The stubbornness of preordained plans prevails. Nothing's going to stop this goddamn luncheon short of catastrophe.'

'So what do we do now?' Tommi said.

'Pray for rain,' he said. He patted the thirty-eight in his shoulder holster and led the way down the steps toward the river as if he personally could halt the destruction he knew was coming.

The boat was coughing and belching black smoke as Clements coaxed it upriver. Water was beginning to collect beneath his feet. The hull had taken hits after all, some of them below the waterline, and now he was urging it on against the current, with G. D. occasionally stirring in the back. Clements was certain by now that he was not going to make it, that everything he had done was all in vain, because somewhere along the Chao Phraya was the third gunboat and it would be moving into position anytime. He could expect to hear the explosion momentarily, for his watch now placed the time at a quarter to twelve and the delegates would certainly be on the lawn.

He took a chance, pushed the throttle all the way forward. The boat shivered and threatened to shake to pieces before it responded and picked up a few knots. And even at this slow speed he saw that he was gaining on the wooden Thai gunboat and he wondered if they had orders to stop him. As he passed them at a distance of ten meters he was aware that they had a cannon which could blow him apart, enough machine guns to strafe his boat to scrap metal, but they ignored him. Shortly he saw the tall monolith of the Empress Hotel off in the distance and heard the strains of a waltz from the Marine orchestra. He was close enough now to make out the tents on the lawn, the umbrellas, the gaily striped colors. He squinted against the haze on the river, his stomach souring as he saw the shape of the other bogus gunboat, painted in the colors of the Thai Navy. It lay to beneath the shadows of a bridge upstream, perhaps a half mile beyond the Empress. It was beginning to move downstream, quite slowly, and he could see now what they were planning to do. There was another chain of barges between them and the hotel, and once the barges had passed there would be a stretch of open river to the place where the green lawn and flowering plants of the hotel grounds met the river. They would wait and then they would make a sweep, cross channel, and taking the force of the current into account, they would launch both torpedoes a hundred feet away from the bank and then make a loop in the river, a tight circle, until the torpedoes exploded and raked the lawns with shrapnel. By that time they would be in a position for a side run and they would parallel the bank, using the fifty-caliber machine guns fore and aft, chewing the canopies and the umbrellas and the guests to pieces.

He looked behind him. The wooden gunboat was still too far off, the officers incognizant of the fact that there were no swift patrol craft in their fleet. and he was the only impediment that lay between the attack boat and the multiple deaths ashore. He pulled upstream, slightly beyond the Empress, thankful for the slow barges which still gave him time, then he reached around and grabbed G. D. by the front of his shirt and pulled him up. 'All right, you son of a bitch,' he said. 'you don't deserve the chance but I'm giving it to you anyway. Get out of the boat.'

G. D. looked at him with uncomprehending eyes. 'What?'

'Out of the boat. Move your ass.'

'I'm not going anywhere,' G. D. said. He stood up, uneasily, and Clements gave him a shove. G. D. tried to hang on to the back of the seat, lost his balance and went over the side. And then Clements had no more time to give to him. Because the barges had passed and the attack boat was revving up, beginning an angular run across the wide river. Almost by instinct Clements opened the throttle and shot ahead on a course angled to intercept, aware that a miracle was taking place because his boat was not shaking itself to pieces. A siren wailed from the attack boat. They spotted him, warned him to get out of the way, corrected their course to port, as if to let him pass through. He grinned to himself at their mistake. For if they had corrected to starboard, moving away from him, he never could have caught them, but now they would not be able to avoid him. He shoved the throttle open. The machine guns opened up on him from the attack boat, strafed the water in front of him, chewed down the side of his hull. He waited until the last moment, until he could see the faces of the

305

men on board, yelling. And at the last minute he went over the side, into the stinking waters of the river, diving to put distance between him and what was coming. The bow of his boat caught the attack boat right in the center of the torpedo tube. For a split second it seemed that it would glance off, splintering under the pounding of the machine guns. And then the torpedo exploded in a great ball of fire and the attack boat was ripped in two. Almost at the same moment the second torpedo was set off, shredding the starboard side of the hull. The shrapnel rained on the river. The fuel tanks exploded as well and black smoke roiled up into the morning sky. The guests on the lawn stood where they were, stupefied, as if witnessing a show for their benefit. The Marine band stopped playing in mid-tune, until the explosions had ceased on the river, and then the leader tapped his baton against a music stand and the tune rose again, ragged.

With his lungs feeling as if they would burst at any moment, his head ringing from concussion, Clements surfaced. He saw the remains of the boat ablaze, the river littered with wreckage. *I'm still alive*, he thought, and he began to swim, slowly but surely, toward the riverbank.

11

There was work to be done in Indonesia, and Clements spent the first week after his return either secluded in his office or receiving emissaries from the Foreign Office or other embassies. He said little, waiting for instructions. He coded one long cable personally to the Secretary of State, a full explanation of what had happened as he knew it, putting the situation in administration hands. For now national policy was involved, and whatever the action, it would have to be instigated in the White House. While he was waiting for his reply from Washington, he talked to the British and the Australians, discussing what difference the new energy policies were going to make, reserving comment on the news as it came over the wire. Within the same week as the Bangkok raid, there had been attacks on a half-dozen offshore rigs with minimal damage.

His most welcome duty was to receive Kemper back at the embassy as he reported for limited duty, his hands still bandaged, and Tommi constantly at his side. It was only with Kemper that Clements could share the whole truth while awaiting word from Washington. They had a drink in Clements's office, the air conditioner purring, Kemper half reclining, studying Clements in the twilight of the room, listening to him talk. And Clements became aware that he was being studied and he stopped, sipped his drink.

'What?' he said, as if picking up the thought.

Kemper smiled. 'I can't figure out who looks worse,' he said. 'You or me. You look like you've been through a meat grinder.'

'I feel it.'

'I owe you an apology,' Kemper said.

'For what?'

'My own stupidity,' Kemper said. 'I somehow thought that you were immune, exempt from pain.'

'How did you come to that conclusion?'

Kemper shook his head. 'It doesn't matter.'

'If anybody ever discovers how to be exempt from pain and shares his secret, the world will make him emperor,' Clements said. 'So what will you be up to now?'

'That depends on what happens,' Kemper said. 'If all hell breaks loose here, then I'm going to stick around. If it doesn't, then I'm going to get married and take a month off.'

'She's a fine woman, your Thomasina Mims.'

'She is that,' Kemper said.

The word did not come by cable. Instead, Clements was notified that the inspector general for the State Department was arriving on the next plane, a no-nonsense man named Campbell, who also carried the rank of Ambassador as well as the confidence of the President. Campbell was in his sixties, silver-haired, indefatigable, and once he was in the limousine, despite the fact he had just disembarked from a flight that had carried him halfway around the world, he got right down to business.

'Are you convinced that what you reported is true, Charlie, beyond the shadow of a doubt?' he said.

'Absolutely.'

'Then you think this was a Russian-inspired operation from beginning to end.'

'Not just Russian-inspired. Russian-planned, Russian-operated. If they had brought it off, the balance of power could have shifted in this part of the world. It would have seemed as if the American oil companies had made a concerted attack on the legally constituted governments. Has the Kremlin commented on Sergei's death yet?'

Campbell nodded. 'Killed by accident in a Thai naval action.'

'And that's all?'

'That's it. No big funeral. No accusations against the West. But they're prepared to defend if we want to play hardball.'

'And does the President intend to play hardball?'

'I'll be frank,' Campbell said. 'This whole thing has come at an awkward damn time. We have your old friend, G. D. Majors, and he's more than anxious to whistle any tune that will get him out from under. And we've got a paper trail that leads from the Singapore bank back to Prague and Moscow and forward to Jakarta. So the whole thing can be proven. You can become a bigger damn celebrity than you are now. The Thai papers are saying you saved a hundred people from death at the hands of Communist conspirators.'

'You mentioned an awkward time.'

'The Russians are claiming that Sergei was involved in negotiating with you and they're anxious to continue that posture. The President seems to think that they mean it. To make an attack on them now, even if we can prove it, would kill any chance of negotiation.'

'Why did you fly all the way out here to consult me about this?' Clements said. 'We've known each other a long time, Howard.'

Campbell looked out at the lights of the city. 'Because you're human,' he said. 'Because you've lost good men and damn near died yourself. And I've known other men in public life who've demanded their pound of flesh for considerably less than you've gone through.'

'And who should I seek retribution against?' Clements said. 'Sergei deceived me and I should feel damn good that he was caught in his own fire, but I don't. I think he was following orders he didn't particularly like. And G. D.? I'd like to see the son of a bitch in prison, but he's totally broke. They burned his place down in Bangkok and I'm sure he didn't have insurance. They would have killed him in the bargain. So he'll spend a miserable time waiting for an attack to come from us, because we have him dead to rights, or from the other side, because he was scheduled to be killed.' He lit a cigarette, smoked in silence a moment. 'Did you find any trace of the assassin?'

'The Thai police searched the crocodile pit. A few bones, nothing else.'

'One other thing,' Clements said. 'We open this up and the Indonesian Government will be incriminated, at least parts of it. And I don't think that will serve any purpose except to ensure that the current government will be fixed in an anti-American position for a hell of a long time to come.'

'A final, delicate matter,' Campbell suggested.

Clements smiled. 'Not so delicate.'

'The woman then.'

'I'll see her tonight.' He shook his head. 'She's no threat.'

'Then I'll leave you a prepared statement,' Campbell said. 'Since we're in agreement. The statement suggests that all this was an action by an Asian Communist faction which was financed by God knows whom but probably Iran. They tried to discredit the United States, to drive a wedge between us and our allies in Southeast Asia. And they failed. But an investigation is under way and results will be announced at a future date. Then the whole business will be allowed to slide into oblivion. Do you think your people can hold to that?'

'I guarantee it.'

Campbell leaned forward, tapped on the glass and then instructed the driver. 'Take me back to the airport,' he said.

'What the hell are you doing?' Clements said.

'As much as I'd enjoy the rest and the visit, I have urgent business in Australia,' Campbell said. 'And I'm finished here. The President sends his greetings and his thanks.'

'You can tell him he's very welcome,' Clements said. 'Very welcome indeed.'

He had Lucy call Madeleine and arrange for her to meet him at the bar in the Indonesia Hotel at ten o'clock. The bar was the center of social nightlife in the capital and he did not have to wonder whether she would show up or not. Because as far as she knew, she was still on the hook. He could have her prosecuted, tie her to the whole plot, discredit her with her own government, thoroughly ruin her Chinese relatives and the Rooseno branch of the family as well. And she was confident enough in her own charms to believe that she could seduce the figure of death himself if she needed to.

He dressed in formal clothes, had his car take him to the Indonesia Hotel and wait in front. From the moment he entered he saw her sitting at a table on the far side, and from his first sight of her he knew the tack she would take with him. Not the seductress this time, no, the victim.

He stopped at a table to shake hands with the British *chargé* and to be introduced to a charming woman who was joining the British staff. Moving on, he spoke to Colonel Mustafa, who had a party at another table. Yes, perfect, enough representatives of the diplomatic community and the Indonesian Government here tonight. He allowed the headwaiter to shepherd him across the room to Madeleine's table. And there he stood a long moment, realizing how awkward this moment was for her, how much she had been dreading it.

'I don't blame you,' she said, not looking up at him.

'For what?'

'I've treated you very badly,' she said. He could see the pulse in her throat by candlelight and he felt a moment of true regret that all this had happened. 'Please sit down.'

He pulled out a chair, sat down. 'I won't stay long. I just wanted you to know that I don't intend to have you prosecuted.'

'I see,' she said. 'I suppose I should thank you for that. But I don't want everything to end here. I behaved badly. I want to make that up to you.'

'And how could you possibly do that?' he said.

She slipped an envelope from her purse and handed it to him. 'This is the check you gave me in Bangkok, the one for fifty thousand dollars.'

'You didn't cash it?' he said, startled.

'That should be worth something,' she said. 'You know how I feel about money.' And at that moment he detected a subtle change in her, for he knew her well enough to know that she was a consummate actress who could manage to generate a single tear which would hold on the lower lashes of her left eye, glittering like a jewel. But she had obviously decided to play this straight with him and he respected her for that. 'I wanted to cash it, I'll tell you that. I'll never be so wealthy that fifty thousand American dollars doesn't mean anything to me. And I would like to be able to say to you that I was filled with remorse and couldn't cash it. But that isn't the case. I don't know why I couldn't cash the check. But I didn't. So . . .' She looked at him directly, dry-eyed, unsentimentally.

'So what?' he said.

'So what we do now is up to you,' she said. She looked around the room, aware of the fact that the two of them were being watched, with all eyes on the ambassador, waiting to see what he was going to do. 'I would like for us to continue to be together, but I won't beg. You know that.'

'I know that,' he said. 'And I respect you for it. So we will make this a parting without recriminations. You have always been quite honest about yourself and what I could and could not expect from you.'

'Then there has to be a parting?'

'Yes,' he said. 'Because I was the one who made the mistake. You told me in every way you could to love you without trusting you, and it turned out that I couldn't do that. I trusted you in spite of all the warnings. And now I've discovered that I really don't want love without trust, that in some peculiar way, I'm incapable of it.'

She nodded. 'Take a few months and think it over. I'm not going anywhere.'

'No need,' he said. He reached out and covered her hand with his. 'I wish you well. Believe that.' He squeezed her hand and then he stood up. 'Good-bye, Madeleine.'

He threaded his way back across the bar, and as he passed the British party, the ambassador stood up and reached out to put a hand on his arm. 'I say,' he said. 'As long as you're not tied up for the evening, old man, why not stop and have a drink with us?'

Clements looked at the charming woman. She had dark hair and eyes and showed her interest in him, and he wondered if she was widowed or divorced, and what kind of mind lay behind those clear blue eyes. But he would have plenty of time to find out, all the time in the world.

The aftermath of a war game that
went terribly wrong . . .

THE FIFTH ANGEL
A ONE MAN KILLING MACHINE

DAVID WILTSE

Sergeant Stitzer, said the officer who'd trained
him, was a hero. He was also one of the most
dangerous men ever to wear a uniform.

These days, they kept Stitzer in the cell at the end
of the corridor. TV cameras watched him night
and day. A broken yellow line on the floor marked
the point of no return.

Five years on, Stitzer had still not surrendered. In
his crazed mind he still had a mission to fulfil. And
the major knew that while Stitzer had breath in his
body he'd find a way to carry out those orders.
And not even the most secure military hospital in
the world would hold him back . . .

'Pacy, original and very readable' THE TIMES

0 7221 9107 3   ADVENTURE THRILLER   £2.95

A selection of bestsellers from Sphere

FICTION

LADY OF HAY	Barbara Erskine	£3.95 ☐
BIRTHRIGHT	Joseph Amiel	£3.50 ☐
THE SECRETS OF HARRY BRIGHT	Joseph Wambaugh	£2.95 ☐
CYCLOPS	Clive Cussler	£3.50 ☐
THE SEVENTH SECRET	Irving Wallace	£2.95 ☐

FILM AND TV TIE-IN

INTIMATE CONTACT	Jacqueline Osborne	£2.50 ☐
BEST OF BRITISH	Maurice Sellar	£8.95 ☐
SEX WITH PAULA YATES	Paula Yates	£2.95 ☐
RAW DEAL	Walter Wager	£2.50 ☐

NON-FICTION

BOTHAM	Don Mosey	£3.50 ☐
SOLDIERS	John Keegan & Richard Holmes	£5.95 ☐
URI GELLER'S FORTUNE SECRETS	Uri Geller	£2.50 ☐
A TASTE OF LIFE	Julie Stafford	£3.50 ☐
HOLLYWOOD A' GO-GO	Andrew Yule	£3.50 ☐

All Sphere books are available at your local bookshop or newsagent, or can be ordered direct from the publisher. Just tick the titles you want and fill in the form below.

Name _____

Address _____

_____

Write to Sphere Books, Cash Sales Department, P.O. Box 11, Falmouth, Cornwall TR10 9EN

Please enclose a cheque or postal order to the value of the cover price plus:

UK: 60p for the first book, 25p for the second book and 15p for each additional book ordered to a maximum charge of £1.90.

OVERSEAS & EIRE: £1.25 for the first book, 75p for the second book and 28p for each subsequent title ordered.

BFPO: 60p for the first book, 25p for the second book plus 15p per copy for the next 7 books, thereafter 9p per book.

Sphere Books reserve the right to show new retail prices on covers which may differ from those previously advertised in the text elsewhere, and to increase postal rates in accordance with the P.O.